PRAISE FOR JEFFERY DEAVER AND ISABELLA MALDONADO

Fatal Intrusion

"Slick, cinematic action and fastidiously detailed investigative work bring this series launch to life. Deaver and Maldonado make a good match."

—*Publishers Weekly*

"Deaver's interest in social media and Maldonado's law enforcement background blend well in this fast-paced crime novel."

—*Library Journal*

"This novel is captivating, detail driven, and intentionally misguiding until the final reveal. Although left on somewhat of a cliffhanger, this novel can be read as a standalone book."

—*Booklist*

"*Fatal Intrusion* coauthors Jeffery Deaver and Isabella Maldonado have created a 'whodunnit' murder mystery that rises to the level of an extraordinary literary elegance. Especially and unreservedly recommended."

—Midwest Book Review

THE GRAVE ARTIST

OTHER TITLES BY JEFFERY DEAVER AND ISABELLA MALDONADO

The Sanchez & Heron Series
Fatal Intrusion

Also by Isabella Maldonado

The Daniela Vega Series
A Killer's Code
A Forgotten Kill
A Killer's Game

The Nina Guerrera Series
The Falcon
A Different Dawn
The Cipher

The Veranda Cruz Series
Death Blow
Phoenix Burning
Blood's Echo

Selected Short Fiction
I've Got Your Number
Smart Woman (in a Real Short Skirt)
The Hand of Fate
Cleañoritas, Inc.
Diablo Ranch

Also by Jeffery Deaver

The Colter Shaw Series
South of Nowhere
Hunting Time
The Final Twist
The Goodbye Man
The Never Game

The Lincoln Rhyme Series
The Watchmaker's Hand
The Midnight Lock
The Cutting Edge
The Burial Hour
The Steel Kiss
The Skin Collector
The Kill Room
The Burning Wire
The Broken Window
The Cold Moon
The Twelfth Card
The Vanished Man
The Stone Monkey
The Empty Chair
The Coffin Dancer
The Bone Collector

The Kathryn Dance Series
Solitude Creek
XO
Roadside Crosses
The Sleeping Doll

Stand-Alones

The October List

Carte Blanche (A James Bond Novel)

Edge

The Bodies Left Behind

Garden of Beasts

The Blue Nowhere

Speaking in Tongues

The Devil's Teardrop

A Maiden's Grave

Praying for Sleep

The Lesson of Her Death

Mistress of Justice

The Starling Project, a Radio Play

Selected Short Fiction

The Rule of Threes

The Broken Doll

Scheme

Cause of Death

Turning Point

Verona

The Debriefing

Ninth and Nowhere

The Second Hostage, a Colter Shaw Story

Captivated, a Colter Shaw Story

The Victims' Club

Surprise Ending

Double Cross

Stay Tuned

The Intruder

Date Night

JEFFERY DEAVER

THE GRAVE ARTIST

ISABELLA MALDONADO

THOMAS & MERCER

Text copyright © 2025 by Gunner Publications, LLC, and Isabella Maldonado
All rights reserved.

No part of this book may be reproduced, or stored in a retrieval system, or transmitted in any form or by any means, electronic, mechanical, photocopying, recording, or otherwise, without express written permission of the publisher.

Published by Thomas & Mercer, Seattle

www.apub.com

Amazon, the Amazon logo, and Thomas & Mercer are trademarks of Amazon.com, Inc., or its affiliates.

EU product safety contact:
Amazon Media EU S. à r.l.
38, avenue John F. Kennedy, L-1855 Luxembourg
amazonpublishing-gpsr@amazon.com

ISBN-13: 9781662518751 (hardcover)
ISBN-13: 9781662518737 (paperback)
ISBN-13: 9781662518744 (digital)

Cover design by Caroline Teagle Johnson
Cover image: © Andy Kennelly, © diyun Zhu / Getty

Printed in the United States of America
First edition

To Blush and Buddy, our respective four-footed furry muses, who ensure we keep them in the lifestyle to which they've become accustomed.

CHAPTER 1

Saturday, June 20

The man cast his dark eyes approvingly over the bride's white satin dress.

He thought of it as a blank canvas soon to be painted—with the vermilion hue of blood.

In his thirties and handsome in an action hero sort of way, Damon Garr stood on the back lawn of the Hollywood Crest Inn, facing the 1930s stucco structure, as he studied the newlyweds bidding farewell to the guests at their reception.

The Brock party . . .

The time was close to midnight. The musicians were stowing their instruments after playing the tired repertoire of canned romantic tunes for the five hundredth time this season. And the month was only June. Servers and bus people clattered away the dessert and coffee china.

Concealed by the sumptuous California foliage that blossomed over the property, Damon looked past the waning celebration and watched.

And waited.

His patience finally was rewarded when the couple retreated to a bench in a large, landscaped garden behind the inn to steal some time alone. The brunette bride, around thirty, was a bit older than the blond groom. She appeared slightly tipsy, throwing her head back and laughing too loud at something her brand-new husband said. He himself was not the picture of sobriety either.

But weddings were made for indulgence, were they not?

Damon was dressed for the occasion—dark Italian suit, white shirt, burgundy tie—with perfectly barbered hair and a pear-skin smooth shave.

Inconspicuous, as always, when creating his Tableaux.

No one would have paid him any mind. He seemed like any other guest at the Brock reception, one of the three happening at the venue, which offered unreal views of Los Angeles, far below its perch in the Hollywood Hills. Still, he remained hidden in the vegetation—out of the couple's sight and, just as important, out of security camera view—and edged close enough to overhear the groom offer to get them each another drink. His bride laughed again, saying she'd already had too much, but he waved away the insincere protest and rose, promising to return shortly with brandies.

Anticipation quickened Damon's pulse. He'd spent two hours hidden behind plantings, listening to bad music and worse toasts, waiting for an opportunity like this.

Now . . .

He slipped a pair of blue latex gloves from a plastic bag in his back pocket. Snapping them on, he checked the distance between the bench and the bar, calculating how long it would take the groom to reach his destination, via a flagstone path overlooking a large koi pond thirty feet below.

The couple would be separated less than five minutes.

Time to act.

Damon picked up what he'd spotted earlier: a landscaping stone roughly the size and shape of a brick. Remaining behind the trees, he swiftly closed the distance to the waiting bride, noting the moonlight glinting off her dark hair. She looked ephemeral, a vision in white.

He clutched the rock tighter.

And walked past her.

The groom's black tuxedo was hard to see when he moved into the shadows, but his steps were unhurried, and Damon had no trouble catching up to him.

This was the tricky part. Timing, as they say, was everything. Damon darted a glance around the area. No sign of anyone.

He sped up, raised the rock high and brought it down in a sweeping arc onto the top of the groom's head.

A satisfying snap told him the skull had cracked. The groom crumpled to the ground.

Time for stage two.

After tossing the stone into the koi pond, he squatted to rifle through the unconscious groom's clothing, found his cell phone and pocketed it.

Still hunkered down, he grasped the groom's left hand to pull his arm around Damon's own shoulders. Next, he wrapped his right arm around the groom's waist and hoisted his limp body upright. Damon trudged with his burden to the iron-pipe railing separating the path from the cliff over the pond. Had he been spotted, it would appear that he was simply helping a drunken reveler too unsteady on his feet to walk.

But another quick look around assured him that there were no witnesses.

He heaved the groom over the guardrail. A moment later, he heard a thud, then a splash. Damon moved to the edge and peered over the precipice. In the moon's glow, he made out a figure sprawled in the shallow water among the jagged stones.

Luckily the body had landed face down. If the blow and the fall hadn't killed him, he would soon drown. No extra effort needed on Damon's part.

Now for the final phase.

He pulled the man's cell phone from his pocket and checked to see if he'd use plan A or plan B. If it was a model that let you open the camera app without unlocking the unit, he'd take several pictures of the beautiful view, then hit the button to swap lenses, so that it was on selfie mode. If it was locked, he'd leave the phone near the cliff, as if the groom had dropped it and fallen while trying to retrieve it for the selfie.

This was part of the thrill for him. The challenge of planning what he could, but relying on sheer cunning to adapt to unexpected circumstances. He felt it was this skill, constantly honed, that made him successful.

He tapped the screen, which allowed him to access the camera. Plan A then. He got four good pictures, reversed lenses, then tossed the phone over the side. He didn't throw it hard, making sure it landed on the rocks, not in the water.

Slipping the gloves away, Damon strolled back toward the hotel with unhurried steps.

He didn't have to wait long—ten minutes—for the sounds of shouting, the pounding of footsteps and the wail of a siren. He joined the throng on the lower-level garden, where the koi pond was located. A shiver of pleasure ran through him when he witnessed the expressions of horror as onlookers watched rescue workers hurry to the body. Within minutes, their urgent movements became methodical. There was no need to rush.

He eavesdropped on two police officers talking nearby. They concluded that the groom had wanted to take a selfie near the edge of the cliff with the moon over the city. The guy clearly had too much to drink and leaned back too far against the guardrail. Such a shame.

Damon stayed long enough to watch the bride, now *widow*, push past the workers, drop to her knees and embrace the body, blood staining the front of the satin gown precisely as he'd imagined earlier.

Exhilarated, he walked to the parking lot to collect his car, tucked away in a spot not covered by security cameras.

Damon Garr was pleased. If there was any phrase to describe the evening, he decided, it was this: a good start.

CHAPTER 2

Tuesday, June 23

"Everybody, down!"

Jacoby Heron grabbed the arm of the man next to him—a twenty-something in jeans and a gray hoodie—and tugged him behind the car.

The other pedestrians on the dusty street of this working part of Santa Monica had already crouched at the sound of the bang.

Jake, in his thirties, was tall, over six feet, and he hunched to keep behind the vehicle. He had dark hair and a beard that was somewhat less dark. He wore black jeans and a dark-blue windbreaker, logo-free. His shoes, also black, were scuffed.

He darted a glance over the hood of the Jeep Wrangler and shouted, "Sanchez!"

But Carmen Sanchez remained slumped over the wheel of her Suburban, whose rear passenger window sported a large bullet hole, spidering the glass.

"No," Jake muttered, closing his eyes briefly.

The man beside him asked in a trembling voice, "What's . . . what's going on?"

Jake ignored the question and patted his pocket. Frowning, he looked toward the street.

His phone lay where it had fallen when he leaped to the sidewalk. He turned to the man squatting beside him. "What's your name?"

"Um, Tim. Tim Bancroft."

"I need your phone, Tim," he said urgently.

"You want me to call 9-1-1?"

"No, I've got a direct line to a response team." He took a quick look at the SUV, caught another glimpse of Sanchez, still motionless, and gestured impatiently for the phone. "Now, dammit."

Tim unlocked his mobile and handed it over.

Jake punched the keypad, then lifted the phone to his ear. "This is Jake Heron. We need an ambulance and backup at"—he looked around—"4495 East Sunset, Santa Monica. A federal agent's been shot. She's bleeding out. Neck wound. I can't get to her. The shooter's still in the building." He chanced another peek over the hood. "I can see him." He called out to everyone in the vicinity: "He's aiming this way. Stay down!"

Turning to look at the black Suburban once more, Jake yelled, "Sanchez, can you hear me? Don't try to move. The shooter's still active. Medical and backup are on the way."

Tim flattened his body on the sidewalk, completely prone. "What the hell's going on?"

"That's my partner in the SUV." Jake's voice caught.

"You're cops?"

"Federal. Terrorist detail." Jake was breathing hard. "The shooter came from nowhere. Behind us. We never saw him." A moment passed. He called out to Sanchez again but got no response.

He ducked. "Jesus, he's aiming this way again!"

He then looked down at Tim, who tried to make himself less of a target yet. His cheek was pushing hard into the concrete, his hands continuing to cover the back of his head.

It was then that a huge man in black tactical gear, which included a watch cap and ballistic vest, strode up to the pair.

"Thanks, Jake. You did all the work for me." The baritone voice was gruffly cheerful.

Liam Grange, a massive wall of a man, had his cuffs out.

"Hey, wait." Tim's eyes widened as realization dawned. "Oh, shit . . ."

He must have seen Grange's boots, noted the man was obviously unafraid of any shooter and realized something wasn't right about the situation.

Before Tim could make a move, Grange, who was head of Tactical Response for the Long Beach office of Homeland Security Investigations, had pulled Tim to his feet and cuffed him, without resistance, which was, for the suspect, a good thing, since Grange could have accidentally—well, *probably* accidentally—snapped the man's wrists if he'd resisted.

Jake said, "You want to do the honors?"

He was speaking not to Grange but to Carmen Sanchez, who had joined them.

She was about Jake's age, wore black slacks and a white blouse ironed as stiff as Sheetrock and had pinned her glossy black hair atop her head. Her only adornments were a necklace and some rings, all silver, but the most prominent accessory was on her right hip, a Glock 17. Her fingers were wrapped around the grip, an instinctive move, Jake knew. She assessed the situation before relaxing her hand.

"Didn't need it, see?" Jake asked, referring to the blouse. Sanchez had wanted to smear it with fake blood. Jake had convinced her that Tim was probably dim enough to be fooled without garment-wasting props.

Grange patted Tim down and sat him on the curb.

He looked up at them and repeated his earlier question. "The hell is going on?"

"I'm Special Agent Sanchez with Homeland Security Investigations," she said. "Timothy Bancroft, you're under arrest for violations of 18 USC Sections 1961–1968, Racketeer Influenced and Corrupt Organizations. You have the right to—"

"You set this up." He was looking around and clearly noticed the other pedestrians standing and dusting off their palms and swiping at their knees to dislodge the irritating Southern California sand. "You all did! They were in on it too."

True. They were employees of HSI as well. Now that their fifteen-minutes-of-fame performance was over, they'd gone back to being clerical and admin staff—chatting excitedly about the operation.

Tim turned a furious gaze on Jake. "And who are you?"

Jake might have explained that he was a civilian consultant working on a pilot program in the National Security Division of HSI. But he was not obligated to. Nor inclined. And therefore he did not, but remained silent, while Sanchez finished the rest of the Miranda rights recitation and asked if Tim wanted to make a statement.

He did, though it was more of an exasperated question. "But the gunshot? I heard it."

What he heard was Sanchez detonating a flash-bang grenade to signify the start of the undercover scam operation. The bullet hole was quite real but had happened yesterday at a DHS range near the Mojave Desert, when she let go with a shot out the back window into a sand dune. She had been doubtful the government would pay to have it repaired but agreed that the op needed the credibility of at least one live round.

Tim closed his eyes. "This is goddamn entrapment."

"No, it's not," Sanchez said matter-of-factly. She recited the rest of the Miranda warning and jotted some notes about the operation on her tablet.

"You're not getting, like, one single word out of me."

Sanchez looked toward Jake, who said, "All done."

"Perfect." She smiled. Then to Tim: "We don't need *any* of your words. Single or double or more. We got what we wanted from the phone."

"What? No, man. No. This is, like, totally illegal and against, you know . . . some law."

"Both illegal *and* against some law," Jake said thoughtfully. "Sounds pretty bad."

"Heron," Sanchez said, trying not to smile. Meaning, he guessed, don't needle the suspect. Though it was always fun.

To Tim, she continued, "We know you hired Tristan Kane to hack financial services accounts. Kane's under federal indictment, and that makes you a coconspirator under RICO. So we've got search warrants."

Serving one, though, would have given Tim at least a few seconds, maybe more, to wipe the phone. Or at least lock it down. They needed to take the device by surprise.

When Jake was pretending to call for backup, he was really uploading the contents of Tim's phone onto a secure server at their organization's headquarters.

"That means . . . No! You got *his* account? Tristan Kane's account? Because of me?"

All of that was true, Jake reflected, and obvious. Again, no need to reply.

"But when he finds out . . . I'm a dead man."

Sanchez said, "The silver lining is you'll be safely behind bars for the next five to seven years, depending on how lenient your judge is." She nodded to Grange, who led the man away.

"How was my acting?" Jake asked.

She would have heard the whole thing. They had all worn earpieces. "Sounded good to me. And how'd *I* do?"

He said, "Academy Award. Best corpse in a drama series."

And he was relieved he didn't blurt what first occurred to him, using instead of "corpse" the word "body."

CHAPTER 3

Wednesday, June 24

The attack began at 8:00 a.m. on the dot.

A faint ping sounded from the largest of three laptops sitting on the desk in Jake's workstation. He was staring at white letters on a black screen, the place where serious communications occurred between human and machine, not Windows, not Apple, but the naked command prompt that all hackers love, C:\.

Incursion Successful

System log reports:

Pinging J2607:f6b0:4004:c06::8b with 230 bytes of data:

Reply from 2607:f6b0:4004:c06::8b: time=18ms

More messages followed.

"Sanchez," Jake called over his shoulder, keeping his eyes on the screen.

A moment later she walked from her adjoining workstation to his. She stepped close to him and bent down. He smelled a familiar scent. Lavender.

Now a special agent with DHS's enforcement wing, Homeland Security Investigations, Sanchez had formerly been an FBI agent in their cybercrimes division. Jake saw from her expression as she followed the lines of type on his monitor that she understood exactly what had just happened.

"Yes!"

Yesterday's scam, where they emptied the data from the phone of Dim Tim, as Sanchez had dubbed him, was a success. They had breached Tristan Kane's computer defenses.

"Where is he?" she asked.

Jake had launched a multipronged attack. "Don't know yet. The physical address bot's still looking. But another one got into his bank accounts. I'm having them emptied—found three so far. It's all going to FCEA."

Financial Crimes Evidence Account. Where funds confiscated from suspects were parked pending trial. The account in the case of *United States v. Tristan Kane* was well into eight figures.

They had done this several times—turned him into a pauper and, after discovering his location, tried to have him arrested, though he always managed to escape before the authorities broke down his door.

Tristan Kane . . .

One of the world's most nimble, and certainly one of the most amoral, hackers. A man with shifting nicknames. Presently his handle reflected the new technology of the battlefield: DR-one.

As in drone. A weapon far more efficient, and capable of causing far more pain and death, than a knife or firearm. And there was also something indefinably creepy about the prefix letters, "DR," as if it were an homage to someone medically trained and prone to dark

11

experimentation. Kane himself leaned into the image, wearing not hoodies and cargo pants—the couture of most hackers—but black suits and white shirts. He was tall, slim and pale, not unlike Jake himself. The complexion was de rigueur—hackers did not sun.

Kane would break into systems for whoever paid his substantial fee. Sometimes he would help terrorists wreak destruction in the name of their ideology—whatever it might be, however simpleminded, as it usually was. Sometimes he would help the more sophisticated clients plunder wealth from governments, companies or the rich.

Never content just to complete the mission, Kane reveled in inflicting gratuitous harm. If innocent bystanders died to more effectively destroy his targets, so much the better. Victims were nothing more than the two-dimensional characters he gunned down in his beloved first-person shooter video games.

Kane had recently been in the process of executing a for-hire project—involving both money and murder—when Jake and Sanchez had joined forces to stop him. His clients had been collared but Kane had escaped.

That incident had not been the first run-in he'd had with Kane, who a few years before had used Jake the way astronauts use the moon's gravitation to catapult them into space. Jake had been unwittingly tricked into helping Kane succeed in a terrorist hack that resulted in a half dozen deaths.

Afterward, Kane couldn't resist slamming Jake with a taunt sent via anonymous messaging:

How does it feel to kill someone, Jake? Did you enjoy it as much as I do?

And how *did* it feel?

There were no words to describe the despair. And the anger.

At Kane.

And at himself for letting his ego override his better judgment.

Jake was going to find the man and bring him to justice.

Whatever that justice might look like. Traditionally, as Sanchez would have it: arrest, trial and conviction.

Or . . . some other way, a more direct means perhaps. Jake Heron believed rules and laws could also be viewed as mere suggestions.

Which was why if someone had asked him a month ago if he'd consider working with federal law enforcement, he would have replied, "Not just no, but hell no."

Yet circumstances change—sometimes dramatically—and now he and Sanchez were in an open-plan government facility that resembled any other office in this no-nonsense Southern California city of Long Beach. It had until recently been a garage—and that had become its nickname, which he and Sanchez spelled with an uppercase "G" to give it the gravitas of an official workplace. Much had been done to convert it to the space it now was, decked out with hastily plasterboarded walls, gray tile floors as yet unscuffed, energetic lighting in the ceiling—where steel beams remained. The scent was of *new*: paint and tile adhesive most predominantly. And, if you were aware of its prior incarnation, you might detect a faint lingering scent of automotive grease or oil.

The windowless fifty-by-fifty-foot area held four workstations. Only two were occupied. Most of the remaining space was empty, though functional shelves lined the walls. Some were bare but others contained office supplies, digital storage media, computers and parts, all neatly labeled.

A vertical storage unit in the corner featured two locks. Inside were assault rifles, pistols, ammunition, Tasers, tactical comms gear and flash-bang grenades.

To say the space was decoration-free was not quite accurate. Mounted on the south wall were three enormous video monitors, two presently in screen saver mode, one showing a time-lapsed video of a seed germinating into a yellow flower, the other filling with numbers of pi being calculated ad infinitum. The third was the case board of the Tristan Kane investigation—a digital version of the whiteboards seen in every law enforcement office worldwide, displaying the details like connections between suspects and bios of unsubs and witness accounts, photos of the hacker's former residences, maps.

One other decoration: characters stenciled in black paint on the opposite wall.

i²

Also known as "I-squared," which stood for Intrusion Investigations, it was a pilot program so small that only he and Sanchez were on the team.

The first word in the name was the key to its purpose. It derived from Jake's real profession. Dr. Jacoby Heron was a self-described "intrusionist" who made his living as a penetration tester—hired by government and corporate entities to breach their physical and internet facilities and report back on vulnerabilities. That paid the rent and was fun. More important, to him, was teaching at a small San Francisco college and giving public lectures, warning of the dangers of government and corporate intrusion (he never pen tested for any company he knew was guilty of such practices). Much lecture time was devoted to domestic abuse, which he considered one of the most dangerous and widespread forms of intrusion that existed.

Jake and Sanchez had managed—*largely* managed—to overcome their complicated past to investigate that recent case involving Tristan Kane. The partnership proved to be successful, and it was natural they would be asked by senior Justice Department officials to work together again.

Sanchez frowned at his screen. "We got his money. I want his *where*. But *don't* contact HTW to give us a hand." Her frown melted into a sly glance.

He sighed at the reference to a fellow hacker from his former life, whom Sanchez always referred to as "Hot Tub Woman." Would he ever live it down? "It was one night, Sanchez."

She put her hand to her chest. "You and a beautiful blonde in a hot tub overlooking the Matterhorn. Maybe it was only one night, but I'll bet it was a memorable one."

"It was Monte Bianco, and she wasn't blonde. At least not then."

"Did your fingers get very wrinkled?" Sanchez pursued.

Engendering another sigh.

The individual in question was a woman of both mysterious origins and undisclosed residences. Aruba—a nickname that had attached based on one of those locations—was in her early thirties, with features that bore the graceful hallmarks of her Caribbean heritage and, yes, was occasionally blonde, though her waist-length braids were sometimes red, brunette, blue or purple. She was renowned on the dark web for being a hacker of extraordinary skill, which, Jake admitted, was probably superior to his.

Sanchez was referring to the fact that the warrant out on Kane permitted intrusion by official law enforcers. It did not extend to international hackers hiding somewhere in Indonesia or Sweden or, for all they knew, maybe in nearby Laguna Beach.

Sanchez's concern was understandable. Her philosophy was to follow the letter of the law to make sure the results of an investigation could be admitted at trial over defense objections.

Jake's attitude was, again, to do whatever it took to find the bastard and worry about the niceties of jurisprudence later.

Otherwise seemingly compatible, Jake and Sanchez were forever at loggerheads on this issue.

"I won't ask Aruba to do anything illegal," Jake assured her.

She squinted his way. "That's a sentence with so many exceptions you could drive a lawyer through it."

He gave her a sardonic glance.

A voice intruded. "I told him you need a *real* plant in here. Not a virtual one."

Jake turned to see a slim young woman in her twenties. She had just entered the Garage from the main Homeland Security Investigations building, which was attached by a short hallway. Her dark-blonde hair was in a messy bun held in place with a lacquered wood chopstick. Her attire was typical of what she usually wore: jeans and a gray tee. Her footwear consisted of retro bright-red Chuck Taylor All Star high-tops that zippered up the side. Her feet were forever busy, tapping slightly. Fingernails black. She must have owned a thousand earrings, because he couldn't recall her ever wearing the same pair twice.

Her eyes, intense blue, were on the looping germination monitor.

"Declan picked the screen saver?" Sanchez asked.

"Who else?" she offered, lifting two hands, palms up. Her given name was Alwilda, but she was known universally as Mouse. The reference was not to the rodent but to the user interface device. She'd earned the moniker by spending inordinate amounts of time online assisting her boss, Sanchez.

"Real plant?" The agent scanned the Garage. "Nothing would grow. No light."

"Oh. Forgot about that. I don't grow things. So, he wants to see you both."

"What's up?" Sanchez asked.

"I'm not sure. But from what I could hear—nobody's ever seen anything like it before."

CHAPTER 4

Was someone following him?

Damon Garr thought: Possibly.

The same color car—dark blue—had appeared twice in the rearview mirror as he drove the short route from the strip mall off the 101 back to his home.

How many automotive paint colors were there? It wouldn't make sense to have too many. Cost efficient to keep the shades limited.

And if somebody *were* following, who would it be?

Some young detective who became suspicious about the death at the inn in the Hollywood Hills Saturday night? Or, he supposed, someone private could have connected him with the murder and scored his license plate. And, with a grand or two to a PI, got his name and address. But to what end? Blackmail? He would have heard by now. And he hadn't seen anyone at the inn following the murder, and his car had come and gone out of view of the security cameras—he'd checked. Also, at the moment, he was in another car, his silver Mercedes, one of several vehicles he owned and kept in a storage garage.

It was four days after the delightful night of the reception. Media outlets were covering the death as accidental, which meant that was how the authorities were treating it. Had there been even the slightest suspicion of a murder, they would have made an announcement asking for anyone with information to come forward.

And the reporters would be all over the story like rooting pigs.

No, he was just feeling a little paranoid.

Being cautious, nonetheless, Damon drove past his house and took several meandering roads through Malibu before he finally decided it was his imagination.

He returned home, pulled into the carport and parked. Few garages here. It was Southern California. No need, given that only seven snowfalls have resulted in accumulation in the past hundred years.

Climbing from the Mercedes, he retrieved two shopping bags from the back seat. Presently he was dressed casually but, as always, in quality clothing, a size and cut to accentuate his athletic build. The path to the front door wound serpentine through dense vegetation in varieties of green, the verdant monotony broken with dozens of yellow and red and blue floral accents. He noted footsteps in the sand dusting the tile, coming and going, but there was no worry. It was just a delivery.

His heart tapped a bit faster as he saw the small package left on the porch.

Damon's house, custom built to his specifications, was typical of dwellings in Malibu, a beach town on the Pacific Ocean about thirty miles west of LA. It certainly had its share of sprawling, luxurious estates owned by nine-figure businesspeople and A-list celebrities, but most were like Damon's, gorgeous places certainly, but on a more modest scale: medium-size lots with manicured gardens in which nestled ranch houses.

One difference: everyone else wanted more windows than walls— so they might peer at floralscapes and the placid ocean. But Damon had ordered only a few small panes installed, much to the builder's surprise. He didn't explain that not only might sunlight be a problem, considering what he planned to fill the house with, but, most importantly, privacy was paramount.

If one can look out, others can look in.

The crash of surf sounded from the beach about three hundred yards west. The original inhabitants of the area, the Chumash, called the settlement Humaliwo, which meant "where the surf sounds loudly." Over time, the native word had morphed into Malibu, where the ocean still roared.

Damon had no more interest in the sound than in the view. Or in the beach. He'd picked the spot and the architecture of his home because it was the exact opposite of the columned colonial estate in Brentwood where he'd grown up. Such specifics in his choice of housing might be the kind of thing he'd discuss with a therapist, but he no longer saw one. Shrinks wanted you to dish and, in Damon Garr's case, sharing was not wise.

He slid an electric key fob from his pocket and tapped it on the lock to unlatch the front door. Inside, he entered a code to deactivate the alarm. The house was clean and neat and ordered. The four dark-haired, short women who descended onto the property weekly, always when he was present to make sure they did not go where they should not go, worked with energy and apparent devotion to their tasks.

They were not, of course, Miss Spalding, but then no one would *ever* be Miss Spalding.

He caught a glimpse of himself in the smoky mirror that dominated one wall of the entryway. Damon was big, six two, weighing around 210. His square face and precision-cut sandy hair would be considered handsome by most. The adjective had been first offered by Miss Spalding, when he was about ten, and she reiterated the assessment often enough that he'd come to believe it. Certainly, that seemed to be the view of the women in the community college classes he taught (art history not being a big draw for men).

He spent four days a week working out. All the best serial killers were strong as sin. The Bind, Torture, Kill murderer easily overpowered his victims, using ligatures to restrain and eventually suffocate them. The Boston Strangler needed a strong upper body based purely on his MO. And Ted Bundy whacked his victims heartily with blunt objects, rearranging their features in horrible ways, thanks to his toned muscles. Damon hated gyms and used free weights in his bedroom and ran along the sandy jogging trails in and around Malibu. And even on nonworkout days, his push-ups numbered two hundred, his sit-ups twice that.

Damon put away the groceries he'd bought—cold cuts and frozen dinners, along with Little Debbie and Hostess snack cakes. Miss Spalding had frequently indulged him when he was young, and the habit remained.

A sudden thought, cloned with a memory, occurred—possibly because of his Hollywood Crest wedding night adventure on Saturday: Felicia would have put him on a diet of greens and lean, steamed entrées after they got married.

But, of course, that never came to be.

He poured a glass of 2 percent milk and drank it down. He then washed his hands, dried them thoroughly and, with eager anticipation, opened the small box that had been delivered earlier.

He looked at the contents, razor blades, each one wrapped in clear plastic. They were German and hard to find in America, but Damon had located a source. There is nothing magic about the sharpness of razor blades. They are honed like any other metal edge: stone first, then finally leather. The trick is the alloy. You could, in theory, make a razor-blade dagger, but the edge would not last, and it would be so brittle it would probably break when it struck bone as you were exploring the torso of someone writhing on the ground before you.

But Damon Garr had no need for a knife. These blades did the job just fine.

A glance at the box of blue latex gloves nearby, the razor blades and, finally, the secret door, disguised as a mirror in the living room wall, leading to his den.

He pictured Her inside.

The downcast eyes, the troubled mouth.

Her smooth arms.

In particular the nape of Her neck, prominent because Her back was bent in misery.

He rattled the box of double-edge blades like a smoker from the 1930s might to see how many matches remained.

But now was not the moment. There wasn't time to do a proper job on Her.

Damon had someplace to be.

A glance at his watch, elevating his heart rate still higher. Anticipatory joy filled him.

He walked into his bedroom and showered quickly, giving an approving glance at his washboard abs. He dressed in a dark-gray Canali suit, which had cost $2,000, and a perfectly smooth starched white shirt. From the small shopping bag he'd brought in earlier he extracted a box and, opening it, drew aside tissue paper like a theater curtain parting at the start of the first act. Inside was a supple silk tie.

The rich violet shade of the accessory, Damon had heard, had become associated with mourning because it's the color of the Catholic church's vestments and coverings during Lent. Or that was one theory. Damon liked his own better: it was the hue of death because the shade resembled the color of lividity, caused by settling blood in a corpse. Although he also entertained the possibility that it signified asphyxiation.

A final look in the mirror.

Good.

With a glance toward the German razor blades on the kitchen counter, then the secret door to the den, he whispered to Her, "I'll be back soon . . ."

After setting the alarm, he walked outside to his car and pulled onto the sandy road in front of his house.

No cars nearby. Definitely no one was following now, if indeed someone had been following before.

Still, he took his time as he wound out of the canyon to the highway and remained vigilant.

A more cautious man might have called off the events planned for today, after having seen the quasi-suspicious vehicle earlier.

But not Damon.

A good start.

Yes. And now more victims awaited. His addiction was such that nothing would stop him from what lay ahead: putting into practice what had taken him years to perfect.

Damon Garr was the man who had invented Serial Killing 2.0.

CHAPTER 5

Carmen Sanchez wasn't accustomed to her boss making leaps in logic, and this was a doozy.

Nobody's ever seen anything like it before . . .

Mouse's words rang true.

Carmen glanced from Heron to Supervisory Special Agent Eric Williamson. "An international serial murderer called 'the Honeymoon Killer'?"

She and Heron were seated at a small conference table in Williamson's office, which offered a stellar view of the Long Beach docks, among the busiest in the world. You could see a hundred or a thousand or a million of those massive cranes that the longshoremen deftly manipulated to move containers between trucks and ships.

"Apparently so," said Williamson, a massive man who had the same physique now that he'd had as a star football player in college. Always in a suit and tie, he'd allowed himself a slight indulgence given the anemic government-issue air-conditioning on this hot June day and rolled up the sleeves of his baby-blue shirt and told his tie knot: At ease.

With a frown, Heron said, "And we're running it?"

Williamson grunted. "What, you wanted our first assignment to be an enemy-state-actor conspiracy to take over the White House with space lasers and paratroopers? A terrorist cell pumping cyanide into the LA drinking water?"

Carmen didn't expect *that* exactly. Newly minted I-squared was meant to investigate alternative threats to national security. Williamson had developed the pilot program for situations that required some creative thinking to unearth them. But a homicidal wedding crasher?

"It was a coin toss, frankly. There's another situation we're keeping an eye on, but for now, our mission is HK."

Carmen got it. "Honeymoon Killer. You come up with the name?"

"That was Declan."

Figured. Declan could be creative in addition to analytical.

"He made the connection yesterday and I sent a notice to Main Justice. They want us to run this one because of an international connection."

"Morning," came a voice from the doorway.

Carmen turned as a solidly built man in a rumpled suit stepped into the office. His dark hair was a week late for a trim. An HSI visitor ID dangled from a lanyard around his neck and an LAPD gold shield decorated his belt.

She gave him a nod. "Hey."

Frank Tandy was a well-regarded detective in the elite Homicide Special Section of the Robbery Homicide Division. His assignment there gave him free range to investigate cases citywide.

"Carmen." His face broke into a broad smile as he looked her over. Then: "Eric."

Williamson motioned Tandy toward an empty chair at the table before turning back to Carmen and Heron. "When I contacted LAPD about Declan's catch—his *possible* catch—Frank here volunteered to be liaison."

No surprise that he'd jump at the chance to work with I-squared, Carmen thought wryly.

She introduced him to Heron, who stood to shake his hand.

Williamson said, "What did the brass tell you, Frank?"

"Just that the fatality at the Hollywood Crest was probably a homicide and HSI was looking into an international angle. If it turns out to be a murder, we'll run it task-forced with you. You Feds'll be primary on any foreign stuff."

After the detective took a seat, Williamson brought him up to speed on the Honeymoon Killer and then resumed his briefing. "Declan spotted two other similar incidents."

Carmen asked, "Overseas?"

"Right. Now, on the surface they looked like accidents, but taken together, likely not."

Heron gave his head a small shake. "Declan can be something of an alarmist."

Carmen agreed.

"Who's Declan?" Tandy asked, glancing back briefly into the HSI office and seeing no other agents lurking in the background.

As the "assistant" fell within Heron's realm, he was the one who explained to Tandy.

Declan was not a time clock–punching employee of the federal government. The name was an acronym for Decoder-EnCoder Language-based AI Network. A large language model computer sophisticated enough to border on sentience, or so it, or he, seemed to feel.

She and Heron had worked with Declan to design an analytical tool called the Obscure Major Crimes Relationship Indexing System, which examined data in the US and around the world for anything suggesting incidents that were, or could be, threats to the country. Declan scavenged data from every imaginable source, including law enforcement databases, traditional and social media, podcasts, online groups and chats and content creators.

"Looks like HK was the first fish he caught," Heron concluded.

"So, three incidents," Williamson said. "The groom who died this past Saturday on his wedding night at the Hollywood Crest Inn, just after the reception. A bride died in Verona, Italy, three weeks ago, and a groom in Florence four days after that. All three victims were knocked unconscious and drowned after they were married and about to begin their honeymoon."

Carmen said, "With that MO, are we thinking our unsub is a man? Unless we find otherwise."

They agreed a male was more likely.

Heron tapped the info into his ubiquitous tablet. It was like an iPad but had no brand name. He'd made it himself. He started a case board, like the one in the Garage, the wall monitor that described the Tristan Kane investigation.

"Are we *sure* they're murders?" Carmen asked. "Couldn't they be real slip and falls? Coincidences? Declan's had some false positives."

Williamson pursed his lips. "I wouldn't have called you all in without good reason."

And she regretted her comment, which, in truth, she hadn't thought through. There was a secret lottery in the halls of HSI about who would be the first to catch Williamson making a mistake. The unclaimed year-old pot was over $500.

He continued, "After spotting the incidents, Declan ran a statistical analysis. He concluded there was a 96.5 percent chance they were intentional and related. I ordered a copy of the Italian police reports, but nothing's come in yet."

Tandy asked, "How did Declan learn about the deaths overseas?"

"Not from Europol or Interpol databases," Williamson said. "Nothing there. He found stories in the news, social media."

The same sources, Carmen knew, where agencies like the CIA and MI6 got the vast majority of their intelligence. Spies had a lot of subscriptions.

Williamson continued, "If this turns out to be part of the 3.5 percent chance that it's a coincidence, you can get back to your hunt for Tristan Kane. And, Frank, you get back to serving and protecting LA. But if it's a serial actor I want all hands on deck. This'll be a perfect chance to test-drive I-squared."

After hearing his assessment, Carmen agreed.

Williamson turned to Tandy. "Do you have any preliminary info on the incident?"

Whether a death is intentional or not, local cops have to run the scene.

"Afraid to report the ME treated the death as accidental," Tandy said. "Just another selfie casualty. They happen more than you'd think. She released the body, which was immediately cremated."

Carmen stifled a groan. There went *that* evidence. She could guess what had happened. "And since no one was aware a crime had been committed, nobody cordoned off the area where he died."

"Nope," Williamson confirmed.

Tandy was quick to reply. "I'll declare it a crime scene and secure the perimeter." He called his supervisor to request some uniforms to tape it off.

After four days, though, Carmen knew the scene would be contaminated to the point where it would produce no helpful trace or impression evidence. But this investigation was vital, and she would check all the boxes.

"Most of the guests are long gone," Williamson went on. "But the widow is still in town. There's a memorial this afternoon. You can interview her and anybody else who was at the hotel around the time of the death."

Carmen's heart went out to her. Imagine . . . a bride and a widow. On the same day.

She said, "Security vids?"

"They're being sent to Heron," Williamson said, turning to him. "Maybe you can get a decent facial image."

Heron said, "I'll take a look as soon as I get them."

Williamson looked thoughtful. "I don't know what HK's agenda is. But the fact he's hit three times in under a month tells me he might be in an escalation phase."

Then the big man fell silent and absently glanced at a cluster of family pictures on his desk: his handsome wife, a US attorney, and four sons, ranging from four to fifteen years old. He sighed and addressed the group again. "There's something I haven't mentioned yet. A glitch. Detective Tandy, cover your ears. I mean that figuratively, of course. You should hear this—but don't repeat it."

The detective lifted a brow. "Ah, we're treading through the minefield of politics, I have a feeling."

Carmen didn't like the sound of her boss's comment, or the annoyed expression that went with it. She could guess the source of the irritation. "I'm assuming you mean Reynolds."

Eric Williamson was well regarded, and usually didn't have any issues running the Long Beach branch of the National Security Division on his own authority, with the singular exception of someone near the top. Deputy Secretary Stan Reynolds, second-in-command of the Department of Homeland Security, made it a point to question nearly every decision Williamson made and seemed to look for opportunities to countermand him.

He nodded. "Reynolds read the memo on the three incidents I sent to Main Justice. He emailed me about it yesterday."

"Hold on a sec," Heron said. "When the servers were down?"

HSI's Long Beach headquarters computer servers had been experiencing random shutdowns over the past two weeks. They might have been typical glitches that occur in all large networks, or they might have been attacks, which were common against federal government systems. Heron—admittedly given to paranoia about such things—told Carmen he thought it was the latter but hadn't found any proof.

"Afraid so," Williamson muttered.

Heron closed his eyes and pinched the bridge of his nose. "So he used the unsecured server."

The one that HSI employees used to share recipes, jokes and reels about cats befriending turtles.

Eyes still closed, Heron asked, "Did it have your original copied?"

"Yep."

"Shit." Heron dropped his hand, lifted his tablet and began typing.

Seeing Tandy's confused expression, Carmen explained: "The bottom line is, thanks to Reynolds, a good hacker could backdoor their way into HSI's system. All of it."

To Heron, Carmen knew, external emails were a serious PPI, or Point of Potential Intrusion, to be avoided at all costs. He called them "Ebola."

He looked up. "I've just sent a bot to scour all our systems to check for incursions."

"How soon will we know?" she asked.

"If nobody exploited the breach, hours. If they did and cloaked the script? Days. Or we may never find it."

"What did Reynolds want?" she asked Williamson.

"To ride herd. Or shotgun. Or at least be kept in the loop. Or whatever other irritating bureaucratic cliché you want to use. Apparently, the groom who died Saturday, Anthony Brock, worked for the Government Accountability Office in Washington. Reynolds thinks he was killed because he had access to sensitive information."

Tandy said, "GAO? Ninety-nine percent of what they do is public."

Carmen added, "And Brock was young, so he probably wouldn't be handling anything requiring a high level of clearance, not top secret, definitely."

"I hear you," Williamson told her. "I made some calls and you're one hundred percent right. He was a minion. Parks Department auditing. But Reynolds loves his grand conspiracies. And he also wants to know if the victims in Florence or Verona were connected to a government agency. He said we should concentrate on the spy angle."

Carmen muttered, "You mean concentrate on the helping-my-career angle." She said to Tandy, "Reynolds is the deputy director of Homeland, but he wants the number one slot. A while back, he filled in as *acting* director, but the Senate wouldn't make it permanent and gave the top job to someone else. He's still licking his wounds." She glanced back at Williamson. "I have another cliché, sir: 'feather in his cap' if he catches that Russian spy he's been after."

"He's got one in particular?" Tandy asked.

"He does indeed. Sergei Ivanov. Has businesses around the world, but he's based in DC. Mini oligarch."

"And he's a suspected Russian asset?" Tandy asked.

"Zero evidence," Williamson said. "But that won't stop Reynolds." Then he addressed all three. "And before you ask, yes, he expects regular briefings."

She cut her boss a look. "Peachy."

Heron was more to the point, reprising his earlier sentiment. "Shit."

"Navigate as best you can," Williamson said. "I'll run interference . . . as best *I* can. That's all I have for now." His abrupt turn to his computer keyboard signified that the meeting had concluded.

The three left the office, walking down the hallway leading to the Garage. Tandy had been to HSI—he and Carmen had run a few cases together—but not to the Garage, so Carmen showed him around, pointing out a workstation he could use. He sat down and placed a call to Robbery Homicide to give his people an update.

She returned to her own desk and glanced at her computer screen, scrolling through messages.

She froze. And gasped.

Heron asked, "Sanchez? You okay?"

She continued to stare. "They sent it."

He asked, "The file?"

"That's right. *Dios mío.*"

A file she'd gone to great lengths to find.

A file she half hoped would remain hidden forever.

A file whose contents would force Carmen Sanchez to relive the worst day of her life.

CHAPTER 6

The digital file Carmen had received didn't involve Tristan Kane or the Honeymoon Killer.

Or anything else I-squared was investigating.

Though it did relate to a homicide.

Her own father's murder.

Three years ago, Roberto Sanchez, a widower, had devastated Carmen and her younger sister, Selina, when he took his own life. Or so it seemed. But, thanks to Heron, she'd learned the death had merely been staged to appear like a suicide.

She had then asked for a copy of the investigative file from the police. She'd been forced to dance around some awkward questions when she made the request. The lead indicating foul play was not obtained through official channels, and she wouldn't have been permitted to investigate a family member's death anyway. And there was the embarrassing fact that the police had come to the wrong conclusion, not something she wanted to share with them without solid proof.

So she'd told them she simply wanted to review the case "for closure." Some would call it a lie by omission, but Carmen preferred to think of it as a "strategic deployment of the truth."

Either way, she now was in possession of scanned documents that could provide answers to the mystery.

She tapped the file icon and began to scroll through the contents.

A financial adviser, Roberto Sanchez had made some bad decisions while investing clients' money. Some had lost their life savings. Unable to handle the shame, he'd flung himself from his office window in Whittier, a suburb of LA.

Or so went the official account.

Carmen had always thought it strange that Roberto, otherwise healthy and not prone to depression, would take such an extreme measure. But all the facts pointed to suicide, and Carmen, suddenly forced to play the role of parent in her sister's upbringing, and executor of their father's will, accepted the facts laid out before her at the time.

Then to her astonishment, Heron found some anomalies about Roberto's death that piqued his curiosity. He had enlisted Aruba's aid to dig further. Carmen might have ribbed Heron about her, but she respected Aruba—who could penetrate systems to her heart's delight as long as official investigations weren't compromised. She truly appreciated the elite hacker's efforts and teased Heron about his relationship with her only as a joke (at least, she *thought* it was a joke).

Together Heron and Aruba found truly shocking news: evidence that someone had hired a contract killer to murder her father.

This was a game changer in many ways, not the least because it would go a long way toward healing a rift between Carmen and her younger sister. Roberto had died just before Selina's seventeenth birthday, emotionally scarring her at a vulnerable moment in her life. Carmen had, over time, forgiven him. Selina had not. Nor did she forgive her older, and more worldly, sister for reconciling herself with the suicide.

Carmen was thrown into turmoil when Heron told her what they'd uncovered. Her father murdered by a hit man? That fact begged her to go into action and track down the killer. But it was a crime over which she had no jurisdiction.

Jake Heron—the man for whom lines existed to be crossed—had considered this. In one of those rare moments when they spoke frankly about personal matters he'd said, "Sanchez, you're a cop. Go do cop stuff and find the son of a bitch."

She had decided to do just that, under the radar of her superiors in HSI.

Now she had the file, which would be the starting point for the clandestine investigation.

Was there something in the matter-of-fact cop-speak that offered up insights into the murder?

As she scrolled, the curt phrases she was all too familiar with—and that she had mastered as well—slid past.

Decedent . . . cause of death . . . velocity of impact . . . responding medical personnel . . .

She stared at her screen as if she could make answers materialize by sheer force of will. But nothing more revealing came forward.

Then she scrolled to the next page and came to an abrupt stop.

Before her was the suicide note. Her hands began to shake as she read her father's familiar scrawl, bringing a lump to her throat.

No priest would give me last rites before what I am about to do, so this will be my final confession, which I will have to give in seconds:
Please forgive me once I reveal my true guilt under oath.
I violated my clients' trust by investing their savings in a risky fund, and I cannot go on in the knowledge of what I have done and the misery I have caused.
I now can admit to hoping that you, my goddesses, can ever live in peace, amen.
—Roberto Mateo Sanchez

"Hard to look at."

She started at the voice, not having noticed Heron slip behind her to read over her shoulder.

He continued, "I mean, hard under any circumstances, but particularly now—that you know he was forced to write it."

While he was facing his own death.

Yes, it was hard.

No denying that. Carmen Sanchez was a human being and moved by loss like anyone else.

But she was also a law enforcement officer, and it was impossible for her to shut out completely doing the "cop stuff" coldly and objectively.

In an instant, with the abruptness of a finger snap, a thought struck her.

Heron noticed. "What, Sanchez? You're onto something."

Maybe . . .

She moved slightly to give Heron a better view of the screen. "Those goddesses, that reference? Our dad read Greek and Roman myths to Selina and me a lot, but he never called us his goddesses. Why say that?"

"And why underline his middle name?" Heron asked. "Is that something he usually did?"

She found it odd that he noticed something that had made her wonder as well. "No. It's a strange thing for him to do, but then again, I'm sure he was under an incredible amount of pressure."

The kind of pressure few people would ever know.

Heron tapped the lower-right corner of the screen with a pen. "What's that?"

She squinted at the area and saw some nearly indistinguishable marks. "Looks like the crime scene tech cut off a fraction of the bottom edge of the note."

The original had been collected by forensic techs, so the detectives had shown Carmen only a copy when they interviewed her shortly after her father's death. She had never seen the entire page before.

"Is there another image?"

Of course there was. CSI took a hundred photos when ten would do. She scrolled through the other images until she found one that included the tiny writing scrawled at the bottom corner. "Can you zoom in?" Heron asked.

She used her index finger and thumb to expand the view.

$$Δ:Iθ$$

"I would say it's Greek to me," Heron said, "but I think it really is."

He was right. Her father hadn't only read them mythology but taught his daughters a bit of Greek history, including some of the language.

"It is. Ancient. But I don't know what it means."

She maximized the image until it pixelated but saw nothing that would explain the strange characters. She thought for a moment and then typed some keystrokes. "I'm sending it to my sister. See if she has any ideas."

Selina called back almost immediately and said, "You got the file?" Her voice was filled with excitement.

"Yes, everything. You're on speaker with Heron."

"Hey, Jake."

"Hi, Selina."

Carmen asked, "Do you know what the reference to goddesses is about? I don't remember him ever calling us that."

A pause. "No. He never did."

"What about the tiny letters in the lower-right corner?"

"They're Greek. But they don't mean anything to me."

"Me either."

Selina sucked in a breath. "It sounds crazy, but could he have been giving us a message?"

"About his death, a clue?"

"Yes."

"It's possible," Carmen said, reading the note again. "I was hoping you and Dad might have had some conversations that'd shed light on it."

"No," Selina said. "But you'll find out. Where are you going to start?"

Carmen was silent for a moment. "I will, honey, of course. But I can't do anything now."

Silence pulsed from the other end of the line. "What do you mean?"

"Lina, I'm working a big case." She added "Homicide" and felt bad about including the troubling detail. She realized she'd done it to justify her decision not to drop everything to follow up immediately on Roberto's murder.

"What're you talking about? This is our father!"

"Lina, we've got an active serial killer in LA. We have to stop him. Dad's is what we call a cold case."

"Did you really fucking say that?"

Carmen was taken aback. "It's just a term we use."

"I know what it means. I watch TV. A cold case is still a case. And you're saying you don't care enough to look into it."

Now Carmen was angry. "Of course I do. And I'll make sure it gets investigated, but I have to be careful. I don't have jurisdiction, the state-federal thing."

"That hasn't stopped you before."

Heron and Carmen first combined their efforts while she undertook a case that did not technically fall within the boundaries of DHS's remit. Some even thought it was wrong for them to handle the investigation.

Deputy Director Stan Reynolds, for instance.

"I'll call some people."

"When you find the time."

"Lina, you don't under—"

"I can call people too. Just as easily. Like Ryan."

Ryan Hall was a detective both sisters had met on that recent case. Carmen found him a competent investigator, if young.

Selina had found him considerably more.

And the feelings were mutual.

But Carmen pointed out, "He's Riverside County. The murder was in Orange. He doesn't have jurisdiction either."

"Another excuse . . . Is there some reason you don't want to get to the bottom of it?"

"*What?*" Carmen sputtered. "It's about priorities."

The Honeymoon Killer could be targeting another victim even as they spoke.

"Look, Carm. You've made yourself perfectly clear. You have more important things to do."

"That's not fair."

The ground felt like it had shifted beneath her feet. For the past few years, Selina had been furious with her for forgiving their father and moving on. Now, she was angry that Carmen wouldn't drop everything to vindicate him.

"I'll do what I can when I have the time," she said. "And listen to me, Selina. You are not to do any investigating on your own. You want to figure out what Dad meant by 'my goddesses' and check out those symbols, okay. But that's it. Understood?"

Selina was a student in Perris, California, about ninety minutes from downtown LA. On summer break at the moment, though, she was in a temporary apartment in Fullerton, smack in the middle of Orange County—exactly the spot where she would be able to play amateur detective to investigate the murder.

And that was not going to happen.

"Whatever," her sister said, flinging the word out like the verbal slap it was.

"Listen to me, Selina. He was *murdered.* And whoever did it isn't going to appreciate somebody—"

The line went dead.

Carmen let out a few choice words in Spanish, then tapped the screen to close the digital file.

Frank Tandy disconnected from his phone call with his team at Robbery Homicide and glanced over at her. "You all right, Carmen?"

She cleared her throat. "Fine. Just some personal stuff."

"I heard 'Selina.' Problem with your sister?"

Tandy had met her several times.

"It'll get worked out."

She hoped.

She glanced at the virtual murder board on the wall near the workstations, headed *HK*. The completed fields were pitifully sparse.

Eyes on the board, Tandy asked, "Where'd the software for that come from? I've never seen anything like it."

Filling in some information on his tablet, which immediately appeared on the wall, Heron said, "I wrote the script."

"Where can we buy it?"

"Buy? I don't charge. Give me your email. I'll send you a copy."

Tandy gave a disbelieving laugh. "You could make loads selling it."

"I don't sell software or code. I give it away."

"Why?"

Carmen noted Heron blinking, as if the thought had never occurred to him.

"Don't know," he said. "I just do. Better to send it to your personal account. The LAPD firewall would probably stop script attachments."

Carmen said, "I have Frank's address."

Heron glanced at her and nodded.

Then her thoughts returned to the prickly conversation she'd just had with her sister. "Hey, Heron. Didn't you say that the worst kinds of intrusion happen within families?"

"Not necessarily the worst, but, sure, families come with built-in PPIs. Because that's where we lower our defenses time after time. And, what's more, loving somebody gives us inside information about the best way of getting under each other's skin."

She felt a gravitational tug toward following Selina's suggestion to pursue her father's murderer. Reflecting that she might even find some basis for federal jurisdiction once she started digging. Title 18—the federal criminal code—was as complicated as the myths about ancient labyrinths Roberto had read to his daughters in their youth.

But determining that would take time.

And time was precious at the moment—now that they were operating on the assumption that the Honeymoon Killer was a serial perpetrator and could be poised to strike again.

She said to both men, "Let's get started on that canvass. Where's the widow?"

Tandy said, "At the Hollywood Crest."

She rose and started for the door.

Pausing only once.

Her eyes were drawn back to the computer that contained the police investigation into her father's death—a murder disguised as suicide.

Her gaze met Heron's.

It was as if he were asking, Are you sure you don't want to look into it?

Her response was: "HK's out there somewhere, Heron. I want to find him. Now."

CHAPTER 7

Being in the ever-dangerous job of law enforcement, where one strives for anonymity, Carmen never understood the appeal of selfies, especially if taken near the edge of a thirty-foot drop onto sharp rocks.

Which made the Honeymoon Killer's setup for the murder a little suspicious from the beginning, in her mind. Natural selection was a rule of the universe, but people were not, in general, complete fools. Could Anthony Brock have gone for the photo on the precipice? Maybe. Was it likely? No. Responding officers probably should have been a bit more suspicious.

She, Heron and Frank Tandy were at the opulent Hollywood Crest Inn, which dated to the era of old Hollywood—a time she knew mostly from artifacts like *Chinatown*, Humphrey Bogart movies and the gritty fiction of James Ellroy and Raymond Chandler. She was peering over the guardrail where the groom, Anthony Brock, had been pushed to his death.

Tandy told them about his conversation with the responding emergency medical techs.

"One of them had said, 'What was he thinking?'

"'Thinking?' a seasoned cop had replied without missing a beat. 'The better question is, What was he *drinking*?'"

Clever, and typical of the dark humor of those for whom death and violence were a daily fact of life.

Now they knew the truth, of course. It wasn't a drunken misstep.

Or, as Declan would have it, 96.5 percent truth.

The upper patio, where Brock and his bride had sneaked away after the reception, was roped off with yellow tape. The LAPD had worked fast, she was pleased to see. This was half of the homicide scene. The other was the pond below. She noted that the patio had been closed by the hotel—sandwich board signs proclaimed UNDER CONSTRUCTION—presumably so guests would not be troubled by the fluttering tape.

She got a text and read it aloud. "Tox shows no drugs. BAC is .12."

"The ME didn't conduct an autopsy," Tandy said. "But I found out she did a basic screen on the victim and asked for the results to be sent to Agent Sanchez. Now we know HK didn't use poison or narcotics."

Carmen considered the rest of the message. "And with a blood alcohol content of .12, Brock would be legally intoxicated, but that wouldn't be enough to qualify him for an extreme DUI charge if he'd been driving."

Tandy summarized: "In other words, he was drunk but not shit-faced."

Looking at the water below, at the huge, slow-moving fish, brown, white, yellow, Carmen explained that alcohol had still contributed to Brock's death. Not because he'd made a poor decision taking a selfie near a cliff—which he didn't—but because his level of inebriation would mean the blow to the back of his head would render him even more helpless than if he'd been sober.

She thought a moment, then added, "We've been thinking HK targets weddings because of the newlywed thing, but maybe it's because people are drinking, and he needs them in that state."

Tandy turned to Heron. "Let's put it on the murder board."

He pulled his tablet from his backpack and added the notation. It uploaded automatically.

As if mocking them, sprinklers suddenly came on, drenching the scene. Water can contaminate and obliterate evidence nearly as efficiently as fire.

Carmen's cell vibrated with another text, this time from the head of HSI's Long Beach crime scene unit. Su Ling had sent a team to search the pond for a squarish rock, which had to be the murder weapon because the indentation in the groom's skull matched the corner of a paving stone from the garden rather than the smooth, rounded river rocks in the shallow water. As Carmen read the message, a humorless laugh escaped her.

"And get this," she said sardonically to Heron and Tandy. "The fish ate off all the organic material from the rock. Which would include the killer's DNA and any skin cells or hair—provided, of course, they'd made their way onto it in the first place. If this shows up in a Discovery Channel true crime special, bet we see an uptick in murders around fishponds."

Tandy chuckled as he cut a glance her way.

The situation sparked another idea. "What if this is somebody acting like a serial doer, to kill him for another reason—and not some phantom Russian spy. Insurance?"

Tandy said, "I like it. Should have thought about that before. The most common reasons for murder are sex and money. And we can rule out the first motive."

Heron said, "I'm on it." He did some rapid thumb-typing on his tablet.

A moment later, he looked down. "Declan. It says, *'Regarding your inquiry about Anthony Brock's insurance policies. He is covered by Federal Employee Health Benefits, GEICO automotive and the federal employee plan for his home. USAA is not an option as he is not presently nor was he ever enlisted in the military. There are no records of any life insurance.'"*

"Thank you, Declan," Carmen said.

Amusing her, Heron lifted an eyebrow her way. She knew he lived and breathed computers, and to a certain extent he slept computers.

He did not, however, thank them.

Their large language model assistant was not quite finished, it seemed. Heron read another missive. "It's got something else. *In addition, I was unable to locate any filings of real or personal property in the names of revocable trusts with Anthony Brock as grantor/trustee, or wills in the name of Anthony Brock. This does not preclude that such documents exist, but as of 2.5 seconds ago, none were on file in the courthouses of any of the fifty states, and US protectorates, Canada or Mexico.'*"

"Wills," she muttered, frustrated at herself for the oversight, though traveling to Italy to murder just to cover up a financial crime was a bit far-fetched. "Good catch."

Heron looked away from them and his eyes swept the garden and the stucco rear of the inn. "This place is ninety percent blind spots. No wonder the security vids were pretty useless."

HK had been careful to avoid being seen. But Heron, who'd reviewed tapes on the way here, had managed to isolate a few frames of an indistinct figure that appeared to be a White female with an average build and long, dark hair in the upper-level garden near Brock and his bride not long before he died.

But if so, then why hadn't she come forward? Although it wasn't thought to be a crime until just now, on Saturday night officers had sought out anyone who might have knowledge of the incident.

Carmen explained that the subject in the picture was now officially a person of interest and offered a couple of possible reasons she hadn't spoken with officers. Maybe she'd left before the death, or before the police started questioning those present.

Or maybe she was connected with the killer somehow.

"Somebody to keep watch?" Tandy mused. "Strange. But so is everything about this. Two people killing newlyweds? *Natural Born Killers* . . . I'd vote no, but let's keep it in mind."

Heron added another note to the virtual murder board.

They had sent the picture to the hotel with instructions to show it to the staff, in hopes it might trigger a recollection. There had been no response yet.

Heron glanced at his tablet as a message came in. "Declan again. About the image of Ms. Person of Interest. *'In an effort to provide a forensically useful image, enhancing the definition of pixels—as is often an overly convenient and unconvincing trope in popular crime fiction—will not produce meaningful results in this instance, due to excessive noise.'*"

Large language models, despite access to all the world's data, were not miracle workers.

Carmen frowned as she gazed around, the sprinklers, the grass trampled by mowing and weed-whacking workers. A mute crime scene. She said, "Nothing for us here. Let's go talk to the widow."

CHAPTER 8

Followed by Heron and Tandy, Carmen walked into the cavernous lobby, where they were quickly approached by the hotel security director. The huge man with a deadpan expression nodded to the trio. His name was L. Jackson, according to the badge affixed to his suit. Introductions were made.

"Agent Sanchez. I got that picture you sent. Showed it to the entire staff that's here. Unfortunately, doesn't show much."

"I know," Carmen said. "But sometimes people can recognize a pose or just a silhouette. That can lead to recalling something about the individual."

Jackson nodded. "Guess so. But, sorry to say, didn't jog any memories. You really think it was a murder?" His voice dropped on the last word, and she supposed he'd be thinking that a homicide at a wedding venue equaled a public relations disaster of a high magnitude.

She employed the typical evasion tactics to avoid revealing specific details of an ongoing investigation. "We're still gathering facts at this point. But it seems likely."

"Man . . . we should've . . . I don't know . . ."

Carmen leaned in. "This wasn't on you or your staff. We think the subject is an organized offender. He was careful to avoid security before he acted."

His face revealed that this was faint comfort.

Jackson said, "Mrs. Brock is waiting for you in one of our private meeting rooms."

The designation was a sharp reminder that she had become a widow immediately after becoming just that: a *Mrs.*

They were ushered through a corridor and into a wood-paneled room with leather chairs surrounding a glossy cherrywood table.

In a close-fitting, high-necked and sleeveless black dress with a brocade belt, Allison Brock was sitting on a tapestry divan, looking somewhat regal, Carmen thought. The lean woman wore her black hair in a sleek chin-length bob. Her bright-blue eyes were in stark contrast to her dark brows and lashes. She had an aloof beauty Carmen had seen on the covers of magazines like *Vogue*, where models seemed to scowl at the camera. She wasn't sure what she'd been expecting, perhaps sobbing, wailing or hysterics, but she supposed everyone handled grief in their own way. Perhaps the bride was the type to put on a brave front and break down in private.

If Carmen read anything in her taut expression, it was anger.

Frank Tandy, who'd spoken with her earlier over the phone, made the initial introductions. Allison acknowledged their words of sympathy with a stoic nod.

The door opened once more.

Allison said, "Thanks for coming, Ben."

The burly, barrel-chested young man was introduced as Ben Sutton, Anthony Brock's college roommate and the best man at Saturday's wedding.

Allison's face softened. "He's been such a comfort to me." Ben sat beside her, and she leaned against his shoulder.

After she disengaged and sat back, Ben said, "Allison told me there's some bullshit about Anthony being murdered?"

Again judiciously, Carmen said, "That's where the facts are pointing. We found a probable murder weapon. And we've learned something else. There were two similar killings. In Italy."

"Similar?"

"A bride or groom killed on their wedding night. Blow to the head. Near water. They drowned."

"No!" Allison's eyes widened.

"Jesus," Ben whispered. "So this is some kind of sicko? A serial killer?"

"We don't know, Mr. Sutton," Tandy said. "Sometimes individuals stage killings to look like part of a series to cover up the real motive."

Echoing Carmen's thoughts from just a half hour before.

"But Anthony? No way. I can't believe it."

"First," she said, turning to Allison. "Did you see anyone in the garden when you two were up there?"

She looked off, her eyes hollow. "No. But I was . . . I was just focusing on Anthony, the night. It was so beautiful." A brief hesitation. "And, okay, we'd been drinking. More than a little."

Tandy asked, "Did you have a jealous ex-husband or lover? Stalkers?"

She scoffed. "No. My last relationship ended nearly a year before I met Anthony. We parted on good terms."

"Anthony?"

"No. Not that he ever mentioned. And he shared everything with me."

"Was he ever in Italy?" Heron asked.

"I don't know," Allison said, looking at Ben.

Ben said, "Years ago. A couple of us went to Europe. We stopped in Rome, Paris and Prague. But it was just a vacation."

"Did he know anybody in Italy?" the detective continued.

"No. And we were together the whole time."

"Any issues at work?" Carmen asked. "Did he handle sensitive information?"

Ben laughed sadly. "No. He was a CPA. Basic work for the government." The smile faded and he choked back tears. "He loved his job. He was career government. He could have gone to work for one of the

Big Five or Big Six—or however many big accounting firms there are. But he wanted to stick with civil service. Felt he had a higher calling working for the public rather than a hedge fund. He was going to run GAO someday. Or Office of Management and Budget, or something."

Allison glanced at each of them in turn. Her eyes had narrowed. "Okay. We've got federal agents and LAPD. Do you have leads?"

Carmen studied their reactions while Heron displayed screenshots of the person of interest.

"That's a *clue*?" Allison muttered, confused. "Who's that supposed to be? You can't see anything."

"That's what we're trying to find out."

She looked at Ben, who shook his head. "You think she's a witness?"

"We don't know," Tandy told her. "She was in the garden not long before he died."

Allison examined the images a moment more and then waved a dismissive hand at them.

Carmen asked the names of everybody who had remained at the end of the wedding reception and might have been present around the time of the death.

"Most everybody had left," Ben said, glancing at Allison. She nodded.

On the drive here, Carmen had spoken to Anthony's parents, who had taken the red-eye back to their home in Florida, then returned immediately the next morning after learning the news. They knew nothing helpful.

Tandy said, "And I called his sister, Lauren. Never heard back."

"I think she left right after the reception," Allison said. "Before . . . it happened."

Tandy said, "Still like to talk to her. Mr. Brock might have said something—that he was being followed or threatened. The memorial this afternoon? Will she be there?"

"Doubt it." Allison explained that Lauren took the death very hard, and she had tried to connect with her new sister-in-law in the days since the death without success. "Given her background, I'm afraid she might be on a bender."

Carmen asked, "Lauren has substance-abuse issues?"

Allison nodded. "Anthony saved her life, got her into rehab. They were very close. And now with him gone, I'm sure she's having trouble coping."

She realized Allison hadn't mentioned her own family and asked if they were still in town.

"My parents have passed," she said. "And I was an only child."

"I'm sorry."

"Thank you," she said quietly. "They would have loved Anthony . . . and as for me?" Allison muttered, with more ice in her voice than self-pity. "Everything's gone. All the plans. All my future. I have to start over again. Now, forgive me. We need to get to the service."

"Where is it?" Carmen asked.

"You might've heard of it," Ben said. "A place called Cedar Hills Cemetery."

CHAPTER 9

Standing within a line of boxwood and topiary in Hollywood's expansive Cedar Hills Cemetery, Damon Garr noticed a teenage girl. Damn if she didn't look like his very first kill.

Eerie.

A sign, he would have thought, if Damon had believed in signs.

Which he did not.

Still, it was too curious a coincidence to pass by.

And, more important, the sight had ignited the urge to create a Tableau, his word for his masterpieces—scenarios that were horrific to ordinary people, but brilliant works of art to him. They were visual feasts designed to evoke powerful emotions, as all truly great things did.

He leaned forward, watching her closely as she stood beside a young man who appeared to be her brother due to the resemblance. They were not particularly upset to be at the funeral and, judging by the ages of those present, Damon guessed it was a grandfather or great-uncle or the like who was no longer among the living.

She looked just like Sarah Anne Taylor.

The *late* Sarah Anne Taylor.

Damon glanced at his watch.

The Brock funeral party would soon arrive for Anthony's memorial but until then he had some time to kill . . . Yes, he actually thought the terrible play on words (Miss Spalding always said he had a wicked sense of humor).

He had parked a safe distance away from the cemetery, a half mile north on the far side of a city park, and had walked here via a camera-free jogging path, to the grounds' utility entrance, where the staff came and went, as well as the heavy equipment and the occasional coffins that did not arrive via hearse through the front gate.

No cameras there either.

He studied the girl again. About thirteen, wearing a black short-hemmed dress and black tights, younger than Sarah, but the facial structure and hair and figure were similar.

Eerie . . .

From time to time she would step away from her brother and send a text or two, read the reply.

Each time she seemed to step farther away from the milling mourners, who were waiting for the others to assemble and a ringleader—priest or minister—to arrive.

She'd be completely isolated soon if she kept up her pattern.

Please . . . just walk a *little* farther.

His heart thudded harder with anticipation.

A Tableau was in the offing.

This was, of course, Magic Day Four, and though he'd made specific plans for later, they did not preclude a little aperitivo.

With a lovely little thing like her.

Sometimes you just couldn't pass up a chance opportunity.

What direction should it take? he wondered.

There was always the old standby.

Murder.

Damon Garr had known for a long time that he was born to kill. Brilliant even in early teen years, he researched this *proclivity* (the very word he used, at thirteen, no less) to kill. He learned of the Macdonald triad. This was a psychological profile used to identify potential serial killers, who often exhibited a cluster of three childhood behaviors: bed-wetting, committing arson and hurting animals.

The famed triad was not conclusive, of course, but Damon refrained from acting out on the latter two, concerned about drawing a counselor's or doctor's attention. As for the wet sheets, Miss Spalding took care of those and never told a soul.

There was also medical proof of his pathology. This came out as a result of his extracurricular activities at school. He was arrogant and impatient and tended to bait bullies. He held back when fighting—his lust to kill might carry him away—but his size and ferocity resulted in some severely injured students.

Once, he put a boy in the hospital. (It didn't help his situation to stand over the screaming boy with a smile of curiosity, marveling at the angle of the broken fingers.) School resource officers and counselors contacted his father, William—his mother, Sydney, having passed—and recommended tests. His father had made millions as a ship charterer, leasing out huge vessels for transporting oil and containers. He said to the school, "Yes, run the tests. All of them. A full battery. Whatever it costs."

The stocky, chain-smoking man was otherwise utterly uninvolved in his son's life, and young Damon thought it was moving that he'd been adamant about getting him help.

Only later did he come to understand his father's true motive. William Garr wanted the tests in the hope that the results would mean he should be institutionalized, removing the last thread of parental responsibility.

The conclusions of the tests were supposed to be kept from the underage patient, but Damon, of course, broke into the doctor's office and read them.

Quite intriguing.

Structural and functional MRIs revealed abnormalities—in the portion of the cortex that can cause the patient to act out aggressively.

The doctor reported he was surprised to find that, despite the patient's sociopathic tendencies, a particular behavior remained solidly normal: impulse control. This observation was listed as "an interesting fluke."

So, Damon was by nature a killer—and a particularly efficient one too, given that he was able to rein in the impulses that prompted others to kill without careful premeditation, making it more likely they'd get caught.

So much for the wiring. But as any shrink will tell you, that alone doesn't make a serial killer.

Nurture plays a role too.

It certainly did in Damon's life.

Enter Miss Spalding.

After his mother passed when he was eight, his father was not going to waste any time raising the boy, and rather than foist him off on his late wife's sister, a loving woman with a family, in Portland, he hired a governess and walked away from the boy completely.

Wiry and severe looking, hair always scraped back into a tight platinum-blonde bun, Miss Spalding never married and, always hoping for a child, did all she could to glue the boy to her side and make sure he spent every waking minute—and more than a few nonwaking moments—with her. This meant indulging him, particularly with those temptations that a doting older woman assumed a young boy would want: ultra-violent games, like *Grand Theft Auto* and *Red Dead Redemption*, slasher movies and any damn thing he wanted to watch in the darkest corners of the internet.

The golden boy could do whatever he wanted. Discipline did not enter into his life once Dad was gone (except that *other* type of discipline, viewed with hungry pleasure on sites he logged on to by adding ten years to his age).

Nature, nurture and a dash of cool impulse control.

A perfect storm of murder, just waiting for a chance to get to work.

At eighteen, it happened. He knew it was time. Maybe like birds suddenly know it's time to leave the nest.

The A-plus student put his calculated plan in motion.

Damon had taken pictures of Sarah with a digital camera using a cash-purchased chip, metadata disabled, in advance. On a carefully chosen afternoon, he took surface roads to Thomas Jefferson High, didn't buy gas and bought no food. There would be no evidence of his presence anywhere in the vicinity.

Next, he followed a football player home from practice, collected a discarded McDonald's wrapper and soda cup and straw from the boy's parked car with latex gloves, then waited until the student had left his house again and was out driving by himself—so he would have no alibi.

He'd taken the time to memorize Sarah's schedule and found her walking home alone from band practice as she always did on Wednesday evenings. She lived less than a mile from the school and had no car.

He came up behind her. Wearing leather gloves over latex, he pulled a thick plastic bag over her head and dragged her from the sidewalk into an adjacent wooded park. She kicked and thrashed, but he easily overpowered her.

He stabbed her in the chest several times, then enacted the second part of his plan. To ensure DNA transfer, he rubbed the food wrapper and straw from the boy's car over Sarah's skin. He drove away, constantly checking to be sure he wasn't seen. He waited an hour for the boy to come home, then hid the knife, leather gloves and SD card under the back floor mat of his car.

Finally, he called the local police precinct on his burner phone to give a partial license plate number for a car driven by a boy carrying a bloody knife near the park an hour earlier.

Just the right number of clues. Not wise, he decided, to draw too clear a line.

Drove home.

A month of planning. One dead, one serving thirty years.

More perfectly plotted and executed than anything Ted Bundy or BTK or the I-5 Killer had ever perpetrated.

Sarah . . .

Picturing her face, first horrified, then desperate, then forever still.

A face that so resembled the girl he was gazing at presently in a sparsely populated part of Cedar Hills Cemetery.

He was about to send a silent plea for her to step just a bit farther away from her family when she cooperated on her own. She muttered something that appeared to be snide to her brother, who fired back a retort and joined the rest of the mourners, leaving his sister to step away from the party altogether.

Which placed her no more than thirty feet from Damon Garr's eager eyes.

CHAPTER 10

"Sit."

Jake took the chair at the small conference table in Eric Williamson's office. Sanchez sat beside him. They had just returned from the Hollywood Crest Inn and had been interrupted by a summons from Mouse once again as they'd been entering information on the digital murder board.

The supervisory special agent flipped through papers and set them down in an orderly pack, like a huge deck of cards. "You two ready to brief me?"

Sanchez paused. "Ready as we can be. On a case that's about three hours old."

Implying that they were being interrupted from an important task for one far less so.

A cool glance in return, as if he'd caught the tacit criticism.

Very little got past Eric Williamson.

"Where's Detective Tandy?"

"Frank's back in his office," Sanchez said, "at Robbery Homicide."

Suddenly the monitor on Williamson's wall brightened to life, at the same time that a blue light on a camera above it began to glow.

Did Williamson sigh?

To Jake's surprise—and dismay—filling the screen was the clean-shaven, narrow face of Stan Reynolds.

He was the one they were to brief.

A word, if it *were* a word, came to mind: *Ugh.*

The deputy secretary of Homeland Security was bathed in light, then not, then bathed again, and Jake realized he was on an airplane. A government one, of course. Reynolds would not demean himself with public transport, even in first class.

"Eric," he said, eyes swiveling to Williamson. Then: "Agent Sanchez. And Professor Heron. Our intrusionist. That is *quite* a job description. Could one major in it? Ha."

Jake gave a polite—and completely inauthentic—smile.

While someone else might have doffed their suit jacket on a flight, Reynolds still wore his. And a white shirt and dark, unstylishly narrow tie, maroon, which was held in place with an accessory you never saw anymore either: a bar, clasping it to the shirt. The getup was, if nothing else, unique, which meant it was a display of power—that elusive magical substance Reynolds had surely been obsessed with collecting throughout his career, all the more so since being passed over for permanent director of DHS.

Williamson voiced the question on Jake's mind: "Where are you, Stan?"

"Jetting to, jetting fro. I actually *was* taking some hard-earned time off when I got a call from the director. Apparently a Senate subcommittee wants a little explanation about our doings."

I-squared had been approved at high levels—the White House was Jake's guess. Since Congress had not been involved in its creation, there were some grumblings that the executive branch had usurped the legislative by whipping up yet another outfit that would be standing in line, cup in hand, for limited tax dollars at budget time.

Reynolds sipped coffee from a china cup. Was he not worried about the combination of brown liquid, white shirt and turbulence?

"I'll do an admirable job defending the team, though. I've got my cheerleading moves down. Not. To. Worry." He suddenly dropped the smarmy attitude that was his trademark. "I'm serious, Eric. I've been prepping all night."

Since they were on a secure video call, with high-def cameras going both ways, Williamson did not cut a glance toward Sanchez and Jake, though it felt like one was almost forthcoming. This was curious news. Reynolds was going to bat for I-squared? He had opposed it from the moment Williamson had drafted his white paper for the Department of Justice, proposing an operation like it—then dubbed Project X—to take on just the sort of enemies that the Honeymoon Killer represented. After all, organized terror attacks in the country ranged from 9/11's more than three thousand fatalities to a few dozen every year. On the other hand, twenty-five thousand people were murdered annually in America by solitary or small groups of actors.

Did his willingness to uphold I-squared under a barrage of queries at a congressional hearing suggest a change of heart?

Maybe so.

Jake and Sanchez had just had a big win in that criminal investigation involving Tristan Kane, which, not to be too cynical about the matter, Reynolds might be happy to coattail on. Whatever his motive, it was good their nemesis might be warming to their pilot program.

"So, now tell me where we are in this present case of yours."

Sanchez gave an update, some of which Reynolds would know, but it never hurt to repeat yourself when dealing with government minions. The unsub they were dubbing the Honeymoon Killer had struck twice in Italy and once here. The deaths were meant to look like accidents, but it was now clear they were homicides—the team had eased beyond Declan's 96.5 factor. They had learned of the overseas crimes by scraping data from the press, largely. A request for information from the Italian authorities had not been answered yet. Williamson hoped for a response any day.

Reynolds jotted notes. He looked up. "The congressional oversight committee will want to know why this is a national security threat and not an ordinary psychopath."

Sanchez was bristling, Jake noted. She said coolly, "You get killed by an ordinary psychopath, it's pretty much the same as getting blown up by a White supremacist. And the country's psyche takes pretty much the same hit."

Reynolds conceded. "Of course."

Williamson added, "National security *is* at risk. And when word gets out, weddings and other events will be canceled. The consequences will be logarithmic."

"Interesting," Reynolds mused. "I never thought something like this could be so disruptive." He was interrupted briefly as a flight attendant brought him a fresh cup of coffee. "Thank you, my dear." He sipped.

Sanchez continued to tell him about the status of the investigation. "We've been canvassing those at the wedding. We have some video captures. We're trying to track down potential witnesses." She shrugged. "HK—"

"Who? Oh, Honeymoon Killer. Got it."

"He's unique. Never heard of anything like this."

Reynolds was looking thoughtful. "What on earth is his motive for targeting newlyweds?"

"Unknown," Sanchez said. "Is the purpose social disruption? Or is that a by-product? He's a serial actor, sure, but not for classic serial killer motives—sexual gratification in the case of male, revenge or money in the case of female—statistically speaking, anyway. For this case, we need more facts."

"And you, Master of Intrusion? What are your thoughts?"

"He was savvy enough to dodge security and video. Not easy nowadays. Highly intelligent."

"Fair enough." Reynolds was jotting again. "All right. Grist for the mill of Congress." A frown. "Their questions can be *so* tedious. They positively make love to the cameras. Oh, one thing . . . don't know if it means anything, but I mentioned it to Eric. The victim? He worked for the Government Accountability Office. Any chance he was targeted because of that by a foreign state actor? He spotted something on a spreadsheet that a contractor or—heaven forbid—a turncoat government employee didn't want found?"

Ah, the elusive Russian spy, Sergei Ivanov, had made a reappearance, Jake thought wryly.

"We looked into that," Sanchez said. "He wasn't doing anything critical. He was working on audits for the Parks Department."

"Parks, ah. Of course, could be a clever cover." He let that linger. "Any connection with Italy?"

"None that we could find. And Declan was full-on deep dive."

"All right. I'll toss it in the unlikely pile. Just as important to eliminate suspects as discover them. Well, you folks are doing a stellar job. And I'm sure our congressional colleagues will get tired of the whole thing in record time and move on to something else that's pointless to everyone except glassy-eyed C-SPAN addicts." He dabbed at his lips with a dainty napkin. "One other thing, Jake. I appreciate your information about my emails and encryption. I've learned my lesson."

Jake nodded in response. This seemed like a whole new Stanley R. Reynolds. And, in fact, his diagnostic bot had not found evidence that the misstep was a PPI that had let a virus into their system.

Reynolds then looked out the window with a distressed expression. "We're about to land. I'm a bit of a nervous Nellie on planes. Gravity and all that, so I'll disconnect and hold on to the armrests for dear life. Thank you, gentlemen and lady. I'll let you know how the inquisition goes."

The screen showed the message: *The meeting has ended.*

"Well, shit," Williamson muttered. "Can you believe that?"

Sanchez scoffed. "Not the Reynolds we know and hate."

"I thought he wanted to toss us in the dustbin of bureaucracy," Williamson said. "Now he actually used the word 'cheerleading.'"

In a cool, analytical voice, Jake said, "Let's accept that Reynolds still is a two-faced, power-hungry narcissist—"

"Don't sugarcoat it, now," Williamson said as he chuckled.

Sanchez continued his thought: "Which means he sees I-squared as a way to get noticed. Does it really matter if he's a champion because he loves us or he's *using* us? I don't think so."

"Maybe you're right." Williamson's expression grew concerned. "Congressional hearings. Those are always trouble. So much grandstanding and political gamesmanship just for the sake of constituents back home—and for voters in the next election cycle. Just once I wish a witness would say, 'In response to your self-interested and simpleminded question, Senator, why don't you answer *mine*? Would it have killed you to do the research a middle schooler would do, so that you could ask something intelligent?'"

Jake had to smile. Sanchez did too.

Then her phone hummed with a text. She glanced at the screen and blinked.

Jake noted her entire demeanor change. "Sanchez?"

"What?" Williamson asked impatiently.

She got to her feet. "Ben Sutton? Anthony Brock's best man. He's at the memorial service at Cedar Hills. A friend from the wedding party told him there's somebody there who he thinks was in the upper garden not long before Brock died. He's acting funny, staying out of sight, or trying to. White male, thirties."

She fired off a text. "I'm telling Ben not to give anything away, or approach, but just keep an eye on the guy until we get there." Without further words to her boss, she strode out the door, Jake following.

He glanced at his phone for the location of Cedar Hills. They would be there in twenty minutes.

CHAPTER 11

For Damon Garr, murder was always an option.

The old standby . . .

But here, at the cemetery, *that* Tableau would add considerable complication to his life.

Besides, the homicide was planned for later.

So this work of art would involve the thirteen-year-old girl's destruction in a different way.

The aperitivo . . .

A look toward the wall where the urn containing the cremated remains of Anthony Brock would be set. Yes, the mourners were gathering. But a number had yet to arrive, it appeared. No minister, no priest.

He had some time.

And so he rehearsed the lines he would tell the girl.

Walking up casually, a big smile, friendly eyes.

Oh, hey, hi! A surprised look, as if he hadn't been expecting to see her here. *I'm so sorry for the loss . . .*

TammySammyKelli, as he dubbed her, would be confused by his familiarity and why she didn't recognize him. And wondering too why he was, in effect, hiding out in the glen and not with the others.

But she would examine the suit, the trim hair and the beautiful tie, and deduce that he was here legitimately.

She would relax.

And he would attack.

So sad what happened, but I wasn't surprised when your mom told me. He wasn't a young man.

The portrait on the graveside easel was of some old codger who probably should have died ten years ago.

How're you holding up? . . . Cool, good to hear . . . Anyway, I'm hanging back here because, yep, ta-da, I'm Bill.

He pictured her frowning, at which point he'd elaborate. *Bill, you know . . . Your mother* did *tell you about me, right? When she and I had dinner last week? At the hotel? She said today was the day she was going to introduce us. We'd all go out together, the three of us. Get some drinks, well, ice cream for you, and you and I would get acquainted.*

At her continued confusion, he'd widen his eyes as if alarmed. *Shit, she* didn't *tell you! God, I'm so sorry. I shouldn't've said anything. I just assumed . . .*

Her face would turn from confusion to troubled, perhaps to glorious horror.

Look, really, please, don't tell her I said anything. Just have her call me, okay? On the special number. I should go now. Really, sorry. But you and me, I know we're going to hit it off just great.

And TammySammyKelli's life would go off the rails, now convinced that her mother was having an affair. A confrontation between parent and child would ensue and, given the girl's age, it would be spectacular.

A smaller Tableau than one that created a herd of mourners, but not every canvas was painted on a large scale.

Serial Killing 2.0 had always been about more than just a cracked skull and water-filled lungs.

Damon Garr always thought expansively.

A glance behind him. Good, the Brock event had yet to begin.

He had time for the girl.

Damon walked up to her and gave the familiar smile he'd just planned. "Oh, hi there!"

Pausing, she looked up.

Dark-gray suit, handsome and kind face, beautiful purple tie.

He was about to deliver the tragic news about her unfaithful mom when motion caught his attention.

Wait, no . . .

What was *this*?

He gasped. Police were here!

Uniformed and plainclothes. They were moving into the cemetery quickly from the two entrances—the north service entrance he'd walked through and the front gate in the south. And they were speaking to people in the Brock party. Their body language was tense.

Impossible!

He turned and walked quickly away from the confused girl.

Think, Damon raged to himself. Think!

Had they figured out that Brock's death was not an accident and somehow linked it here?

He didn't see how.

But maybe, despite his infinite care about cameras at the Hollywood Crest, he had been spotted.

Did this have anything to do with the dark-blue car he'd seen earlier?

He sprinted toward the line of limos and other vehicles here for the second funeral. On the far side, using them as cover, he turned north and, staying low, returned to the back gate. He couldn't get through, because a young cop was stationed there, eyeing those nearby. So he ducked into the shed, unnoticed. It smelled of fertilizer and damp earth and grease and oil. Two backhoes were parked here. He squinted in the dimness and when his eyes grew accustomed to the faint light, he saw that there were no windows through which he could escape.

A burst of anger snapped within him.

He returned to the shed's door and gazed out.

If there was any doubt the police had been tipped to the idea that the groom had been murdered, that was now put to rest. One man in the party was pointing to the exact spot where Damon had been standing just before making the assault on the teenage girl's psyche.

So, yes, he had been made at the wedding.

He continued scanning the perimeter . . .

Could he scale the wall? He was strong but the stone was smooth. He could get no grip. And even if he found a way to boost himself up, he'd be noticed immediately and tracked down outside, within a dozen feet of the wall.

He looked at the front gate. Eight, ten squad cars and other official vehicles.

At the rear, nearby, there was no car, but that youthful officer continued to guard the exit with the alertness of a Secret Service agent on the lookout for an assassin.

Glancing back to the main grounds, he could see a dozen tactical officers slowly moving through the brush and around trees and cars and past mausoleums, hunting, hunting . . .

Here, in the shed, anything he might use to escape? A row of hooks against one wall held workers' uniforms, vests . . . and one other thing.

An idea formed.

Despite his anger and frustration at this turn of events, Damon actually smiled.

Yes, it might work. Depending, of course, on the amount of blood, and the volume of the screaming.

CHAPTER 12

Jake Heron was not a small man—over six feet and fit from his physically demanding work as a pen tester breaking into corporate facilities like a cat burglar. But Special Agent Liam Grange was enough to make anyone feel inadequate.

Six feet four, clocking in at around 250, 260 pounds, the wall of a man was sporting a brown buzz cut and full beard. With aviator sunglasses seemingly permanently attached, the head of HSI's Long Beach field office tactical team put his former Special Forces training to good use arresting terrorists, bombers, human traffickers and anyone else who showed disregard for Title 18 of the US Code—like Dim Tim, just the other day on the streets of Santa Monica.

He was presently directing his tac operators through the cemetery to the spot where a possible suspect in the Brock killing had been spotted.

The agents were complemented by LAPD uniforms requested by Frank Tandy.

Jake stood with Sanchez and the detective near the front entrance of the place, which to Jake had an eerie, Gothic look, with imposing iron gates, dark stone walls and moss-covered statues and effigies.

The best man, Ben Sutton, had introduced them to Evan, a slim balding man, who looked troubled.

Evan said uncertainly, "I saw a man hanging around in the garden before Anthony died, and I'm not sure, but I think the same guy is here at the service." He mopped his brow with the back of his hand. "But what if I'm wrong? I've screwed up the whole ceremony."

Allison Brock was not, in fact, very pleased by the guest's news. The short, intense woman was looking at the witness and muttering, "Are you sure, Evan? Absolutely sure? Because look what's happening." Her plans for a respectful, stately memorial had gone down in flames.

"After the reception, I went back to get my wife's purse," Evan began. "In the upper garden, there was this guy. In the bushes. He was kind of crouching, and I thought he was being sick. You know, from drinking. Anyway we left and drove back to Santa Barbara. Then I heard from Ben what happened and *where* it happened. And now I see the same guy again, I'm pretty sure. I'm sorry," he finished sheepishly.

When Allison's cold stare showed no signs of thawing, Ben tried to placate her. "Alli, you asked about leads. This might be one."

"I was just trying to do the right thing," Evan said.

Allison's tone then shifted. She looked around at the dozen officers and her eyes settled on Sanchez. "I want to pay respects to Anthony properly. Of course I do. But if that son of a bitch is here, get him." The last two words were a growl.

"We will, Mrs. Brock," Sanchez reassured her, then asked Evan, "Wearing?"

"What every other man here is. Dark suit, white shirt. Tie. Purple, I think."

Grange radioed the description to the agents conducting the canvass. He added, "Be courteous. And not obvious."

The radio clattered back with a "Yes, sir, Agent Grange."

Tandy did the same with the LAPD uniforms present.

Sanchez and Tandy joined the searching officers.

Jake added the details to the murder board on his tablet and wandered off in a different direction, looking for video cameras. And finding none. Not surprising. The eight-foot walls were a deterrent to vandals, trespassers and thieves, although he guessed grave robbery went out of fashion in the nineteenth century.

And then a scream came from somewhere behind him.

Spinning about, he saw that the hearse from the other funeral had rolled onto the grass and was aimed toward the front gate, driving through the plantings and directly toward the Brock mourners.

The long black vehicle gathered speed as it trundled over freshly laid flowers and knocked over funeral wreaths, and the rows of chairs, while people shouted and scattered.

Of course, Jake recognized immediately it wasn't a mishap, and the suspect wasn't trying to escape that way—a hearse made a very poor getaway vehicle.

But it sure created one hell of a good distraction.

Jake turned again and rushed toward the back of the cemetery, the north side. He spotted a shed near the fence line. Was it only for storage, or did the structure have a back door that exited to the street? At the very least it would be a good spot for HK to hide until he could seize a chance to get away.

He reached the shed, yanked open the door and started forward, looking for a light switch.

And just as he found it and clicked the overheads on, his feet hit a cable, probably used to lower coffins, strung like a tripwire six inches above the ground. Instinctively he flung his hands out before him to cushion his fall—and caught a glimpse of the hedge shears, propped point up between two bags of fertilizer, the sharpened ends placed at just the spot where they would pierce the eyes of anyone caught by the simple, but effective, trap.

CHAPTER 13

Damon was striding quickly along a jogging path that ran through the park north of the cemetery.

He listened for screams from his booby trap in the shed.

Didn't hear any.

But then the hedge shears might have struck the falling victim in the throat, in which case there would be only a gurgle.

In any event, his plan to draw the LAPD officer away from the back gate to tend to a wounded colleague turned out to be unnecessary, because apparently a hearse driver had panicked at the sight of so many police, thinking it was a terror attack or something. Leaving the vehicle in gear, he'd climbed from the front seat, Damon speculated, and the vehicle had begun to roll into the cemetery grounds, drawing everyone's attention.

Including that of the young cop guarding the back. He ran forward to look for the fleeing suspect, leaving the north service exit completely clear for Damon, in Carhartt overalls and matching cap, to waltz right through.

An atheist, Damon nonetheless whispered to the copper angels on the back gate, "Thank you."

As he walked quickly along the path through this forested area of the park—though not so fast as to draw attention—he reflected on his newfound enemies. By the time he made it to his car, he'd formed a plan. He drove to the top of a nearby hillcrest overlooking the cemetery, set his phone camera to telephoto and took some pictures while he watched the cops work.

Three people seemed to be in charge, all in plain clothes. One was a Latina with a badge and a gun on her hip. The second, who seemed to be her partner, was a man of a serious demeanor in dark clothing, but with no visible weapon. The third was a handsome but slightly disheveled man in similar dark clothing, but he had a sidearm.

Damon assessed the first two of the trio were the biggest threat. They appeared driven and intense. Unlike the third cop, who seemed more jaded, they were wholly focused on the task of finding him.

He zoomed in and took more photos capturing the pair's expressions, the way they caught each other's gazes. Their nods of agreement. A familiarity that transcended a working relationship.

Now he wanted their identities.

And he would do whatever he could to find out who they were.

Serial Killing 2.0 was his mission in life. Nothing, and no one, could interfere with it.

And that would mean murdering one of these two pursuers, who were clearly determined to stop him.

One or the other, but not both.

This was the better strategy. The death would eliminate half the threat right off the bat, but more than that, having observed their connection, it could very well paralyze the other with grief.

He would wait until the excitement at the cemetery had dissipated some and then go on the offensive.

The only question: Should he eliminate the man or the woman?

No answer occurred just yet. Maybe he'd simply flip a coin.

CHAPTER 14

Carmen and Heron lay on the floor of the work shed at the back gate of the cemetery, gasping hard. She was on top of him and their faces were inches apart. She smelled his shampoo. Had to be that. Jake Heron was not an aftershave kind of guy.

"The hell, Sanchez. You tackled me? I saw the shears. I was going to roll."

"A homicide suspect on the loose and you go charging into a closed-door facility without armed officers clearing it first? And no backup? What, you have a death wish?"

"HK wasn't going to wait around. Everyone else was busy with the hearse. I had to do something." He let out a small groan. "How 'bout getting off me?"

She realized she hadn't moved. And climbed to her feet.

She should have known that Heron—a professor and penetration tester and hacker by profession—wasn't used to working with a partner and would act on his own.

Years of law enforcement had taught her to be a team player, especially when dealing with a deadly situation. You didn't leave your partner hanging, you communicated what you knew and, if at all possible, you called in for assistance and you waited for it.

Not Jacoby Heron.

Seeing him start for the shed, she had broken into an all-out sprint, reaching the open doorway at the same instant Heron was pushing in. She barreled into him, knocking him sideways and sending them both crashing to the cold cement floor.

Her hand had automatically found the grip of her pistol and she looked for threats, then noted that the small shed was empty.

Though she couldn't look away from the trap he'd set. The shears that would blind and, if he'd fallen in such a way that his throat was slashed, kill.

Then her anger faded and reality set in. She asked, "How did he engineer it, Heron? The hearse was near the front gate. How did he put it in gear and get back here in time to escape through the gate?"

"Agreed. Don't see how. Maybe a coincidence. The driver screwed up."

Frank Tandy arrived. He looked at the booby trap. "Jesus. You okay?" He put this question to Carmen, who nodded.

Heron said, "I am too, by the way."

"Good. Meant to ask." Tandy actually blushed at the faux pas.

Carmen looked at the detective. "Escape routes."

Tandy pulled his radio from his belt and called in checkpoints a half mile east and west on Cedar Hills Road and north on Parkside Drive.

She said, "I'd do a mile. He's had six, eight minutes."

"Sure." Tandy corrected his order.

Then she made another call, to Grange. "Liam, we're in the shed in the back."

"Copy that. On my way."

Tandy said, "I've been interviewing people from both funerals. Brock's, and the one to the south. Elderly man in his nineties. Somebody said our boy was talking to one of the attendees at that funeral. A girl. Teenager."

Carmen winced at this news. "A serial killer chatting up a kid? That's not good."

Tandy continued, "I'm trying to track her down now. She might've left with her family. Some people got the hell out of Dodge when we showed up." He flipped to the murder board on his own tablet—Heron had sent him a link to the app. Then he regarded the others. "I also asked if Brock's sister showed up, after all. But she didn't."

Carmen remembered that Lauren Brock had likely experienced a breakdown of sorts and might have fallen off the wagon with drugs and alcohol following her brother's death. Allison had reported she'd probably left before the attack, but Carmen still wanted to interview her. This was the agent's way—to never forgo a single lead, if possible.

Liam Grange's massive bulk filled the small doorway. "Carmen." He nodded to the others and lifted an eyebrow at the trap. "Well . . ." He noted everyone on their feet and no blood. "We got the hearse secured. The driver's sure he left it in park, and nobody saw anyone else near it. You think it's on purpose, a diversion?"

Heron shrugged. "My vote. Though how he managed it and got back to the rear gate in time, I have no idea."

Carmen said, "We need canvassers immediately." She nodded at the back gate. "He went out this way. Then probably turned east or west on Cedar Hills Road or north on Parkside to pick up his vehicle. I'll take a team east. Liam, you go west. Frank, north?"

He nodded.

It was then that a uniformed LAPD officer came to the doorway. She said to Tandy, "Detective, don't know if it's important but a witness said they saw something weird. One of the mourners near the Brock funeral? A woman in a black dress and hat with a veil. Probably dark hair, long. Sunglasses. She wasn't too far away from our unsub. But she was kind of in the bushes too, like she didn't want to be seen. And she left by the service entrance after the hearse incident. She left fast."

Carmen glanced to Heron, who said, "Ms. Person of Interest?"

He nodded. "Any other description? What was the hat like?"

"Wide brimmed, black veil. Oh, the shoes. They were interesting. Black, except a bright-red stripe down the back of the heels."

"High heels?"

"No, thick. About three inches."

"Mid heels," Carmen said.

Heron quickly keyboarded. A moment later, looking up, he said, "Here's the response. *'In answer to your inquiry regarding the heels of shoes captured in the screenshot at the Hollywood Crest Inn you submitted two hours and seven minutes and twenty-two seconds ago, my conclusion is that it is a 44.2 percent likelihood that the individual was wearing shoes of the sort you describe with a stripe down the heel. The variegation of shading suggests it is possible the color of the stripe is red, though that fact cannot be ascertained beyond a reasonable doubt, as would be required if the information were to be submitted for evidence at a criminal trial.'*"

"Ah, Declan, what would we do without him?" Carmen mused. Then: "Okay, we'll assume Ms. POI was here. Acting odd. And she left by the same exit our unsub did. Let's find her. She's hiding something. And I want to know what."

CHAPTER 15

Well, they had moved fast.

Looking in his rearview mirror as he sped away from the hilltop where he'd been taking photos, Damon noted a squad car skid to a stop about a block and a half behind him.

A roadblock, looking for him, of course.

They had arbitrarily picked a mile from Cedar Hills for their perimeter, thinking they'd been fast enough to trap him.

Mistake, obviously.

But it was a calculated decision, a reasonable one. Adding to his understanding that they—the Latina and her bearded partner—were smart, and they were formidable.

And needed to be stopped.

He drove a few miles to his car-storage garage and swapped out the Mercedes for another set of wheels, an "invisible" Honda. The adjective referring to the fact that there had to be a million of them in this silver shade on the streets of LA. Nobody paid a lick of attention to Accords.

His next stop was a flea market in East Hollywood. It was a permanent one, not just set up for weekends. This was where he bought many of the things he used in his work that could never be traced back to him. The market also was camera-free. There, he bought a used hunting knife with a wickedly sharp blade. Then, reflecting, he bought a second one, deciding he might have to discard the first one after he had used it, and there might be additional people to cut.

He returned to his car.

His MO for Serial Killing 2.0 was blunt object and drowning, meant to give the appearance of accidental death.

But now the truth was known, since the police were involved: the death at the Brock wedding was murder and perhaps they had tipped to the ones in Italy as well.

Which meant subtlety was out the window.

Leisurely deaths from rock and water were out. It was time for blood.

CHAPTER 16

Ms. Person of Interest . . .

The silhouette woman who wore black shoes with the red-striped heels.

Who are you? Jake wondered. Just a witness? An accomplice—willing or coerced?

Where have you gone?

And then there was the big question: Had she been the one at the hotel when Brock was killed? Declan's opinion was tepid at best.

Sanchez had taken a team along one canvass route, looking for HK and what kind of car he was driving. Big Liam Grange another. And Tandy a third.

Jake had been left out of the equation when Sanchez charged off on her mission.

Leaving him free to . . . well, do what Jake Heron did best.

Out came his tablet and he typed quickly. He preferred actual keys, rather than digital ones, but he was still lightning fast on the screen's virtual QWERTY.

He read the results.

Ah, here's something . . .

He crossed Cedar Hills north of the cemetery and started up Parkside Drive, the row of beautiful homes that bordered the west edge of the park.

He found Tandy walking down the serpentine path from the doorway of the house nearest the cemetery.

"Jake."

He nodded to the impressive dark brick Tudor structure. "Any luck there?"

The detective shook his head. "They've got a doorbell cam. But nobody's home."

"No worries." Jake lifted his tablet. "I've got the vids of everybody along the street here who has doorbell or porch cams."

"What?" Tandy was laughing in surprise.

"It's about eighty percent of the houses."

"But how the hell did you guys get paper this fast?"

Jake paused. "You can get warrants for the central server."

The detective began scrolling through the vids. "I know, but, man, it'd take me hours to write up my petition and affidavit and find a magistrate I could convince to sign off. How'd you do it so fast?"

"Carmen's pretty well known."

"I guess so. Damn."

Everything he had just told Tandy was true. You can get warrants for central security system servers to see what's on doorbell cams.

Though he had not.

And Carmen Sanchez was pretty well known.

Though Sanchez had not applied for warrants to look at the doorbell cam videos, so therefore her popularity within judicial circles was a factoid of no relevance whatsoever.

Because they needed to find Ms. POI immediately. Witness or accomplice, she might be a necessary component to the case.

And so he was using an effective technique to avoid any consternation or conflict about unauthorized hacking.

He simply didn't tell anybody that he'd done it.

There were no images of HK, though he could have used the dense foliage in the park for cover.

But they did score something.

"Hey," Tandy said, eyeing Jake's screen as he held it up. They were looking at an image of a woman walking down the sidewalk dressed in black, wearing shoes with the infamous red stripes. "We got her."

CHAPTER 17

My goddesses . . .

Selina Sanchez could not get the two words out of her head.

They were what Carmen had pointed out in their father's supposed suicide note from three years ago.

Seemingly innocuous. The kind of endearment any father might use when referring to his girls—the sort that Roberto Sanchez had used frequently.

But he had never used this particular phrase.

And so it wasn't too far-fetched to wonder if maybe, as she'd told her sister, the words were a signal of some kind. A code. A message. She considered the symbols scrawled at the bottom corner of the note. Maybe they would lead her to more direct answers.

$$\Delta:\text{I}\theta$$

Selina was in her temporary digs, an okay rental she'd taken for her summer job between college terms. It was in an LA suburb she called Functional Fullerton, northeast of downtown. The decor was simple: schoolbooks, a plastic ficus, a long-abandoned Christmas wreath, a medium-size TV monitor, a poster of Simone Biles and one of Nadia Comăneci—gymnasts she worshipped.

Those idols were hardly surprising. Slim, strong and with raven hair often bunned up atop her head, as now, Selina was a competitive gymnast herself, the floor routine her specialty. Presently she was sitting cross-legged in a chair before the kitchen table, perfectly upright—natural athletes like Selina do posture like no one else.

Her Dell was open and her long fingers tapped assuredly on the keys. She did a quick online search to see what the characters meant. Yes, as she'd thought, they were Greek—but there was a twist. Professor Google informed her this was part of the Milesian system—a way to write *numbers* using the Greek alphabet.

"What were you trying to tell us, Dad?" she murmured.

She looked up the symbols and came up with 4:19. She left the colon in place, because it was not part of ancient Greek lexicon, but was clearly inserted for a reason.

She leaned back, perplexed. Was he killed at 4:19 p.m.? Did she need to look at the videos to see what happened at 4:19?

Stop.

She forced her racing thoughts to calm down. Think logically. Her father would not have known the precise time of his demise, or the moment the killer would have been caught on some camera. The numbers must mean something else.

Her eyes were drawn back to the sentence with the word that had grabbed Carmen's attention.

I now can admit to hoping that you, my goddesses, can ever live in peace, amen.

She supposed he was referring to her and Carmen, but, again, he'd never called them his goddesses, so why would he do it in his final communication?

She paced and let her mind wander. She'd heard Carmen talk about how she investigated. Often, viewing a situation from the perspective of the suspect, victim or witness helped her gain clarity about what happened.

What if Selina tried to put herself in the mind of her father?

A highly intelligent man, Roberto would know that writing the note would be the last thing he did. Selina crossed the room and dug a pen and notebook from her backpack, then sat down at the unsteady table once more.

"Someone's forcing me to write a note," she muttered. "And they're watching me do it. This is my only chance to communicate, so I have to do it on two levels. How?"

She tapped the pen against the page that was as blank as her mind, whispering, "If I'm going to hide a message, it's got to be complex enough so whoever's watching won't catch on, but simple enough that I can create it on the fly—while I'm under extreme stress."

She'd put down the strange wording of the message to that very stress, but what if the odd expressions were due to a hidden meaning?

Goddesses.

The word stuck out like the frayed end of a thread. A thread she would pull until the entire secret unraveled.

What kind of code would be so simple anyone could do it without having to perform complicated calculations?

An anagram?

She ran the word "goddesses" through an anagram generator online but didn't come up with anything meaningful. Then "my goddesses." Nothing. What else?

Putting herself back into her father's mind, she thought aloud, "I have to leave the key to the puzzle, but where?"

Arriving at the most logical conclusion, she referred back to the first sentence.

No priest would give me last rites before what I am about to do, so this will be my final confession, which I will have to give in seconds:

Roberto Sanchez, a man of faith, referred to a holy sacrament he would not receive, since his death would appear to be a suicide. Then he'd mentioned having only seconds to make his confession. That was because someone was holding a gun on him. But it was still an odd way to put it. She knew how her dad talked, and he would have said he had only a minute, or that he had to hurry. Not that he had to give his confession in seconds. It was too specific.

In seconds . . .

Could it be that simple?

What if reading every second word created a message?

Far-fetched, but give it a shot. She had no other ideas.

Her heart began to pound as she read over the entire note again.

No priest would give me last rites before what I am about to do, so this will be my final confession, which I will have to give in seconds:

Please forgive me once I reveal my true guilt under oath.

I violated my clients' trust by investing their savings in a risky fund, and I cannot go on in the knowledge of what I have done and the misery I have caused.

I now can admit to hoping that you, my goddesses, can ever live in peace, amen.

—Roberto <u>Mateo</u> Sanchez

Her gaze lingered on the signature. Why had her father underlined his middle name? She couldn't recall him doing that before. With a resigned sigh, she decided to focus on the body of the message first and printed the words on the blank paper in her own neat writing.

priest give last before I about do this be final which will to in . . .

Made no sense to her.

Okay, what if the second *letter* of every word spelled out a clue? She scanned the note again.

ORETOLGVMATIEBFR...

Well, guess not.

Still, she felt like she was onto something. Her father had to quickly come up with something that would be easy to write but difficult to catch without the key. And she was convinced he'd explained the code in the first sentence.

The first sentence.

She figuratively smacked her forehead. Why hadn't she seen it before? The clue would be given in every second sentence.

She copied the note, but this time she numbered each sentence, and underlined the second word in every second one.

1. No priest would give me last rites before what I am about to do, so this will be my final confession, which I will have to give in seconds:

2. Please _forgive_ me _once_ I _reveal_ my _true_ guilt _under_ oath.

3. I violated my clients' trust by investing their savings in a risky fund, and I cannot go on in the knowledge of what I have done and the misery I have caused.

4. I _now_ can _admit_ to _hoping_ that _you_, my _goddesses_, can _ever_ live _in_ peace, _amen_.

Still nothing. Not words. But what about first letters of the indicated words? She jotted.

FORTUNAHYGEIA

She actually let out a whoop.

Fortuna and Hygeia were goddesses.

They were who he was referring to!

This had to be it.

Given the family tradition of his reading to the girls from the Greek and Roman pantheon, Roberto had found a way to leave a clue that only they would understand.

She felt a twist in her belly, of love and pain. It was as if her father were here in the room, smiling and offering the clues, seeing if she could figure them out.

I will, Dad, she thought.

And suddenly another emotion flooded through her.

Anger. Pure raw anger.

She turned to her computer and with a heavy touch on the keyboard began a search.

CHAPTER 18

According to the videos that Jake had hacked, Ms. Person of Interest was walking steadily north from the cemetery, head down, her features completely obscured by the hat, veil and sunglasses.

The red stripe on the heels was clear, though.

"Nice shoes," Tandy offered.

The two men scrubbed through the tapes quickly. Ms. POI, captured on six of them, walked to the end of the block, then unfortunately vanished from view—no doorbell cams after that point and therefore no leads to cars she owned or Ubers she hailed.

But there might be other ways to find that information, of course, and they kept at it. The men started north in her direction, stopping passersby and asking if anyone had seen the woman in Jake's video. Some individuals were helpful—eager, in fact. Others were: Oh sorry can't help you good luck have a nice day.

But whatever category they fell into, none of the pedestrians could provide any information whatsoever about Ms. POI.

Still, they persisted. Police work, Jake had learned, was like writing computer code. Every line, every *character* was vital.

As the men walked along the street, continuing the canvass, Tandy asked, "You mentioned your specialty? You're with I-squared, but not sworn law, right?"

"Have some past experience with LEOs," Jake said, referring to the shorthand for law enforcement organization, or officer. He did not elaborate on what that experience was. Instead he mentioned his pen-testing business, then added that it was mostly to pay the bills. His real career involved the courses he taught and his public lectures about keeping safe from overreach.

"An 'intrusionist,'" Tandy chuckled. "Is that a thing?"

"It is now."

Jake added that you could analyze all of world history in terms of intrusion. "By my count, there've been five hundred and twelve major wars and twenty-two thousand significant battles. And each one is an intrusion. So is every criminal offense—either in its own right, like murder, or to facilitate another crime, say, breaking into a warehouse to steal TVs."

"Pretty interesting. How'd you get into that line? If it *is* a line."

"Just fell into it."

Without, of course, explaining. Sanchez knew the answer to Tandy's question. His brother knew. A few other people.

He heard the words he thought about maybe once a week and had for many years.

It's a big day. A special day! Everybody up!

The story was not for Frank Tandy, though.

The man, clearly a natural detective, continued to be curious, it was obvious. He'd sensed something evasive about Jake's answer.

One of the best shields against intrusion is to deflect. Jake had learned that it took very little to change the course of conversation. People—whether egotistical or modest—tended to talk about themselves if given just a pinch of encouragement.

"How about you, Detective?"

"Make it 'Frank,' okay? That way I don't have to call you Intrusionist Heron."

"All right. Frank. And you? Why'd you become a cop?"

"Fell into it."

Both men laughed.

Tandy continued, "High school. Junior year. A buddy of mine was driving like an asshole. Impressing girls, what else? By doing the one thing guaranteed to *not* impress girls. Anyway, Jimmy was my bad boy homie. We all had one, right?"

Jake didn't. But then he had very few homies, good or bad, at that or any other age.

"I told him to cool it, but he wouldn't. Laying donuts, solo drag racing. The more I told him to stop, the worse he got. You can guess what happened."

Jake foresaw several outcomes.

"We went off a bridge, but the axle got caught in a guy wire. That was just dumb luck. Dangling thirty feet over a canal. It had flooded and the current was moving pretty fast. My friend begged me to switch places. He had a suspended license because of a DUI I hadn't known about. He was crying—or *seemed* to be crying. You could never quite tell with him. I was a soft touch then. Maybe still am . . . ha! So I said, 'Oh, hell,' and agreed. A patrol car comes up and this cop gets out. He's a big beefy guy. He gets a rope from the trunk and rappels down and saves us."

Jake had to ask, "Did the car fall dramatically the instant you two were safe? Thriller movie cliché number ten?"

"Nope. It just hung there until they winched it off. So after he pulls us up, we're standing on the bridge and he's looking us over and asking what happened and before I can say I was driving and I lost control— what I'd promised Jimmy I'd say—he says to me, 'Lying to police is obstruction of justice. And you can go to jail for that. I hope nobody's going to lie about who was driving. Because modern cars have cameras in them—to tell if drivers are nodding off. So there's a video of who was in the driver's seat.' I just look at Jimmy, and don't say anything, and he confesses.

"The cop writes him up and is going to drive us to the station so our parents can come get us. And I ask the cop if he's going to get the tape out of the car, but he says, 'Oh, there's no camera.' Jimmy looks all shocked, but the cop says, 'I said *modern* cars have cameras. That piece of crap isn't modern.'

"I knew that minute I was going to be a cop. Saving lives. And fucking around with people to get to the truth. The best job ever." Another laugh. "So. See, I *literally* fell into it."

The men stopped at an intersection of a major road.

"Which way?" Tandy asked. There were stores and parking lots in all three directions.

Jake noted no street cams, but he saw a camera in the window of a warehouse. It was closed for the day. He looked up the company. They weren't part of the city's voluntary surveillance system.

Though they were about to be. Even if they didn't know it.

Jake didn't need any of Aruba's savvy or some supercomputer's muscles. He ran the hack himself and in ten seconds he was inside. The system's security software was based on Windows Vista, a dinosaur of operating systems, which was still common, shockingly, in many modern smart appliances—like internet-enabled refrigerators and stoves. The owners of those clever machines, which could tell you when you were low on milk and if your stove needed cleaning, had no idea that those very same devices could be hacked with a few keystrokes and used as portals to inundate the world with spam and phishing scams that originated in Nigeria and Russia.

But sloppy security was all to the good for Jake, since he now had eyes on the intersection.

He nodded to an image. "She went thataway," he said, pointing west.

"Yep, pahdner," said Tandy, slipping into a bad Texas drawl.

Jake laughed. He eyed all the stores and restaurants spreading out away from them.

"A lot to canvass," Tandy said. "Feels like a StaleState."

Jake blinked.

"Oh, sorry," the detective said. "It's a phrase from—"

"*World of Stone.*"

"Shit," Tandy said. "You mean, you're a nerd too?"

"Have a degree in it."

WOS was an online role-playing game of geopolitics and domination—like a more subtle version of the famous Risk.

"StaleState" was a term that meant two countries or armies were at loggerheads.

"One of my faves." A shrug. Followed by a pause. Then Tandy asked, a bit awkwardly, "Maybe sometime you want to go online as a team? Or have a beer and watch the pros on Twitch?"

Jake had played the game with his brother and his niece, though that was years ago. He was suddenly looking forward to the idea. "Sure."

"Good."

As Jake put his tablet away and slung his backpack over his shoulder, his phone rang. He answered. "Sanchez. Have any luck?"

"None. Liam either. You at the cemetery?"

A pause. "I'm with Frank. You're on speaker. We've got a lead to Ms. POI."

A delay in her response too, then: "You're in the field?"

There was no answer other than yes, and so he told her that.

She seemed to sigh. Sanchez hadn't exactly told him to stay put and not go in search of a murderer, but that was clearly the implication.

"Frank."

"Hey, Carmen."

"Where are you?"

"North of the cemetery a half mile. No sign of HK. But Ms. POI went this way around the time your suspect disappeared. But a lot of people left so it's not necessarily suspicious."

"Okay. Reason I called, I heard from one of Liam's people at the cemetery. They found that girl that HK was talking to. The teenager. She's there with her family. She's willing to talk. I'm a half hour away. Can you get over there and start interviewing her?"

"Sure," Tandy said.

"Her name's Sylvie. She's thirteen. Sounds older, so I'm hoping what she has to say will help."

"Maybe better if Jake goes? I might need to flash my badge to get store clerks and pedestrians to talk about Ms. POI."

A pause. "Okay," Sanchez said. "Just make sure she and her parents stay put. I'll be there soon."

They disconnected.

As Jake turned and started back toward the cemetery, Tandy said, "Ask you kind of an odd question?"

"Does anybody ever say no when somebody asks can they ask an odd question?"

"Of course they don't." Tandy's grin didn't last long. And he was suddenly uneasy—in a youthful, embarrassed way. "So. Are you and Carmen a unit?"

"Unit?"

"You know, going out? Dating? Or, I don't know, living together?"

He found himself blurting a quick denial. "No, no, no. We just work together."

"She's divorced, right?"

Jake said, "My understanding."

"I hear her ex was an asshole."

"I wouldn't know about that."

"She seeing anybody?"

Surprising himself, surprising himself a great deal, he was suddenly reluctant to answer with the truth—that, no, she was not.

"Couldn't tell you much about her personal life."

Tandy was nodding. "You're new to this. After a month or two, walking or riding a beat, you get to know everything about your partner. I mean *everything*. Lot of times more than your wife or husband."

Jake said, "Well, I'm new. Like you said."

"So you don't know if she's interested in anybody, or anybody's interested in her?"

"Not a clue."

They shook hands and, as Jake walked through the park, he was thinking of one of the questions he would ask his students in class: Did anyone know what type of intrusion was both the most common and the hardest to detect?

Typically no one raised their hand.

He always paused a beat before giving the answer. "Lying."

CHAPTER 19

Having changed into a light-gray windbreaker, jeans and a cap, Damon Garr was walking through the park, north of the cemetery, looking at a bench where three nannies sat talking. Before them were strollers, which they ignored as they chatted and scrolled on their phones.

The scene brought back Miss Spalding's hoarse yet oddly melodic voice, drifting to him from the past. "They don't love their little ones the way I love you."

Ten-year-old Damon and his governess were passing through a park. She walked him back from school, which was an embarrassment, but she wouldn't have it any other way.

Gesturing at several similarly indifferent nannies, she had spoken loudly enough to be overheard. "See, they're not paying any attention. A stroller could roll down the hill and then who knows what might happen?"

Here, the three women in front of him weren't paying any attention either, but then there were no hills and, besides, strollers were considerably safer nowadays, having been designed by lawyers as much as by engineers. Runaway babies seemed unlikely.

After her observation about the negligent caretakers, Miss Spalding had paused and turned, bending down—only a bit, as he was a tall child—and said, "Come here, my Little Pup. Give me a hug."

And young Damon had endured the embrace, the way he endured the coddling walk home, and all the talk about baby carriages.

He endured a lot from Miss Spalding because there were other benefits.

Thinking of the den where her Little Pup would spend many of his afternoons.

And this reminded him of something else, something certain to distract him from the troubles caused by the officers determined to destroy him. He thought of his den behind the secret door, in his house in Malibu.

And who awaited him there.

Her . . .

And the delightful razor blades, sharpened on stone and honed on leather.

Then he tucked away thoughts of women with pale skin, hunched over in sorrow, and blades and Miss Spalding too, and eased into the brush, following the man he was about to stab to death, as he walked back to the cemetery from an intersection to the north where he and the other investigator had been poking their goddamn noses into Damon's business.

Nearby was a statue of William Shakespeare. He was not a person you saw memorialized in bronze much like here—he was a *painting* kind of historical figure—and Damon wondered who had erected it. And wondered too: Why Southern California?

His victim was on his phone, though not speaking. Looking down, reading texts.

This was like fishing.

His father had never taken him. Of course.

But Miss Spalding had done so—several times—because he'd asked, and she did almost anything he had the least interest in. In a grim suburban lake in San Fernando Valley he'd caught a big sunfish and then hadn't known what to do with it.

She looked at the thing distastefully and rather than take the hook out, she dropped it onto the ground and with a big rock smacked it into death.

"Didn't want it to suffer," she said, as if to allay his concern for the creature's murder.

Though watching the fish die didn't trouble him any more than it did her. He did not, however, gaze down at the guts and the final twitch with a gleam in his eyes, like her.

Maybe it was just the sunlight, that gleam. Or maybe not.

A jogger trotted past and vanished.

Alone now, Damon was free to attack.

He moved in fast, silently, and brought the hunting knife down hard between the man's shoulder blades.

A shout from the pain.

The blade went straight in, through the dark cloth of the jacket. Deep.

He yanked the knife out, then plunged it in again, feeling the satisfying resistance as the blade pierced skin and organ. In seconds, the man was lying face down, hands clenching and relaxing spasmodically, feet kicking.

Motion from nearby.

Another jogger. Damon had planned to do a bit more stabbing, but he was satisfied he'd done sufficient damage. He turned and jogged away, glancing back to survey the Tableau. All was good. The figure was lying motionless. The jogger had jogged elsewhere, unaware of the attack. No one else was present.

Well, that wasn't quite accurate. William Shakespeare had witnessed the whole thing. Damon glanced at the dark metallic face. It held a curious expression, as if the violence the eyes had just witnessed were a thing of familiarity.

Which made sense, considering that here was a man who had, in his literary imaginative mind at least, engineered a hundred bloody murders.

CHAPTER 20

Carmen had hit the twentieth shop or restaurant along Cedar Hills Road during her canvass.

Asking about: A White man. A dark suit. White shirt. Purple tie. Dark hair. Thirties, ish.

"Uhm, well, I guess, I think I saw a bunch of guys like that."

"Thanks. Have a good day."

She hated canvassing.

Carmen was about to turn and head back to the cemetery to help Jake interview the girl witness, Sylvie. Her phone vibrated in her pocket. She put it to her ear without taking the time to check caller ID.

"Agent Sanchez."

"I figured it out, Carm." Selina was breathless with excitement.

Apparently the girl had gotten over whatever had made her hang up so rudely not long ago.

"The 'goddesses.' In the note. But I need to run the last part of the clue by you."

She shouldn't have been surprised her highly intelligent sister had figured out what the mysterious reference might be. But, for some reason, she was. Perhaps because a part of her still thought of Selina as her little sister, a child. Would she *ever* see her differently?

She was tempted to say she was busy but remembered Selina's reaction when she had dismissed the matter of their father's death earlier. A few minutes couldn't hurt. "Cool, Lina, what did you find?"

"Just texted it to you," Selina said, then launched into an explanation of how she'd realized their father had used the first letter of every second word in every second sentence to spell out the names of two goddesses. She could see how Roberto would have easily been able to construct the note on the fly without anyone suspecting it held a secret message.

Fascinating. Carmen actually laughed at the discovery. "Fortuna and Hygeia. Where does it lead us?"

"I looked them up," Selina went on. "Fortuna is the Roman goddess of wealth. Hygeia is the Greek goddess of health and cleanliness."

"Wealth and health?" Carmen muttered, turning the concepts over in her mind.

"I kept getting stuck there." Selina went on. "Did Dad ever read to us about them? I can't remember."

"No, I don't think so."

What would his point have been?

Selina suggested, "Maybe a client with a health problem did something illegal to get money for experimental treatment? Dad found out and the client killed him."

"Maybe. But I don't know how he'd find out. HIPAA, you know?"

"Right. Let's keep going."

Despite the pressure of the case—and the vital need to interview Sylvie—Carmen couldn't help but be drawn into the puzzle. "Any other thoughts?"

"The English word 'hygiene' is obviously based on Hygeia's name. So let's think about cleanliness," Selina said thoughtfully. "And Fortuna was also luck and money."

An idea rippled through Carmen's subconscious, working its way to the surface. Something Selina said resonated, but it wasn't quite there yet. She repeated the three words silently.

Money, luck, cleanliness. Money, luck, cleanliness.

And then the thought that had been a ripple now geysered up.

Not "cleanliness" the noun. But the verb: "Cleaning."

"Money and cleaning," Carmen blurted. "Money laundering."

A pause. "My God, Carm, yes! That's got to be it," Selina said. "Dad realized one of his clients was cooking the books, and they found out."

Damn, Carmen thought, as if punched in the gut.

Another idea occurred. "Any luck with the symbols in the corner?"

"I sent you another text," Selina said. "It probably means '4:19,' as near as I can tell. Mean anything to you?"

She thought for a moment. "No. Nothing. But the money-laundering lead is credible. And could make the crime federal, honey. RICO—the corrupt organizations law—at least. I still have contacts in the FBI, but we have to give them something more than Greek myths to go on. And I guarantee, no federal judge would issue a warrant based on speculation like this."

And a warrant service on whom? They had no suspects.

Selina blurted, "Then let's go and get them what they need."

She admired her younger sister's enthusiasm but had to be straight with her, once again. "Lina, this is brilliant. But you're talking a huge amount of work. And I told you before I can't run with it."

"Yeah, yeah, your un-cold case." Her voice had gone from enthusiastic to snide.

"Lina!"

"Nothing's more important than finding Dad's killer. I can't believe I'm having to say this to you. You just told me no one else is going to investigate this case until we do. Now you still want to shove it to the back burner after what I told you?"

"Yes, something *is* more important. Finding a killer who's going to kill again. Maybe any day now. There's nothing that tells us Dad's killer is going to murder anyone else."

"You can't be sure of that. For all we know, whoever it is could have killed twenty people over the last three years since Dad died. And maybe he *is* about to kill again!"

Carmen calmed and said reasonably, "You're right. It's just, I can't be sure of it. But what I can be sure of is that another innocent person will die if I don't follow up on this one."

"Why does it have to be *you*, Carmen? Aren't there thousands of agents assigned to HSI? Can't one of them take over the case from you?"

Actually, they couldn't. "Jake and I are the only ones running it on the federal side. And I'm the only LEO assigned to I-squared. He's a civilian."

"Well, if you're not going to follow up on this, I'll do it myself."

That again . . .

"Lina, I told you: no."

"You're not my mother," she snapped.

This cut deep. Because, yes, Carmen *had* been her mother, since she'd raised her after both of their parents had passed.

Still, reasonable. Still, even tempered. "You don't have the training or the authority to—"

"Then why did you teach me everything you know?"

Yes, she'd taught her sister many things about being a law enforcer. But it was mostly for her own defense. And her "lessons" were no substitute for years in the academy and the trial by fire on the street.

It was then that a single long tone sounded from the police band radio clipped at her waist.

"What's that sound?" Selina asked.

"An emergency signal. The dispatcher uses it to get attention before making an announcement."

"What kind of announce—?"

"Shh!"

The dispatcher's voice cut through the silence that followed the tone. "All units, code 3. Two forty-five in progress. The park north of Cedar Hills Cemetery. Subject is stabbing a victim near the north entrance of the grounds. Suspect is a White male, six two, two twenty, wearing gray windbreaker and jeans, baseball cap."

A flurry of LAPD patrol unit transmissions reported that officers were en route to the scene. Carmen abruptly ended her conversation with her sister. "I gotta go, Lina. Leave Dad's case alone. I mean it."

Without waiting for an answer, she disconnected. She listened as the dispatcher delivered an update, indicating the suspect had left the scene. Then an addition:

"Responding rescue personnel, be advised that the victim is near the north entrance to Cedar Hills Cemetery. Victim is described as a White male, tall, average build, early thirties, brown hair."

No!

The site of the stabbing was the exact spot where Jake Heron would be on his way to interview the girl.

She began to sprint.

CHAPTER 21

Her stomach in knots, Carmen held up her creds as she sprinted past the local PD officer posted at the perimeter of the park.

Please don't let the wounds be fatal.

She had seen death while serving on the FBI's Los Angeles field office SWAT team and now picked up the odor of blood in the air as she approached the paramedics hunched over the inert form lying on the grass near a statue of William Shakespeare.

The contrast between the three busy EMTs and the stillness of the body they worked feverishly to save struck at her very core.

The Honeymoon Killer had caught Heron from behind.

Please don't let him die.

She pounded to a halt and sank to her knees beside one of the medics, a burly balding man in his twenties who was the definition of "unflappable." Gasping, Carmen asked, "Have you got a pulse?"

No immediate response, which she took as a good sign. Experience had taught her that when an ambulance crew moved slowly, that meant the patient's terminal outcome was a foregone conclusion. This team, however, was working feverishly.

She didn't want to interfere with what she'd overheard EMTs refer to as "thumping and pumping," which meant chest compressions and squeezing air into an oxygen mask over the patient's face, but she was desperate for an assessment.

She looked at the closest paramedic and decided to try again. This time she restricted her question to one word. A word that should elicit a response as if a doctor or charge nurse had demanded an answer. "Status?"

"Attempting to stabilize for transport."

That didn't console her at all. The word "attempting" implied they weren't having success, after all. Then again—

"No . . ." A voice, laced with dismay, came from behind her.

She swiveled to the speaker.

It was Jake Heron.

Overwhelmed with shock and unable to form words, she stood and reached out to grasp his arm, assuring herself this was not an apparition. Then she stepped to the side to peer around the paramedic and took a closer look at the victim's face, which was still partially concealed by the oxygen mask. What she saw sent alternating waves of relief and dread rushing through her.

Frank Tandy was the one who'd been stabbed.

Carmen had known the detective for years. They had participated in joint federal-local training, served on a few multijurisdictional task forces and, after major incidents, had occasionally seen each other at one of the local watering holes favored by law enforcement, where beer selections were long and wine short.

"How is he?" Heron asked.

She shook her head.

He said in a strained voice, "That could have been me. *Should* have been me."

"What happened?" she asked.

"I started toward the cemetery to meet the teenage girl, then I got a phone call." He hesitated. "Family matter. I couldn't let it wait. I told Frank and he said he'd interview her, and I could take over on the canvass."

"Family matter?"

Heron said nothing more about it. But simply stared at the medic hovering over Tandy's form. He whispered, "Son of a bitch." Then heaved a sigh.

"Heron."

He slowly lifted his gaze to meet hers.

"What-if's a game you can't play in law enforcement," she said. "You'll learn that as you go along."

"Did he have a vest?"

She nodded. "But ballistic armor doesn't do much good against edged weapons. HK stabbed around and through it."

The paramedics positioned Tandy on a board, lifted it to the gurney and ran a line. They wheeled him to the ambulance. An LAPD sergeant strode forward, and Carmen briefed him. He took custody of Tandy's service weapon, asking Carmen, Heron and the medics, "He describe who attacked him?"

"No," a woman EMT replied as they loaded Tandy into the ambulance. "Nonresponsive when we got here."

Without another word, she slammed the rear doors, and soon the vehicle was gone. Carmen explained to the sergeant about the task-forced case, and suggested Tandy's captain contact Williamson for next steps regarding liaison.

She then called Williamson to update him on the disturbing developments. He was out at a meeting with other DHS officials, but Destiny Baker, his assistant, promised to relay the information to her boss.

Carmen disconnected and turned to Heron. "That teenager. We need to talk to her."

"Right," he said firmly, his face grim. He seemed as deeply troubled by the attack as she was. Maybe he felt guilty, but Carmen thought it was more.

Battling together in the trenches does that, forging connections that might not otherwise exist. And forging them fast. She suspected this was what had happened between the two men.

Carmen called Liam Grange and found that when the teenager's family learned of the attack, they immediately returned home to Brentwood, fearful for their safety.

Heron considered this news. "I know you like to interview wits in person, but we don't have time to drive over to their house."

She said absently, her mind still on Tandy and his condition, "'Wit.' Instead of 'witnesses.' You're turning into a cop, Heron."

He offered a wistful smile.

Carmen placed a call to the number Grange had given her. A woman's smoky voice answered, and after a few minutes of setting the ground rules, which included the nonnegotiable condition that her daughter would never testify in court, the girl joined her mother on the line.

"Hello, Sylvie. You're on speaker. I'm here with my associate."

"Yes, ma'am."

"You can call me Carmen."

A pause. "Okay. How's that guy? You know, the one who got stabbed?"

"He's alive. In the hospital and they're operating on him now."

"Okay. Good. Cool."

"Now, we're ninety percent sure the man you saw was the one who stabbed him."

"Shit."

"Syl." From the mother.

No response from the daughter. She had been tangentially involved in a knife attack. Carmen guessed the teen would have no time for parental corrections.

"Can you describe him, Sylvie?"

"He was White and *old*—maybe, like, thirties."

Despite everything, Heron and Carmen shared a brief smile at this.

"But he was still kinda hot."

"Syl!"

Everyone ignored the mother. Carmen continued, "What was his hair color?"

"Dark, I think. And he was big but not fat. He wore a suit, like all the men. My dad calls it charcoal gray. And his tie, I kept looking at his tie. It was purple. Like the wizards wore in *Harry Potter*. You know, to signal each other they were wizards."

"What happened when he talked to you?"

"He saw me and walked up, all friendly. And I thought it was weird because, you know, my grandpa—it was his funeral—he was *really* old, and we knew he was going to die. But everybody was still real sad looking. Kind of like what you do, you know. At a funeral you're supposed to look all sad, even if you don't really care. But he wasn't sad at all. He looked happy."

Carmen had her tablet out and made a note. "And what did he say?"

"Just a couple words. Like, 'Hey there. How you doing?' That kind of thing. Then he freaked. I think because those cop cars, I mean *police* cars, showed up and he just turned around and walked away. Fast."

"You remember anything else about him? Jewelry, scars, tattoos, cell phone?"

A pause. "No. Definitely no tats. I always notice body art."

"Did you see him with anyone else?" Heron asked.

He'd be thinking of Ms. POI.

Who was maybe a wit.

Maybe something more.

Sylvie seemed to think it over before responding, "No."

"Did you see him later?" Carmen asked. "After he walked away."

"No, ma'am. I didn't."

"What did his voice sound like?"

"A man's voice. I don't know. No accent or anything if that's what you mean."

"Exactly."

Heron asked, "You saw the hearse that started driving by itself?"

"Yeah, totally fu—totally friggin' weird."

"When he left you, did he walk in the direction of the hearse?"

"I . . . geez. I don't know."

"Hey, listen, Sylvie. You're being super helpful."

Heron posed a question. "Did you see a woman in black heels with a red stripe down the back?"

"No." The girl's voice brightened. "But I would've remembered those."

Carmen then asked the ever-important final question in an interview. "Anything else?"

A pause, then: "Yeah. It was funny."

"Go on."

"Yeah. He wasn't a perv."

"Honey!" her mother said.

"Mom," she said, sighing. "Come on."

Heron was about to ask her to explain but stopped when Carmen lifted a hand. He understood. This topic was a topic discussed among women.

"Okay, I'm, like, a teenager, right?" Sylvie said. "And we get . . . girls, mostly, we get guys coming up to us—sometimes older dudes like this guy's age—and they act all nice and smiley and chatty, you know. But we just *totally* know they're pervs. You can tell. We call it our pedar."

Carmen thought she understood but got clarification anyway. "Pedar?"

"Pedophile radar," Sylvie said. "Like a built-in perv detector. Only this dude wasn't that way at all. Which I thought was funny, because why come up to *me*, some stranger at a funeral and just go 'Hey there.' I was thinking he wanted something. But not *that*. You know what I mean?"

Carmen jotted this down too. Was it significant? She had a feeling it was, but nothing immediately came to mind.

After a few more questions, they said goodbye and Carmen disconnected.

"'Pedar,'" she said to Heron. "Clever. But also sad kids have a word for it."

"Don't get me started on the subject of sexual intrusion. We'd be here all day."

"Well, what do you think, Heron? What the hell *was* he interested in? He approached her for some reason."

"Agree it's significant but, as my colleagues in academia would say, I'm lacking sufficient data to form a hypothesis."

She knew Heron was avowedly anti-speculation. He never made a decision or offered an opinion without a basket full of data points.

As they walked back to the cemetery, Carmen frowned. "Heron?"

"What's that?"

"How the hell did he know you or Frank were coming here to interview that girl? Only one answer."

And Heron provided it: "He's been watching us. It's not just honeymooners he's after. We've made it onto his hit list too."

CHAPTER 22

Eric,

Good news from the Eastern Front! Have had some chin-wags with the powers that be, and it looks like Congress is on our side. Going to move forward with I-squared. Make it official. Assume you want to keep your present status as lead, so they'll need some signatures.

Somebody is coming by your office today. Can hardly believe they want to move as fast as we do.

Lots of chatter about your recent big win!

Congressional Liaison in LA will be in touch.

BTW: One can complain about pollution in the City of Angels, but did you know that Washington DC literally was a swamp once! And I'm not speaking of politicians and lobbyists. Ha.

Thanks, Eric. Talk soon.

SR

Eric Williamson read the text once more—yes, the highly encrypted text. Stan Reynolds had indeed learned his lesson about security from Heron.

So it was going to happen.

"All right, Eric, what's that Cheshire grin all about?"

Williamson looked up from his desk to see his assistant in the doorway. Destiny Baker wore a perfectly shaved buzz cut that emphasized a perfectly shaped head and face, and the smile was remarkable, set off by the stunning crimson hue of her lipstick.

"I wasn't smiling."

"You weren't frowning and for you that's a smile."

Williamson had no problem with her quirky nature. Baker set the standard for personal assistantness.

"Looks like it's happening."

She blinked. "My God. Official?"

"Official."

"So I don't have to start an online Etsy business to make ends meet?"

"Your employment wasn't in danger . . . at least not much." Now he offered a true, if brief, grin.

"Congratulations, Eric."

Nothing jokey now. She opened her mouth to say more but was interrupted by a trilling phone.

Williamson momentarily closed his eyes and rested the back of his head against the massive chair, a black leather swivel rocker that he'd purchased out of his own pocket because there was nothing in the government warehouse that could handle his bulk.

The pleasure he felt was diminished by the news that HK had attacked and severely injured Frank Tandy, whom Williamson had worked with several times in the past. He placed a call to Tandy's captain at LAPD, who told him she had spoken to the hospital, but had no updates about his condition. She added that she would look for another gold shield to serve as liaison, but for the time being, the LAPD and I-squared would have to work independently and share information as needed.

He told her he would keep her informed and they disconnected.

Baker appeared once more at the door. "Congressional Liaison office. Somebody's coming by with paperwork."

"When?"

"Probably ten or fifteen."

"How did they know for sure I was here?"

Baker shrugged. "They know *everything*, Eric. Key cards, all that. The US Congress doesn't have time to waste. If they're coming to get your signature, they're going to know exactly where you are."

"I'll need to draft a memo to everyone. Could you hang around—"

"Not going anywhere till I see a congressional ass in this doorway. I wonder if they look like everyone else's ass." She zipped back to her desk.

Williamson picked up his landline phone. He had never in his life asked a secretary or PA to "get so-and-so on the line for me." It was demeaning to everyone. He aimed a blunt finger toward the speed-dial list. The names beside the buttons were printed in his own clumsy script—a hand injury had forever affected his writing. One might think it was from eight years of line- and quarterbacking football, or eight years as a field agent, but that would be wrong.

He hit button number one.

A ring, then: "Honey!" Camille's breezy voice was sweet and satin smooth, utterly disarming to defendants on the stand—who, upon hearing it, expected a shy schoolteacher when it came to cross-examination. They got instead breathtaking speed and precision of delivery, as she wielded verbal knives with which she cut their legs—and the foundation of their case—out from under them.

"All good?" she asked.

Both parents spent equal time marshaling, nurturing, educating and chauffeuring the four boys—with the help of an impeccable nanny. A call to his wife during office hours, a rarity, might have to do with a problem at school, a medical issue or the like.

"Fine." A pause. "I just heard. Looks like it's going to happen."

He offered no further explanation. Sure enough, Camille instantly understood.

"Oh, my!"

"A congressional aide or somebody is on the way over here with the paperwork."

"So I-squared will be permanent?"

"That's right."

Camille said, "Is this where I mention that you've damn well earned it?"

"That's what the script calls for. Along with how wonderful I am in general. And an irreplaceable asset to King and country."

"Handsome too," Camille said coyly.

"Forgot that one."

"What, the best part?"

Williamson wondered how his agents—say, Carmen Sanchez—would react, hearing him talk like this. Like a normal husband. And not the gruff bull he was in the office.

Camille asked, "What're the details?"

"Don't know yet. My request for expansion's still on the table."

I-squared's temporary pilot program was authorized for two operatives—Sanchez and Heron—and access to HSI support, like tactical and forensics. Williamson had originally requested dozens of agents and an entire division of HSI personnel.

Maybe the new Stan Reynolds had twisted arms and made that dream come true.

He said as much to Camille.

"Stan? Playing your wingman?" Her voice exuded astonishment.

"Miracles happen. Chill that champagne we've been saving."

"Eric, we're not *saving* it. It sits there because you don't like champagne."

"It's great—if you mix it with a little Jefferson bourbon."

"Ouch."

"Better go. The emissary will be here soon."

"Emissary. That makes it sound special. And it is, Eric. You should be proud. Love you."

"Love you too . . ."

After disconnecting, he sat back. He knew he should get to work on the stack of files heaped on his desk, but he simply stared out the window at the shipyard. His massive right hand clenched and relaxed. Some days it was better than others. He'd tried to correlate the pain to the weather. That didn't seem to be the case. Sometimes it hurt worse when he was stressed out.

But *that* of course lacked any basis in medicine.

Essentially, his hand hurt when it decided to hurt.

He scanned his desktop. Those file folders sitting there—twenty-seven of them—contained details of the cases that his agents in Homeland Security Investigations were running. HSI's jurisdiction ran parallel to that of the FBI and other law enforcement agencies, but it specialized in crimes with an international element. The files were representative of the cases HSI handled: human trafficking, child exploitation, weapons, corruption in labor organizations, financial fraud, computer crimes and—being with the Department of Homeland Security—big T. Terrorism.

Williamson didn't deny the importance of HSI's work—it was the backbone of the organization—and his department's arrest record and the more-important conviction-to-arrest ratio were the envy of every federal LEO in the country.

Yet when he'd ascended to his current senior position, he did so with the awareness that there was a gap in HSI's mission. And that awareness on his part could be traced to, of all things, a song.

Shall we gather at the river?
Where bright angel feet have trod,
with its crystal tide forever
flowing by the throne of God?

The hymn, more memorable for its tune than lyrics, revolved through his mind like a carousel's organ music several times a week. And what had seated it there was a performance he had attended three years, five months and four days ago.

That day in early October, he and Camille and their three children were in the second-to-last pew on the right side of the modest Ezekiel Brethren Church in Inwood. They'd been late—shoes had gone missing, and the youngest had further delayed them with a last-minute bathroom stop.

Upon arriving, they found a pew and sat in their accustomed order: Marcus, Eric, Aaron, Peter, then Camille, who together with Henry counted as one because she was not due for another two months.

The choir—and yes, they were astonishing, the bass especially—had just struck up the melodically infectious river-gathering song when Williamson noticed that the door behind him—the front door—had opened, painting the interior in a brief swath of cool white light.

He leaned over to Camille and whispered, "So we're not the last in."

"Points are still deducted for being *penultimate*," she joked and sat back, resting a hand on her belly. Henry apparently liked the music too and was, maybe, kicking out the beat.

Yes, we'll gather at the river, the beautiful, the beautiful river . . .

The late entry, standing in the aisle just behind their pew, was a young White man in jeans, a dark-green windbreaker and a baseball cap with no logo.

That he was White was not unusual. The Ezekiel Brethren congregation was only about 80 percent people of color. Williamson knew most of the parishioners well, but he didn't recognize the newcomer.

There were plenty of seats, but the man continued to stand in the middle of the single aisle, gazing about, searching for congregants he was supposed to meet, Williamson assumed. He concentrated on his own singing. Reverend DeKalb encouraged everyone to join in.

A full two minutes passed and still the young man did not sit, and Williamson noted something—he *believed* he noted something. As the man scanned the church, he was not looking at the clusters of White congregants but only those of color—Black and a few Latino families.

The beautiful, the beautiful river . . .

And then it happened.

The man crouched, and Williamson recognized the way his hand disappeared into his jacket in a way that meant only one thing—he was cross-drawing a weapon.

Williamson was instantly on his feet, covering his wife and the boys beside her and flinging his son Marcus, closest to the threat, behind him. The boy actually caught air before Camille fielded him.

"Shooter!" he yelled in a booming baritone.

Williamson carried a .40 Glock—a powerful round—but there were parishioners behind the gunman. At this range, his bullet might tear through his target and strike innocents.

As the shooter's weapon swept out—a Glock 9mm—Williamson launched himself forward. While some of the muscle from his college football days had pastured into fat, most remained rock solid. He slammed headlong into the perp. They both crashed into the pew on the other side of the aisle and sprawled to the floor.

The attacker was scrawny, but he twisted and slugged and kicked like someone possessed—no doubt trying to injure Williamson and get some distance so he could start shooting the other congregants.

Williamson shouted at Camille: "Get the boys out of here! Call it in!"

And he was infinitely grateful she didn't hesitate but quickly shepherded their children to safety.

As the two men grappled, Williamson began to twist the gunman's wrist, grunting with the effort as he issued a guttural command through clenched teeth. "Drop it."

Rather than comply, the shooter used his left hand to pull the gun from his right and swung the muzzle back and forth as he looked for targets.

Some fled the church, but many remained, hiding behind the pews. Williamson had no way to warn them that a 9mm round could penetrate the wooden benches.

And more troubling, Mrs. Abbott, a grandmother who took six-year-old Mary to church when her mother worked, was panicking. She had simply dropped to the middle of the aisle not twenty feet from the gunman, using her body as a human shield to cover her screaming granddaughter.

The shooter noticed and smiled as he shifted to aim his weapon at them.

Williamson cried, "Get out! Run!"

But Mrs. Abbott was paralyzed with fear.

The big agent released his grip on the gunman's right wrist and caught the left an instant before he pulled the trigger.

Williamson had been in plenty of fights. The familiar mix of sweat and body odor assailed his nostrils as he kept trying to wrestle the gun away. "You don't . . . want to . . . do this," he muttered, between grunts. "It's not too late."

The shooter spat in Williamson's face, then blurted the familiar slur—the last resort of the ignorant and the desperate—after which he redoubled his efforts to point the muzzle toward the Abbotts.

A jerk of the trigger.

The explosion of sound and the muzzle blast so close to Williamson's face forced his eyes shut and snapped his head back.

The bullet ended up somewhere in the ceiling.

Then a searing wave of pain, breathtaking, as the attacker's teeth sank into the flesh just below Williamson's thumb.

He howled in agony, but didn't let go, and he felt the recoil in his throbbing hand as the man fired another two shots. They too missed their target, one slamming into the altar, the other shattering a stained glass window depicting Jesus on the cross.

Williamson's left hand was free, and he drew it back to plow the heel of his palm into the man's nose in an attempt to break the excruciating grip with his teeth. A scream—a satisfying scream—resulted.

The strike didn't force the gunman to release his bite, and it had unintended consequences. Blood from the man's freshly broken nose flowed onto Williamson's right hand and the slippery liquid broke his grip on the shooter's gun hand.

At that moment, little Mary managed to wriggle out from under her grandmother and scramble to her feet. Before Mrs. Abbott could pull her back down, the gunman aimed at the girl.

It was a shot even an amateur could make.

Williamson shouted, "No!"

A word that was lost in the thunderous blast, which deafened him and brought tears to his eyes. Gunshot residue spattered his forehead and cheeks.

In the ringing roar that followed, Williamson watched the shooter silently slump to the floor.

A .38 special round is roughly the same diameter as a 9mm, but the shell is longer and has more mass—as well as a lot more gunpowder behind it. When the bullet strikes the temple, death is instantaneous.

He knew what type of ammo had killed the shooter because of who had pulled the trigger. His wife, Camille, a federal prosecutor, was permitted to carry a weapon, and she did with some frequency. She put away sicarios and OGs and young banger punks from South Central and Mafia wannabes from the docks. From time to time some foolish—and now incarcerated—soul threatened her or put a price on her head.

The shooter was down, but procedures were baked in. Instantly Williamson was on his feet, securing the man's weapon, unloading it and locking the slide back before pocketing it and verifying there were no other weapons on him.

He scanned the church for accomplices. None that he could see. A quick check of the man's vitals confirmed he was dead.

He then checked the man's phone to see if there were texts about others he might be working with for coordinated attacks. But he couldn't access messages in the password-protected device.

Paramedics and LAPD soon arrived to take charge of the scene.

This incident was the spark that gave life to the organization destined to become I-squared.

And yet, the shooting itself was not the genesis.

What spurred him to act came days later when he learned the shooter, John Ray Hobart, had been active on a website.

Williamson had logged on to check it out. The site had a chan chat board and an imageboard that were filled like a hornet's nest with hateful rants, angry diatribes, disgusting cartoons and pictures. Racism and misogyny-fueled conspiracy theories abounded.

The shooter at the church had been called a hero.

And the site was not even hidden in the corners of the dark web. It was free for anyone to access by using simple search terms.

Williamson sucked in a breath—a rare show of emotion—when he read some of the posts about Hobart and the shooting. Hundreds extolled him as a martyr to the "cause."

One began: *All he was trying to do was kill a bunch of . . .*

And of course the vile word made yet another appearance. On that page alone he counted it two dozen times.

As a senior agent in Homeland Security, he was more than aware of terrorist threats against the country and the efforts by the federal government to identify and thwart them. But after the shooting at the church and his discovery of the website and many others like it, Eric Williamson came up with a new concept: micro threats to national security.

Not hatched by enemies overseas or domestic extremist organizations, these were perpetrated by lone actors or small groups. Each incident might account for only one or two deaths—but those crimes, in the aggregate, were as much a threat to the fabric of America as a coordinated attack planned in some far-flung terrorist enclave. Williamson wanted a rapid response team that operated independently to find and thwart them before they carried out their deadly plans.

And so began his quest to create a dedicated group. The new unit would devote itself to searching for these micro threats by scouring the web, NCIC, social media and regular news sources for any hint of brewing danger. He would then send the rapid response team to stop it.

Which was why he'd been delighted to score Professor Jake Heron—the best on the web he had ever met. Carmen Sanchez too, who not only had a background in cybercrime but had served on the FBI's LA field office SWAT team.

Until Williamson had recruited her for Homeland.

Then came Declan. Williamson was the first in the Department of Justice to employ a large language model this way, searching for any traces of a micro threat.

But resistance within the DOJ was fierce, especially from the man who could give the yea or nay to the program he'd proposed, none other than Stanley Reynolds. A new, streamlined unit that operated independently and moved fast, without involving endless chains of command, was "out of the ordinary." It threatened both the status quo and his bailiwick. Reynolds apparently believed, inexplicably, that an outfit like I-squared would endanger his ascension to the top spot at Homeland.

But because of the positive attention garnered after a case Carmen and Jake had recently concluded, somebody over Reynolds's head had authorized a pilot program to test the concept.

A step forward.

But not enough for Eric Williamson.

He wanted—needed—I-squared to be permanent, and not implemented by executive order, as it had been, but by Congress.

Now it was clear from Reynolds's message, Williamson had succeeded.

And with some luck, the subcommittee might have also approved the staff expansion he dreamed of. He envisioned Carmen overseeing a dozen field agents. Heron in charge of I-squared's cyber operation, white hat hackers and penetration testers just like him.

Williamson heard voices just outside his office and looked up to see a man of around thirty and a slightly younger woman, both with dark-blond hair in, respectively, a businessman's trim and a taut ponytail.

Destiny Baker spoke to them, and she walked to the door. "You free now?"

You bet he was. A nod.

She escorted the two inside.

"Agent Williamson. I'm Steve Mehlman. And this is my associate, Karen Winters. Office of Legislative Counsel."

The men shook hands, she nodded.

"Please, sit."

"We can't stay, sir. We're only here for some signatures." The man glanced to Winters, who dug into a shoulder bag and withdrew an 8½ × 11-inch envelope and two sheets of white paper. She gave them to Mehlman, who completed the hand-off to Williamson.

"If you could sign both copies. One's for your files."

It was a receipt saying he acknowledged accepting delivery of certain documents listed below.

He looked at the first item on the list and the smile of anticipation faded.

Wait . . . no!

He tore open the envelope and read.

It was the worst news he could possibly imagine.

CHAPTER 23

Selina Sanchez hadn't gotten where she was by sitting around and waiting for others to do things for her.

Or by asking for permission to do them herself.

She was a champion gymnast with an athletic scholarship. She was also an A student, mastering tough subjects like organic chemistry and advanced calculus using what she called her "mental muscle."

She was an intellect who'd begun to crack the Da Vinci code of her father's supposed suicide note.

And now was playing ace investigator, pursuing the case her sister would not.

Selina was sitting in the office of her father's former business partner, in Whittier, a suburb of LA.

Dapper, sixty-year-old, balding, solidly built Carl Overton—who always wore dark three-piece suits—looked at her with dismay. "Someone's stalking you? One of your dad's former clients?"

"I think so." A hedge that sort of defused the lie. "I've gotten messages about how Dad ruined their lives with his bad investments. And now they want to ruin *my* life."

"What does your sister say? Or the police?"

She scoffed and tried to remind herself to be a talented—that is, understated—actor playing her part in the role she'd created. "They don't care. There's no proof a crime was committed. They can't devote resources until something actually happens."

"Yes, I've heard about that. Domestic abuse and stalking. The police need concrete evidence before they do anything."

"Exactly."

"What do you want to do?"

"Get financial statements from back then. See who lost money in the bad fund, and how much."

"Well, I'm sorry, honey. But I have a fiduciary responsibility. I could lose my license, and get sued, by revealing confidential client details without a subpoena. If I were served with papers, I'd have cover for turning over sensitive information."

She countered: "But I don't think there's enough evidence for that. Just some phone calls I've gotten. Some mean comments on social media. Posted from anonymous accounts."

"Well, I can't give you records. I'd get in really hot water." A wan smile. "As hot as the tea your dad used to drink."

She plastered on a smile that matched his. Hiding the fresh surge of anger that someone had killed her father.

And Carmen's refusal to do anything about it. She was certain her hard-charging sister could finagle a subpoena if she really wanted to, with only the thinnest of evidence.

"Well, Mr. Overton, what about just a list of names? Then I could go online and see if any of them had records. Previous stalking. Abuse. Anything violent."

Or had a history of goddamn money laundering.

Which, of course, she did not add.

Carl Overton had been like an uncle to her and Carmen. Not immediate-family close, but he'd always treated them kindly and been generous with presents at birthdays and around holidays. He'd put together the funeral reception, which was held at one of the fanciest restaurants in the city—and was attended by CEOs of major companies and even some Los Angeles city officials.

It appeared he really did want to help but could not quite reconcile the legal and ethical issues.

She tried another approach to push him over those hurdles. "It's like what happened with that guy, Bernie Madoff. He lost all his clients' money, and they came after his family, even if they hadn't done anything wrong. There was a TV special on him."

He nodded in understanding, but clearly still wasn't convinced.

Selina sat forward and lowered her voice to a conspiratorial whisper, as if government regulators lurked nearby. "You know, my dad probably still has some of his own files in the effects Carmen and I have."

Though they had nothing to do with his work. His financial advisory files had all disappeared—and she now knew why.

But she continued, "And if anybody asked, well, I could just tell people that I found them there. On his old laptop at home."

Would he understand that she was giving him cover?

"Probably," he said uncertainly.

"And they'd never know." She waved a hand at his computer. Finishing the sentence with a silent "where any files you gave me came from."

"Hm." His dark eyes swiveled from her to the computer and back again.

Her older sister had taught her that when you were interrogating a suspect, silence could be your friend. Shut up until they feel compelled to fill the awkward pauses.

Overton hesitated for a long minute and then, apparently coming to a decision, began typing on his keyboard. "It'll take a while. And there'll be gaps. Roberto's clients all moved on—those who still have money to invest, anyway." He grimaced. "Sorry. That came out badly."

"It's okay," she said. "It's simply the truth."

He turned to his computer.

Overton had been referring to the bum investment her father had persuaded people to sink their money into. Normally he wouldn't have counseled such a lopsided portfolio, but this fund had been vastly out-performing the market for several years.

Roberto had done nothing illegal, and he wasn't the only adviser who'd been stung by the choice. The disaster could be traced to the fickleness of the stock market—and by the stroke of terrible coincidence that the three largest companies in the portfolio had all suffered financial disasters simultaneously. Two went bankrupt and the government sued the third for unfair trade practices.

But that knowledge had been of zero comfort to those who had lost their life savings and were too old to earn it back.

Yet the tragedy now worked to Selina's advantage, creating the basis for the fiction that a resentful stalker had targeted her. A fiction that Overton had apparently bought.

"Thank you," she whispered.

He gave her a curt nod in response.

She got to her feet. "Is the bathroom still in the hallway?"

"That's right. The code is one two three eight."

After leaving his office she walked down the corridor, passed by the restroom and continued toward the door to what had been her father's office, now sealed off from Overton's but accessible from here.

Was it occupied? What would she say to whoever was inside?

If it was empty, would the door be locked?

Didn't matter.

Locked or not, she would get in.

She reached the closed door and looked at the sign above it.

STORAGE

Of course, no one else had wanted to work in a space that had seen such tragedy.

She twisted the knob. Locked. But it was a simple mechanism and, after making sure no one was around, she removed a flexible plastic rectangle—a sporting goods store loyalty card—from her wallet. Using an old burglar's trick her sister had casually mentioned to her years ago, she kept working the card against the dead bolt until it was pushed from the hole in the frame. The door swung open. After casting another furtive glance over her shoulder, she slipped inside and pulled the door shut behind her.

Gone were the pair of black leather chairs she and her sister would lounge in, playing video games or reading books on the Saturdays and Sundays Roberto came in to get work done and not have to be concerned about client visits.

Gone were the modern desk and sleek credenza.

Gone were the empty file boxes the girls had stacked to build fortresses.

Gone, the family pictures that were everywhere, from walls, to filing cabinets to credenza, to desk.

Ah, the desk, she thought, blinking back tears. The desk with the dent in the front that Carmen said looked like a belly button, making Selina dissolve into giggles.

The desk where Roberto had been forced to write the note, a copy of which burned in her pocket.

My goddesses . . .

And the anger returned, nearly blinding her.

Slowly, she turned to face the window.

After a steadying breath, she walked toward it. Her fingers, suddenly cold and nerveless, fumbled to release the latches. She grasped the metal hooks at the bottom of the sash, but it was stuck. After a considerable amount of tugging and cursing, the lower pane slowly squeaked up. A cool breeze blew over her sweat-damp skin, raising goose pimples.

Swallowing the bile creeping up the back of her throat, she bent and leaned her upper body out. Her gaze traveled to the parking lot far below. Carmen had gotten the entire police file, which contained the crime scene photos, Selina was sure. But her sister had sent her only the note.

Just as well. She didn't want to see her father's body bloody and broken.

But now, she did have to see the place where he died.

What had he been thinking as he sailed through the air? Had he been conscious or, as Carmen believed, had the killer knocked him out after he wrote the note? Although, privately, Selina wondered whether her sister had told her that to spare her the horror of imagining their father's last moments of sheer terror as he plummeted to his death.

And how had he been coerced to write it? Carmen had shared her theory that someone must have threatened the only thing he cared about more than life itself—his daughters.

Who the hell was the killer?

Carmen said Jake Heron and a friend had discovered that it was a professional hit man. What had he looked like? Was his voice high or low? Did he feel any remorse?

But, most importantly, who hired him?

A creak behind her. She whirled around.

Carl Overton was staring at her. His gaze traveled to the open window, then returned to her. "You shouldn't be here."

He must have heard the pane squeak.

She realized he'd closed the door behind him and swallowed the lump in her throat. "I had to see."

He gave no reaction. His expression hardened a fraction, and for a moment it was as if he didn't believe her—about what she was doing here in the first place and what she wanted the names for.

And worse, that he resented her mission altogether.

"How did you get in? The storage room is supposed to be locked." He walked toward her, and she stepped back, nearer to the window.

Before he reached her, a noise from the hallway drew Overton's attention, stopping him in his tracks. The door opened and a member of the cleaning crew stepped inside. She glanced at the two of them, then began to empty a waste bin.

Overton moved past Selina, then closed and locked the window. He gave her a meaningful look. "My office."

He left. She followed.

Inside, he returned to his desk and said, "I didn't know what dates you wanted for the client list."

Was this the reason he'd gone to find her? Wasn't it obvious? He clearly knew when Roberto died and who his clients were at the time.

She gave it some thought and said, "For the twelve months leading up to his death?"

A slow nod. He resumed typing. Several sheets hissed from the laser printer beside the desk.

He handed them to her.

And for the first time, a thought occurred. Yes, Roberto had invested badly—but only he and his clients had suffered. Was Overton wholly innocent of the decision? The men had very likely discussed the fund. What had the senior partner's opinion of it been?

And why had Overton not invested in the fund too?

She decided that maybe he had, but didn't recommend that his own clients put *all* their savings into it.

She scoffed to herself. This investigator stuff was making her suspicious of *everyone*.

Overton regarded her carefully before saying, "I wish you all the best with your mission."

"My mission?" she asked softly.

"Finding your stalker, of course."

"Oh, sure. Thank you."

CHAPTER 24

"What is this?" Eric Williamson whispered, staring at the documents the congressional liaison attorneys had just delivered.

Mehlman blinked, apparently because it was obvious. "It's a subpoena to appear before the Congressional Subcommittee on National Security."

Words failed him momentarily. The appearance was set for tomorrow morning at nine. Factoring in a five-hour flight to DC, and a three-hour time zone difference, he would have to leave now. As in, right now.

About fifty pages of exhibits, reports and sworn affidavits and other supporting documents accompanied the short subpoena.

He glanced up at them. "The hell's this about?"

Both visitors remained calm. One thing was clear from their expressions. The pair were utterly bulletproof to any insults and anger fired their way. They were the government equivalent of the hit teams called in by human resource departments to fire employees.

"You'll have time to read everything on the flight—there's a government jet standing by at LAX. But the gist is that the subcommittee plans to fold this I-squared program into DHS at a higher level than HSI."

"But . . . I can't leave HSI."

Winters offered, "Oh, that's not a concern, Agent Williamson. You'll remain here. There's no change in your job status whatsoever. But you'll no longer have the added burden of I-squared."

"Burden? It's the whole point of what I've been trying to put together for three years."

Mehlman jutted out his lower lip. "Then kudos to you that it's going to a higher division." He looked at his watch. Was he late for the next meeting in which he'd destroy someone's life? "If you could acknowledge receipt of the subpoena, sir."

"I'm not doing that." He pushed the two slips of paper back toward them.

Mehlman shrugged. "All right." Delivered with the practiced air of a process server who had heard it all before. He glanced at Winters. "Please record."

She lifted her phone and hit what was presumably the video button.

Mehlman spoke in a carrying voice. "The federal subpoena issued by Magistrate Joanne Visconte in the District Court of Washington, DC, dated this day has been duly served on Supervisory Special Agent Eric Williamson." He looked back at Winters and added, "And duly witnessed."

No . . . this can't be happening . . .

His mind spun. A million thoughts. "Well, I can't just leave with these active investigations going on."

"The director will be in touch about that. You don't need to worry."

Williamson resisted an urge to tear up the subpoena as Winters frowned wrinkles into her young face. "Agent Williamson? I should mention. The plane is wheels up in forty-two minutes."

Mehlman added, "If I were you, sir, I'd get a move on. You miss your appearance and you'll be held in contempt of Congress. Could get you a year in prison. We wouldn't want that now, would we?"

CHAPTER 25

Jake stood in front of the digital murder board on I-squared's otherwise unadorned walls. There was a lot of text, a lot of pictures, a number of maps. Some sketches.

Nothing was proving helpful, though.

Sanchez disconnected a call. "Not having much luck with Lauren Brock."

The elusive sister of the victim at the Hollywood Crest.

They had gotten pertinent information about her from Allison and Ben, Anthony's best man. Lauren worked as a bookkeeper at an automotive parts supplier in San Fernando Valley. She rented a small house in Van Nuys, a modest region of LA, also in the Valley.

Sanchez continued, "Her boss said she called in the day after Anthony's death to tell him she was taking the week off. He advised her to use as much time as she needed. He didn't say anything about substance issues, and I didn't mention it.

"Sheriff's deputies stopped by her place, but nobody was home. And the neighbors hadn't seen her since the weekend. I tried the rehab center Anthony put her in, but she's not there and hasn't been in touch."

Jake sighed. "Hate to picture her with a bottle or a bunch of dirty needles, holed up in some sleazy motel."

"Tough, yeah."

He noticed her face had stilled and wondered where her thoughts were.

The answer—possible answer—came a moment later. "I'm going to see Frank."

They'd gotten no updates on Tandy's condition.

"Sure. Give him my best."

"Will do."

After she'd left, Jake gave one last look at the uncooperative murder board and sat down at his workstation. Sanchez's comment brought to mind the phone call that made him swap tasks with the detective in the park north of Cedar Hills Cemetery—the call that had saved Jake from a vicious stabbing and maybe death.

The buzzing of his cell phone pulled his mind from dark thoughts. He glanced at the caller ID, smiled and tapped the screen.

"Uncle Jake!"

His niece's cheerful voice always lifted his spirits. "Hey. I got your message."

Julia Heron—his brother Rudy's daughter—was presently in his apartment in the Bay Area. He was letting her stay there, as he had relocated temporarily to Southern California to take on the assignment with I-squared.

"I'm glad you called back," she said.

He looked at his phone's screen, taking in the miniature image of a slender woman in her twenties, with freckled cheeks. Julia was on the other end of FaceTime—only it wasn't FaceTime because Jake would never ever conduct a conversation on a commercial app. Madness. He used a video comm app of his own making.

With pixie-cut blonde hair (the opposite of Jake's and Rudy's—shades could apparently skip generations), intense blue eyes and gray, logo-free hoodie, she looked every inch the earnest, no-nonsense grad student. In truth, those days were behind her, having graduated early from Stanford with degrees in computer science and electrical engineering and—because why not?—fine arts.

Her message, which had derailed his trip back to the cemetery to interview Sylvie, was both simple and earth-shattering—to Jake, at least. *Your mom came here to your apartment. I wasn't home. She left a security cam message. Wants to talk to you.*

His mother.

Returning as if from the dead.

"Did she contact your dad?" Jake asked. His brother was currently in Africa on business.

Julia shook her head. "I asked him, but he hadn't heard from her. I think it's only you she wants to see."

"Play it."

His niece was sitting at his desk, dominated by several large monitors. Behind, unseen from this angle, was a beautiful view of the bay, with Alcatraz as the focal point. Jake rarely looked that way. Scenery didn't interest him.

Julia entered a few commands on the keyboard and the security cam video appeared on the biggest screen. She turned her camera lens toward it.

Jake was taken aback by the sight of his mother. Lydia Heron appeared gaunt, pale and somber, and the high-definition video revealed her to be makeup-free. She was in a floral dress, the sort of garment he associated with Amish teachers, though he had never seen one in person. The burgundy-and-black frock had a high collar and was accessorized with several prominent necklaces. Her head was covered in a dark-brown ski cap, which unsettled him. Mothers should not wear such things unless they were skiing.

Her voice was both familiar and eerily alien. "Jacoby . . . Jake, it's me." A pause. "It's been so long . . . I know. Life has been so crazy. In so many ways . . . but I want to see you. It's important." Then peering closer into the lens: "Are you there, Jake?"

She hit the door buzzer button again.

A moment later she did something curious. As he watched, she looked around, slowly pivoting in a 360-degree circle, then going back for a second glance up the street in both directions.

Her body language and her face, when she returned to the camera, radiated fear. Was she being followed? Was she in danger?

One more press of the button. "Jake, please . . ."

A huge interval passed, though the time stamp revealed it was a mere ten seconds. "I'll come back, Jacoby. I love you."

Then she was gone.

Julia said, "I didn't recognize her at first. I haven't seen her since I was little."

His parents, Lydia and Gary Heron, had not been fixtures in the extended family for ages.

His niece's brow furrowed. "How do you think she found your address? You told me it was super secret."

The ownership of his apartment was hidden in layers of corporations and trusts, which Jake himself owned. Completely legal.

And not a foolproof way to disappear.

"Mother's brilliant. The smartest one in the family. If she wanted to find me, she'd find me."

He didn't add the obvious—that she clearly hadn't wanted to before now.

Julia winked. "So that's where you and Dad got your brains."

This was probably true, though their intelligence was different in kind: Rudy was an owl. Jake was a fox.

"Uncle Jake, did she ever consider going into computer science? Or was she just interested in doing good? At that nonprofit she and your dad worked for."

"The nonprofit," Jake answered. And he didn't elaborate.

"I remember they didn't come by during Christmas or other holidays very much. Always out helping the homeless."

"That's right."

Doing good . . .

"Wouldn't she leave a number?"

"You'd think."

"Well, I guess you can get in touch with her through the foundation, the nonprofit, right?"

"Yes. I have their information."

She asked, "And where is it, exactly?"

"North of San Francisco."

"Cool! Wine country?" Julia said this wistfully. "Miss seeing you, Uncle Jake. When are you coming back to the Bay Area?"

"Don't know how long this project will last. But, yeah, miss you too."

Julia had always been a favorite. They understood each other and spoke the same language—English, as well as C++ and JavaScript. He noted now she was wearing the present he'd designed especially for her: a gold reproduction of the very first microchip in history, made in 1958 by a Texas Instruments engineer, Jack Kilby. It faithfully re-created the exact location of the transistors on the original.

Curiously, owing to complications at the time, it had been Carmen Sanchez who had played Santa on his behalf.

"Hey, Uncle Jake, got a question."

"Sure. What?"

"Have you asked out Agent Sanchez yet?"

This was the last thing he'd expected. *"What?"*

"I think you should. I like her."

Twice in one day. What the hell?

"We're colleagues. That's all. It never ends well when work partners start dating. And, anyway, didn't your dad tell you? I don't date. Don't have time. Maybe someday—"

"You're rambling, Uncle Jake. People ramble when they want to deflect the conversation. Okay, I'll consider myself deflected—for now." A laugh. "Love you."

"Love you too."

The memory of the phone call ended, and his eyes once more took in the murder board. Julia's call—and his personal life—were now distant memories, and hardly even those. A killer roamed the streets of Los Angeles.

And it was time to stop him. Whatever it took.

CHAPTER 26

Serial Killing 2.0.

Why should the darker tendencies of human nature not evolve?

A question Damon Garr frequently considered. We progress from Gutenberg to typewriters to invisible bytes making up letters. We progress from oxcarts to horse-drawn buggies to internal combustion to battery power. We progress from passbook savings accounts to credit default swaps (okay, bad example, but the point was otherwise valid).

We progress from ash on cave walls to oil paints to acrylic to Dall-E and Stable Diffusion large language model art generators.

It was geniuses with foresight, or at least dogged *entrepreneurs* with foresight, who tugged society forward—Sisyphus pushing a rock that never rolls backward, always up the hill.

Now examining his computer, as he sat in his car overlooking Santa Monica Beach, Damon reflected that this described him perfectly. With some pride—why not?—he decided that he was among those innovators, both genius *and* dogged, who move society forward. In his case, it was simply that his specialty was a bit different: evil.

And once he'd hit on his theory, he felt an urgency to push forward up the hill, to refine, to perfect.

And, of course, to enjoy.

Planning now, scheming.

Which was part of the fun.

Damon loved social media. It was one of the factors that made Serial Killing 2.0 work. The information people carelessly shed about themselves . . . astonishing. They were like heretics in the Middle Ages, camping out in front of the local church, wearing the Latin equivalent of an I HEART SATAN button.

Next stop, bonfire.

Did they not comprehend that there might be consequences for being so foolishly candid?

He now continued to update information. For the past few days he'd been checking out another soon-to-be-wed couple, blond and jovial. They had throngs of friends, to judge from the posts of the bachelor and bachelorette party pictures. Lots of family too.

And mundane jobs in the food service industry, not law enforcement (he *always* checked that first).

By rights, Damon might have taken a breather after the killing and the funeral at Cedar Hills and the knife-fest with the cop afterward. He was still traumatized by the appearance of the police. They'd nearly caught him when he was on the brink of his next evolution. What if Thomas Alva Edison had been arrested a week before he'd discovered the filament that worked in the incandescent light bulb?

But this was not a day of rest, a day to lick wounds.

This was Day Four.

Magic Day Four, and he was required to strike again. The aperitivo with the teenage girl at the cemetery hadn't worked out. No matter.

Damon had those other plans.

James and Robin . . .

Damon was pleased with his selection of the couple for one other reason. The choice of venue for the wedding, which was scheduled for today.

The location itself.

If there was one place that offered the intriguing combination of challenge and convenience, this was it.

A glance at his phone to check the time.

Damon put the car in gear and sped onto the street, heading for his home. He had some unusual preparations to make before the world said goodbye to James or Robin.

CHAPTER 27

Jake returned to his workstation, cradling the coffee he'd made in the Keurig machine upon entering the Garage.

He set the cup down and before he took a sip, he called the hospital where Frank Tandy had been admitted. He'd wanted to talk to Sanchez, but she'd left. The nurse or administrator he spoke to wouldn't give him any information about the detective's condition, even after Jake lied, claiming he was a relative.

He said, "When he wakes up tell him Jake Heron called. And he's looking forward to gaming with him as soon as he's out of StaleState."

"Out of—"

He spelled the word.

And they disconnected.

Maybe we could go online as a team sometime . . .

One sip of coffee. Another.

Sanchez walked into the workstation and sat heavily in the chair across from Jake's desk.

He recounted his failed attempt at information gathering.

"I just came from there. He's still in surgery."

"How'd you get in?"

"Badge."

"How's he doing?"

"They won't say anything until he's out. They're as stingy with info as cops are." She made a coffee too.

"Could he give you any statement?"

"No. He's been out the whole time. I don't know what he could say, anyway. The scenario was pretty clear. HK got him from behind. He never had a chance to turn around. Jake . . ."

Something odd about this, using his first name, unsettling. They were a surname-only pair. An unspoken habit between them, maybe to maintain a certain emotional distance. Keep things strictly professional.

After a pause, as if she too realized what she'd done, she continued, "When I first heard about the attack, I thought it was you. I mean, *you* were supposed to go talk to the girl in the cemetery."

The sentence carried a particular tone. And it defined Carmen Sanchez to a T. She was, in her typical understated way, expressing how relieved she was that he was safe, how devastated she would have been if anything had happened to him. It was how they communicated about matters between them—personal matters.

Obliquely.

He asked, "You know Frank well?"

"Pretty well. We were on a couple of task forces together." A faint laugh. "He's been working up the courage to ask me out."

Jake hesitated a moment, recalling the detective's questions about Sanchez's relationship status. "You think so?"

"You never noticed?"

"Not really."

Her eyes narrowed, ever so slightly. Understandably. As his response was neither yes nor no.

But the question he wanted to ask—you plan to go out with him?—remained unspoken.

And Sanchez was apparently not inclined to volunteer anything. "Did you come up with any leads to Ms. Person of Interest with the red-stripe shoes?"

Understanding the prior subject to be closed, he refocused his attention on the case at hand. "She turned west on Harrison Street. Retail district. I've been searching for cameras but not having much luck." He nodded to his screen. "A street vid showed her ducking into a cosmetics store. Didn't buy anything. And there was only a fake camera inside."

Half the cameras in retail stores were for show only. A monthly security surveillance system with cloud storage could cost hundreds. For thirty bucks you could buy a plastic mock-up of a camera with a battery-powered blinking red light. Savvy criminals knew the difference, but for the most part, using such a cam was a solid deterrent.

His computer chimed with an incoming message.

As he read the words, his gut twisted.

"We have a lead, Sanchez." A whisper.

"HK?"

"The *other* one."

Tristan Kane.

"You heard from Hot Tub Woman?"

Jake didn't bother to sigh. The truth was it *had* been quite the memorable evening, snow falling, the Italian Alps in the background, bubbles in the hot tub roiling excitedly . . .

But that was his business.

Like her relationship with easygoing, gaming Frank Tandy was hers.

"Yes, Aruba gave me the info."

She continued, "I *told* you. The warrant doesn't extend to her."

"All she's doing is pointing us in a direction."

"She's going to point us right to a not-guilty verdict by reason of fucked-up evidence."

"Let's find Kane first—"

"And worry about the trial later," she cut in. "Broken record, Heron."

"I used that phrase with my niece once and she asked me what a record was."

"Heron, don't change the subject." Then she peered over his shoulder, sighing in surrender. "As long as she's got it . . . Show me."

Someone with Kane's digital signature recently chartered boat in Managua, Nicaragua. Company used is known for ferrying illicits to Oaxaca in Mexico. Possibly Bahias De Huatulco International Airport. Hub for moving persons out of Mexico and Central America. Generally, used for transporting cartel people to Europe and the Far East.

Got a hit on male passenger Kane's age and description on flight to St. Maarten, Dutch West Indies, onward to Amsterdam. Charter tourist flight. Would have landed there by now. No record of "Tristan Kane" in Dutch customs but he creates identities and passports as needed. Will keep digging.

He looked at Sanchez. She nodded. He could tell she was pleased at the intel.

Jake replied:

K

Running a search like Aruba was conducting would have been impossible a few years ago. But now she knew the access codes to the world's most powerful supercomputers. Her favorite was the famed Japanese Fugaku, whose initial performance was an astonishing Rmax of 416 petaflops, rising to 442 after an upgrade.

A number that to a lay person was gibberish, but to a geek translated into an awestruck "Fuck me."

"What kinda pods *you* guys have?"

The low female voice pulled him from the mesmerizing visual lull of code on the screen.

He glanced up to see an athletic woman in a pale-blue jogging outfit printed with Marvel comic characters, black ankle boots and a pink bow in her straight jet-black and shiny hair. The ink on her neck and back of her hands were the only tatts visible, and Jake often wondered what the rest of the body art might be. On the job, thirtyish Su Ling wore conceal-ing clothing suitable for her position as head of HSI Long Beach's Crime Scene Unit. Some of the work involved taking photos of crime scenes and she was known as one of the best in the business. In fact, she occasionally channeled that skill into fashion photography. Su's pictures had graced spreads in *Vogue*, *Elle*, *GQ* and *Marie Claire*—impressive, Jake supposed, but as he was not a subscriber, he had to take Sanchez's word for it.

The MIT valedictorian was also an extreme marathoner . . . and a devoted mother.

How she found the time . . .

Sanchez waved toward the Keurig in response to the question. "Help yourself."

Su strode to the machine and rummaged. "No hazelnut. What's the point?" She found one that apparently suited her taste, though, and brewed.

"All right. I just scored something about Kane."

Su had been parsing the evidence recovered from Kane's last known location, in Trinidad and Tobago, where he'd fled after his recent failed mission in the United States.

Jake nodded to his computer. "Just got a message from an associate. He might be headed to Amsterdam."

"Could be related," Su said. "Let me tell you what I found." She gestured to his computer. "May I?"

"Sure."

She spoke as she typed. "This was in the hallway of his hotel in Trinidad the day he skipped town when he found out you and Carmen were onto him. Near his door."

The photo was of a PCB—a printed circuit board. Green in color, it would have been made of the substrate FR4, a composite of fiberglass and epoxy resin. He shrugged. "One of about twenty million in the Western Hemisphere."

"But how many are made by Systèmes de Circuits Spécialisés de Lyons?"

Jake felt his heart tap hard. "What? How can you tell?"

"Micro etching. Invisible to the naked eye." She sipped more coffee. "Though I'd prefer to say unaided eye. The idea of an eyeball wearing clothes is just odd. Is it significant, Jake?"

"Oh, yes. It's a company that works almost exclusively with CERN." The European Council for Nuclear Research is an international organization that runs the largest particle physics laboratory in the world. Located in Meyrin, a western suburb of Geneva, Switzerland, it's been the site of dozens of particle accelerators since the 1950s and presently houses the Large Hadron Collider, the biggest and most powerful such device in the world.

Su said, "Particle acceleration's a research tool. If you're thinking Kane could weaponize a collider, I don't know how."

"No," Jake said. "The problem's something else. A lot of people don't know CERN is also one of the largest computing networks in the world. Last year they generated more than fifty petabytes of data."

Sanchez said to Su, "He talks this way sometimes. Heron?"

"Fifty petabytes would be—" He glanced at Su. "You have children. Fifty petabytes of YouTube videos would keep them busy for five million years."

"Lord," she muttered. "And I cut them off after an hour."

"The World Wide Web was invented at CERN."

Sanchez said, "So the internet traffic going through CERN is massive. If Kane could get access to that . . ."

Su said, "It's a short flight from Amsterdam to Geneva."

Jake muttered, "Does HSI have a presence there?"

"Yes," Sanchez said. "I don't know if it's Geneva or Zurich. But I'll find out. And get a notice to the supervisory special agent. They'll contact CERN and the Swiss and French intelligence forces."

Su was studying him. He could feel her eyes. "You really want this guy Kane, don't you?"

How does it feel . . .

He offered only a nod.

After she left, Sanchez took a call and Jake deduced from her end of the conversation that the canvassing LAPD officers were having no luck learning where HK had gone after attacking Tandy.

Her shaking head confirmed his deductions. After disconnecting, she said, "We really need Ms. Person of Interest, Heron. She was at the murder scene. She was at the funeral. She knows *something*."

"That she clearly doesn't want to share."

Jake returned to his computer. His chaining bot was working. Like Tarzan swinging through the jungle from vine to vine, chaining is when a bot looking for a particular subject spots something that could be related to it and then makes a determination about where to go next. In this case, it meant the next logical video camera that might pick up an image of Ms. POI on Harrison. The bot would keep up the chaining until the subject vanished completely or it scored ID information, like facial recognition or a license plate.

This particular search would not raise any Fourth Amendment issues with Sanchez. It was completely legal. The procedure involved using both public and private security cameras in commercial stores along Harrison Street—unlike his illegal hacks earlier.

This time, merchants had willingly—with a little pressure from police—given access to their videos. Most were aimed at tills and counters, meant to capture the bad guys during a stickup, or employees trying to palm cash from the register. But a few were angled in such a way that they caught small swaths of the street and sidewalk.

Still, the algorithm was having no luck finding a tall woman in funeral black, face obscured by an old-fashioned veil and hat and wearing stylish shoes—described simply as "black mid-height heeled shoes featuring a bright-red stripe down the heel." He had decided to omit in the search the term "kick-ass" on the theory that the phrase was a bit too human for even the worldliest bot.

CHAPTER 28

"He's moving on someone again."

Carmen was looking at the digital murder board on the wall of the Garage, though her focus was elsewhere.

"A hunch. But . . ."

She rocked back and forth in the springy office chair.

"And?" Heron asked, attentive.

In the time they'd spent working together, he'd clearly realized her intuition paid off most of the time.

"Total organized offender. HK. Unusually high impulse control, but with a ritualistic MO. Some behaviors he can't ignore. Even if they mean creating detectable patterns for us to find."

Heron said, "Assault with a blunt object, drowning. Not the most efficient way to kill but he's sticking to it."

"What if he's controlled by the schedule? Two murders in Italy that weren't far apart in time. Then none, and then he starts up again here."

"So you think he won't go to ground."

"No, not yet."

"He almost killed Frank. And he used a totally different MO."

"That's the key. He needed to throw up a hurdle. Slow us down."

Heron too studied the board. "While he attacks somebody else."

"Declan?"

On the screen: *Yes, Carmen?*

When the words appeared, the murder board automatically minimized. It was irritating. "Declan, can you turn on voice function?"

Somewhat startlingly, they heard: "Voice function is now activated. I was going to suggest doing so myself. It is a more logical way of communicating with you. Is this voice acceptable?"

It was a man's low tenor with the neutral pronunciation referred to as the General American Accent.

She glanced at Heron, who shrugged.

"Yes, it's fine."

"Jake and Carmen. I can tell you're both present. I would like to ask a question."

"Go ahead," Heron said.

"I have recently become aware of a study in which humans who interact with computers prefer the responses to be more vernacular and less computerese. I have been tailoring my responses to include contractions. Do you prefer that, or should I avoid them?"

Heron and Carmen shared yet another glance. She thought it was good Declan could not see them, as an eye roll was involved. She said, "Contractions are fine."

"All right. I'll log that and modify my default template accordingly. What about slang?"

Carmen said, "No slang" as Heron began to say the same.

"All right. Now. You have a request, I believe?"

"We're considering the possibility that HK will strike again. We're looking for patterns. What days of the week did the cases in Italy occur?"

"The two were four days apart, the first on Saturday and the next on the following Wednesday. The killing here was on Saturday of this week, so if you are looking for patterns, it is logical to posit that he will attack again today, four days later."

Carmen wondered how many weddings there were on a Wednesday. She recalled her own ceremony many years earlier, in which she'd been forced to reserve a church and reception hall months in advance to be assured of a coveted slot.

"Worldwide, most Christian marriages occur on Saturday, and Muslim on Friday," Declan said. "But other days are gaining in popularity due to availability issues and cost savings. Social media suggests that elopers and impulsive individuals get married on weekdays."

Carmen said, "Let's take people who elope out of the mix. If we can't find them to protect them, then HK can't find them to attack. No, we need traditional, scheduled—announced weddings. Something that HK could find online, wedding announcements, social media, like that." She was curious. "How many weddings are in LA annually, Declan?"

"Last year, 54,744."

"How many of those were in June?"

"On a national level 10.8 percent of weddings occur in June, which means in LA that number would be about fifty-nine hundred."

"How many on Wednesday?"

This took some calculation. "I can only answer from a statistical perspective. Given that weekday weddings are less popular, it's reasonable to estimate 190 weddings on any given Wednesday in June in Los Angeles. Factoring in the freeway system and extreme mobility of residents, it would be logical to consider other cities in Los Angeles County. There are eighty-eight of them. I estimate the total number of weddings in the county at 265."

She considered the possibility of HK striking today. How could she narrow down the list of potential targets? "Declan, of the weddings today in LA County, are any taking place at venues with water features where a victim could be intentionally drowned, with the death appearing to be an accident?"

"But not swimming pools," Heron added.

He was right, Carmen thought. For one thing, nearly all venues would have pools, and at the height of the summer season, the deck around it would be too populated to be an efficient murder site.

They waited a few seconds for Declan to scan through social media, and whatever other sources of information he could access.

"Seven. One at the Grand Palace in Venice. Two at the Sunset Gardens. One at the Malibu Hills Inn. One at the Beverly Glen Resort and Spa. One at the Hollywood Crest Inn. One at the Chinampas Grand Resort in Bel Air. I've selected them, as they all have secluded grounds with lagoons or ponds on the property, according to their sales material. Note that there will be others, but I am limited by the amount of public information I could access."

"Understood," Carmen said, then added: "He's already hit the Hollywood Crest, so we can eliminate that. Gives us six possibilities."

Heron said, "That's doable. Declan, can you give us an overview of each ceremony?"

"All are occurring in the next one to three hours. Couples are scheduled to renew their vows for their wedding anniversaries at the Grand Palace, the Sunset Garden and the Malibu Hills. The others appear to be traditional weddings."

"I'd put the vow renewing lower on the list," Carmen said.

"Agreed," Heron said. "Doesn't fit the pattern of him targeting classic newlyweds. But which of the others?"

Carmen's eyes were on the murder board. "I want profiles of the brides and grooms."

"What exactly would you like?" Declan asked. "There's a great deal of information on social media, and in their résumés. Hundreds of pages."

Frowning, Carmen asked, "You have their résumés?"

"LinkedIn, Carmen."

"Oh."

She'd been thinking that Declan had done some unauthorized hacking à la Jake Heron.

She asked, "Were any of the brides and grooms married before?"

"I don't have that information, Carmen."

Heron then asked what she'd been about to: "Ages?"

"At the Beverly Glen, the second Sunset Garden and the Bel Air events, the bride and groom are, respectively, fifty-four and fifty-six, forty-nine and sixty-three, and twenty-four and twenty-two."

Carmen said, "So possibly—likely—the first two are second marriages."

"That's logical," Declan said. "Or they might be third. Statistically, the number of third marriages in America—"

Heron interrupted. "Declan, stop generating."

Half smiling, Carmen said, "Declan, were any of the Honeymoon Killer's prior victims over forty?"

"No."

She and Heron shared a glance. "Probably the Bel Air event," she suggested.

"It's a good bet," Heron offered.

Declan, unasked, chimed in with, "I assess it is the most logical."

"What are the details, Declan?"

"It was described as a ceremony at sunset, which today would be at 1934 hours and twenty-eight seconds, although it would be logical to assume the actual commencement time would be different, given the human factor."

An hour and a half ago. The reception would probably still be going on.

"So, we send in Grange with a team," Heron said.

She hesitated, eyeing the board.

"What is it, Sanchez? We need to move."

"We have to handle it right. Our tactical people storm a wedding venue based on what amounts to pure speculation, and we're wrong? That's a media circus, and senior brass get involved. I-squared's still on probation."

But she didn't share the second reason she wanted to tread carefully. She remembered that she'd once been a young bride, filled with hope and excitement over her special day. People had flown in from around the country, and untold money had been spent by her parents and guests to bear witness to a union that should have brought love and joy.

A few years later the marriage had ended in divorce when her husband left her. He'd demanded that she give up her career after a bullet pierced her abdomen during a shoot-out with a bank robber.

Carmen Sanchez did not respond favorably to ultimatums.

Heron looked at her as if he understood there was something more involved here. Well, let him think what he wanted, but she was sticking by it. If she could protect the couple from the destruction of the most important day of their lives, she would.

"We'll have Grange and tactical stage nearby, and survey the streets leading to the resort. As for an inside operation, we need more facts before we can put one together." She tilted her head back, addressing the intercom. "Declan, call the Chinampas in Bel Air."

"Yes, Carmen."

CHAPTER 29

Carmen was speaking to Adam Zebrowski, the evening manager. He had a faint eastern European accent, Polish probably, given the name.

"Sir, I'm a federal agent. I have you on speaker with my associates." Plural, since Declan was listening too. "We have reason to believe the couple who was married there today, the sunset ceremony, might be in danger."

"What?" Zebrowski sounded startled. "How do you mean?"

"No time to go into specifics now. What's the status of the wedding?"

"It's over. The guests have already left. It was a small ceremony—like most of them on weekdays. James and Robin work in the restaurant business and their weekends are too busy to take time off."

"Where are they now?" Heron asked.

Carmen added, "That's Jacoby Heron, my associate."

"In the honeymoon suite."

She checked her phone. Liam Grange and a dozen tactical operators were mobilizing.

"Do you have armed guards?"

"Yes, two."

She continued, "Place one in the corridor outside their door."

"I can't."

Can't or wouldn't? she wondered. "What do you mean?"

"There is no corridor. This is the Chinampas Grand Resort."

Carmen scrunched her eyes shut, frustrated with herself. "I should have realized."

"Sanchez?" Heron asked.

She said, "Chinampas were the floating gardens of the Aztecs in their capital, Tenochtitlan."

"Exactly," Zebrowski said, seemingly surprised she knew this esoteric fact. He continued, "The most exclusive suites are in the water. They're miniature islands. It's one of our big selling points. James and Robin are in the biggest one—and the most remote. It's at the far end of the lagoon."

"Do they have a boat?"

"No. We have small ones our staff uses to ferry them to and from the main lodge."

"Can your security people see it?"

"Yes."

"Have one of those armed guards watch it. And call the couple but just make up something innocuous. I want to know they're all right."

"Shouldn't we tell them about it?"

"No," Carmen and Heron said simultaneously. She continued, "They'll want to leave and probably call friends and family. That could scare the person we're after. He might hurt another guest or staff member trying to escape."

"Whoever this person is," Zebrowski said, "you really think he's here?"

She and Heron shared a look.

It was a damn big assumption.

She said, "Yes."

Much of policing was mindset. You had to believe your suspect was real and was dangerous and was nearby. Otherwise, you might let your guard down.

"Hold on a minute, please," Zebrowski said.

For a very tense minute Carmen waited. Nothing but silence.

Were they not picking up because they were wedding-night indisposed?

Or because they were dead?

Then, *gracias a Dios*, they heard Zebrowski saying he was sorry to interrupt but was just inquiring whether the room was satisfactory. A pause, then: "Very good. Have a nice evening. And, again, congratulations."

Heron blew out a sigh that reflected her own relief.

"There'll be some officers arriving soon," she told Zebrowski. "They'll be discreet. They won't bother your guests. They won't even be seen. And my associate and I will be there in a half hour."

They disconnected.

Heron regarded her thoughtfully. "We could get them out now if you really wanted to. But you don't, do you?"

She fired a look his way.

He continued, "You're using them as bait."

This was the third reason for keeping the operation on the down-low. True, she did not want to ruin their day if it turned out to be a false alarm, but mostly she wanted this son of a bitch.

Wanted him bad.

"Say we get them out," she snapped. "And HK sees and gets even more pissed off that we're fucking with his plans. He changes his plans, follows them home and stabs both of them to death for the hell of it."

Silence between them. Finally he broke it with, "That's the way you want to play it, Sanchez, okay. It gives me an idea."

"Good."

"Maybe. Maybe not."

"What do you mean?"

"I don't think you'll like it."

"What're you going to hack, Heron?"

"Nothing to do with that."

"Then why wouldn't I like it?"

"You'll see."

CHAPTER 30

Jake Heron hated suits. He didn't own one.

As for ties? He believed he had one he'd been given as a present once but had no clue where it was. And, needless to say, bow ties did not even enter into his universe.

He had to look the part, however, so he forced himself to cinch the strip of black polyester tightly around his buttoned shirt collar.

He stood beside Sanchez in a small windowless room off the lobby of the Chinampas Grand Resort in Bel Air, one of the posher sections of posh LA.

"I'm only doing this for the investigation, Heron," Carmen said. "I'm a walking stereotype." She made a sweeping gesture up and down her body.

He took in her maid's uniform and privately admitted that she'd gotten the worst of the deal.

He'd warned her that she wasn't going to like his plan. "I do this all the time. Pen testing. Camo and disguises. Playing a role. You do the same thing, don't you? Undercover?"

She made no reply.

During their drive from headquarters to Bel Air, Declan had forwarded them photos of the Chinampas Grand Resort—including the floating gardens in the huge lagoon. Only accessible by boat, the honeymoon villa was every bit as isolated as Zebrowski described. With the water surrounded by a rainforest, the resort would have huge appeal for those wishing to get away to an exotic location without the time or money to jet to Mexico or Costa Rica.

They walked into the lobby proper and looked over the expansive lagoon shimmering in a slight breeze and reflecting colored lights into fractals.

"The chinampas in Xochimilco are the most famous," Sanchez said. "Mexico City. There used to be thousands, precolonial portable farmland. Now they've kind of grown together. Still about two hundred. Tourist and eco thing these days. You can take gondolas around them."

"You've done that?"

"Sure. When my family went, our favorite was the Island of the Dolls. The place is filled with them."

"It's either cute or spooky."

"I'm talking Hitchcock . . . We loved it."

Jake nodded toward the distant honeymoon suite, a large tiki hut with a fake-grass roof, sitting on a landscaped island that measured about forty by forty feet. "It's the perfect place for HK. He'd slip in by boat and look for an opportunity."

"What's his strategy, Heron?"

Jake squinted as he gazed over the mesmerizing lagoon. "A slip and fall. But somehow, he'll have to get one of them alone. He was lucky with Anthony Brock. The groom went for drinks by himself. Here? I don't know. But if your four-day pattern is right, he'll have it carefully planned already. Impulse control, remember?"

Zebrowski appeared and gave them both a quick perusal. "Your tie is crooked. Our bell persons do not have crooked ties." He was dead serious. The manager himself was perfectly assembled, from his sparse, slicked-back hair to pointy shoes that shone like black mirrors.

In a touch of domesticity, Sanchez reached up and adjusted Jake's tie.

"And me?" she asked the manager.

"I would hire you in a minute."

"I'd make a bad maid. I don't vacuum, don't polish and don't make beds. At least not very often."

Zebrowski seemed unsure how to respond, so he motioned toward the exit. "Your boat's here."

The vessel was a small pontoon variety with a flat deck about six by eight feet. The driver sat on a bench at the rear and operated a quiet electric outboard.

They stepped on and Zebrowski handed Jake their props: a bottle of wine and a basket of fruit. It looked like any other evening at a ritzy hotel. The bell person bringing a bottle for the couple and the maid coming for the turndown service.

They began to cruise across the glass-flat water, a small wake V-ing away behind them. Jake scanned the shore but most of it was impenetrable vegetation and if HK was there, he could see no trace. He noted that Sanchez was doing the same. Her body language casual, her eyes intensely focused.

"Nothing," she whispered, barely moving her lips. "Goose chase?"

He paused to consider. "No."

The driver slowed the craft until it thudded gently against the dock. Sanchez clambered out of the boat, walking through a gate into a grassy yard. Jake followed.

She glanced over her shoulder as they approached the door. "Me first."

"Because you're armed?" Had she seen evidence of HK's presence and not mentioned it?

She gave her head a shake. "Because I'm a woman."

"I don't see what—"

"Exactly my point. You *shouldn't* see anything." She gave him an amused glance. "If they're busy doing . . . whatever . . . the groom will come to the door in a robe. He sees you, he might not undo the chain. He wouldn't want you checking out his bride in a state of undress. If it's me, he won't care. I served my share of no-knock warrants in the middle of the night. Believe me, men are less self-conscious about their bodies. They're all about fight, flight or freeze."

Jake shook his head. "The fine art of policing. Not sure I'll ever catch on."

They arrived at the front door—the jamb decorated with pink-painted hearts—and she rang the bell. "Housekeeping."

The sound of fumbling came from inside. "Be right there," a male voice called out.

A pause, presumably while the groom robed himself and looked through the peephole. Then the clatter of the chain—Sanchez had been right—and a man in his twenties appeared, head and terrycloth-covered shoulders only.

"Thanks, but we don't need turndown." He peered over her shoulder at Jake. "And no more champagne or anything for now either."

He gave a small finger wave and started to close the door, but Sanchez stepped in quickly, slipping past him.

The groom was too shocked to muster more than a feeble protest. "Hey . . ."

Jake followed, clutching the wine and fruit.

A slender woman about the same age with long blonde hair was tying the sash of a matching plush robe around her waist as she emerged from the bedroom. "What's going on, honey?"

"They've brought us more stuff, but . . ."

His voice faded as Sanchez reached behind the starched white apron at the front of her maid's uniform, pulled out a slim leather badge case and opened it. "Agent Carmen Sanchez, Homeland Security Investigations."

The groom blinked, then recovered, his expression morphing from shock to amusement. "You're punking me. Who put you two up to this?" He focused on Jake. "Was it Todd? Because that asshat is going to pay when I—"

"This isn't a joke," Jake said evenly. "You might be in danger."

That stopped all traces of humor.

Sanchez said to Jake, "We'll have to move fast. Real employees would only be here ten minutes, tops."

They had to assume HK was somewhere nearby, watching his prey and preparing for the attack.

Sanchez outlined the situation, leaving out references to a serial killer. He was impressed with her storytelling ability, making the whole thing sound like a follow-up to a singular but nonspecific threat.

"Have either of you seen anyone who might be watching you? White male, average build, dark hair?"

Jake added, "He'd have been paying a little more attention to you than normal."

Robin and James looked at each other. The groom ran his hand through his mussed hair. "No."

His bride agreed.

Sanchez frowned in thought and said, "I'm curious. You mentioned not wanting *more* champagne or anything else. Some was delivered before?"

The bride's mind seemed elsewhere—digesting the news of the threat, undoubtedly. James answered, "Somebody at the hotel missed the note that Robin's diabetic. We got a box of chocolate anyway, along with champagne."

Jake's eyes snapped to Sanchez. Hotels rarely missed information about medical conditions and allergies. The risk of liability was too great.

Sanchez asked, "Where's the candy and wine now?"

James opened the door to the minifridge. A bottle of California sparkling wine and a box of Godiva chocolates sat inside.

"They were delivered after you checked in?"

"About an hour ago."

Sanchez pulled out her cell phone, tapped in a number and put it on speaker. "Mr. Zebrowski. Agent Sanchez. We're in the suite. Robin and James are here. Everything's good. But I have a question. Did you send another bottle of champagne and some chocolates an hour ago?"

"Let me check."

After an eternity, the manager came back with a response. "No one took anything to that suite. They're scheduled for an excursion in a glass-bottom boat tomorrow morning. No one is supposed to contact them until then. And there's a note to the restaurant and room service that Ms. Schwartz is diabetic."

So HK *is* here.

"This is Jake Heron. Can you connect me with your security cameras? I'll need the IP addresses of the ones focusing on the shore near the honeymoon suite and the lagoon between the two locations."

"Sure. I'll do that."

"Call it in to Agent Sanchez's number."

"My God, this is serious!" Robin was visibly shaken.

"Who exactly is this guy?" James asked.

So their special day would be tainted, after all. On the other hand, the groom's eyes sparkled with excitement. Maybe the trade-off for the disruption was that he'd have a story to share about their honeymoon for the rest of his life, even if his bride wished the incident weren't happening.

"We'll go into details later," Sanchez said, and was saved from dodging more questions when her phone vibrated. She held it up for Jake, who typed in the appropriate information on his tablet.

Within minutes he was reversing through the surveillance footage to a point that was about ninety minutes in the past. Then slowly the video rolled forward. Soon they saw another watercraft leave a different dock—one not far from the honeymoon suite. This was not for guests, but a small outboard. It navigated to the suite, and a figure climbed out. Left the wine and chocolates at the door, rang the bell and quickly departed.

Too dark to see any details.

Sanchez tapped the service dock. "He's probably waiting there."

"Waiting for what?" Robin asked, her voice unsteady.

Jake said, "We think he spiked the champagne or the chocolate. Roofies maybe. Something stronger. To knock you out."

"Oh, shit," Robin muttered, looking at the gifts as if they were explosives. "And then he was going to come back and . . . what?"

Sanchez didn't answer. She nodded to a wall clock. "Time's up. We have to move."

Jake said, "Wait here and stay away from the window."

"Where are you going?"

"Into the bedroom." He glanced at Sanchez. "We need to strip."

CHAPTER 31

In under three minutes, the switch was done.

Carmen had traded her maid's uniform for Robin's terrycloth robe, and Heron had done the same with James, who now wore the bellman outfit.

Carmen wasn't thrilled at the idea of wearing only her skivvies underneath the plush terry, but the rule for working "sets"—Special Enforcement Teams—was that you looked the part to trick the bad guys. Presumably, this was true for pen testers as well.

There was, however, a major difference. The robes concealed the body armor both she and Heron had worn here. Covering front and back, it was specially designed to ward off both bullets and bladed weapons.

The memory of what had happened to Tandy was prominent in their minds.

"You should go now," she said to the couple. "The manager has a room in the resort proper. You can stay there if you like. Or go someplace else."

Robin said, "We're not staying here."

James was a little less certain. As if he was enjoying the adventure. But his new wife's mind was made up, and Sanchez knew he'd comply.

"We can't take anything, can we?" Robin asked.

Carmen told her, "Wallets, phones. That's all. Whatever fits in your pockets. You have to be a maid and a bellman, returning from an errand."

"Won't he see we're different? You're taller, and I'm blonde."

Heron said, "It's a risk, but a small one. It's so dark I don't think he'll be able to see more than your silhouettes."

Carmen shooed them out the door and watched as they stepped onto the ferry and vanished toward the main building.

"I'm really not liking this, Heron."

"We don't have a choice. The best chance of catching him is on the water, when he moves in for the kill. If Grange and the others try to hunt for him in that vegetation, he'll spot them in a minute and vanish." He glanced at her with a smile. "If the plan's going to work, we both have to be bait, me included."

She understood. But she didn't like it: using a civilian to draw out a suspect. She was trained law and used to roles like this. He was not. Pen testing wasn't in the same league.

"I'm not in any danger." Grange and another tactical operator had a speedboat hidden at the far dock and would be on HK as soon as he showed.

She countered with: "Patterns, Heron."

"You mean, his MO?"

"Right. What if he doesn't stick to it? Bludgeoning and drowning. What if he gets cautious and decides he's too vulnerable on the floating island, so he simply pulls out a sniper rifle and shoots you in the head?"

Heron shrugged. "You're the profiler. What're the odds of that?"

"Not likely. But . . ."

"Anyway, Sanchez, what other options do we have?"

He was correct there.

Her shoulders slumped. "All right. We go forward. Well, it's your plan. What's next on your agenda?"

Heron said, "We have to convince him that his scheme is working. We've had some of the funky champagne and chocolate he delivered earlier and we're getting drowsy. We make him think we fell asleep."

He opened the bottle—the one he'd brought, not the likely spiked one in the fridge—and poured two flutes. "Now, let's go sit on the deck and let him see us."

"And what do we do out there?"

He answered quickly as if it was obvious. "Act like newlyweds."

CHAPTER 32

Quite the place, Damon Garr was thinking, as he hunkered down in the bushes and watched the couple on the shadowy deck of the honeymoon suite, standing close, sipping the nighty-night champagne.

Floating islands . . .

Amazing.

It was like the place Felicia had chosen for their wedding venue. Lush, secluded.

Unique.

The thought came to him without sorrow or regret. He'd mourned her death and emerged a better man for it. Truer to himself. Had they gotten married, Serial Killing 2.0 might never have been born.

Funny how fate took over sometimes.

He eyed the villa and the honeymooners once more, recalling his earlier assessment: convenient yet challenging.

Convenient because the room was surrounded by water and would not require any stretch of effort for one of the two to fall in and drown.

Challenging for exactly the same reason: the villa was surrounded by water.

How would he get there, how would he engineer the death? He had spent some hours speculating.

The solution he'd come up with was tricky, but he believed it would work. After the couple had retired to their room and the shuttle boat had returned to the lodge, he had taken one of the small utility vessels—from the dock right in front of him now—and glided over the water to the suite. There he'd left a basket containing a bottle of champagne and box of chocolates, both of which were spiked with propofol, enough to put an adult asleep in ten minutes after a single glass or several bites of candy.

He'd then headed back to where he now crouched on the secluded grounds.

The couple would indulge, then pass out. He then would return and use the maintenance key he'd stolen earlier to get inside. After that, he'd remove the candy and wine and leave an envelope of propofol caps on the bed—recreational drugs brought by the happy couple themselves for the happy night.

And he would then drag the bride outside and ease her into the water—the coin toss had decided that she would be the victim.

He'd remain long enough to make sure she was dead before boating back to the dock.

Mission accomplished.

The original plan called for them to be inside. But now they were conveniently standing right near the handy dock. He could easily see that they'd succumbed to the drugs.

He watched the couple closely.

Sipping the champagne.

Getting drowsy.

Good.

It was time to get ready for the next step.

CHAPTER 33

Jake Heron was not much of a romantic.

Those lost in the rabbit hole of the internet are the definition of "loner." As a young man, he'd told his close friends—when asked—that he'd had exactly 101 partners in his life . . . before adding that 1-0-1 was the binary version of 5.

For various reasons those five relationships had not flourished.

To put it mildly.

Computers were often to blame—well, computers combined with his reclusive nature and his purpose in life: to expose the dangers of intrusion. All three aspects of Jake Heron wore thin with four of the women. One was different. She felt the same. About intrusion. About a lot of things. But then Saoirse was gone. For reasons he didn't like to think about.

Now, though, he found himself on the deck of a floating island, in the honeymoon suite of a luxurious resort, a beautiful evening, the nighttime chill of the fragrant air mediated by the thick robe and the warm wool slippers.

Standing close to Carmen Sanchez.

He took a sip of champagne. She lifted the glass to her mouth and pretended to drink (in HSI there was no drinking on duty, and while Sanchez bent some rules, this was immutable, because she carried a firearm).

She cocked her head, apparently receiving a message through her earbud, hidden by her thick dark hair.

Hair he remembered cascading over his face not long after their first meeting as she lay atop him.

She said softly, "Copy that." Then to Jake: "The last agent just got in position. We're good to go."

The plan was sound, and they had all the backup they needed. He noticed Sanchez visibly relax. The trap was set. Now all they had to do was wait until HK appeared on a utility boat, totally vulnerable in the middle of a placid body of water.

They were both acting drowsy, and she pointed to a bench in a small garden, which was, he couldn't help but notice, filled with rocks that were the perfect size to cave in a skull.

Perhaps HK had thought the same, as he delivered the champagne and chocolates and anticipated what would happen later that night.

They sat and both lifted their flutes to their lips once more. He took another sip. Why the hell not? It was Moët, true French champagne, which was about the only alcohol Heron drank. They set the glasses down.

"Act drowsier," Sanchez said. "We've got to convince him it's working."

It was his play, but he was happy to have her be the director. He dropped his shoulders a bit, lowered his head. Then, as if battling to stay awake, sat up straighter. Sanchez did the same.

"Do you think HK is falling for it?" he muttered under his breath.

"Don't see why not. Though . . ."

She said nothing more, but he got her meaning. That the theater perhaps called for more "newlywed behavior."

He put his arm around her. He'd hesitated at first, but when she nestled closer, he gripped her shoulder more firmly.

She turned to face him, tilting her head back slightly to meet his gaze. The smell of her shampoo—her favorite, lavender—drew his eyes to her hair, and he felt a compulsion to run his fingers through it.

He thought of Tandy's comment about the two of them being together.

And his hedging response that he'd never thought about it.

Lying . . .

But did he truly want to? Given their history, and their partnership at I-squared, and their personalities . . . Did he want things to progress further?

His urge to proceed and his urge to stand down were in perfect balance.

Of course, relying on these circumstances wasn't playing fair with the decision. They were acting. A kiss, however passionate on the surface, would be no more than stage direction between two actors.

Wouldn't it?

Yes.

No.

Then he told himself impatiently: Stop generating! Just do it.

He reached out slowly, giving her plenty of time to object or turn away, and brushed his hand against the silken strands that framed her face. When she made no move, he traced a fingertip along her jaw and under her chin, lifting it slightly as he leaned toward her.

Her lips parted in invitation, and he lowered his hand from her shoulder to the small of her back and pulled her closer. For a long time, he'd wondered what it would be like to kiss her.

He knew Grange and the tac team had them under observation, making sure HK didn't sneak up on them from an unexpected route.

But it was dark here. The operators couldn't see much, other than two silhouettes getting close to each other.

Besides, Jake didn't care.

Their lips had nearly touched when she sighed. And tapped her earbud.

Then grew alert. "Copy."

Jake felt the moment slip away.

She continued to speak to Liam Grange. "Where is he?"

He followed her gaze as she looked out over the water and noted a small outboard heading their way. A utility boat, like they'd anticipated HK might use.

"Copy that. We're going defensive."

Sanchez was instantly in motion. He barely registered what was going on before she grabbed him by the elbow and yanked him to the ground with considerable force.

His knee collided with the table beside the bench, bringing out a curse.

He glanced up and saw the HSI motorboat, Liam Grange at the wheel, speed up to the smaller craft. There was a brief exchange and the person in the utility vessel was hauled aboard the HSI boat, which spun around and accelerated toward the dock behind the resort proper.

She cocked her head, listening once more. "K," she replied. Then to Jake: "One in custody." She smiled. "Official for: We fucking got him."

CHAPTER 34

Carmen's sense of unease increased as she sat across from the man plucked from the boat cruising toward the honeymoon suite. The resort's manager had directed her and Heron to a private meeting room to conduct an initial interview.

During which it became clear the evening had not turned out as they'd hoped.

Got him?

No.

Zebrowski had confirmed the man Grange hauled from the boat was Hal Pratt, one of their employees.

So, 99 percent likelihood he wasn't HK—who was too smart to hunt this close to home.

Of course, he might be an accomplice, or a witness, but even if so, he was not in a cooperative mood.

She gave him a stern look. "Mr. Zebrowski told me no one was scheduled to be out on the lagoon at night unless they were making a room service run. Which you weren't. That's for the guests' privacy. Explain."

Pratt's knee bounced up and down as he sat in the swivel chair across from hers. "Is that, like, a crime?"

The color had drained from his face, making his freckles appear livid against his pale skin. He was tall and stocky, although, at twenty-four, he already had the look of a former high school athlete gone to seed.

"'Crime'? How's that responsive to my question? It's against your employer's policy. So, again, explain."

More knee bouncing. More thinking. "I'm supposed to take the honeymoon couple out on an excursion in the morning. I wanted to get everything prepped ahead of time."

She recalled they did have a trip planned. But she had to ask the obvious. "At nearly midnight?"

"I'm kind of a night owl. I'd rather stay up late than get up early. So I was out at a bar, just hanging, you know? Then I figured I'd stop here and get the boat ready on the way home. That way, I could sleep in longer." Speaking fast, and overexplaining.

"Name of the bar?"

"Um. The Rabbit's Hat. Alvarado Street."

"And if we contacted them, will they confirm you were there tonight?" She gave Heron a significant look and he began typing on his tablet. Which probably was gibberish and only for show.

Pratt stared at him and fidgeted some more. "I was kind of sitting near the back. Could be nobody saw me." He swallowed. "I'm the kind of guy people don't notice."

"What about the server?" she asked. "And your check?"

"I paid cash."

Convenient.

"When did you deliver the champagne and chocolates to the honeymoon suite?" She looked at her own tablet. "The exact time."

She had phrased the question as if the answer were a foregone conclusion. During an interview, it was important to keep the subject in the dark about how much you knew. They were aware of his actions and would make him try to justify them. On the other hand, he would have no clue what she meant if he hadn't done it.

"What? No, no, I didn't take anything to the honeymoon suite. The kitchen and room service staff are the only ones who do food and beverage. I do the entertainment packages, that's it."

She wasn't surprised, and moved on, switching subjects to keep him off-balance. "Where were you last Saturday night?"

The change in direction sparked a blink. "Um, Saturday? Working."

She stood and stepped to the corner of the room. Heron followed. She said softly, "He's not HK, obviously. But something's not right."

He said, "You want me to get a phone call?"

"Yeah, good."

She returned to Pratt and started to ask him about his employment history, observing him closely—and making sure he saw *her* doing so.

Even in the chill of the room he was sweating, and there wasn't a square inch of the place that his nervous eyes had not darted to.

She heard a trill and she and Pratt looked toward Heron. He had hit a ringtone button and was pretending to take a call. He made a few sounds along the order of "uh-huh," and "yeah," all the while frowning as he stared at Pratt. He disconnected and crossed the room to whisper in Carmen's ear. "How was that? I'd say it was another Academy Award performance."

She nodded and turned stern eyes on Pratt, rising and packing up her tablet. A glance at Heron. "So. That confirms it. Which detention center?"

Heron said, "La Brea, I'd say."

"There? They'll eat him alive."

Pratt's eyes were wide. "Wait. Who was that? Who was on the phone?"

She spared him a glance. "Hush."

Heron said, "You were telling me just the other day, Sanchez. You hate being lied to."

She then nodded. "You're right. La Brea it is."

Pratt wrung his hands. "I'm sorry, okay. You don't understand!"

She gave him her coldest glare. "Fill me in. You have five minutes. And if you lie again, you're going straight to La Brea."

Which was a perfectly fine street in Los Angeles, home to office buildings and the famed tar pit, filled with prehistoric, fossilized creatures, and, as far as Carmen knew, not a single detention center or jail.

"I was lying. I'm sorry, but I'm scared. He's going to hurt my family!" Tears dotted his eyes.

They had finally gotten to the truth, and she could see where Pratt was going. She sat down. "Tell me." Softer now.

Carmen Sanchez was often good cop and bad cop in the same interview.

"Okay, there was a man." His eyes didn't waver. "He was by the dock where we keep the service boats. Thirty, forty minutes ago, I was going off shift. He came up to me. He kept a flashlight in my eyes. He said he had a gun."

"Shit," Carmen muttered.

She called Liam Grange and told him what Pratt had said. The tactical leader and his team would search, but she was certain the instant the HSI boat appeared, HK had fled. Other officers would secure the scene until Su Ling and her evidence-collection crew arrived.

She then turned back to Pratt, whose voice cracked as he continued, "I thought I was being mugged. He asked for my wallet. Only he didn't take any money or credit cards. He had me pull out my driver's license and he took a picture of it."

The ID with his home address meant HK could find, and hurt, Pratt's family if he helped the police. A well-used gangbanger tactic to keep witnesses silent. They almost never acted on the threat, but the technique was powerful leverage.

"And he wanted you to take a boat out to the villa." Heron was nodding with the same understanding Carmen now had.

"That's all. Yes. Take it out and back."

"Shit," Carmen said. "He was testing—to see if it was a trap."

Heron asked, "What else do you remember?"

"The light, my eyes. I really couldn't see anything. I swear! His voice, I think he was White. Tall, from the silhouette. That's all, and he was like, I'll fucking kill you and your family in a minute, and I don't care. I mean, he didn't say it, but that was the tone, you know."

She said, "We can protect your family."

"He disappeared but maybe he waited around to see if I talked to you."

"He didn't," she assured him. "But call your family and have them spend the night with friends or relatives. You're not in danger but it'll give you some peace of mind. Anything else you can remember?"

"No. I swear!"

Often those two words are an indicator of deception. Not now. He was telling the truth.

"He give you money?"

"No! Really. Here's all I have on me." He opened the wallet and showed a couple of twenties and dug a crumpled wad of cash—about forty dollars—from his pocket.

She believed HK hadn't paid him. After all, why fork out money when it costs nothing to threaten violence?

"Where was he standing?"

Pratt stood and pointed out the window. "There. Can you see it? The lawn."

She suppressed a sigh. The crime scene techs couldn't lift footprints from grass.

Not that they'd be much help anyway.

"Where should my family go? My mother-in-law in San Diego?"

Was he asking permission? "That'll be fine," she said, then asked, "Do you know which boat he took earlier to deliver the wine and candy?"

Pratt said, "There's just the one at that dock. The one I was in."

Maybe they could lift prints.

Pratt frowned. "You know, there's one thing I can say about him. One thing I noticed."

"What?"

"He wore gloves. Those blue latex ones the bad guys always use on TV. So they don't leave fingerprints. The wife and I, we watch all those shows."

But of course. Why should anything be easy?

"Get on home," she told him.

"Look, I'm sorry I lied."

"It's all right. If you remember anything else, give me a call." She handed him her card.

He hurried out.

She and Heron met with the manager, who looked a bit more edgy and a bit less coiffed than earlier. Carmen supposed a tactical operation on the grounds of your hotel will do that. She assured him Pratt was in no trouble.

"Will this . . ." Zebrowski began hesitantly. "Will this make the news?"

"Doubt it," she said. Police scanners were generally legal in California, but HSI used specially dedicated frequencies so reporters could not pick up transmissions about operations. That was the reason the Hollywood Crest killing was not yet public knowledge. Carmen's—and Williamson's—theory was you kept the media out of the picture for as long as possible. On the whole, reporters screwed up investigations more than they helped.

"Why is he doing this?" Zebrowski asked. "What's the point?"

"I wish we could answer that," Heron said.

"So he's a serial killer. Like Ted Bundy."

"Smarter, more careful. But yes, similar."

"Lord."

She and Heron walked outside into the cool night.

She called Williamson to give him a report and was surprised to hear a message that he was out of town for a few days. Send any reports in writing to him, copying Destiny Baker, his assistant. For emergencies, call HSI's or DHS's regional offices. He gave the numbers. She left a message.

"Williamson's out of town. I'll write up a report and send it over to you to fill in, then can you get it to him?"

"Sure. Tonight."

They walked to their respective vehicles, parked beside each other and stopped before getting in.

The operation had been so consuming, she had not had time to check personal messages. She did so now and felt a surge of relief reading the first one.

"Frank's okay. 'Satisfactory condition,' whatever the hell that means. But I'll take it."

"Really." Heron's face showed his own reaction. Guarded but pleased.

One thing was curious, though. She had not received a call or text from her sister. She supposed Selina was still angry that she hadn't dropped everything to pursue their father's killer.

Siblings, she reflected with a sigh and couldn't help but think of their father's message about the money-laundering goddesses from mythology.

Heron caught her expression and lifted an eyebrow.

Not in the mood to elaborate, she said nothing.

Los Angeles is the definition of ambient light and usually even on the clearest of evenings stars are nearly invisible. Here, though, because of the tropical vegetation and towering trees, you could see thousands of bright-white pinpricks overhead. She noticed Heron was also looking skyward.

Her thoughts moved from her sister to a very different memory: the near kiss an hour earlier, as they sat outside the honeymoon suite.

And what, she wondered, was going through his mind just now?

She turned to him.

To see Heron tuck his tablet into his backpack and give her a businesslike, almost formal nod as he climbed into the driver's seat. "I'll look for that report."

"I'll get it to you ASAP."

And she watched him slam the door, throw the vehicle into gear and speed from the lot, leaving behind a trail of mist that soon vanished into the timeless vegetation.

CHAPTER 35

War.

Damon Garr had officially declared war.

Somehow the pair of investigators—the woman cop and the man probably-not-a-cop from Cedar Hills Cemetery—had struck again.

And this time it wasn't a question of spoiling his enjoyment watching the mourners at the cemetery or tormenting a teenager to tears, but actually preventing the murder in the first place. On the special day, no less. The Fourth Day.

Not acceptable.

Damon was taking his typical circuitous route home, keeping an eye out for that mysterious—and probably unthreatening—car from earlier. But now, no tail. He'd gotten away from the Chinampas Grand Resort safely, thanks to the precaution of sending that employee out in a boat to, literally and figuratively, test the waters.

And the cops had moved in.

Hands kneading the steering wheel compulsively, he realized that they were a threat to not only his life and freedom but to Serial Killing 2.0 itself. He thought of the great rivalries in the art world. Da Vinci hated Michelangelo. Lucian Freud versus Francis Bacon. Van Gogh versus Gauguin. There had once been an exhibition about these famous rivalries. The show was entitled *You Were Shit in the 80s*.

Now he had his rivals too. The pair were practicing their own art, you could say. While rivalries like Picasso and Matisse and most of the others were simply verbal, with the occasional absinthe- or wine-fueled brawl thrown in, some were lethal. The sixteenth-century craftsman Cellini, in Italy, murdered a competitor . . . and thought about dispatching another man, a sculptor, simply because he'd "gotten on my nerves."

Damon would be ensconced in his small enclave in thirty minutes. He thought briefly of Her.

In his special room. His den.

And of the box of precious razor blades.

Tonight? No. He was too upset to enjoy the cutting.

In the morning.

His thoughts returned to the pair who had defeated him. He had resolved to fight back—hence, the knife attack on the man he thought was the woman cop's partner, though, according to the news, it had not been him, but an LAPD detective named Frank Tandy. And the photo did not match the image of his intended target, although there was a distinct resemblance.

So his rivals remained alive.

That would not—could not—last. After war had been officially declared, death always followed swiftly.

CHAPTER 36

Doing the Garage one better, there was only a *single* decoration on the wall of Jake's month-to-month rental in Venice Beach, south of downtown LA.

It was a poster of the movie *The Matrix*. Extremely faded. It had come with the place, ironically, given his career.

The movie, Jake maintained, had consummate style and great tension but a plot that not a soul on earth had adequately described to him.

But there the poster hung, slightly askew, on one of the yellow-painted walls in the eight-hundred-square-foot place.

He was presently at his impromptu desk—from IKEA and built with only three pieces of hardware left over. It was solid enough. Before him, on one of the laptops, was Sanchez's after-action report. He added to it before firing it off to her, Williamson and Destiny Baker.

After what Sanchez had told him about their boss's trip, he wasn't surprised to get one of those out-of-office replies. The report had still gone to him, though, and he was sure Williamson would read it promptly.

He stood and stretched. Jake's space was cluttered with clothes in gym bags, toiletries in boxes and shopping bags, Mountain Dew twelve-packs, chip bags. And, as always, hovering around him like planets around a red star, computers and components and allied systems were present. Cords too. Many, many cords in all different thickness, colors and lengths.

One would think he aspired like the rest of the world to go wireless, but that was not the case. Hacking airborne signals was infinitely easier than hacking copper wires, so Jake skewed to the early-twentieth-century technology in this one instance.

He glanced at his screen and noted the time. Midnight was creeping close. A long, exhausting day. He pulled his jacket off and tossed it on Pile Number Two, the Mount Everest of clothing.

Despite the clutter, or maybe because of it, his place had a certain appeal. It featured a small deck offering a pleasant view of the palms and the sand and the Pacific Ocean, which guests might enjoy.

If he were ever to entertain guests.

As for Jake himself, well, placid scenery appealed no more than the drama of Alcatraz and the turbulent San Francisco Bay outside his window at home.

More to his liking, this place was not far from I-squared.

Or from Carmen Sanchez's house.

He showered and then collapsed in bed. Thinking yet again he had been meaning to get a new set of springs and mattress.

Jake also knew he would forget about that mission by the time he'd woken and then would have the thought again tomorrow night.

Anyone else might enjoy the sounds of lively inhabitants of Venice at midnight. And, later, when the town dozed at three or so, the sound of the ocean coaxed to gentle hushing with tides and a delicate wind.

Not him.

But there *was* a soundtrack looping through his mind. One as indelible as the sound of midnight waves to a surfer impatient for the first breaker in the morning.

A voice.

From more than twenty years ago.

Clear as could be.

The ethereal woman in yet another of those Amish teacher dresses flits about the bedroom, waking up a ten-year-old Jake and a twelve-year-old Rudy. "It's a big day," his mother says. "Come help me, gentlemen!"

And, after a high five between brothers, and morning bathroom visits, they walk from the room they share into the living room, where a wrapped present sits on the unsteady coffee table, and the aroma of cooking coming from the kitchen, where Lydia Heron is hard at work, fills the suburban split-level house.

Thin, a slip of a thing, her voice soft, she is nonetheless a force to be reckoned with in the kitchen. Jake wonders what the smells represent.

A birthday feast.

Jake turned two digits at midnight.

Unable to wait, Rudy gives him his present early. It's a graphic novel Jake had mentioned he'd like. Money is tight in the Heron household. But Rudy has done some extra yardwork and saved up. Jake hugs him.

And he looks again at the present on the coffee table, wrapped in turquoise paper. A handwritten tag, a cheerful reindeer—left over from Christmas—reports, *"Happy birthday, Jacoby. From Mother and Father."*

He caresses it.

Then he joins Rudy in the kitchen, where his brother is pouring cereal into bowls for both of them. Their mother's cooking is for later, a roast and some vegetables. They've been asked to help out, and, after chowing down the Wheaties, they take to their task—scrubbing the dirty pots and utensils their mother has left in her wake. She's a good cook, and a bad cleaner.

They then retire to the living room to do some gaming. Lanky Rudy is the athlete among the two—Jake is bored playing catch and, well, every other sport—but he excels with the joystick.

They laugh and shoot and speed their cars around the beautiful deadly landscape of *Grand Theft Auto*.

Their mother appears in the doorway and says she and their father are going out. They'll be back later. She is soft-spoken but when she summons Gary from the den, he appears instantly, tugging on his brown sportscoat.

Then they're gone.

A few minutes later, Rudy nudges him. "Open your present. Go on. What do you think it is?"

Jake would like to wait, but he really can't. He walks to the table and picks it up and returns to the couch. It's very light. What could it be?

Money, maybe—in a big box as a joke. Money would be good. There is so much he wants and so little they can afford. Enough to buy a secondhand laptop?

Even thirdhand?

That would be heaven.

He runs his hand over the sides.

He carefully unseals it, as if it would be disrespectful to tear the ribbon off, which he really, really wants to do.

Then he looks at the naked box and lifts the lid.

Inside is a card.

Not a birthday card, just a three-by-five index card.

A donation of $100 has been made in your name to the Family.
Happy Birthday, son!

Rudy says, "Fuck."

Jake is silent and manages to control most of the tears. He doesn't know why he bothers. He's cried in front of his brother before, as Rudy has with him. And there is no one else to witness the emotion.

He can't help himself. He rises and walks to the kitchen. The savory aroma lingers but the food is gone, and he understands that what she cooked will be part of a potluck supper for new recruits they hope to bring into the same organization that is now $100 richer, thanks to young Jacoby Heron's generous "gift."

Lydia's voice faded into the past.

Along with his brother's sympathetic gaze.

And his own quiet tears.

Jake had returned to the present, once more in his small apartment overlooking Venice Beach.

The "nonprofit foundation" his niece, Julia, mentioned earlier was not that at all. It was very much *for* profit—as the IRS and tax court decided in the losing battle for tax-exempt status.

Nor was it a beneficent foundation, as Julia believed, "doing good." The Family was a cult. His parents had been seduced into joining the group by the founder, Bertram Stahl, a failed professor, failed entrepreneur, failed bartender, failed real estate investor and failed author . . . and those were just the job descriptions that appeared on his résumé (minus the "failed," of course).

But the ageless man had excelled at one thing: corralling those with the tiniest modicum of gullibility or insecurity into signing on to his group and forfeiting any shred of self-worth and dignity.

Along with most of their money.

His parents were recruiters—a vital function—and they would prowl the streets looking for easy marks, the lonely, the confused, the damaged, both physically or psychically.

It was the irony that his parents had abandoned their own family for a cult that called itself a Family, with a capital *F*, that taught Jake the evil of intrusion and started him on a route to study the phenomenon in all its incarnations. And fight it.

From what he'd studied about the dangers of cults he'd learned that with very few exceptions, one did not step away voluntarily. You might be kidnapped by a relative and deprogrammed.

But leaving of your own accord, rarely.

And so now—lying in his *Matrix* room on Venice Beach—Jake could only wonder what his mother was doing tracking down his apartment and making a heartfelt plea, a woman in midlife crisis wearing a hat that put him in mind of the revolutionaries in eighteenth-century Paris, herding Robespierre and Marie Antoinette and Louis to the guillotine.

Then he chided himself for the diversion.

More important matters existed than the disaster that was his family.

Tristan Kane was still at large, playing a dangerous game of internet—and possibly nuclear—roulette in Switzerland.

And the Honeymoon Killer was in the wind too, probably targeting other couples on the verge of embarking on a life together now that Jake and Sanchez had thwarted tonight's attack.

And they knew he had a different couple in his crosshairs. Jake and Sanchez themselves.

He was compelled to act, and that meant he would be compelled to stop those dedicated to preventing him from acting.

He debated rising and sending her a text reminding her to be careful. He was sure it would be redundant, though. He had been to her house and knew the address was as secret as addresses could be nowadays and the security system was sound.

Besides, she surely was fast asleep by now.

Then he speculated—and if she were *not* asleep, was she thinking of something else that was going through his mind too?—that if the Chinampas Grand Resort employee hadn't decided to make his midnight run at the moment he had, what would have happened next between Jake and Sanchez?

He knew what his answer was.

Hers?

Did she believe that "newlywed behavior" and "kiss" were in fact merely part of the undercover set in the plan he himself had written?

Or was she thinking of that moment too—if sleep were eluding her, as well?

Of course not, he chided himself. Her mind would be on more important things, like catching the Honeymoon Killer.

And, likely, on Frank Tandy.

Finally, sleep approached, slowed by only two things. One was his wrestling with a strategy to find their prey tomorrow.

The other was the persistent scent of lavender, though this, Jake later decided, was probably his imagination.

CHAPTER 37

Something was wrong.

Sitting at her kitchen table desk in her tiny rental in Fullerton, Selina Sanchez stared at her laptop screen.

It wasn't anything specific, not like an imbalance in some combination of the four key aspects of organic chemistry: carbohydrates, lipids, proteins and nucleic acids. An anomaly easily isolated and dealt with.

This was more of a feeling.

Which had no place in her discipline.

Her main discipline, that was. College studies.

But her other avocation? Oh, yeah, feelings played an important role, a vital role.

Being an investigator.

Only her approach wasn't working. She'd gone to all the trouble to put on an act for Carl Overton, to score the list of clients, and yet here she'd spent hours googling and DuckDuckGo-ing the names—and the names those searches had led to.

And more names after that.

Resulting in a big bowl of nothing.

Her hunch was that the list had answers, but she was trying to find them in all the wrong ways. Carmen had told her once: If what you're doing isn't working, try something else.

Good advice.

And she followed it now.

She sent a brief text.

Can I come over?

A reply came in less than thirty seconds.

Working late but yeah, sure, good.

Selina had to smile.

Throwing the laptop and list, and a copy of the suicide note, into a backpack, she locked up and hurried down to the parking lot.

Energized by her mission, she sped out onto the streets a little faster than she needed to. Soon she was cruising north toward Riverside County.

Thinking of the list put her in mind of her father. And she gripped the wheel uneasily, reflecting with some shame that she'd been such a hard-ass when it came to Roberto—and to Carmen. Recently Selina hadn't even been willing to attend a small memorial gathering for him on the anniversary of his death. She'd been filled with righteous anger at what she'd perceived as his abandonment.

Now she knew that not only had he never forsaken his daughters—he'd likely sacrificed his life to save theirs.

The enormity of her guilt nearly overwhelmed her. She had believed the worst of him, when he was not only blameless, but deserving of her utmost honor and respect.

Honor.

That was how she would honor him. She would find the person or persons responsible and bring them to justice.

A car slowed in front of her and, her focus divided, she had to brake quickly.

It was then that she noticed the lights of a car behind her doing the same. Hardly suspicious. Except that most other vehicles were changing lanes to speed around her. This vehicle—she couldn't see what it was— kept up the slow pace, then accelerated when she did.

Was he following?

No.

Was she sure?

Yes.

Pretty much.

Then those headlights were lost amid all the others on the inundated byways of Los Angeles. Locals called it Carmageddon.

Soon she was through the mountains and pulling up in front of a trim ranch house in a trim yard, located in a trim suburb. Selina leaned toward the funky and this was a very un-her kind of place.

Still, she found it immensely comforting, especially after her day playing amateur cop—and confronting painful memories of her father's death.

Walking to the front door, she slipped a key from her purse and opened it, then stepped inside and hit the five-digit alarm code.

The door swung shut behind her.

Riverside County Detective Ryan Hall kept a neat house—likely due in part to his military background. A place for everything, everything in its place.

A tap on her ankle scared the hell out of her. She gasped and looked down. It was only Ryan's cat, Caliber, a name she thought didn't fit at all. Apparently he'd inherited the feline from an ex he didn't talk about, though Selina was determined to learn all the deets.

The gray-and-black kitty rolled over for a belly rub, which Selina dutifully provided.

It was then that she heard a noise from outside, that guttural hum that a gas-powered vehicle makes.

She rushed to the window in time to see a black SUV driving slowly down the opposite side of the street. It was a smaller model, a Ford Edge.

The vehicle glided by, then turned the corner. She heard its engine rev as it accelerated away.

At first, she was troubled.

But then she did as her sister recommended and analyzed each fact carefully. First, nobody knew she was looking for the hit man who killed her father, other than Carmen and Jake. Even Carl Overton had no clue why she wanted the list of names.

Second, she had seen no one outside her apartment, much less anybody in a telltale black SUV. There was no indication the lights behind her earlier belonged to this vehicle, nor that the driver was anyone but a person as cautious as she was.

So, next steps: pour a glass of wine, lie back on the couch and summon Netflix.

Or go through the client list one more time. And study the "suicide" note again, on the assumption there were other clues it might give up in addition to RICO-offending goddesses.

There was, for instance, the unknown reason why her father had underlined his middle name as well as the equally mysterious Greek characters.

Δ:Iθ

Which—probably—translated into the no-less-mysterious numbers 4:19.

What the hell did that mean?

Okay. The decision was made: no wine, no streaming.

She plopped down on the couch, assembled a makeshift office on the coffee table and, with a purring feline beside her, got back to work.

CHAPTER 38

Thursday, June 25

Jake heard the urgent voice from behind him.

"Found something." Su Ling was walking into the Garage. She was dressed in a lab coat over a bright-green spandex running outfit.

He recalled she had a race planned for today but had canceled it to analyze the evidence collected at the Chinampas Grand Resort.

"Tell us," Sanchez encouraged.

Su gestured to their computers. "Just uploaded the lab reports. The champagne and chocolates were doctored with liquid propofol. A few sips or bites would put you out for ten, fifteen minutes."

"Source?" Sanchez asked.

"The drug's adulterated, so it's from the street. Untraceable."

"Dead end," Jake muttered. "Then the prop's not what you're talking about."

"Right." Su lifted an eyebrow. "You know in forensic work we want something unique that can point to a specific location. Well, that's what I found on the candy box. Now, a little bit of organic chemistry and I have to go back in time. During the High Renaissance, the most common type of varnish that painters used for their works was called a drying oil. It's a substance that hardens through internal bonds, which form when water evaporates.

"The composition varies but typically it's linseed oil, polyurethanes, alkyds and organic solvents. Art restorers often have to remove aging drying oil and replace it with new varnish. And how *do* they remove it?"

"Don't keep us in suspense," Sanchez said.

"Aliphatic and lipophilic solvents. Which is what I found traces of on the candy box. Only there, nowhere else at the resort. Those chemicals are fairly common, but what's unusual is that these were found in combination with molecules of four-hundred-year-old alkyd residue."

"On the murder board," Sanchez said and typed in the words, after getting the correct spelling of "alkyd" from Su.

"So he's an art restorer?" Jake asked.

"Not necessarily, but he's been around art restoration. Collectors or museums that specialize in High Renaissance art."

"Italian?" Sanchez asked.

"Likely."

"Our boy's first murders," Jake muttered.

"You ever hear from the police there?" Su asked.

Sanchez shook her head. "Five or six phone calls and emails. Nothing. My guess is that they're not convinced their cases are connected to ours, so collaborating isn't a priority. They may not believe in micro threats either."

Jake had been impressed when Eric Williamson had told him of the phrase he coined and how it was I-squared's mission to find and neutralize them.

"Thanks," Sanchez said to Su. "This is helpful."

It was only one new data point, but his partner seemed pleased. She had told him that building a case was like constructing a wall. Every brick laid, no matter how small, was important. Like writing code. They'd shared this observation over a glass of wine a month ago.

Which brought to mind the near kiss.

The reverie vanished when his computer chimed. He glanced at the screen. "Results from one of my bots."

"Which one?" Mouse asked.

There were two. The first was the one he'd sent out to scout for viruses on the HSI server after Stan Reynolds's fumble in sending the unencrypted email. The second was the one searching cameras for Ms. Person of Interest.

It turned out to be the latter.

"Got her."

Sanchez rose and joined him.

He explained that his chaining bot had swung along the vines of servers on Harrison Street and had spotted her walking into a coffee shop, farther along Harrison, after she left the cosmetics store. Significantly, the bot had not caught her *leaving* the shop.

"Look."

Sanchez leaned close to his screen, hair tumbling, and again he was momentarily awash in the scent of lavender. Dismissing the sensation, he scrolled quickly through the video over the course of three hours from the moment Ms. POI entered. Few people linger in a coffee shop without a book or computer. Either she was an employee, or the place had a back door to a parking lot or another street.

If there were a security cam in the shop, it was not part of the voluntary surveillance program. Jake was not inclined to hack any video systems at the moment. Not only would it aggravate Sanchez and start another debate about his stepping over legal lines—he was already on thin ice—but also there was no need. They could just drive over to the shop, a mere thirty minutes from where they were at the moment, and ask to see any recordings.

In the hacking world, like every other, for that matter, the simplest solutions were often the best.

CHAPTER 39

Now, at last, time to visit *Her*.

A trip to the special room Damon loved, his den, armed with the imported razor blades.

Yesterday had not gone as planned and, though he was safe, he was still shaken.

And so he needed the comfort of doing some cutting.

In his kitchen, which was suffused with morning sunlight, Damon pulled on the latex gloves and picked up the box of blades. Then he ambled to the huge living room.

There was no secret code or anything like that to enter his den, though the door was not obvious. It seemed to be yet another floor-to-ceiling mirror. A simple push on the frame and the heavy panel swung inward. He flicked on the light and entered what appeared to be a space typical of an art gallery or museum. Prints and paintings covered the walls. A comfortable light-brown leather couch in the center, some armchairs, a few end tables, and nods to the business side of Damon's life: shelves, a scanner, a computer, a file cabinet, a worktable, an office chair, which could scoot across the tile floor fast as a sports car.

At the back was the special room, partially hidden by a thick purple (what else?) curtain.

Where *She* waited.

A rattle of the razor blades.

His eyes drifted to a print—a good one—of Vasili Pukirev's painting *Unequal Marriage*, which portrayed an elderly nobleman marrying a young woman, possibly a teen. His expression was haughty and imperious. Her downcast eyes radiate sorrow. She is undoubtedly poor and forced into the union by circumstance.

As he sat down at the workstation, his thoughts were, not surprisingly, drawn instantly to September 15, some years ago, the day that changed his life.

For certain reasons, after Sarah Anne Taylor's murder, Damon had decided to try leading a normal life. Why not? Many serial killers were able to juggle. He had finished his courses, with honors, and started teaching at a community college. Then he met someone, an elementary school teacher and part-time grad student, Felicia McNichol. He began dating the willowy brunette.

Not a bad life.

It was faculty dinners, finding a town house, Sunday-morning sex, movies, drives to San Simeon . . .

He still lived in his dreaded family home but, on the plus side, was tended to by Miss Spalding, who would not hear of him staying on campus or in an apartment.

He proposed to Felicia, who was working full-time at an elementary school in Hollywood. She preferred teaching sixth graders, explaining that they were at that perfect age, *past* babbling silliness and *before* hormonal dystopia.

And to Damon's delight, she said yes.

September 15 was the day they would exchange vows, sealing their love in the bonds of matrimony. And begin their new life together—never to be alone again.

The ceremony was to be small. Both their parents were gone at that point, and they were only-children. So the guests would be mostly friends.

That fateful morning, Damon had gone to the hotel to see about final arrangements, while Felicia remained at her house in Beverly Hills to await girlfriends who would help with the hair and makeup.

They had discovered a wonderful venue for the ceremony and reception: a hotel and spa with a pavilion on a lake, offering lush gardens providing the perfect backdrop for an array of beautiful bridal photos. There, he made a few last-minute decisions on the menu, the decorations and the seating, then returned home to put on his best suit.

Miss Spalding greeted him, and he knew instantly something was amiss. It wasn't her face—which was a constant somber mask. No, it was her clothing. By then she should have changed from her typical floor-length gray frock to the pastel taffeta she'd selected for the wedding.

She had not.

She gave him one of her solid embraces—which lingered a bit too long—and said, "Come inside and sit down, Little . . ."

She'd stopped short of calling him her Little Pup, that nickname from his early childhood. Her instinctive move to comfort him with the familiar term reinforced his sense of foreboding.

Damon had not taken a seat but stood with arms crossed over his chest as she delivered the news. There had been an accident, Felicia was dead. Before her friends arrived, she'd gone for a swim and slipped climbing out. Her head hit the travertine coping, knocking her unconscious. Then she'd fallen back in the water and drowned.

Damon had mutely stared out the window. He waved away Miss Spalding's offer of iced tea and cottage pie. She suggested some junk food, candy, always good for comfort.

"No," he'd exhaled.

She said she knew how upset he would be, so she would handle notifying everyone of the tragedy, and would field any calls, if he liked.

That was fine. He didn't want to speak to anyone. Something odd, something significant, was occurring within him and he wanted no distractions.

He went into his room—a large space, as big as some bungalows whole families lived in. He paced slowly past the contents: the many books of art for classwork, the framed posters and prints that were the souvenirs of the visits to art museums and galleries Miss Spalding had taken him to from almost the first week she had moved in: the Getty, the Broad, the county museum, those in the various colleges in the area.

An observer might be curious to see the high art was interspersed with the low: racks of DVDs of slasher films and violent computer game cartridges—all of which Miss Spalding was happy to let her Little Pup indulge in.

Damon stopped pacing when he came to his desk and gazed at the one photo that sat upon it: Felicia's graduation picture.

And realized with a jolt what that sense of significance was, the one that had been wafting about him since Miss Spalding had delivered the horrific news.

He was experiencing something unprecedented.

Sorrow.

Of course, he'd been sad and disappointed at times. He'd been close to his mother before the pills and mental illness took over. And when she died, his main thought was that he was partly sad and partly relieved—and more than partly horrified that the buffer between him and his father was gone.

And when the man himself finally died, he'd idly wondered if *The Evil Dead* was on Amazon Prime, and then laughed, realizing the unintended and possibly subconscious joke about the classic horror film's title.

But Felicia . . .

At her loss, he felt raw, unadulterated grief.

Fascinated with the new sensation, he researched the subject.

Damon had been surprised to learn that sorrow had a close relationship to art.

First, as a theme: mourning the death of Christ, for instance.

Second, as therapy, in a way. Artists often expressed their personal loss on paper or canvas or in marble as a way to cope. Given that there was often a tortured element to being an artist, this therapeutic technique was widespread. Käthe Kollwitz, for instance. And particularly Frida Kahlo—whose lifelong battles with physical and emotional pain, from respectively a bus accident and a turbulent relationship with muralist Diego Rivera, were reflected in the majority of her haunting works.

Yes, Damon Garr had become quite the expert in grief.

He now found he was looking again at the Russian painting of the sorrowful marriage, which was directly across the worktable from him in the hidden den.

Grief . . .

And, in fact, studying its many iterations had led directly to the most significant moment of his life, to—

"Hello, Damon," came a quiet voice from behind him.

Gasping, he rose and spun around. The chair rolled away.

A man in a black suit stood in the doorway of the den. Tall, lean and pale, he looked like a mortician.

Damon struggled to come to grips with the fact that a total stranger had somehow gotten inside his house. He wasn't physically imposing, yet there was an air of subtle menace about him. His lack of concern about the potential threat posed by Damon, a much larger man, attested to either supreme confidence or foolhardy arrogance.

His unexpected visitor strolled over to the wall and squinted as he regarded a print of *La Douleur* by Paul Cézanne, which depicted a man beset by sorrow, with a deformed version of Mary Magdalene in the corner as she mourned the death of Jesus.

Damon demanded, "Who . . . who the hell are you?"

The man turned to face him. "My name is Tristan Kane. And I have a proposition for you."

CHAPTER 40

"How did you . . ." Damon began, his heart slowing after the shock.

"Get in here?" Tristan Kane studied more prints. "Like everybody else in the universe you believe what advertisers tell you. They've convinced you their product is easy to use, it's technological, it's digital . . . and according to the commercials, you're endangering your family if you don't buy it."

"You mean my locks and security."

"Hm." Kane seemed pleased that Damon had understood. As if he'd been uncertain of his intelligence. "If you'd put a padlock on your front door, I'd still be sawing away. But you have an off-the-rack system that took me about . . . six seconds to open."

"But the camera—" Damon looked at a nearby monitor. The scene was still, despite the omnipresent breeze from the Pacific Ocean. A dead giveaway that he should have spotted. He tsked his tongue. "You loaded a screenshot, and waltzed right in, directly in front of the lens. Clever. You're good."

Kane shrugged as if bored with the praise. He scanned the walls, where his eyes settled on the Goya, then the El Greco. Trubert's *Weeping Madonna* held his attention for a while. He stepped close to a high-quality reproduction of Hopper's *Automat*, which depicted a woman sitting alone at a table in one of the coin-operated restaurants that were all the rage when the artist painted the work in the 1920s. It was described as embodying the essence of urban alienation. Eyes still on the seated woman, he said softly, "I did some research. You teach art history. Yet you've never published. That's curious for an academic." Then the man turned to him. "I suppose you want to draw as little attention to yourself as possible."

True enough, but rather than respond verbally, Damon walked to the filing cabinet. With deliberate casualness, he pulled open the top drawer and reached in as if retrieving a stack of bills that needed paying.

He lifted out the pistol he kept inside and pointed it at Kane. "We're talking about security systems and my career, but not about who the fuck you are and what you're doing here."

The man gave no visible reaction. He glanced at the weapon and then continued to take in the paintings as he spoke. "Are you aware the authorities call you the Honeymoon Killer?"

This struck Damon like a fist. "How do you know that? There's been no coverage in the media. Wait, you hacked the *police*."

"I'm always monitoring your friends, Jake and Carmen."

Damon's heart gave another thud—this one of pleasure. Could these be the names of the pair who'd been thwarting him at every turn?

Kane continued, "A colleague of theirs, named Reynolds, sent some emails asking about two murders in Italy and one here. Killing newlyweds preparing to begin their honeymoon. He was careless about encryption and security. I got into the government's servers. The door's closed now. But the access was helpful while it lasted."

He had to know. "The two you mentioned. Do you have pictures?"

"A few." Kane pulled out his phone and scrolled. He held it up. The "few" was an entire album, which contained seemingly thousands of images of the two people who were Damon's enemies.

"Who are they?"

"Jake Heron and Carmen Sanchez." Kane explained briefly about HSI, and this outfit called I-squared.

Apparently Damon was considered a risk to national security. Seriously? He only wanted to practice the fine art of Serial Killing 2.0.

"You're a micro threat," Kane explained. "It's not an insult. It's just a classification. The sort usually back-burnered by the FBI, CIA and NSA. But you fall squarely within I-squared's parameters." He gave Damon an appraising look. "They're good, Jake and Carmen. But your ID is safe."

"Not from you. Obviously."

"They have to play by the rules. I don't."

"Then tell me how you found me."

Kane seemed proud to do so. "After I read Reynolds's report and checked out popular news stories about the deaths overseas, I wrote some script that hacked every Italian traffic camera record in and near Verona and Florence around the time of those killings. I collected twelve million facial images, upscaled them from 512 to 1024 to improve quality and ran them through a comparator program I also wrote."

Damon felt his jaw slacken. He'd heard students around campus talking about world-class hackers they referred to as "elite," but had never met one. If Kane were one of those, he could break into nearly anything.

Kane was still in full flow about his exploits. "Yours was one of 853 that were statistically similar. They went into a face rec farm I use. Based in eastern Europe. They have four trillion facial images . . . nearly everybody on earth who's ever walked near a camera. It could identify most of those images, but only one lived in Southern California, near where the third killing took place."

That was downright alarming. "But if *you* did it, then—"

"Jake and Carmen could never get warrants to pull that off. And even if they did? I paid the farm to wipe every image of you. And I scrubbed the traffic cam archives in Italy. You no longer exist, my friend."

Damon shivered with anger. "They stopped me. Yesterday. And it was the Fourth Day. Doesn't mean anything to you, but it's significant to me. Now my . . . schedule is off. That's not good."

"No, I imagine upsetting you would not have felicitous consequences. But I can help."

"And now we've come full circle back to why."

Kane seemed amused. "You really don't need that." A glance at the gun. "May I sit?"

Damon nodded to a couch. Still holding the pistol, he resumed his seat in the rolling chair beside his worktable and waited for Kane to continue.

"We have a mutual goal. You know *Moby-Dick*?"

The epic novel written by Herman Melville in the 1800s, about a captain obsessed with killing a white whale that was as massive as the book. Damon did not know anyone who had finished the story. He, on the other hand, had. The combined themes of obsession and loss resonated.

He nodded.

"I'm Jake Heron's white whale. I exploited a weakness of his a few years ago. Not a weakness in his coding. You'll never find that. A *personal* weakness. Ego. People died. And now, he's teamed up with Carmen Sanchez. They stopped a project I was working on recently. My clients were arrested. It . . . damaged my reputation."

So he wasn't the only one at odds with this Carmen and Jake team. If this conversation went the way he thought it was headed, his situation might improve dramatically.

"Destroying me is their mission," Kane went on. "They pulled a scam on another client of mine recently and got access to my main banking accounts. Drained them in seconds. And they're searching for me. I have various emergency plans and already put one in play."

He was intrigued. "What did you do?"

"Left evidence that points the dogs in a different direction. Sent them sniffing around Switzerland, a research facility. They have no idea that I'm in their backyard."

Damon concluded that the gun was unnecessary after all. If Kane wanted to hurt him, that would have already happened. He returned it to the cabinet drawer.

"First name okay, Damon?" Kane waited for him to nod, then added, "Good." He regarded Damon for a long moment, then said, "I don't really get what you're about. Some kind of sociopathic fetish? There are so many, one loses track. I don't care. But, as I said, we have something in common. Heron and Sanchez are rooting around like pigs after truffles, looking for you, looking for me."

"I have a plan," Damon said, curious to hear Kane's thoughts. "Kill one of them. Only one, which would sideline the other. A one-wheeled motorcycle."

Kane, Damon guessed, did not smile much. But he seemed to come close to doing so, upon hearing this. He took this as approval.

"I can get into most security camera servers ever made." Kane nodded to the monitor. "And make you disappear. I can break into a lot of email servers and phone switches. Find out what they're up to."

"I-squared? That place you mentioned where they work?"

"That's sealed now, as I was saying. By Heron. Cracking would take weeks. And we don't have that kind of time, do we?"

Damon shook his head.

"But I can break into their comm systems and regular police servers. I can find addresses they think are cloaked. I can find out what cars they drive, where those cars are going. Dozens of other things."

"Fact is, I *am* having trouble locating them."

"Figured as much. That's why I'm giving you a present, as a show of good faith. To prove you can trust me. And give you a chance to have some fun."

Damon took the folded sheet of paper Kane had held out with his long, pale fingers.

He read the name and address. "Selina Sanchez? Sister, I assume?"

Kane nodded.

Damon glanced at the purple-curtained room. Felt the weight of the razor blades.

Her . . .

The cutting could wait a bit longer.

He looked at Kane's note and mentally called up a map of LA. He did the calculations. He could be in Fullerton in forty-five minutes.

CHAPTER 41

Selina tilted her head back to look up at Detective Ryan Hall, who was a foot taller. "I'm no investigator, and I need help."

He gave her a lopsided smile that tugged at her heart.

Hall had gotten home around four in the morning after wrapping up a lengthy investigation. She and the cat had fallen asleep on the sofa, and she had a vague memory of Ryan spreading a blanket over her before he kissed her forehead and vanished into the bedroom.

She'd awakened at six and continued to pore over the notes and list of clients, Googling name after name and going down rabbit holes after the cryptic Greek characters, 4:19 . . . and getting nowhere.

Now that he'd emerged from his room, tousle-haired and jonesing for coffee, she filled him in about the case and her mission to find the hit man and whoever had hired him, adding her theory about money laundering.

"A code?"

She set the note in front of him.

No priest would give me last rites before what I am about to do, so this will be my final confession, which I will have to give in seconds:

Please forgive me once I reveal my true guilt under oath.
I violated my clients' trust by investing their savings in a risky fund, and I cannot go on in the knowledge of what I have done and the misery I have caused.
I now can admit to hoping that you, my goddesses, can ever live in peace, amen.
—Roberto Mateo Sanchez

His eyes widened. "Damn. That was smart."

"There are still some mysteries." She pointed out the Greek letter/numbers, 4:19, in the corner. And the fact his middle name was underlined. "I can't figure those out yet. I've been online looking for dirt on Dad's clients, to see if one of them has a record or some mob connection maybe."

She added that Carmen was busy chasing a serial killer. "So I came to the one person I thought could help. My own knight in shining armor, who also happens to work homicide in the Riverside County Sheriff's Department."

"Who's that? Maybe I work with him."

She kissed him again. Harder. With better aim.

She and Ryan had been dating only a short time, but she already knew he was the type to pitch in when he saw a need. In other words, he was one of the good guys.

As he opened a can of food for the cat and plopped it onto a plate, he asked, "How'd you get the list of clients? I'd need a subpoena for that."

"Fell into my lap."

"Then don't tell me any more."

"Deal."

Hall was wearing dark slacks and a white shirt. He tried twice to knot his tie. Selina took over and got it done on the first attempt. Now *he* initiated a kiss. It landed on the top of her head.

Not her first choice, but still it sent that wonderful jolt through her. She nodded to the coffee table, where the list of names sat.

"Find anything?"

"No," she conceded.

"We always start there too."

"The police use Google?"

"Yep. Hardly ever does any good, though."

"Maybe you could run a background check," she offered with a coy smile.

"I could. If a case were open in Riverside County. Which it isn't. And if I had the staffing to run fifty names." He was looking at the list. "Which I don't."

"It's only forty-eight." She refilled his mug from the fresh pot of coffee she'd made when he woke up. "What do I do, Ryan?"

"Forget background. Start at the beginning. So, Jake was the one who found out your dad was murdered, right?"

"His associate—someone called Aruba—was investigating a dark website where people hire contract killers." She swallowed the lump forming in her throat at the thought. "And Dad's name was on it."

Ryan reached out and pulled her to him. She leaned against his chest, finding comfort in his strength. She wasn't normally the type to simper and fall into a man's arms, but this investigation was more personal, and more emotionally taxing, than she would have believed.

"Good. A starting point. The hit man. We always work up the chain. In drugs, it's user to street dealer to wholesaler to importer to cartel boss. That's what you and I'll do."

Selina thrilled at the two pronouns. "How?"

Hall released her to take another sip from his mug. "He died here, right? LA?"

"Whittier."

"Still Southern California. Lot of crime, lot of homicides, but there's still a finite number of professional killers." He leaned against the kitchen bar. "There's somebody I want to talk to. Guy I put away my first year on the job. A fixer named Everett Judd." He pulled out his phone, scrolled and sent a text.

"What's a fixer?"

"Like a broker. He puts together buyers and sellers—drugs, guns, hit people."

"So he's not a killer himself?"

"No, but he's handled some deals with a few. I remember his ads for hits on the dark web."

"You're not serious. Advertising?"

"Yep. Look it up. 'Silk Road.' There are others too."

"Can I talk to him?"

"No." Hall was texting.

"But—"

"I'll do the talking. Judd's a three-time loser. He's doing a twenty-fiver for conspiracy and state RICO. The man doesn't play well with others. He just shanked his cellmate last week. Nobody died but he's in solitary." He nodded at his phone. "I just texted a buddy who's a supervisor at the prison. Maybe he'll agree to a video call."

Selina continued briefing Ryan for another twenty minutes before his phone vibrated on the coffee table.

"It's him." He picked it up and tapped the screen. "Hey, Tal. Thanks . . . Five, ten minutes . . . Okay, thanks . . . yeah, this number."

He disconnected. "My friend. He's head of the block that includes solitary. Cal State Prison."

"Will Judd answer your questions?"

"Maybe. You never know. The thing you have to remember: Criminals at his level? They're mostly sociopaths. Sometimes you have normal conversations, sometimes things take a dark turn. But always— and I mean always—they try to manipulate you."

He finished getting dressed while Selina continued to stare at the list of names.

Had one of them hired Roberto's killer?

Caliber jumped up and purred and rubbed his head against her leg. She absently stroked the soft fur.

Hall's phone hummed once more and he walked into the living room, clipping his gun onto his belt. He glanced at the phone and, answering, gestured her to join him, but to stand to the side. "It's a video call. You can listen, but I don't want him to see you. A woman would be a distraction." He added under his breath, "Especially you."

Fine with her. She had no desire to see Judd. "All right."

She listened as Ryan navigated his way through the Corrections Department's communication system. After a couple of minutes, he held the cell phone up in front of him and she knew the video link was live.

A deep, raspy voice sounded through the tiny speaker. "Well, well, well. My old buddy. What do you want, Detective?"

Ryan's expression hardened. "Information."

"Like everything else in this world of ours, it's gonna cost you."

"After that stunt you pulled last week, there's no way you'll get your sentence shortened. In fact, it'll be extended considerably."

"You think I'm stupid? I know there's nothing you or the DA can do for me that way. There's something else I want."

"Before we get to haggling, let's see if you have anything to trade. You know anything about a contract three years ago on a Roberto Sanchez? Whittier. An investment adviser."

"No, nothing."

"Okay. Let's talk about that site on the dark web where you brokered your last deal."

"You mean the job that landed me in here?" When Ryan nodded, Judd said, "That site was taken down."

"I know. What I want are the names of other pros who used sites like that for pickup jobs."

"Well, that's quite a few people. Gotta give me more to go on."

"Was there anyone who specialized in staging a hit to look like something else?"

"There was one dude had been a medic. He could get this shit that made people look like they had a heart attack. And somebody else we called the mechanic. He knew how to make brakes fail without cutting the line. That didn't usually kill you, you know, airbags and everything, but then he'd follow 'em in his car and break their necks after. Oh, and he could also make an engine explode and it looked like a bad gas line. The guy was a freaking genius."

Selina felt bile rising to the back of her throat as she listened to Judd's recitation of—and admiration for—how ruthless killers ended people's lives. She detected no sign of remorse, judgment or any other emotion as he spoke. He might have been discussing players with varying degrees of skill on a sports team.

Ryan pressed for more. "How about making the death look like a suicide?"

A long pause. "Now you're getting into very specific territory. That's hard to pull off. Cops like yourself and coroners, they're trained to catch that. But if you can do it, it's a fucking good cover. The vics are usually involved in something that could ruin their lives, so everybody's more inclined to believe they offed themselves. I know this one asshole who was good at it. How was it done?"

"A jumper."

"Oh. Him."

She saw her own shock reflected in Ryan's face as he urged, "Keep going."

"Tossing people out the window was his signature move, and before you ask—yeah, he advertised on a dark website."

"What's his name?"

"Now see, Detective, that reminds me of the favor I need. The thing about last week? My cellmate? He got a little familiar, so I had to remind him to behave himself. Simple little correction. The screws didn't see it that way. And they're gonna send me to some supermax."

"The Q?"

"Naw, someplace else." He paused. "I've been to one of those before. Didn't like it. I like it here."

"You don't want to be separated from your crew. You'll have to start all over in another place to run your hustles."

"Hm. That's a cynical way to put it. Let's say a home is a home."

"I'll be straight with you," Ryan said. "I can't make any guarantees."

"You got cred, Hall. You're young, but your word is good. Probably you'll find somebody who'll listen. All I want."

"Okay."

"Say it."

"I'll talk to the DA and DOC about keeping you here instead of sending you to supermax. Now spill."

"I don't have a name to give you."

"Then you'll be on the next prisoner transport bus, Judd. We don't have anything more to talk about."

"Hold on. I just mean his *real* name. I've got his handle. Sweeney. And where he hangs. Or used to. It's a bar in North Hollywood called Paquito's. A bartender named Nando works every night. He can hook you up with him."

"Give me something on Nando. Pressure point."

Silence for a moment from Judd. "He wants to buy the bar from the owner. To make extra money, he over-orders the booze, then waters it down and lines his pockets with the difference in cost. Oh, and he's an asshole."

"The last one kind of went without saying."

"Yep."

"Describe him."

"Bald vampire."

"What does that even mean?"

"You'll get it."

"We're also after whoever hired Sweeney. You know who took out the contract?"

The big question. Who had wanted their father dead?

But Judd said, "No clue. You'd have to ask Sweeney that."

"Okay, Judd. I'll make the calls for you."

"Thanks, Detective. Hey, lot of assholes in your business. You're not one of 'em. Oh, and one more thing? About pros like me? We don't give a shit about anything. This Sweeney? He'd just as soon dust you as look at you."

"Weapon of choice?"

"If it can be used to fuck somebody up, *that's* his weapon of choice. Glock with a Yankee Hill suppressor or a Home Depot screwdriver. Watch your back. And front and sides."

As he disconnected, Selina thought: one crazy life. She'd just seen two men haggling over stone-cold murderers as if they were on a car lot settling on a price for a used Volvo.

She asked, "We heading out?"

"Not yet. I've got to get to the office."

"Then I'll go home to change." She grabbed her purse, kissed him goodbye and then walked out to her car.

She climbed in and started the engine. Before pulling into the street, though, she checked her surroundings.

No sign of any black Ford SUVs.

She committed herself to stay alert on the drive home, keeping an eye out for the Ford, and any other cars that seemed to be tailing her.

Now that she knew the sort of people she was dealing with— Judd and Sweeney and whoever had hired him—she'd have to be extra vigilant.

The last thing she wanted was to lead anyone to her apartment in Functional Fullerton, her enclave, her sanctuary in this Wild West city.

CHAPTER 42

Carmen sat down at a table in the coffee shop.

Heron joined her a moment later with two steaming mugs.

The place was not a chain and seemed to date to the pre-Starbucks era. Mismatched tables and chairs, faded posters of coffee estates in Central or South America, a bulletin board that customers used to post cards for guitar lessons, house painting, math tutoring.

This was the place where Ms. Person of Interest disappeared after the funeral at Cedar Hills and never returned. Shortly after arriving, they'd learned there was a back door to a parking area and, better yet, a working camera aimed outward into that part of the lot. According to the barista, many people used that exit.

With luck, they might score Ms. POI's tag number.

They'd have to wait to find out, though. The manager was not there, and only she could give them access to the security system. She would be in soon.

They sipped their coffee—filtered brew, nothing fancy. Heron claimed it was quite good. She knew that hackers may avoid liquor but were connoisseurs of all things caffeine. He would recognize superior java when he tasted it.

He put his mug down and checked his tablet. "Nothing from Switzerland."

"HTW."

"DGT," Heron replied.

Carmen frowned.

The hacker said breezily, "Don't go there."

"That's funny, Heron. For a minute I thought it was referring to whatever you two got up to on your infamous moonlit night."

"Anyway, no, it's not Aruba," he said, not taking her bait. "I'm getting real-time updates from the Swiss authorities, monitoring all the traffic into CERN."

She recalled that CERN housed the world's largest nuclear collider—and was a place Tristan Kane was apparently quite interested in.

Disturbing, to say the least.

Heron continued, "But there've been no breaches. Digital or physical."

"Right." Then she asked, "What the hell does he have in mind?"

Heron shrugged. An appropriate gesture. After all, what was the point of speculating?

"What does an accelerator do?" She could google it but wanted a quick and succinct answer rather than scrolling through screenfuls of information.

"Smashes atomic stuff into other stuff to make smaller stuff."

Heron could be a bit too succinct. "And how is that helpful?"

"CERN cost five billion, so somebody must've thought it was worthwhile."

A troubling thought popped into her mind.

"What?" he asked, clearly reading her expression.

"I'm pissed off," she announced, nodding at his tablet. "The Swiss are cooperating. Why not the Italians?"

She and Williamson had both sent multiple requests for information on the cases in Verona and Florence. All were ignored. "I've worked with MI-5 and -6 in England, Police Nationale in France, Bundespolizei, Germany. Never a problem. But nothing from the Polizia di Stato and the Carabinieri—"

"The military police that helps out in civilian criminal cases," Heron cut in.

Carmen lifted an eyebrow. "How do you know them? Get into trouble over there too?"

"Video game I play."

"Well, the Italians are as good as the other LEOs, so I can't understand why they're not taking the crimes seriously. Or taking *us* seriously."

"Excuse me, ma'am?" A barista, a slim man with elaborate body art, gestured toward the door, through which a stocky woman with short blonde hair was walking quickly. She wore jeans and a black blouse and had already donned her beige work apron.

Mary Nance, the manager, had spoken to Carmen from her mobile on the drive here and was aware of what they needed. She had come in a half hour early to meet them.

After introductions, she said, "This is about that officer who was stabbed at the cemetery?"

"That's right," Carmen said.

"Terrible." Nance's face showed concern.

Carmen understood why—sympathy for the victim, but more than that. "You don't need to worry. The person in here wasn't the attacker, but we think she may have some helpful information. Can we see that video?"

The relief was clear.

"Sure. Come with me."

Nance led them down a corridor past a storeroom filled with bags of coffee beans and sugar, plastic utensils and other disposable wares. In the cluttered office, Carmen was amused at the frame on the wall, a shadow box holding what would have been the currency used to make the first purchase. It wasn't a bill, but two quarters and a dime.

Definitely pre-Starbucks.

Nance booted up a Lenovo several years out of date and the screen flickered to life. She logged in and found the security system files, then began searching for the date and time in question.

The trio stared at the scrolling screen, on which a clear, high-def image of the counter was visible in one window, the parking lot in another.

Heron said, "Good system. I know it. Over a hundred thousand are sold every year."

Carmen noted his body language as he spoke, a compressing of the lips and tightening of the shoulders. She could guess what he was thinking. He'd told her that someday, nowhere on earth would be free from surveillance. But he'd also acknowledged his own hypocrisy, admitting that he'd welcome the technology if it helped them stop criminals.

"This is her," Heron said.

The interior video depicted Ms. Person of Interest approaching the counter. The veil was lifted but she still wore the wide-brimmed hat, obscuring her face.

He nodded at the computer. "Can I?" He was a deft scrubber of video.

Nance vacated the chair, and he took her place.

"Do you know her?" Carmen asked, hoping she was a regular customer.

Nance didn't.

At Heron's suggestion, she left the office and asked one barista, then the other, to come in and look at the video. The inked barista was the one who had served her, but he could not recall her ever coming in before. The same with the other employee.

Heron typed some commands. Seconds later, a printer in the corner spat out several pictures of Ms. POI from various angles. "Keep those," he told Nance. "Show them to the other employees when they come in for work. Let us know if anybody recognizes her."

"Of course."

Carmen stared at the screen. She lifted a frustrated arm, scoffing. "Hell. Everyone else looks up at the menu on the wall. She keeps her eyes down. I'll bet she knows there's a camera."

Heron said, "Maybe we'll get lucky . . . ugh, no dice."

Carmen knew he'd been referring to their hope she would pay with a credit or debit card. Ms. POI remained unhelpful, paying cash.

After collecting her order, she stepped quickly to the back exit.

Heron maximized that window. A recording that depicted a twenty- or thirty-foot section of the parking lot began to play. Their target walked into view, the red stripes down the back of her heels clearly visible.

And finally their elusive target cooperated.

At least to an extent. They saw her climb into the driver's seat of a white Toyota Camry. A moment later the vehicle backed out, turned and then sped forward and down a side street.

Heron whispered, "Shit."

Carmen too was disappointed. They could see neither the front nor the rear plate. California required both.

Heron pulled his tablet from his backpack and looked at a map. "No cameras in the direction she headed."

They thanked the manager and returned to Carmen's SUV. She said, "At least we have the make, model and color of the car."

After they climbed into the big vehicle, Carmen saw Heron looking at his tablet and shot him a questioning glance.

"Thought I'd look to see how many such vehicles are prowling the California highways."

A good question. And the answer would indicate how much work they'd have to do searching for the one Ms. POI was driving.

"Bad news. There are more registered vehicles in California than any other state. That includes well over a quarter million Camrys. And guess what? The vast majority of those are white. I hope Declan doesn't mind the grunt work."

She imagined him doing the large language model computer equivalent of cracking his knuckles before getting down to business. She chuckled. "Just the sort of thing he lives for."

CHAPTER 43

Where are you, my dear? Damon Garr was thinking.

He was standing behind a renegade shrub of some sort on a side street in Fullerton, studying the small, pocked-stucco apartment building whose paint job was the color of bubble gum with turquoise trim. More Floridian than Pacific. The windows in the unit he gazed at were intact. Some in other apartments had been "repaired" with plywood.

He guessed that Selina Sanchez, who was a student, would be perfectly happy in the place, even if it was not an architectural gem like the mansions a mere thirty minutes away.

But where was she?

Her car was not in its assigned spot.

His thoughts slipped to that Tristan Kane guy. Odd duck, Miss Spalding would have said. But Damon had an instinctive feeling that he could be trusted—and helpful, since he clearly knew security systems cold.

Then too, there was the gift he'd presented. Selina's name and address.

Damon's hatred for the pair of investigators was at a fever pitch. And killing—or otherwise "debilitating"—Carmen's sister would provide a major advantage in the war against them.

And give you a chance to have some fun . . .

He could—

Damon was suddenly aware of shouting from a construction site across the street—a small apartment complex, work on which had been abandoned years ago. A sign advertised a bankruptcy sale and a number to call if anyone was interested. The sun had bleached away all but the last two digits.

Curious—and ever fascinated by violence of any kind—he crossed the quiet street, stepped into the lot and peeked behind the cinder block wall that outlined a building that would never be. He saw a struggle between a heavyset man and a woman in a formfitting dark-red sweater and leather, or faux, miniskirt. Black tights and high-heeled shoes of the same shade completed the outfit. A purse lay on the ground.

The man gripped the woman around the waist and was trying to kiss her. The maneuver was sloppy and uncoordinated. Drunk undoubtedly, even at this hour, he was persistent. The woman batted at his hands and tried to twist out of his grasp, but his thick fingers scrabbled at her clothes. Suddenly the sweater tore wide open, exposing a sheer black lace bra and ample cleavage.

Damon took in this view for a moment, then remembered his mission and glanced back toward Selina's apartment. No sign of her.

Might as well continue to watch the show.

"Stop it!" the woman yelled. "I said no, asshole!"

He gave up on the kiss and devoted all his efforts toward getting her on the ground.

Damon noted two things. First, she was stunningly beautiful. Her long dark hair contrasted with her alabaster skin, and her figure was both voluptuous and athletic. His second observation: she hadn't panicked and was keeping her wits about her. In fact, she was doing a pretty good job fending the man off—so far.

No stranger to assaulting people, Damon noted that the attacker had made a tactical error. He had become distracted by the sight of the lingerie and the flesh it barely contained. The instant his guard was down, his intended victim kneed him in the groin with the speed and force of a striking snake.

Damon gave an involuntary wince as the man grabbed his crotch and doubled over, collapsing onto the ground. "Bitch, bitch, bitch . . ."

So the assault was over. Next, she would run to the street and call 9-1-1.

He was wrong.

She gazed around. For a weapon? Apparently. Not finding any rocks or metal pipes nearby, she improvised.

Damon looked on, transfixed, as she ripped the high-heeled shoe from her left foot, dropped to her knees and began to bring it down on her attacker's head, repeatedly.

He couldn't see clearly—her back was to him—but once, she paused and scanned the area. He retreated into the shadows, though he caught a brief glimpse of her face. He was close enough to see a demonic madness in her eyes, which seemed to be cobalt blue.

The image gripped him, and Selina Sanchez slipped from his mind entirely. The Tableau this woman was creating was not in his style, but what artist didn't enjoy watching a skilled colleague at work?

The man was now unconscious, lying helpless and bloody. Damon was sure that *now* she would flee.

But he was wrong again.

The spike heel had broken in the onslaught, and she simply dropped the left shoe and pulled off the right.

Damon debated. She was intoxicated with bloodlust and if she carried the assault to its natural conclusion, she would likely end up in prison for murder. Ordinarily he wouldn't care, but this woman was not only a kindred spirit but too beautiful and intense to waste her best years in a cell for zero reason.

Which would inevitably happen. Any claim she had of self-defense ended when her attacker passed out. And she was not done yet. She positioned herself to impale him with the equivalent of an ice pick once more.

What was the word that he was thinking of?

Ah, yes . . . in Damon's experience, the only reason for such excess was *passion*.

He knew this because he had a curious relationship with the emotion himself: wholly absent in 90 percent of his life, it utterly possessed him when he was crafting a Tableau. He knew exactly what she was feeling.

But it was clear she did not have that magic element that made him so utterly dangerous: impulse control.

Damon stepped away from the corner of the building. The woman clocked the motion in her peripheral vision and looked up at him.

A sharp gasp of shock escaped her lush mouth.

Their gazes locked. He thought her initial reaction would be to cover her chest, but no. She scrutinized Damon and the surroundings, perhaps to see if he was a cop. Or another threat.

He cast his gaze down at the prone figure before he spoke to her. "These circumstances? If you kill him, it's going to take a lot of work to get away with it. I'm not even sure you could, at this point."

An array of expressions passed over her lovely face, but she said nothing. Then she seemed to process his words.

Breathing hard, she regarded him a long moment, composed herself and answered in a calculated tone. "I always figure something out."

Her response caught him off guard.

"Always?" He raised a brow. "You make a habit of bludgeoning people to death?"

"Only the ones who have it coming."

He should have been repulsed or even afraid—he was bigger and, after all, a shoe is not the most formidable of weapons, but she could do some damage if the rage returned.

At the very least the script called for him to walk away.

Yet just as she had chosen not to flee, he followed suit.

And to his shock, as he took in the bloody, barely moving victim, and the feral gleam in her eyes, he found himself, of all things, keenly aroused.

Watching her approach, he stepped fully from the shadows, unable to resist the image that came to mind: that she was one of the frightening yet beautiful Furies, out of William-Adolphe Bouguereau's painting *The Remorse of Orestes*, a work that managed to perfectly capture the unlikely combination of unholy retribution, reckless abandon and unbridled rage.

CHAPTER 44

Captivated by her magnetism and looks, Damon forced himself to give no quarter. He knew that retreating in response to her advance would only strengthen her position in the silent power struggle that had unexpectedly materialized between them.

And he wanted to establish equivalence, if not domination.

She stopped just three feet from him, well within his personal zone.

What came next was as surprising as the footwear assault.

Nothing.

No pleas, no excuses, no tears, no threats.

She simply looked him up and down with apparent amusement.

He found himself asking a cocktail party question. "So. What's your name?"

"You first."

Okay. This was how she wanted to play it. Her words were a challenge, and they sparked an internal debate.

Damon had been very careful with his identity, taking pains to ensure he could never be connected with any of the locations where he'd created a Tableau. On the other hand, this woman had no clue about his avocation. Should he tell her the truth? He performed an analysis in seconds.

Pro: She might see him drive away and get his license plate number. Someone with her determination would easily find a way to get his registration information, which would include his name and address.

Con: If she learned his secret, she could lead the cops right to him. Which meant he would have to kill her. And that would be such a waste.

Conclusion: Either way, he had nothing to lose. It was worth the risk because an image had popped into his mind. An image of her back at his house. An image of her in his den.

He smiled. "Damon."

She lowered the hand holding the shoe. "Maddie Willis."

He had edged ahead in the power game. Those who knew last names were at a level higher than those who only knew first.

He flicked a glance at the man she'd just incapacitated. She did too and said, "You're right. They make a big fucking deal out of murder. *Beating* assholes? Not so much."

"Is he going to cause trouble for you after he wakes up?"

Her lip curled. "What's he going to tell the cops? He can't admit to attacking me and he's not going to say some random woman kicked his ass for no reason—with her shoe. Men're too proud to admit that."

Fair point.

She gave her head a disgusted shake. "He'll slink to some ER and tell them he got mugged by a whole crew."

Damon cast a covert glance at Selina's apartment. No car had arrived, and the lights were still dark. He debated. Then thought: Okay, sis. It's your lucky day. He turned back to the beautiful woman before him. "The cops'll come sooner or later, and we shouldn't be here."

He'd deliberately used "we" to subtly reinforce that they were in this together. He was on her side and would help.

The next part required finesse. "Can I give you a ride somewhere?" he said quietly, then allowed his eyes to drift lower. "I have a spare shirt in my car." The thought of her wearing his clothes nearly stole his breath.

She followed his gaze and tugged the ragged edges of her sweater together. "I can't walk around like this, can I?"

He pressed his advantage. "If that asshole dies, he might have some fibers from your sweater under his nails. You need to ditch that thing immediately. We could use my fireplace to burn it."

Her gaze grew calculating. "How come you know so much about it?"

He stifled a curse. He'd been so determined to get her to his place that he'd overplayed his hand. Now he needed a good answer. Something that wouldn't frighten her off. He considered various options:

Could he be a huge fan of true crime? Nope, too risky. She might ask him about the shows he watched or the books he read—and he'd be left staring at her, slack jawed.

Could he be working on a crime novel that included research on forensics? Nope again. She'd keep probing out of curiosity. Or suspicion.

And then it came to him. "Got a buddy who's a criminal defense attorney," he said. "We get together and the guy spills all his war stories. I've heard how his murder clients got caught. And how they were convicted—or not. There've been dozens."

He watched her carefully as she processed the explanation, which should have put any doubts to rest. Hell, the "buddy" sounded like the exact person she'd want in her corner in the event the sack of shit lying on the sidewalk died and LAPD Homicide came to visit.

"Makes sense," she said slowly. "But still, you're inviting me to your house?" She lifted her shoe. "After what you just saw?"

She had a fair point. He'd sized her up, however, and figured he could take her . . . if it came to that. "I'm not worried."

She snorted. "Either you're incredibly confident or you're completely nuts."

"Does it have to be one or the other?" He kept a straight face while the joke settled. Then he smiled. "Look. It was just a thought. Good luck."

Like a prospective buyer in a used car lot, he knew the best tactic in a negotiation was to show no interest. And to turn and walk away, which was what he did now.

"Wait."

He made sure to stifle a grin before turning to face her again. Just then the man lying nearby let out a groan.

She flicked a glance at him and chewed her lower lip. "Let me get my purse."

He watched her hurry over to snatch up her bag as his thoughts raced ahead to the next few hours he would spend with her. It was a good thing he'd received the German razor blades yesterday.

Because he had big plans for Maddie Willis.

CHAPTER 45

"Is he back from wherever he went?" Jake asked Sanchez, as they stood in front of his workstation in the Garage.

He meant their boss, of course.

"Don't have a clue. Never heard back from him."

They had just set Declan to work, tracking down cars that might be traced to Ms. POI.

"Not like him to go silent," Sanchez noted. "You know, let's go talk to Destiny. Maybe he's sick or one of the kids is."

Jake nodded.

Together they walked out of the Garage and up the short, gray-carpeted corridor to HSI proper.

"Notice anything?" he asked.

Sanchez looked around. "Quiet."

"It is."

As they approached Williamson's office, he glanced ahead and saw Mouse at the far end of the main hall. When she saw them, she began jogging their way.

Odd, Jake thought. She was excitable but not given to this kind of behavior.

Or panic, as her expression suggested.

They stepped into Williamson's ante office, where Destiny Baker was on the phone. She was surrounded by dozens of slips of paper covered with handwritten scrawls. Many Post-it Notes too.

Her look of dismay mirrored Mouse's.

Jake and Sanchez glanced at each other.

Which was when they heard a voice from inside their boss's office.

"Ah, Agent Sanchez and Mr. Stealthy Intrusionist. Pray enter."

"The fuck," she whispered.

Deputy Director Stanley Reynolds was pouring bottled water into a potted plant in the window. Williamson did not decorate his office with greenery. Which meant Reynolds had brought his own. And that implied he planned to stay awhile and was making himself at home.

This was why Mouse was doing her sprint—racing to warn them of the disaster.

Reynolds put the water down and motioned to the small round conference table in the corner. They sat and he joined them. The office seemed naked without Williamson's massive presence.

"Where is he?" Sanchez asked.

"Eric? Ordered to Washington. Hauled before a meeting with Justice and a congressional subcommittee hearing, so I'm at the helm for the time being."

It was all clear now. Reynolds had likely been working his dark magic and convinced the subcommittee that *he* was responsible for the recent win that Sanchez and Jake had managed to pull off. He was leveraging that for another shot at the director position when it opened again and, at the same time, stealing I-squared out from under Williamson. If he didn't dissolve it outright, he would make sure it was absorbed into another Justice operation like the FBI or NSA—where the whole point of the pilot program, rapid response to micro threats, would be ignored.

And the palace coup grew even sneakier. Jake was thinking of yesterday's video, Reynolds on a plane. But not going to Washington, DC, as he'd implied.

He'd been headed to LA.

"Shit."

He'd meant to whisper. He caught Sanchez's eye, and she gave a brief nod.

Reynolds frowned. "Say something, Mr. Heron? Something I missed?"

"No, Stan."

Intentionally not using his title, or even the last name.

Reynolds then began once again to push his theory that Brock had been murdered, for some reason, as part of a Russian spy op, involving the oligarch Sergei Ivanov.

Sanchez sighed. "Remember, we did look into it. And HK made another attempt, last night. A couple on their honeymoon in Bel Air. That would've made that killing, and the deaths in Italy, collateral damage to sell the deception."

Reynolds wasn't put off in the least. "Exactly. Clever, aren't they? Ivanov and his hit man."

Jake weighed in. "What we told you on the plane—when you were headed out here." He couldn't let that one go. "Is still true. Nothing suggests that's why Brock was killed. He didn't have access to sensitive information, and he wasn't assisting with any federal investigations. There's no motive for—"

"This is where you have the disadvantage of being, as they say, out of the loop. I'm privy to information you don't have. For example, Mr. Brock was being considered for a spot in a section tasked with analyzing foreign financial influence. The team would report directly to the top." He leaned forward. "The Comptroller General of the United States. I can't say more than that."

"Only being considered?" Jake asked.

Sanchez now voiced another logical parry: "But if *we* didn't know about the promotion, and we work for the federal government, how would an outside asset know?" She shook her head, a bit more enthusiastically than necessary. "And, Stan, I still don't see what killing Brock gets Ivanov. Wouldn't the Russians want to *turn* him?"

Reynolds blinked, as the idea zipped by. He said, "Ah, well, that's the mystery we need to unravel, like an onion."

Jake didn't dare look at Sanchez for fear she would mouth, Can you unravel an onion?

"And you're just the two to do that." Then he grew serious. "Look, doesn't this whole idea of a serial killer who gets off on murdering newlyweds seem a little far-fetched? What could his motive be? It's not sexual. It's not money. Then what?"

"We agree there are questions," Sanchez said.

"Which are all answered, nice and tidy, as soon as we agree that he's being paid by Ivanov to kill Brock and lead the investigators astray.

"Now, here's our strategy. Ivanov's assets. He's a tech billionaire but that's just a cover. And his money is going to lead us to his employer. GRU, the SVK, the ABC—some outfit we don't even know about yet. We're going to squeeze him. And find out. I want enough evidence to freeze Ivanov's bank accounts and some of his goodies. He's partial to his G7 jet and his Bentley. You look blank, Mr. Heron. You've presumably never seized anything . . . legally. Ha, that's a joke. I'll explain.

"There are three types of forfeiture," Reynolds began in a gratingly superior tone. "Criminal, administrative and civil. The first two don't apply to this situation, not yet. But we can pursue him through the civil avenue. We don't need to prove criminal liability, just some criminal activity. I want to pressure him—I want him to sing like a little birdie. He gives up his handlers here and in Moscow and we bring down the whole network."

"But forfeiture's a complicated process," Sanchez said. "It takes a long time. And we need to establish criminal behavior and trace specific assets to it. And with a Russian national? It'll mean an international investigation, with dozens of agents. Usually 981 actions take months or years." She waved a hand toward him. "We're only two people, and neither of us has a background in accounting or international finance."

Reynolds said coolly, "Thank you for that fine law school class description, Agent Sanchez. But I'm confused. Didn't Eric tell me that I-squared's whole thrust was speed? Targeted raids? Precision strikes? If you want to move fast, you'll find a way."

Jake said, "Not my area of expertise, Stan, but just thinking out loud—once we make any move at all on his assets, he'll have to be put on notice, won't he?"

"You can be forgiven for not appreciating how due process works, Mr. Heron. Most hackers don't. But, yes, he'll be on notice—and that's when he'll make a mistake."

Silence. Jake and Sanchez now regarded each other once again. It was Sanchez who asked, "And what mistake would that be, Stan?"

"I don't know. But you'll be there to find it. Bigger operations have failed, and I won't stand by while he continues to thwart me—and embarrass me at every turn."

And then Jake got it. With that last sentence, Reynolds had given himself away. Jake would bet a year's salary the deputy secretary had been part of that task force earlier in his career and had never gotten over the fact that Ivanov had outmaneuvered him.

"You contact Main Justice," he said to Sanchez. "And see if Ivanov has filed as a foreign agent and if so with whom. Then dig up everything you can about every single one of those organizations. His principal employees too."

Jake knew nothing of this process either, but it sounded like a tremendous amount of work.

"If he's stumbled, that'll be enough to start forfeiture proceedings. And you, Professor, you're going to locate exactly what we will forfeitize—ha, I know that's not a word, but it should be. Now how's this plan? You do some of your pen testing at Ivanov's facilities. You should be able to find bank accounts, the aforementioned vehicles, some properties that we don't know about. All kinds of goodies."

Jake could not suppress a sigh. "The subject's company hires me to pen test. I can't initiate it on my own."

This would surely amuse Sanchez, Jake thought, since his position was exactly the opposite of what he usually said.

Reynolds bristled. "Obviously, Professor. It's going to require a little work on your part to convince Ivanov and his operating people they need to hire you. Do some salesmanship. Isn't this what they call social engineering?"

Yes, it was. And in fact Jake Heron was damn good at it. But the art and science of social engineering took weeks, if not months, to ply successfully.

And besides, did Reynolds not see the gaping hole in his logic? If Ivanov were a Russian spy, the last thing on earth he would do is hire a private pen tester to assess his security systems.

"I've contacted LAPD." Reynolds frowned. "I do wish they hadn't been brought into any loops. Local police? Positive sieves when it comes to holding on to classified information."

Sanchez stiffened. Even as a civilian, Jake knew that LAPD's anti-terror unit—which had access to as much classified data as the CIA—was one of the premier such outfits in the world.

"But I've made some calls, and they're benched for the time being. Now, run along, both of you. Get to work. I've got to check in with the circus in Washington and see about the latest developments there."

"And Eric?" Sanchez asked.

"He's being well taken care of. Don't you worry." He rose, picked up the water bottle and returned to his farming.

Jake and Sanchez left the office, sliding sympathetic glances at Destiny Baker, still on the phone, still swamped with handwritten notes, which he now knew were instructions from Reynolds.

Jake lifted his hands, asking in effect, What the hell?

Destiny lowered the phone. "Eric's in Washington. A select committee's grilling him about I-squared. I talked to him. He said it's not going well. Reynolds plotted the whole thing."

Her intercom buzzed. "Destiny, could you come in here? And bring your pad and pen again? By the way, did I tell you I really like your name?"

With an eye roll, she finished her phone call and got up, and Jake and Sanchez returned to the Garage. He was thinking that the Honeymoon Killer himself could not have derailed the investigation against him as effectively as their "superior" had just managed to pull off.

CHAPTER 46

Damon had an odd thought: Did Maddie Willis look like Miss Spalding?

Maybe a little.

In a certain light.

He held the notion rather like one of the too-hot-to-eat toasted marshmallows his former governess made for him. Then put it away as he watched Maddie stride into the living room, where he sat on the sofa, waiting for her, as the embers of what had been the crimson sweater glowed in the fireplace.

She'd taken him up on his offer to use the guest room shower, and her long dark hair was half dry. Years ago, Felicia had told him it was an act of intimacy for a woman to greet a man with hair that was not completely dried after she'd bathed or showered. He hadn't thought about her comment until just now.

But he could add a new element to the mix, because Maddie was also wearing the spare collared business shirt he'd given her in the car. He realized with mind-numbing clarity that she would not have put on dirty lingerie after taking a shower, which meant his shirt was the only thing between them. A message even more blatant than damp hair.

She'd rolled up the sleeves and the hem skimmed her thighs. He could barely resist the impulse to lift it a few inches. "Sexy" was not an adequate word.

They had the house to themselves. Tristan Kane was back in the bed and breakfast he had rented, anonymously of course, after arriving in LA to help Damon eliminate his pursuers, Jacoby Heron and Carmen Sanchez. Kane had set up some kind of computer workstation there to monitor the pair's whereabouts as best he could, and prowl through the law enforcement systems in Southern California.

Damon was curious how he was progressing.

But, at the moment, other matters intruded.

He rose. "I want to show you something."

As he stood, he noticed Maddie giving him a slow perusal, her gaze lingering just below his belt. He was certain she'd noticed his reaction to her. In that moment, he couldn't resist joking to himself, if she'd asked him whether there was a pack of razor blades in his pocket or if he was happy to see her, he could honestly answer yes to both.

She looked back up at his face. "Lead the way."

He considered taking her hand but did not. Instead, he walked to the mirror that was the secret door to his den, then turned to watch her reaction when he pushed the side to open the hidden entrance and gestured for her to go inside.

She hesitated on the threshold—the room he was ushering her into was completely black.

He felt that power thing again, tipping in his direction. Then he flicked on the light.

She scanned the walls. "Well." A step farther inside, studying the frames. "I recognize some, but the others, did you paint those?"

He said, "I appreciate art, I know art, I teach art. I can't paint or draw. I tried. I don't have the talent."

Her eyes went to Hopper's *Automat*, the print that had caught Tristan Kane's attention as well. Did the solitary woman remind Maddie of herself?

Urban alienation . . .

She asked, "Was that a disappointment? Deciding you couldn't paint?"

He considered the question. "I had a governess. She raised me after my mother and father were gone."

"You're an orphan. I'm sorry."

"Well, in a way. My mother died when I was a kid. My father assholed his way out of my life. He died when I was older."

She blinked. A smile followed. "I shouldn't laugh, but that's a good expression, about your father. I lost my parents too. An accident. I was twelve." This seemed to be something she didn't want to discuss, and she nodded briskly when he said he was sorry. Then she was moving on. "You had a governess? For real?"

"I did."

"Cool. I didn't know they made them anymore. I mean, not after, like, 1900 or whenever."

"Miss Spalding . . . she said I was good at everything, including drawing and painting. She was afraid to make me feel bad, afraid to, you know, alienate me. But finally a teacher told me I simply wasn't talented. I was *fighting* the sheets and canvas. A real artist doesn't have to."

"You must have been mad."

She'd moved on to *Christina's World* by Andrew Wyeth. Some people thought it was a painting of peace of mind. Damon found it one of the most sorrowful works ever created.

"I was," he said. "But then he told me I *was* an artist. One of the best he had ever seen."

Maddie frowned.

"He explained that there are those who can paint and draw and sculpt brilliantly. But they're not artists. They have technical trade skills. There are millions of them. But only a few people were like me. I understood what art was—it was giving voice to those with profound feelings they couldn't express. That's the value of art. It gives us understanding that science and religion and education can't. It completes us. Without art, we would exist with gaps."

"In what?"

"Everything. Our daily existence, our faith, our souls, our purposes, love. You can't be an artist if you don't understand that."

"But—" Maddie was truly curious. "How can you be an artist and not draw or paint?"

"The teacher said I just hadn't found my medium. It would only take a little time. But one day I would."

"Have you found it? Your medium?"

He didn't answer but redirected her. "What do you think of the art?"

As she looked at each wall in turn, he gazed at her, thinking that she was even more beautiful than he'd initially believed.

She was Felicia beautiful.

Miss Spalding beautiful. In the old photographs, of course.

"They're all so sad," she whispered. She glanced his way. "And appealing. No, more than that. Seductive. Does that sound weird?"

"No, not at all."

Just the opposite. Damon was thrilled at her reaction.

"I love them!"

As she continued to study the pictures, he was thinking:

Have you found it? Your medium?

Yes, he had.

As he'd been reflecting when Tristan Kane interrupted him, the loss of Felicia, and the ensuing grief, was the very source of Serial Killing 2.0.

The reason for the innovation came, as often happens, in a disappointment. An absence. A hollowness that was supposed to be filled but was not.

Sarah Anne Taylor.

Victim Number One.

A death so perfectly planned and executed that he should have been in what Miss Spalding called seventh heaven.

Damon Garr, born to kill, had killed.

And, yet, he felt virtually nothing.

A bit of professional pride. But euphoria? None.

He knew that Ted Bundy and BTK must have felt nearly orgasmic pleasure when they killed. Not so for Damon.

But silver linings come in all shapes and sizes (another Miss Spaldingism), and it was the failure to launch after Sarah's death that led him to try a "normal" life with Felicity.

Which in turn led to her death.

And his discovery of grief as a weapon.

And hence was born Serial Killing 2.0. Get the murder out of the way and revel in the sorrow of the mourners clustering around the deceased's grave.

The study of art had given Damon a deeper understanding of that sentiment, and he'd begun to create his own art form: the Tableaux.

And, like any artist, once he'd mastered his craft, he was compelled to share it with the world. But his form of art hardly lent itself to a museum display. No, his was an interactive and fully immersive experience. As such, it could not be merely seen. It had to be experienced.

To accomplish that, he did not need art critics. He needed mourners.

And so his campaign had begun.

His first Tableau was in the US, at a wedding in Santa Fe, where the bride died in one of the hot springs in the mountains. Then a trip to Europe, Italy specifically, where mourning was a common theme in art. One victim in Verona—the honeymoon capital of the country (thank you, Romeo and Juliet). Another in Florence, ground zero of Renaissance painting and sculpture.

Then back here.

To the Hollywood Crest and poor Anthony Brock.

The memories filled him with comfort, even to the point where he could forget the disaster at the floating island inn.

His eyes now slipped to Maddie as she walked from frame to frame like one of his students trying to decide which artist to write her final paper on.

She was fascinating and unique. A part of her was wild and uninhibited. Her beauty, her decisiveness, her intensity . . . Everything about her pushed him to share the truth about himself. About his brilliant creation.

Ah, but the impulse control told him no. Not yet.

He needed to know more. He had to know more. He'd seen the surface.

What was beneath?

She had returned to the Hopper. He joined her, standing close.

"So. Your story?"

"My story?"

"In the space of two hours, we've advanced from near murder to fine art. I'd like to know a little bit about the person I've shared that experience with."

"Not unreasonable."

She turned those electric-blue eyes on him and for a moment he had absolutely no idea what was going on in her mind behind them.

It was disconcerting, true.

But Damon Garr was not overly concerned.

If worse came to worst, and her dark side erupted again, well, *he* was the one with the imported razor blades in his pocket.

CHAPTER 47

"Well, at least we'll go down together," Carmen said as she put down her cola.

She sat across from Heron at a corner table in a small diner a few blocks from HSI's Long Beach headquarters. They had agreed to have a private meeting to discuss their next steps. It had taken them less than three minutes to decide not to follow the deputy director's absurd orders.

"The dynamic duo," Heron said, touching the rim of his cup to hers in a mock toast. "Or maybe Thelma and Louise—this could go either way."

Since HK had started his macabre spree, the two had eaten next to nothing, and presently were working on a BLT, in her case, and tuna salad in his. Heron was sticking with coffee. She supposed the cola wasn't good for her, but try telling that to a person who wears a semi-automatic pistol on her hip and, occasionally, uses it to defend herself.

"I just hope whatever charges of insubordination we face won't blow back on Williamson," she said. "Reynolds is out for blood."

"I figure we have maybe a day before he catches on," he said. "Let's make good use of our time. So. HK. What do we know about him? Other than that?"

He was pointing to his tablet, on which the murder board was visible. She noticed his eyes lingering on a box in the lower-right-hand corner. It was devoted to the attack on Frank Tandy.

"You go first," she said, aware his mind worked differently than hers and interested in hearing his current theory. "Let's add to the profile."

"I'd say right-handed, with an extremely high IQ. He has some money but he's also successfully self-employed, works out regularly, is short tempered but struggles to control it."

"How the hell would you know all that?"

"I study intruders for a living. And that describes HK to a T."

"Explain." She started with something provable. "How would you know he's right-handed? I looked at the knife marks in Frank's jacket. You couldn't tell from that. Equal number right or left."

"But the footprints. He was slightly to the left of Frank's back."

"Ah. Good." She was impressed but annoyed she hadn't tipped to it too—and that he hadn't shared this previously. "And the high IQ?"

Heron shrugged. "His plans are meticulous. We only know of three people he's killed, but there could be plenty more. He's figured out how to pass murders off as accidents. It's hard to fool detectives and medical examiners with all the forensic capabilities they have. That's also why I think he tries to control his compulsions."

"You believe something drives him to kill, but he puts a lid on it."

"Yep."

"Hm. All the careful advance planning means he forces himself to wait until the right moment when everything is lined up before he acts out."

"Exactly." Heron gave her an appreciative nod. "The temper part? He didn't need to stab Frank—or me, if I was the intended target. But we pissed him off and a part of him, a small part, couldn't let that go."

"His resources?"

"It's not expensive to travel to Europe—everybody does nowadays. But to travel on your own terms—keeping a low profile? Flying where you want, when you want? That takes money. Now, hardly anybody's independently wealthy, so he has to work. And self-employed? I'm thinking that because he feels he's above other people. He's special. Therefore, he feels free to take their lives. Anyone that arrogant wouldn't work for someone else. That would be beneath him."

"And the regular workouts?" she asked. "Are you basing his physical fitness on the vague description we got from the witnesses in the cemetery?"

"Partly. I believe this is his calling. Like anyone else, he's got to train for his profession. Judging by the crime scene pictures at the Hollywood Crest Inn, the groom was knocked out and then thrown over the guardrail to fall from the cliff. The victim was a large man. It took strength for that."

She was impressed. "Nice deductions, Sherlock."

Heron finished his sandwich. "But even if I'm right, Watson, it only helps if we have a suspect."

True. It was like having a DNA sample from a crime scene. If the sequence wasn't in the CODIS database, it didn't do any good without an individual to compare it to.

Her phone hummed. She glanced at the caller ID, hoping it wasn't Reynolds checking up on them.

But it wasn't.

She tapped the screen. "Go ahead, Mouse. You're on speaker. I'm with Heron."

Her voice was taut with strain. "Can you believe it? What Reynolds did to SSA Williamson?"

The answer was yes, Carmen absolutely could believe it. "You tried to give us fair warning."

Recalling her assistant running along the corridor as they were about to enter Williamson's office.

"I've called him three, four times. But he's not picking up." She added, muttering darkly, "I wonder if Reynolds turned his phone into digital oatmeal. Anyway, I've got news. And I've got you guys on speaker too." A pause. Then: "Go ahead, Declan."

Carmen and Heron had to share a smile at this.

The computer voice said, "I have discovered the identity of the individual you have designated Ms. POI."

"Excellent," Carmen said. "Go on."

Declan continued, "First, I have a question. You'll notice that I don't *always* use the contractions we talked about earlier. Would you like me to use more or fewer?"

"It doesn't matter," Heron said bluntly. "Don't focus on punctuation."

"Jake, while contractions are formed by the *use* of punctuation, notably apostrophes, they are not themselves punctuation but rather—"

"Declan, stop generating. And give us the identity of Ms. POI."

"Yes, Jake. Of all the individuals driving white Toyota Camrys in Southern California and western Arizona, there is only one individual who bears any relationship to the case involving the suspect known as the Honeymoon Killer that I could determine. Her name is Lauren Brock. And she's the sister of the victim killed at the Hollywood Crest Inn on Saturday."

CHAPTER 48

Waiting.

Selina Sanchez was not good at waiting.

This was one of the reasons she did the floor routine in gymnastics. It was ninety seconds of nonstop motion.

She was back at Ryan Hall's, after a shower and a change of clothes at her apartment. And she'd made the trip without seeing a single black SUV or other tail. In fact, the only people she'd seen near here were a couple, in the deserted construction site across the street from her apartment. The woman wore a body-hugging sweater, black miniskirt, tights and high heels. Selina was only in the area temporarily, working a summer job in a nearby research lab, and had taken the apartment because it was cheap, convenient . . . and available. The woman's outfit made her wonder if she'd ended up in the red-light district. Did they even have them in Fullerton?

Ryan had texted not long before and reported that Paquito's was open but Nando the bartender had not come in yet.

Selina knew they needed to meet with Nando soon. Word could spread that Judd had talked to the police and the bartender might take a permanent vacation from his job.

Or, worse, warn Sweeney that he was a suspect in the Roberto Sanchez murder.

Which might make the hit man decide to vanish too.

Or to pay her a visit.

She looked at her phone impatiently. Ryan had said he could take some personal time today to get to the bar, but he had a heavy caseload.

Selina wasn't going to complain, though. At least Ryan, unlike her sister, was making an effort to help her.

But please, she thought, hurry back.

And who the hell was this Sweeney? A hired killer who specialized in making murders look like suicides.

Another thought arose. Her sister would—eventually—want to find evidence to arrest and prosecute him. But Selina had fantasized about a quicker and more satisfying resolution.

Sweeney dead.

Followed by whoever had hired him to kill Roberto.

Of course, this was the product of anger and imagination.

Could she kill two people—even if they deserved to die?

No.

Probably not.

Caliber jumped into her lap. Then launched himself off and walked to the food bowl. She remembered Ryan had fed him that morning, but it seemed he wanted more.

Why not?

She opened another of the small cans and dished out the pungent contents. Caliber dug in. As she threw the empty away, motion caught her eye.

She glanced out and it seemed to her that a vehicle was just slipping from view, as if it had been outside, or near, Ryan's house.

Black.

And it might have been an SUV, like the one she'd seen last night.

She was going to step outside to see if she could get a glimpse when her phone hummed.

"Hey," she said to Ryan.

"I called the bar. Nando's there. And I've finagled a few hours off."

She nearly said she loved him. But this was not the time. There'd be a transactional quality to saying it now. So, no.

"We'll be here."

"'We'? You have a secret lover over at my place?" Ryan asked coyly.

"I'm busted. I can't resist a man who wears a collar and chases a laser beam around the floor."

"You'd be surprised what I'm capable of. See you in a half hour."

Selina disconnected and glanced outside. No vehicles of any shade at the moment.

And while the glow from the funny repartee remained, her smile faded, and one thought rose above the others: the hunt was on.

CHAPTER 49

"Start with what happened. In Fullerton."

Damon arranged his features into his best approximation of sympathetic concern. "You and that guy?"

Maddie Willis hesitated a beat before responding. "I was in the coffee shop down the street. He'd been drinking—yeah, that time of the morning. Complete stranger. And he just came on to me. I ignored him. He got persistent, so I shut him down hard. Then I left. Headed to my car. Only he wouldn't take no for an answer and followed me out. I didn't see him behind me. He dragged me over to the jobsite. We both know what was coming next." She crossed her arms. "I had a different idea."

"Earlier, you said something about taking care of people who had it coming . . ." He deliberately trailed off, keeping all traces of judgment out of his voice. He wanted her to confide in him.

She looked down. Said nothing.

Time to blend a bit of fact with fiction. "Look, there are plenty of people out there who are just plain bad. Sometimes, they get what's coming to them." He laid a hand on his chest. "Personally, I think that's a damn good thing." He waited for her nod of agreement, before adding, "You pretty much admitted that you—"

"Have . . . done that before?" Her full mouth hardened into a tight line. She studied him again, weighing the risks, it seemed.

"I'm sure you had your reasons."

"I did. Damn right I did." It was almost a tease. "Want to hear?"

He wanted to say, "Hell, yeah," but settled for a casual "Sure."

"I was in college when a football player spiked my drink at a frat party. Most of the night was a blur, but I had some lovely memories of what he did to me." Bitter sarcasm filled her voice. "The next day, I reported it to the campus police."

"And they didn't believe you?"

"Oh, yeah. They believed me. Hot-button topic at schools now. They called the city police. They charged him with rape. The jock came from a rich fucking family. They hired a famous defense attorney. The prosecutor was fresh out of law school. I think it was his first sexual assault trial. The defense ran over him like a bulldozer." She blew out a sigh. "The judge gave him a suspended sentence of six months."

"So no jail time?"

"It was such bullshit. If he didn't commit any infractions during those six months, his record would be completely expunged. Like it never happened. Like I didn't mean shit."

"But you found a way to get your own justice."

"Someone had to hold him accountable." Maddie's eyes blazed. "I couldn't go to class anymore. It was too much. So I dropped out and dedicated all my time and energy toward getting even. I did some research and figured out what kind of drug he must've used on me and bought some. Then, after spring term was over, I staked out his house. I took my time, studied his routines."

Organized offending. An art and science.

"And waited for an opportunity to come up. Eventually, it did."

Damon was hanging on every word.

"One night he was in the hot tub. All alone. Sucking down a beer and texting. When he got out to pee, I roofied the Heineken and slipped into the bushes. When he got back it took only a few sips for him to get totally groggy."

She was clever, determined and patient, biding her time. It might have taken weeks or months, but she clearly would not let it go. A trait he could appreciate.

"Once he was good and loopy, I came out from behind the bushes so he could see me. You know the first thing that asshole did? He smiled and said, 'Cool. You're back. I forgive you.'"

Damon noticed her trembling with rage, even now.

"Then I told him I was going to kill him. He laughed again before he got that it wasn't a joke. He started to panic and climb out. But, sorry, too late. Bang, he passed out. It was easy to hold him under." She cocked her head. "He was helpless, just like I was helpless after he drugged *me*."

Interesting . . . the Furies had not killed Orestes but had brought him to trial for the murder of his mother. He'd been acquitted. Damon always believed that was a shitty outcome.

"No one found him until the next morning." She lifted a slender shoulder. "Basically, the body spent several hours in a slow cooker set to 106 degrees. And I submerged the empty beer in the tub with him. No way would any trace of the drug survive all the hot water and chemicals bubbling around inside the bottle."

"There must've been an investigation, the police—"

"Ruled accidental."

Damon found the familiarity of her MO delightful: death by drowning. And made to look like an accident.

He studied her for a moment. "Earlier, when we met—"

"That fateful moment," she joked.

"You said you always figure something out."

"Oh. Did I?"

"Yep."

A deep breath. "I was lost in the moment," she said slowly.

"So there were others."

Maddie debated. "The jock wasn't the first. I told you I was an orphan. Had a foster home thing. The family was okay. One of the older boys placed there wasn't. Not sex. He was just a bully. Hurt the little ones. There was something wrong with him. I knew he wouldn't stop. We were walking to school one day. It was along this big highway and we were the only kids who lived on that side of it. A semi went by. I'd gone there earlier and left a twenty under some leaves. When we were waiting to cross, I uncovered it with my foot. I started to pick it up and he pushed me away and bent down." She shrugged.

"You shoved him." He made it a statement rather than a question.

"Under the rear wheels. That was the first. Then, a couple years after the hot tub, I was dating this guy. He turned abusive. In a big way. Put me in the hospital twice. Hurt his two-year-old niece and threatened to kill me if I told his sister what happened. He spent every Saturday working on his cars. You know, sometimes those jack stands can collapse."

Jesus.

A faint laugh. "I'm not normal, Damon. I have to say that right up front. But I guess you figured that out."

"I'm not heading for the hills, am I? What did you say? I'm incredibly confident or I'm completely nuts?"

"And you implied you were both." She laughed.

Damon decided he'd heard enough.

A nod toward the far end of the dimly lit den, the curtained-off special area.

It was where he'd left Her.

"Come on." He rose, smiled and gestured for her to follow.

"What's back there?"

He reached into his pocket and gripped the box of razor blades with sweating fingers. "Something special."

CHAPTER 50

"Yo, you can't park there."

The office maintenance engineer—he preferred that to "janitor"—was calling out to the driver, who had just pulled into the loading zone. He might've shut the engine off. Ramirez couldn't tell because rap was blaring from what must have been oversize speakers.

The driver's eyes, a shade darker than his skin, turned and sliced Ramirez into little pieces before returning to his phone.

No, no, this wasn't going to work. Fuck no.

"Yo, I call the police, have your ass thrown in jail."

The driver frowned. "Yeah. On private property? You can *sue* my ass. But police got nothing to do with it. Course, you could always just whip my ass. In fact, I'd welcome you to try."

Ramirez couldn't see the driver's body, only his head, but it was a big one and the torso it was attached to was probably equally sizable.

But still the guy was breaking the rules, if not the law.

And pissing him off in the process.

Ah, but now the owner of the building had arrived. Ramirez had friends in high places, and he wasn't going to let a suspicious character like this jerk just sit in a no-parking zone.

Not in *his* kingdom.

Ramirez waited for the owner to park his Mercedes before approaching him. He stopped short, however, when the owner got out and headed straight toward the rule-breaking asshole.

Good. Kick the prick off the property.

But wait, what was going on?

The door of the SUV was opening and the driver—a huge man in a black leather jacket—got out. The two shook hands and the building owner handed him a thick white envelope as they exchanged a few words.

The owner nodded goodbye, and the driver got back behind the wheel and piloted the black Ford Edge out of the lot, leaving Hector Ramirez very grateful he hadn't made a stink about anything.

The owner of the complex, Mr. Carl Overton, could have one hell of a temper.

CHAPTER 51

"Who is it?" Maddie whispered, looking down.

"It's Her. With a capital *H*."

They were standing in the workshop area of his den, over a large art table. Sitting in the middle was one of his most precious recent acquisitions.

He continued, "Demeter, Greek goddess of agriculture."

It was an original drawing, 120 years old, in chalk and pencil on gray paper, by the famed British artist Evelyn De Morgan. She had created the piece as a study of what would become her most famous oil: *Demeter Mourning for Persephone.*

It depicted the goddess, racked with misery at the absence of her daughter, who had been seized by Hades and taken to the underworld, where she would remain for six months each year. That original painting, the embodiment of bereavement, was on display at Wightwick Manor and Gardens in Wolverhampton, part of the British National Trust and, sadly, not for sale.

He explained to Maddie that the painting was his favorite piece of all time, and the study was a recent discovery. Damon had used an anonymous broker to buy the work instantly.

He set the box of blades on the table, opened it and mounted one in a matte cutter.

Damon did not trust a commercial outfit to frame the piece. He would do so himself and had ordered special matte boards and these particular razor blades, which were oil-free, to do the job. In addition to his talent as an art lecturer, and as a murderer, Damon Garr was a skilled framer.

He asked Maddie, "Which color matte?" He pointed to the shelves where they sat.

"Me?"

"Sure."

"I don't know. Wait. This one!"

She chose taupe. It was, not surprisingly, his first choice. The color that would complement the gray paper of the De Morgan study. He pulled on cloth gloves and handed her a pair. He nodded to the board and, after donning the accessory, she gave it to him.

He arranged the board on the table and set the cutter to a forty-five-degree angle. Then pressed it down, piercing the cardboard.

"Put your hand on mine."

She hesitated.

"Go on. You're safe. I'm not wearing high heels."

A brief laugh. And she did as he'd instructed.

Together, they moved the cutter upward, in a fluid motion along the right-hand vertical side.

He enjoyed the sound of the cut.

It reminded him of the slasher movies Miss Spalding weaned him on, where you hear the knife make that swooshy sucky noise slicing into the bodies of blonde coeds and their randy boyfriends. But in real life a knife rends in near silence. He remembered this from his encounter with Sarah Anne Taylor and from his run-in with the LAPD detective bleeding massively beneath the enigmatic gaze of a bronze William Shakespeare statue.

"You're strong," she whispered.

He didn't answer.

They made three more cuts on the board. And he held it up, examining the corners.

They were perfect.

"Do we do another one?" Maddie nodded to a print nearby, which featured two mattes, one white and one salmon.

"No. I don't want to draw attention away from Her."

He set the sketch on the backing and placed the matte over it, both acid-free. Pressure held the De Morgan in place. Never glue. Then he mounted the assembly into the frame, which was fronted with carefully dried and polished glass.

"Never glare-free panes," he told her, explaining that diligent curators and collectors displayed the finished pieces on walls where lights were placed carefully to avoid flares.

He rested it on an easel and gazed.

Demeter's sorrow . . .

She took his hand in both of hers. "You know that thing people say when they first meet sometimes, like a blind date?"

"You mean," he said, "'It's so easy to talk to you. I can tell you things I've never been able to tell anyone else'?"

"Yep. Exactly. In our case, that line really takes the cake."

Silence arose. She said, "I want to ask you something, Damon."

A nod. He pulled off the gloves. She did, as well.

"What you told me about your friend, the criminal lawyer. You made him up, didn't you?"

This might be a reason to be afraid.

Or to smile.

He did the latter, and he nodded.

"I think there's more to you than meets the eye. You see me try to kill somebody and you have basically no reaction. Except to tell me how to get away with it."

"I—"

"Shh." She touched a finger to his lips. "Don't tell me anything. Not yet. We've shared enough for one day."

252

She glanced at his phone. The lock screen was a clock.

He saw her disappointment. "You have to go?"

"Beating assholes almost to death with my shoe isn't a full-time job. I work in marketing, and I've got a meeting. But it's in an hour. That leaves plenty of time."

"For what?"

She gave him a do-you-really-need-to-ask look, took his hand and led him from the den, whispering, "Where's your bedroom?"

CHAPTER 52

Carmen wanted Lauren Brock, Ms. Person of Interest, to feel comfortable.

It was always best to start things off in a nonconfrontational manner. That way, if she needed to turn up the heat, it would be even more jarring for the subject of the interview. She'd learned from experience that if you started off yelling, you had nowhere to go.

Not that it would become an issue. Carmen was a bit peeved the woman had not returned her calls and not come forward to help but understood that she'd just lost her brother—the man who had been her savior.

She just wanted answers to some basic questions, the ones she'd ask any potential witness.

Or person of interest.

Carmen assessed Lauren's appearance. Clearly, she hadn't been able to keep up the polished appearance she'd managed at the funeral. Her attractive face was makeup-free, and her dark hair only casually brushed. Her gray blouse was wrinkled and the jeans had two coffee stains on the right leg. Perhaps, as Heron had suggested, she'd been holed up in a motel on that bender Allison had mentioned.

There was no obvious odor of liquor, but Lauren was wearing perfume—a cloying, sweet scent—which was maybe intended to cover up the scent of any booze.

"Now that we've gotten the preliminaries out of the way," Carmen said in a casual tone, "why don't you start by explaining why you were reluctant to talk to us."

Lauren looked around. This was one of the more comfortable rooms at HSI in Long Beach, designed for victims and witnesses rather than suspects.

Heron had made it clear he wanted to participate but satisfied himself with watching the video monitor in another room. The dynamics of a two-interviewer session are very different from a solo.

Lauren fidgeted in her chair, making the faux leather squeak. "I was so shattered, I wanted to be by myself. And, anyway, I really didn't see anything at the hotel that night."

Carmen had been trained to listen for subtle qualifiers when people made statements. In this case, the witness said she didn't "really" see anything.

Implying that she saw something, but didn't think it worth reporting. Or that she saw something, but felt it was against her *interest* to report it.

"I would have told the police if I had. Why wouldn't I?" A bit of an edge to her voice.

But Carmen always cut victims—and Lauren was a victim in a way—a lot of slack.

Still, she sensed something more was going on. Perhaps the woman knew something but didn't know she did.

"Ms. Brock." She moved in closer. "Can I call you Lauren?"

A nod.

"And I'm Carmen. By all accounts, Lauren, you loved your brother dearly."

Her eyes began to well. "He was the only person in my family—the only person in my life—who believed in me. Everyone else gave up." A small sob escaped her. "Even my own parents called me a junkie. Wouldn't have anything to do with me."

"Then you'd want to help find his killer, no?"

Lauren swept at a tear with her knuckle. "Of course."

"Could you tell us where you were when it happened?"

"I'd already left. I didn't know a lot of people. Anthony and our parents live on the East Coast. I'm pretty much out here by myself. And my past . . . well, the substance-abuse issue. You know about it, I'm sure. Allison wouldn't miss a chance to bring it up. So I went there for him, then I left."

"Is that why you went to the service at Cedar Hills alone and stayed out of sight?"

Lauren blinked, clearly surprised at the quality of their intelligence. A nod.

"What's the story about your sister-in-law?"

"Controlling, serious, no sense of humor. And hot. Ah, men . . . my poor brother. I admit I haven't had a lot of luck with money, not with the drinking and everything. That Camry? It's thirdhand and Anthony gave me the money for it. And he was going to cosign on a mortgage so I could buy a house. Allison didn't like that one bit. And she'll freeze me out. I get something in his will, but she'll find a lawyer and look for loopholes, I know she will. I can barely make the rent as it is. Fuck. I'm not going back on the street."

"The street?"

"Yeah. Lost my job, couldn't get off the bottle, the drugs. Living under overpasses. In polite society, we're called 'unhoused.' But it amounts to the same thing. Homeless."

"I can put you in touch with—"

"Shelters?" Another snort. "No, thanks. Besides, I have enough money to tide me over until I can figure something out. I am, most of all, a survivor."

Carmen shifted gears again. "What are you afraid of, Lauren?"

She took a long time to answer. Too long. "Maybe whoever killed my brother *thinks* I saw something, even if I didn't."

"But why would he think that if you weren't even there?"

Lauren was becoming flustered. Carmen knew that emotion would soon turn into anger and when that happened, she would shut down. She needed to move fast.

Carmen took out her cell phone and thumb-typed a quick text.

Lauren watched suspiciously. Less than ten seconds later, Mouse opened the interview room door. Carmen beckoned her over and briefly whispered in her ear.

"What was that all about?" Lauren asked when Mouse left.

"Look," Carmen said, picking up a remote and aiming it at a monitor on the wall.

Both women turned to watch as the screen flicked on to reveal footage of the grounds at the Hollywood Crest Inn.

Lauren swallowed audibly. "Why are you making me look at that? It's where he died."

Carmen froze the frame that showed the silhouette in the garden nearby. "This was just before it happened. And that person is you, isn't it?"

"No! I told you I left right afterward. I wasn't welcome."

Repeating an explanation could be a sign of deception.

"Those are your red-striped shoes, aren't they?"

"What're you talking about? You can't see a thing. You can't even tell if they're wearing shoes. Whoever the fuck they are. You should be spending your time finding them, not bothering me."

Carmen narrowed her eyes. "So, it's not you?"

"No! I swear to God."

With that proclamation, Lauren Brock had completed the trifecta of deception. The only trick she hadn't pulled was suddenly claiming her memory was faulty.

Aware she had no legal justification for holding an uncooperative witness, Carmen tried a bit of shock to break through her defenses. "Whatever you're hiding, you'd better level with me now, Lauren. Because I'm going to find out, and by then your options will be severely limited."

Lauren shot to her feet. "You know damn well I had nothing to do with my brother's death."

"Of course not. I'm not saying that at all. But I think you have information that can help us find who did." Carmen played her trump card. "We have reason to believe he killed two other people. Both of them on their wedding day. In Italy. And he just tried again last night. He's a serial killer and he's going to strike again. It's in your interest—in everybody's interest—to open up. Now."

Lauren broke down in tears. "I'm leaving. And I don't ever want to talk to you again."

With that, she stormed out of the interview room.

A moment later, Heron strolled in. "That went well."

"You're being sardonic, Heron. But the fact is, it went better than I hoped."

"How so?"

She peered around his shoulder to address Mouse, who had followed him in. "Is everything in place?"

Mouse nodded. "They're on it."

When Heron raised an inquiring brow, she explained. "When Mouse came in, I asked her to pull video of the hotel grounds, but I also told her to activate the SHIT detail."

"Excuse me?"

She took a moment to enjoy Heron's confusion before enlightening him.

"You haven't been involved in government operations long enough. Everything has an acronym." She lifted a shoulder. "Granted, it's usually not vulgar, but this unit's unofficial moniker stuck."

"What's it stand for?"

To everyone's surprise, Declan answered first. "Surveillance and Holistic Investigative Technology."

"No shit," Heron said, deadpan.

Carmen said, "What Declan doesn't know is that it has two meanings. In law enforcement circles, any undesirable assignment is referred to as a 'shit detail.'"

Declan's response was instantaneous. "I am aware of that, Carmen."

Mouse grimaced. "He's a large *language* model. Now you've insulted him."

Carmen steered the conversation back to the most pertinent point. "It's a dedicated surveillance team. They're going to tail Lauren."

"Okay, Sanchez, good. You knew she knows something but wasn't going to talk. You flushed her."

She nodded at the screen, the silhouette of Ms. POI. "Maybe that's her, maybe it isn't. Frankly, I don't see any red stripes."

Declan broke in. "I said 44.2 percent, Carmen."

Carmen ignored him and continued, "Zero idea what she's up to. Maybe she's afraid HK's following her. Maybe she's pulling some funny business with the will. We couldn't find one, but she just admitted it exists. And maybe she's got a plan to screw Allison. Will it help us get closer to HK?" She shrugged. "We don't have a lot of options."

Heron was frowning. "This surveillance outfit . . . tell me about it."

"They're practically invisible, and they're damned good at what they do. And they can spy on anything, anywhere."

Mouse chuckled at the look of disdain on Heron's face. She continued, "They use a combination of unmarked cars—that don't *look* like unmarked cars—traffic cams and sometimes even drones, so whoever they're following has no clue."

"Intrusion," Heron muttered. "You're always lecturing me about warrants, Sanchez." He glanced around dramatically. "I don't seem to see any."

Carmen was ready with an answer. "I'd need a warrant to install a GPS tracker without her knowledge or consent, but not to track a car driving around in public, using other vehicles or traffic cameras. This is our only option. Lauren's holding back on us. And I'm going to find out why."

CHAPTER 53

Selina felt guilty. But not so guilty that she'd cave and "be reasonable."

She and Carmen had been raised to be strong. Their parents had taught them from a young age not to be followers. Not to go along with the crowd. Both sisters had taken it to heart, each forging her own path.

Carmen had gone into law enforcement. At first, their parents had been alarmed but gradually had come to accept her choice—and eventually to take pride in it.

For Selina, that had meant pursuing gymnastics, a physically and mentally demanding sport that had given the one they had viewed as their "baby girl" a competitive streak, the ability to overcome pain and rippling muscles.

"Ay, mija," her mother would say when, for instance, she'd sprained an ankle during a floor routine. "You have to stop."

But Selina had asked the trainer to "tape the hell out of it" so she could finish her meet.

This was the spirit of the Sanchez women. A tradition she proudly carried on.

A tradition that was currently driving Detective Ryan Hall to the breaking point, she could see.

"Civilians don't participate in police investigations," he said to her as they pulled into the parking lot of Paquito's Bar in a seedy part of North Hollywood.

"Technically, it's not one," she said sweetly. "Carmen hasn't made it official, and you don't have jurisdiction."

"You know what I'm saying."

"And besides, we're just talking to a bartender, not a suspect."

"It's still an investigation, whoever you're talking to." He shut off the engine and turned to face her. "I don't know how to say this, so I'll be blunt." He looked her up and down. "This is a sleazy joint and you're . . . hot."

He blushed. And she felt a shiver of pleasure to hear him use the word to describe her.

"You'll attract the wrong kind of attention. I'll go in there by myself."

She felt terrible for doing it but played on his chivalry. "And leave me out here in this parking lot all by myself? Anyone could snatch me right out of this car."

She had a brief thought about the black SUV, the Edge, and even looked around for it, but saw no sign.

"It's North Hollywood. True, it's not Beverly Hills, but the odds of getting kidnapped are pretty low. And do you really think there's anybody here you couldn't kick their ass?"

Her sister had taught Selina some basic, but effective, martial arts moves.

Her shrug was accompanied by a plaintive look. "Sorry, there goes your excuse for not letting me come inside. I'll just kick the ass of whoever's wrong kind of attention I attract."

He sighed.

She saw the inner battle raging in his expressive features.

"Just stay close to me and do exactly what I say."

The last part of the sentence was a bit of a speed bump, and irritated her, but she put it down to his legit concern about the dangers of going into a bar where hit men—or one at least—frequented.

They climbed out. She navigated around the car and threw her arms around him. "Thank you." Then she laughed and thumped his chest. "You're even hunkier than I thought."

"Ballistic vest. Lot of gold shields wear them under our dress shirts. It'll come as a shock, but there're a lot of guns in this country. Let's go. And remember our deal."

She tucked away the urge to protest—really? *Do exactly what I say?* But didn't disabuse him of the notion that she would be a meek little lady. "Absolutely."

She glanced up at the sign above the entrance as she followed Ryan inside.

PAQUITO'S BAR

She stayed close on his heels as he made his way through the Lysol-scented and dingy interior toward the bar, which was located in the back against the rear wall.

"What'll it be?" the bartender asked when they perched themselves on two of the torn vinyl-covered stools in the nearly empty space.

Oh, yeah, a bald vampire.

Shaved head, ultra-pale skin, black spooky eyes.

No missing Nando.

Selina looked around. She was surprised to see how few patrons were in the bar. Was it because the place was known to be dangerous, or was it because they were known to water down their booze? Of course, it was early, though places like this drew flies from the minute the door opened to last call.

"I'll have a beer," he said. "IPA. Whatever's on tap."

Nando turned to her with a lascivious grin that exposed a gold front tooth. "¿Qué quieres, mami?"

The barkeep was being a tad familiar, but she pretended to be flattered. "A whiskey sour. Maker's."

"Hey, you got good taste," he said, switching to English. The man's smile widened as he turned to the tap to pull Ryan a house beer before crossing to the whiskey section to prepare her drink.

Even to her unpracticed eye, he seemed to put a lot of booze in the tumbler before adding the other ingredients and shaking it. She also caught the surreptitious wink he gave Ryan.

So this was the kind of bartender who would help get a young woman drunk to make things easier for their dates.

Lovely.

She assessed his height and weight and wondered if a single kick to the cojones would bring him down.

Well, she wasn't here to correct men who needed correcting.

He plunked the glass in front of her, but she merely swirled it around, then pretended to sip.

"You're Nando."

A grunt.

"I hear you can be helpful," Ryan cut in.

Nando gave her another slow perusal, then turned back to Ryan.

"Sometimes. Depends."

"I've got a problem that needs fixing," Ryan said. His voice dropped to a whisper. "I'd like to talk to Sweeney about it."

Nando, who had begun wiping glasses with a grubby rag, froze for an instant before resuming the motion. "Don't know any Sweeney."

Ryan cocked his head. "Funny. I was told he hangs out here."

"A lot of people hang out here."

Selina glanced around the bar, deserted except for one wiry man in a sweat-stained undershirt and jeans and a woman sipping a drink that looked a lot like hers. Ryan shot Selina a quelling look and she refrained from calling out Nando on his dubious assessment of Paquito's popularity.

"Maybe you pass some information to him?" Ryan asked, trying to salvage the mission. "I've got money. You can have a finder's fee."

"Can't help you."

"You sure? I'm talking some serious green."

"No green. No Sweeney."

She couldn't really blame Nando. Ryan looked like just who he was. A cop.

This was going nowhere. Selina decided to enact plan B.

When the bartender wasn't looking, she slowly poured the drink out on the floor at her feet. Ryan was the only one who saw, and he frowned.

She slapped the empty glass down. "Gimme another, huh?"

Nando blinked and picked up the glass. She said, "I'm new here but I like fucking California! Twenty-year-olds can drink."

Nando froze. "What? Hold on a sec, you didn't tell me you were under twenty-one!"

"She doesn't have to," Ryan said, pulling out his gold shield. "It's your job to check."

"This is bullshit." Nando jabbed a finger at Ryan. "It's . . . it's . . . what the hell is the word? Trapping or something."

"It's not entrapment," Ryan said coolly. "Your job is to ask for ID. You didn't. This bar's been fined three times already. Another violation and you'll lose your liquor license for six months." He gestured around. "I don't think customers will keep coming here to sip soft drinks and take in the ambience."

Nando shut his eyes and huffed out a long breath. "I'm trying to buy this place. I got every penny I own sunk into it."

What Nando didn't know was that Detective Ryan Hall of the Riverside County Sheriff's Department was outside his jurisdiction and had no authority to enforce liquor laws in LA County.

Ryan had explained the issue to Selina when she suggested plan B—in the event Nando wouldn't sell out Sweeney for money. They'd agreed on the idea after Judd, the con, had told Ryan how much Nando wanted to buy the bar.

Ryan was taking a massive risk by pulling this stunt but assured her he was willing to do it.

For her.

Fortunately, the bar was dark, and the lights looked like they hadn't been cleaned in years. Nando saw the briefly flashed shield and credentials and took Ryan at face value.

After a fair amount of cursing, in English and Spanish, Nando finally relented.

"Look, I don't know his real name," Nando said. "And Sweeney's just his nick. Yeah, he comes in here some, but I don't know where he lives."

"But you can get in touch with him," Ryan said.

"He doesn't roll like that," Nando said. "He uses a burner and changes it a lot. When someone wants him, I have to wait until he comes around here to give him the message."

"You mean the job," Ryan said. "After which someone either dies or gets hurt. You could be considered an accessory, Nando."

Beads of sweat stippled Nando's forehead. "Hey, I just pass messages. I don't know nothing about what happens after."

Ryan leaned in and dropped his voice. "If you want to keep this bar, and your freedom, talk. Now."

Nando swept his hand over his glistening bare scalp. "He came in here a few weeks ago and I had a message for him. He told me to get back to the client and say to meet him at Fillups in an hour."

"Fillups?"

"It's a gas station on Stone Canyon Parkway. Sweeney told me he was on his way to see a client who lives in one of those mansions up there. Sounded like he goes there a lot."

"What's he driving?" Ryan asked.

"A red Chevy Silverado pickup."

Ryan looked him over closely. "A few weeks ago . . . but you've seen him since."

"What're you, psychic?"

"Yeah, I'm a fortune teller. You want me to tell your fortune, Nando?"

"All right, chill, dude. Chill. He was here about an hour before you came. Had a couple of beers and left."

So Ryan had spotted something in the man's body language. Damn, he was good.

"And when were you planning to share that little piece of info?"

"I don't want no trouble, okay? That's all I know."

No amount of threats could get any more information out of Nando, Ryan apparently concluded. After settling their bill—and promising not to tell the liquor board about the underage drinking if Nando didn't tell Sweeney a cop was looking for him—they left.

Selina waited until they were in the car, then turned to Ryan. "What now?"

"Talk to local detectives. Get a file going on Sweeney and check out where he's going up in the hills."

"So we're not doing anything right now?" The disappointment in her voice was evident.

"No," he said firmly. "No more 'off the book' stuff. Now it's 'by the book.'"

But other events intruded. His phone trilled.

"Detective Hall."

She waited while he had a brief exchange.

"On my way." He disconnected and turned to her. "Triple homicide. I'm not the lead, but they're calling me in to help work it." He put the car in gear. "I'll drop you back at my place. You can keep Caliber company till I get back."

She sat in the front passenger seat as a thought occurred to her.

It was good that Sweeney was driving a red Silverado. Whoever worked at that gas station, Fillups, where he'd gone, would likely remember a nice big garish truck like that.

CHAPTER 54

As Mouse walked into the Garage, Carmen asked, "Are they on her?"

She could only hope Lauren hadn't stormed out of the building too quickly for the SHIT detail to get a bead on her.

"They scrambled three chasers in three minutes." Lifting a blonde eyebrow, Mouse added, "They're good."

"They are," Carmen agreed.

To follow a car in an urban environment, a minimum of two vehicles was required to avoid detection. Their team had been known to use as many as six in rotation, making them invisible to all but the sharpest drivers. Add the ability to coordinate the use of traffic cams and the occasional drone, and no one could figure out they were being followed.

Heron was staring at the murder board.

"What's that look, Heron?" she asked.

"I get it. Streets are considered 'public areas,' but it still feels intrusive to me. I just break out in a sweat when I see 'Big Brother Is Watching You.'"

Mouse asked, "What's that mean?"

Heron said, "From George Orwell's novel *1984*—which was the future when it was written more than three decades earlier. Dystopia. Big Brother was the government and he, well, it, watched everything every citizen did. Everywhere. Gave me nightmares as a kid. Gives me nightmares now. But"—he held up a hand—"we've got to do it."

Carmen nearly laughed. Their roles in pushing the boundaries of the Fourth Amendment had been swapping back and forth all day. She said to Mouse, "And Declan?"

She leaned toward one of the computers at a nearby workstation and typed. The image of a budding flower on the screen dissolved to reveal a map. "He's monitoring all the communication from the SHIT detail and rendering it into a real-time display of the target vehicle's movements."

They all followed a red dot going through the city on a virtual map.

Then Heron took a phone call. She noted surprise on his face, but she paid no more attention and returned to the map.

"We've got some incoming assistance," he said. He tapped keys. "I'm putting him on your screen, Sanchez."

"Hey there, everyone," came a voice from the unit.

Carmen turned and, despite everything, felt a genuine smile tug at the corners of her mouth. She was looking at Frank Tandy on Heron's monitor. He was still in the hospital but propped on pillows in his bed, tubed up, but not looking too bad.

"Frank!"

"I'm out of StaleState," he said. "Ready to help."

No idea what the word meant but it brought a smile to Heron's face.

She would have expected Tandy to be slurring his words, but no. He sounded alert, though his face tightened into a wince when he moved. "Detective work while lying on my ass. Kind of like self-driving cars and artificial intelligence. New state of the art."

Carmen recalled the most recent conversation she'd had with Tandy when she'd visited him in the hospital. He'd taken her hand and in unsteady words said, "Hey, Carmen, probably not a good time for this, but what the hell. Near death and all that . . . How about you and me having dinner sometime? Only rule is—no talk about cases."

"You mean not a business dinner."

"Yeah, that's exactly what I mean."

Her response had been ambiguous. A smile and a squeeze of his hand. Largely because she didn't know what the answer might be.

One thing she did know for certain: there had been two responses in her gut to the thought. One, it would undoubtedly be a fun dinner. The second reaction had nothing to do with Tandy. It was the unexpected memory of the near kiss by Jake Heron as they sat on the deck of the honeymoon suite.

Dispose of that, she instructed. Now.

And Carmen was then focusing once more on the case. She spent some moments bringing Tandy up to speed on the investigation.

She'd just finished when Heron's monitor came to life yet again.

He frowned.

"What?" Carmen had noted the expression.

"My scan of the comm systems after Reynolds screwed up and sent that unencrypted email? The bot found a packet kicker."

Mouse offered, "Not good."

Carmen asked, "How not good?"

Heron said, "Very not good. It identified any email or trunk line calls from Europol and the Italian police coming into our office and routed them to an anonymous server. Anybody who called got a response telling them to leave a message. Anybody who emailed got a return that said, 'Thank you. Somebody will be in touch as soon as possible.'"

"When did this start?"

"Two days after Brock's murder."

"How would HK know how to do that?"

"He wouldn't. There are only a few people in the world who could run a kick like that. It's brilliant. It lies dormant until it reads an IP or a phone call from selected sources—like any Italian law enforcement agency—and then it grabs the message and reroutes it."

"Maybe the Italians have been trying to reach us all along."

Heron's eyes were on his screen. "Yep. Any communications from here to Italy or Belgium—Europol headquarters—got hijacked too."

"So if HK isn't a world-class elite hacker," Mouse said, "that means he's got a partner."

CHAPTER 55

Selina glanced in her rearview mirror. Was she imagining things, or was that a black SUV behind her?

After Ryan Hall had left her with fluffball Caliber, she had waited exactly five minutes before heading out.

There was no way she was going to sit on her hands.

That waiting thing again. Always a problem.

Upstanding soul that he was, Nando might have been lying about having a way to reach Sweeney. And he could be calling the man right now to tell him a cop was looking for him. Their only lead might pack up and vanish.

That was not going to happen.

Ryan had made it clear he wanted to be in her life. If that was true, it was time he learned that the Sanchez women weren't the type to stay home and wait for the men to handle things.

Thoughts of how she'd been raised reminded her of her big sister. Carmen was trained in countersurveillance and had given Selina some pointers over the years.

First, identify if you're being followed.

She'd been driving toward Fillups gas station in the Westside region of LA, in the Santa Monica Mountains. She made four consecutive right turns, effectively taking her in a circle, then glanced up again.

The black SUV, the Ford Edge.

Yes, it was there. Definitely hanging back, allowing several cars between them. Seemed like what a pro would do. Okay, she had a tail. She struggled for calm, recalling her sister's next instructions.

If you are being followed, take streets with traffic lights. If it's green, slow down and wait until it turns yellow, then act like you're going to stop. At the last second, gun it to get through an instant before it turns red.

She did just this at the next light: slowed dutifully at the yellow. Then punched it, zipping through as yellow went to red. She checked, and sure enough, the car directly behind her had stopped, forcing the Edge to stop as well.

Good.

If the tail's forced to stop, immediately turn at the next possible street or alley, accelerate and lose yourself on surface roads.

This she did too.

She sorted through other tricks Carmen had taught her:

Call 9-1-1. But if you can't, drive to the nearest police station or government building and lay on the horn until someone comes out to see what's going on.

Regarding that advice: nope.

She continued on to her destination, Fillups, only now taking side streets, not the highway.

Soon she was cruising in the Stone Canyon hills. Traffic was less congested here, far more vegetation and, in places, an absence of vegetation. Sand, rock, dirt.

After making several turns to be sure no one was trailing her—black Ford, or anything else—she wound her way along Stone Canyon Parkway to Fillups, one of hundreds of independently owned gas stations in California. She saw it ahead of her, dusty and in need of paint and fronted by ancient pumps. She pulled into the lot around back, where her car wouldn't be visible from the main road.

After a brief wait to make sure she was safe, Selina climbed out and walked inside. A forty-something woman with sun-burnished skin and sharp hazel eyes greeted Selina with a nod, when she walked through the smeared, heavy glass doors.

"Hey," Selena said.

"Hey."

Selina's mouth was dry from Ford Edge–induced stress. She got a bottle of water from the second case from the counter (beer was the first). Then grabbed one of Jake Heron's favorites, a Red Bull.

No one else was in the small convenience market attached to the station. Selina walked to the counter, paid for the drinks and sipped the water.

Recalling a conversation she'd had with Carmen years ago about gaining trust with witnesses and interviewees, she tried to personalize things.

"I'm Selina," she said, smiling.

"Wanda," came the automatic reply.

Selina looked around. "You the owner?"

Wanda nodded. "Yeah, I've had this place nearly ten years. Don't want no chain franchise shit."

Selina detected a note of pride. "Well, that's great. I bet you see a lot of things around here."

Another nod. "Part of the territory. No gas today, hon?"

"Fact is, Wanda . . . got a question."

"Hm?"

Selina realized her plan would work only if she came off as young and naive, so she tucked away some of the Sanchez grit.

"Okay." She looked down. "The thing is . . . See, I met this guy at a bar. North Hollywood." She offered her most innocent smile. "I kind of like him. But I lost his number. I didn't put it in my phone. I wrote it on a Post-it. Stupid."

"In the ocean of stupid, hon, that's a pretty small fish."

A smile. "His name's Sweeney. He told me he comes up here a lot. Drives a red Silverado pickup. You know where he lives, where I can find him?"

"Isn't he a little old for you, hon?"

So she *did* know him.

Selina winked. "I like older men. He was nice to me. Not a lot of guys are nice."

Wanda clearly heard that. After a brief pause, she pointed out the front window. "All I can tell you is, he sometimes goes up into the hills. That private drive to the houses up there."

"Whose house?"

"I don't know."

"How many are there?"

"Six, seven, I think."

"He drive up there recently?"

"I haven't seen him. But I got more important things to do than sit and watch rich people coming and going."

"Is Sweeney rich?"

She smiled. "I don't mean him, honey."

"Thanks, Wanda. You've been super helpful."

The woman frowned. "You're a good-looking girl. You're polite. You can do better than him." Then a shrug. "But that's coming from four-times-married Wanda, so what do I know?"

Now it was Selina's turn to smile . . . and slide a twenty to the woman.

She strode out the door. Moments later, at her car, she chugged the Red Bull. Then was driving up the hill Wanda had indicated, which offered a view of the Stone Canyon Reservoirs—the one to the north being a weird football field kind of structure, while the big one to the south was more like a lake.

Situated south of Mulholland and west of Beverly Glen, this whole area was posh city. There was no way a hired hit man would live in a hood like this. She glanced from hilltop to hilltop, each mansion fancier than the last.

So this would be Sweeney's client.

And, possibly, the man whose money-laundering operation her father had uncovered.

Twenty minutes later, so high in the hills her ears popped, she parked.

Where the hell do you go up here, Sweeney?

The cul-de-sac was surrounded by seven imposing gates. She could see several of the houses—mansions. Shit, look at the size of them. Where did people get this kind of wealth?

Well, money laundering was one answer.

Maybe. Of course there was no guarantee that the "client" Sweeney had gone to see was really their father's killer, but what else did she have to go on?

That was how it was in her discipline—scientific research. You followed the most likely route in your experiments. A negative result was just as good as a positive one, a professor had said. It eliminated one possibility and let you pursue others.

But, please, she thought, in a very unscientific frame of mind, let this be the place where that fucker lived.

She drove in a circle.

No Silverados.

She climbed out and walked slowly past the gates to get a better look. No residents. No pit bulls either.

Well, she chided herself. It was pointless to go for a stroll along the asphalt. You're here to investigate, then do some investigating!

There were probably security cameras, but at this point she didn't care. She strode to each mailbox and took one piece of mail, then hurried back to the car.

Damn good thing her sister wasn't running the show. Carmen wouldn't have done this without a warrant, and she probably couldn't have gotten one based on what she had learned so far.

In fact, Selina thought in passing, she'd just committed a federal offense. Well, you've got jurisdiction now, Carm, come and get me.

The thought nearly brought a smile to her lips.

She returned to the car, dropped into the front seat and pulled the client list she'd gotten from Mr. Overton.

She compared the names.

None of the hilltop residents were on the list. Her shoulders slumped.

Until she thought of one she'd just seen. It was Christopher James Fisher, in the house at the end of the circle.

Fisher . . .

No, impossible.

My God.

Her heart thudded.

She was thinking of the other parts of her father's note that no one had figured out. The fact that he had underlined his middle name, and the ancient Greek lettering scrawled at the bottom corner of the page.

$$\Delta : I\theta$$

The characters that translated into the numbers 4:19.

Mateo equaled Matthew in English.

And the answer blossomed. Like everything else her father had been forced to do minutes before he died, the clue was elegantly simple yet easily disguised.

Their parents had taken their two daughters to Mass every Sunday. Selina had attended CCD and catechism growing up. Now that she realized the scripture her father had directed her to, it was obvious. Something anyone raised to memorize sections of the Bible would recognize without having to look it up.

He was directing them to Bible passage Matthew 4:19.

And He said unto them, "Follow Me, and I will make you fishers of men."

Christopher Fisher.

But she grimaced. His name was not on the client list.

Then she scanned it again. And saw that some of her father's clients were companies, not individuals.

And one of those was CJF Enterprises, LLC.

Too much of a coincidence. A fast Google search gave her proof.

Yes, the Christopher Fisher who lived here was the founder and head of the company, which did something called venture capital work.

Okay, she had enough to get started. She'd call Carmen and Ryan and tell them about her discovery.

First, though, put the mail back.

She climbed out and made the rounds once more.

She was putting Fisher's cable TV bill back in when a man's voice made her jump. "What have we here?"

Selina started to turn but froze when the muzzle of a gun pressed against the side of her neck.

CHAPTER 56

"So, HK's got a hacker buddy," Carmen said. "Any ID information?"

"None," Heron told her. "Anonymous."

"Comms still compromised?"

"No. They're open."

"Then let's get started. The police in Florence and Verona. We need to talk to them. I know HSI has an interpreter division. It's in DC. We can—"

"I speak Italian," Mouse offered.

Carmen was surprised. "You do? I never knew that."

"Nobody ever asked." She rocked on her red Chuck Taylor high-tops. "And, if it's helpful, Spanish and German, Russian. Mandarin. I'm a little rusty on my Hindi but I can get by. Oh, and Romanian—the closest to true Latin, not church Latin, still being spoken."

Lord, their assistant was a jewel.

Heron asked, "Which city first: Verona or Florence?"

"Florence," she said, recalling what they'd learned from forensics. "Su Ling found the art restoration chemicals he might've picked up. And Florence seems more . . . arty than Verona. At least from what I've seen on the Discovery Channel."

Mouse began giving orders to Declan regarding law enforcement agencies in the Tuscan capital.

On the screen, Tandy laughed. "You know he's kind of like HAL, don't you?"

The renegade computer in Stanley Kubrick's *2001*.

Mouse frowned. "We're not sure he likes those references. It might just be he's not a Kubrick fan in general—you know, *Eyes Wide Shut*—but to be safe we avoid mentioning *A Space Odyssey*."

Tandy blinked. "Noted."

Declan returned a wealth of information, including several police agencies likely to have been involved in the investigation—if there had, in fact, been one.

"It's late there," Heron pointed out.

"If they're like us, some of them'll be up. There's this line some famous cop said, a long time ago. Like a slogan. 'We never sleep.'"

Declan was in fact-checking mode. "It was not a policeman, Carmen. That was the motto of the National Detective Agency, founded by Allan Pinkerton around 1850. Pinkerton went on to become the head of Lincoln's Secret Service and—"

"Declan," Heron muttered. "Stop generating."

After a dozen calls, assisted by Mouse as interpreter, Carmen was put in touch with Inspector Valeria Fresca with the Polizia di Stato, the Italian police agency tasked with criminal investigation.

Mouse reported that Fresca, who was with the Interregional Directorate of Tuscany, wasn't surprised by their call. She had been expecting to hear from someone in LA for several days.

"They heard a news report of the killing here and contacted LAPD and DHS."

Heron broke the news to her that the communications between the Italian State Police, Europol, Homeland Security and LAPD had been compromised.

The call was on speaker and the inspector was, to put it mildly, pissed off. A sharp few words were muttered in Italian.

"Won't bother to translate," Mouse said.

"Tell her we did, in fact, contact them right away. But never heard back either."

Mouse did.

More stern words, which Carmen thought sounded elegant nonetheless.

Mouse translated. A moment later, she said, "Inspector Fresca is not happy. She will talk to her subordinates, who should have followed up on the absence of a reply to her queries."

Carmen said, "Do they have any leads to their murder?"

The answer was no. They considered it a tragic accident. And when she heard there were related cases, the Verona police weren't interested in starting an investigation and, even though Fresca was, she never heard back from HSI. So they never opened a full-scale investigation.

Heron asked, "Did they look for any video surveillance where the death happened?"

"Yes, but there was none," Mouse said after posing the question. "It was on a deserted walkway between ponds at the inn. One of those was where the victim drowned. But once they learned of the other murders, they began to compile a list of motels and hotels in the area where the killer might have stayed. They've been too short staffed to investigate them all yet."

Carmen asked whether Fresca could send the list to them, and she said she would.

A minute later the file appeared in Carmen's secure transfer inbox.

Carmen and Inspector Fresca agreed to share any other information they had gathered.

Heron said, "Tell her about the art restoration chemicals. Is that helpful in narrowing down the search?"

Laughter erupted from the other end of the call when Mouse translated the question.

Mouse said, "It's Florence, Italy. The presence of Renaissance art evidence is as useless as if we'd found traces of Sangiovese wine."

The inspector then asked a question. Mouse listened and translated, "Do we have any thoughts on what his motive is?"

Carmen and Heron looked at each other briefly.

She said, "No. Never seen any serial killer like him before."

No one had anything else to add and Mouse ended the call with, *"Grazie mille, e ciao."*

Tandy said, "We could try Verona, but let's stick with 'arty' Florence for now. Follow up on the leads we've got from the inspector."

"Agreed," Carmen said. "How would *we* find HK's name if we were Italian police?"

Tandy grimaced. "Canvass the hotels. But we're here, not there."

Carmen tipped her head toward Mouse. "We have a remote canvasser."

The woman beamed.

Carmen told her, "Call all the hotels on the list the inspector gave us and ask about a White male American." A nod at the murder board. "Fitting his description. Around the dates in question."

Heron asked, "How many hotels are there?"

Carmen opened the file from Fresca. "Oh lovely." She looked at the others and then at Tandy. "Ninety-two."

"Shit," Tandy muttered. "Not the Italians' fault there're so many. Blame American tourism."

Heron said, "Signora Mouse, *per favore* . . ."

A smile. "Jake, *you* speak Italian too. Sounds so romantic coming from you, don't you think, Carmen?"

"Mouse. Call."

Mouse consulted the list Fresca had sent and picked up the phone.

Carmen stopped her to add some quick pointers. "Listen for their tone. If they're awkward or hesitant or the pitch of their voice changes, that might indicate deception."

"Accord," Mouse said, well into the game. Then she frowned. "I guess I can't say I'm an HSI agent."

"No," Carmen said.

"But I have an idea. One that won't get any of us arrested."

Again, the hour was late, but at least hotels and motels could be counted on to have one or two clerks on duty.

The first clerk spoke English and so there was no need to translate. Carmen could only be amused by her approach.

"*Signore*, I am calling from America on an urgent criminal investigation regarding an American who may have stayed at your hotel. Have you heard of the IICI? . . . No? It's the Institute for International Criminal Investigations. I must inform you that there will be serious consequences if you do not answer my questions or if you answer falsely. Do you understand?"

Carmen noted that Mouse had not actually said she was with the IICI, which Carmen knew was not a police outfit at all but a nonprofit devoted to information gathering about war crimes.

And it was completely true that if a clerk lied there might be serious consequences—the Honeymoon Killer might strike again.

She and Heron shared a smile.

The man knew nothing about such a guest, however.

Call after call, the same.

Until number twenty-three: the clerk at the Bella Flora Motel off SR222, the Chiantigiana highway, running from Florence to Siena. They spoke in Italian, and after a few minutes Mouse translated. "This could be it. American came in and paid cash in advance. He said his wife had his ID and would bring it before they checked out. But he just left. So they have no record of his name."

"Damn," Tandy said from his flat-screen perch. "But he must remember the name."

Mouse asked the question and received an answer. She turned to the others. "The name he gave was Joe Buck."

Carmen scoffed bitterly. It was a variation on John Doe.

"His car, or tag number?"

"He claimed he arrived by taxi, but the clerk thinks he was lying. He's sure he had a car, but he parked it somewhere else. Not in their lot."

Too suspicious not to be their suspect.

She asked, "Maybe there's something about HK that we can use to track him down. Did he have any particular food he liked? Alcohol?"

The clerk didn't know, though he added that he dressed very well. "His suit was Italian," Mouse told them.

Heron tried another question. "Did he have any friends come to visit?"

A good inquiry, Carmen thought.

But this answer was negative too.

Carmen asked, "Did he ask for directions anywhere? Restaurant, airport, anything?"

After posing this question, Mouse tilted her head. And lifted an eyebrow. "Yes. He asked how long it would take to get to the Uffizi."

The clerk had nothing more to add. Mouse ended with some stern words and disconnected. She smiled at the others. "I told him not to leave town. I always like it when the detective tells the suspect that in a movie, and they look way nervous."

Carmen asked, "Declan, tell us about the Uffizi."

"The Uffizi Gallery, Florence, Italy, is one of the premier art museums in Europe. The Uffizi, which means 'offices' in Italian, was originally the home of the administrative and judiciary services of Florence. Upon the death of the last of the Medicis their collection of art was moved into the structure to make a museum, which has been expanded over the years."

Tandy said, "Let's find out how many people were at the place then."

Carmen asked, "Declan, how many visited the Uffizi on the dates around the time of the Florence murder?"

"I don't have access to that information, but the Uffizi Gallery is the most visited art museum in Italy, with two million visitors a year. That statistic suggests that eleven thousand eight hundred seventy-nine and seven-tenths visitors were present during the time in question."

Silence.

Then Mouse offered the official assessment. "I'd say we're screwed."

CHAPTER 57

Sweeney.

Selina could guess who her kidnapper was.

"Move, bitch." He shoved her into the massive entryway of Fisher's mountaintop mansion.

To open the door, Selina noticed, Sweeney had typed in what seemed like a ten- or twelve-digit security code. Of course Fisher would have an elaborate security system.

Sweeney's hazel eyes narrowed. "Give me your cell phone."

No sense lying about having one. That might earn her a rough pat down or a bullet hole in her body.

She slowly pulled it out of her pocket, wondering whether she could chance unlocking it with her fingerprint and tapping the speed dial for Carmen.

"Please don't hurt me."

"Just do what I say, and you'll be fine. Lay it on the floor."

"Okay, whatever you want, Mr. Sweeney."

"The fuck do you know my name?" His eyes were narrow with rage and concern.

"I just . . . I'm sorry."

"Phone now."

She tried the fingerprint thing.

"Don't get cute. Leave it locked and kick it over here. Now."

"Let me go. The police know I'm here."

"Not unless they've given you the okay to pilfer mail. I'm not asking again: phone."

Selina set the unit down and used the edge of her shoe to slide it toward him.

Without ever taking his eyes off her, Sweeney tapped the toe of his shoe on the floor until he felt the phone underneath his foot.

He ground the device under his heel. "We wouldn't want your big sister calling you, would we?"

A whisper: "You know who I am?"

"Selina Sanchez," Sweeney said. "And your sister Carmen is a Fed."

How had he found out? Nando?

The driver of the black Edge?

Someone else, betraying her?

She glanced around the massive room, the doorways, the windows. He gave a cold laugh. "Don't bother. You can't outrun a bullet."

She was tempted to say sarcastically, "Oh, that was a clever line," but she had to maintain the aura of helplessness.

"Just so you don't do anything that would be stupid for you and irritating for me, sit down in that chair."

"Yes, sure. Whatever you say. Just don't hurt me."

"Don't have your sister's balls, do you?"

She wiped her eyes. "She's a cop. I'm a student."

"Sit." He walked closer to her and put his hand on her shoulder to shove her down.

Which was when the "helpless" girl struck.

The scared attitude was fake, as was the phony crying, which Sweeney might have noticed if he'd bothered to look closely. For a professional hit man he wasn't at the top of his game.

The sobbing young girl turned suddenly into an athlete who had been trained, by her sister, in the devastating Russian martial art of Systema.

She swung in close, grabbed his collar and slammed her sole into his knee. He cried out in pain. Systema is a form of grappling. It has none of the elegance of karate or tae kwon do but is far more utilitarian. It was created during the Mongol occupation of Russia so that soldiers could learn it fast. The system is also known by the Russian words for "know yourself."

He swung a fist, which caught her on the shoulder. She staggered back, pain coursing through her upper body.

But when, enraged, he came toward her it was with a decided limp.

Selina balanced her weight and, as he drew closer, she seemed to go once more for the leg, but when he shied away she slammed the heel of her palm into his nose.

"Don't ever use a fist. You're more likely to break your own bones than inflict any damage on the opponent."

Sweeney staggered back, wiping at the blood on his face, groaning in pain. "You fucking bitch . . . That's it. I've had it!"

Well, I haven't, Selina thought and picked up a small statue, then tossed it at his head. It sailed past and smashed into the window, cracking the glass.

Sweeney charged forward, the gun up.

"No, no, okay . . . okay!" Selina held her arm up as if that would deflect bullets.

"The chair."

Glaring, she walked to it and sat.

Sweeney looked at the blood on his fingers, from a sweep of his face. And bent his knee, wincing.

As she sat staring at him, she said, "I know what's going on."

"Do you?"

"You killed my dad."

"Figured that out, did you?"

"My father was a financial adviser. He found something suspicious with one of his clients' accounts." She lifted her head and looked around. "Christopher Fisher."

The expression that crossed his face told her she was on the mark. "Smart little thing, aren't you?"

"So, it's true."

"That's right."

She looked him over. "I heard you specialize in making murders look like suicides."

"How the hell did you know all this? Tell me!"

She got a small taste of what Carmen must feel like when someone is surprised into making an unintended admission.

"You screwed up, Sweeney. Left a trail so clear even a college kid like me could follow it right to you."

"I'm not fucking around. Tell me who ratted me out."

This was the only reason she was still alive. He had to know where the holes were so he could plug them.

"I'll tell you. But first, I want to know exactly how Fisher did it."

He gave her a cruel look, up and down. "I could just force you to talk."

"If I'm in pain, I might lie. If you tell me the truth, I'll return the favor."

He laughed. "You're a piece of work."

"What did Dad discover, exactly, that made him so dangerous you were hired to kill him?"

"I tell you and you give me the leaky faucet that gave up my name."

"Sure. You're both pricks. I don't care what happens to either one of you."

No smile now. He glared coldly.

"Okay, about your dad . . . well, you're just a kid. I don't suppose you know much about money laundering."

"I've heard of it," she said. "Only I know it by a different name. Fortuna and Hygeia."

And she enjoyed the look of complete confusion crossing his ruddy face.

CHAPTER 58

Jake said, "The museum . . . okay, let's think."

Tandy offered, "We're not going to catch him at the ticket windows. He won't use a credit card. And facial rec's useless with that many visitors. But if we could figure out where he went specifically, maybe he got caught on one of those vids."

Sanchez shook her head. "But there are so many places he could have gone . . ."

Declan had continued his Wikipedia report and told them that the Uffizi held nearly two hundred thousand paintings, drawings and statues.

Both Jake and Sanchez found themselves looking at the murder board. She mused, "What do we know about him that tells us what he might like to look at?"

"No sexual component. Nothing financial."

Tandy added, "And generally thrill killers don't try to cover up the deaths and make them seem like accidents. The pleasure is both in the act of killing—"

"And watching the public reaction," Sanchez added. "But this one's a bit different. He wants the world to know someone died . . ."

Jake added, "But not that they were murdered. He's setting them up as accidents."

On the screen Tandy was nodding. "What else?"

Sanchez offered, "He kills newlyweds, people at the beginning of their lives together."

Mouse threw out, "And at a wedding reception. So a whole bunch of people know about the death."

Sanchez said, "We're getting to something. Keep going."

"He went to the funeral," Tandy said. "What killer goes to the funeral of the victim and risks getting caught? Which he almost was."

Silence for a moment. Then it was broken abruptly by Sanchez. "And he was smiling."

Jake turned to her. "Yes. Sylvie, the girl in the cemetery. She said he was smiling but it wasn't like a formal greeting. He was *happy* to be where he was. At a *funeral*."

"Jesus," Tandy muttered. "Think about this: maybe it's not the murder itself that gets him off. It's what the death does to the survivors. The mourners are his true victims."

Mouse said nothing but she was clearly shaken by the idea that someone would enjoy the sorrow of others.

"Declan," he called.

"Yes, Jake?"

"What are the most famous paintings of mourning in the Uffizi, 'mourning' as in grieving, not sunrise?"

"I deduced that from the context, Jake. There are a number of paintings whose themes are death, sorrow and mourning in the Uffizi Gallery, as those are persistent themes in Italian Renaissance art. It is not possible, according to the information I have, to give you a specific number. But I can tell you the two most visited works falling into that category are Rogier van der Weyden's *Lamentation of Christ*, and Giovanni Bellini's *Lamentation over the Dead Christ*."

"Where are they hung, in the Uffizi?"

"The van der Weyden is on loan to the Vatican. The Bellini is on exhibit in the Uffizi, in the Bellini and Giorgione room. The museum has a 360-view feature of that room on its website. Would you like to see the room?"

"Yes," Jake and Sanchez said simultaneously.

Instantly a 3D image appeared on the monitor. The gallery was smaller than Jake expected. On the tan-colored walls hung only a dozen or so paintings. After circling the room, Declan focused on the Bellini. It was a monochrome of several sorrowful men surrounding the body of Jesus.

"You see any?" Sanchez asked.

Jake knew exactly what she was talking about.

Security cameras.

"Two, I think. Let's find out. Mouse, we need you to be an international woman of intrigue again."

"Bond. Jane Bond." She grabbed the phone and eventually got through to the security office, which was open, though the museum itself was closed. A gazillion euros' worth of art would not go unguarded.

The person in charge, however, did not immediately cooperate. Mouse cited the IICI again, but her sternness did not sway him.

She turned to Sanchez and Jake. "He needs something official."

US-issued warrants have no power in foreign jurisdictions. You need to apply to the local police and they in turn would get a magistrate's warrant from their own court system.

Sanchez thought for a moment, then sat at her desk and pounded out a letter on HSI letterhead. The top said "Law Enforcement Demand for Warranted Information" and requested clips of the security videos from the Bellini room for the days in question.

She saved it as a PDF file and then Jake went online and ordered Stable Diffusion—an art generation program—to "create a stamp that resembles an outdated Italian apostille."

The resulting image resembled the stamp that was affixed to US documents that had been authenticated by the Italian embassy for use overseas—with birth certificates, marriage documents and certain contracts.

He copied and pasted the image into Sanchez's letter, and Mouse got the security man's address at the Uffizi and sent it off to him via the encrypted server.

"What does it mean?" Mouse asked, eyes on the letter.

Jake had to chuckle. "It means your boss and I are dancing on the edge of propriety."

Sanchez shrugged. "Nothing illegal about it. The fact is, it's meaningless. He'll be well within his rights to ignore it. But I'm betting he *wants* to help. He just needs a cover-your-ass document in case somebody asks him why he released the vids. Let's hope he buys it."

Which he did. The letter was all the man needed.

And in ten minutes they received the videos and Jake sat down at his station and scrubbed. They counted about four hundred individuals who had visited the room where the Bellini was hung.

"Declan."

"Yes, Jake?"

"Scan the videos in Heron Secure Folder 89 labeled 'Uffizi' and compile best-quality screenshots of dark-haired White males aged twenty-five to thirty-five who viewed the Bellini."

Sanchez said to Jake, "And add in your Sherlockian deductions about him physically. What we talked about in the coffee shop earlier." She nodded to the murder board.

"Good. Declan, prioritize right-handed individuals in good physical shape."

"I'm doing that now, Jake."

Ten seconds passed. Then:

"I have forty-two, in descending order of seconds spent examining the painting."

Jake nodded to Sanchez, who took over the hunt. "Compare the images with those of passengers in the Customs and Border Patrol database flying into the US from Rome, Milan, Venice or connecting from Italy through Munich, Frankfurt, Brussels, Paris and London."

Declan suggested, "I would add Reykjavik too. Icelandair is a popular carrier for flights into and out of the United States. Would you like me to do that, Carmen?"

"Yes."

Her eyes met Tandy's, Jake noted. The detective said, "The plan, it seems kind of . . . fragile. What if it doesn't work? Do we have any alternatives?"

The answer was no, they didn't.

An endless moment of silence.

Finally broken by the computer's low tenor. "I have one match. Would you like to hear it?"

Now it was Jake's and Sanchez's eyes that met. She said, "Yes."

"The individual fitting all your search criteria is Damon Garr, 4437 Ocean Vista Drive, Malibu, California, 90265."

CHAPTER 59

"I don't know what you're talking about," Sweeney said. "Who?"

"Fortuna, the goddess of wealth, and Hygeia, the goddess of cleanliness. Money and laundering."

The big man still seemed confused. "I don't remember them from Marvel or DC."

Sighing, Selina continued, "My dad realized one of his clients was laundering money. I didn't know which one but eventually figured out it was Fisher."

"You really are something." He shook his head in disbelief. "But we have a deal, right?"

"Oh, plugging the leak. Sure. But tell me more about Fisher."

A nod around the mansion. "Silicon Valley venture capitalist. They call themselves VCs. They raise money for start-ups. Not all of Silicon Valley is a golden goose, and Fisher lost a shit ton of money."

She looked at the mantel. There were pictures of a handsome man in his late forties, trim and with perfect hair. One was of him with a woman about his age, holding hands and looking at the camera from the deck of a yacht. They wore wedding rings. Another photo about the same age showed him with his arm around a pretty girl in her late teens in a cocktail dress.

"Husband and father," she whispered. It seemed impossible that a "normal" man could do what he'd done.

Sweeney chuckled. "You got that part right, kid. Husband, yeah. But that's not his daughter. It's his girlfriend." He snickered. "The missus doesn't get here very often. He keeps her picture there to remind the arm candy she shouldn't expect a marriage proposal."

"Asshole."

Sweeney didn't argue. He shrugged and continued his monologue: "So some of Christopher's lenders came to him and said, 'We won't take everything you own, if you wash a little money for us.' He did a good job. And they wanted more. And he did a better job. That was his real calling. He even ended up working for OC."

"Orange County?"

Sweeney snorted. "Organized crime. The mob. One Marco Mezzo in particular."

This apparently was meant to impress her. Selina simply shrugged, which she believed disappointed Sweeney, for some reason.

She could see how Fisher had gone down a slippery slope until he was completely compromised. But none of it would've happened if he hadn't been greedy and weak. A man with character would have given up all his possessions rather than commit to a life of crime.

"Everything was fine until your dad found some issues. He called Fisher to ask if there was some mistake. Fisher said there was. Had to be some mix-up. Just give him a few days to track down the oversight . . . and then he started going through the dark web for sites where people could find a fixer.

"So, there you have it. Sorry about your pop. He should've stopped asking questions. Never a smart thing. Okay. My turn. Was it that bald fuck Nando snitched me out?"

Of course, if she told Sweeney, Nando was dead.

Nando, the bartender who passed messages about jobs to people like Sweeney who tortured, maimed and killed. Nando, who had surely received a cut of the blood money.

Who had also undressed her with his eyes and liquored up an underage girl.

She said, "Yeah, Nando."

Sweeney's lip curled. "Figures." His phone buzzed, and he checked the screen before holding it to his ear. "Go ahead."

His gaze held hers as he listened. His end of the conversation was minimal.

"Uh-huh . . . yeah. It'll cost extra. Uh-huh. Okay. Deal."

She was certain it was Fisher and that the two men were bargaining about the fee for making her permanently disappear.

He disconnected and gave her a look that was almost apologetic. "Sorry, kid."

Selina was struck by one thought: that she would never have the chance to apologize to Carmen for her mistake—in playing detective.

And, more importantly, for those years when she resented her sister for forgiving Roberto, when Selina could not.

There would never be a chance either to tell her how much she respected, and loved, her.

She dropped all pretense of calm as tears streamed down her cheeks. "Look, please. I did all this on my own. Nobody else knows. My sister doesn't. I wanted her to go after Dad's killer and she said no. There's no need to hurt her. Please!"

She made peace with her death but wanted to save the one person who meant more to her than anyone else.

In that moment, she truly understood what her father had done—sacrificing himself—and was trying to do the same, even though it would seal her fate.

"No one else knows who you are or where I am," she said in a shaking voice. "Carmen can't find you. Let her go. Just . . . let her live. Fisher won."

He gave his head a slow shake as he raised the pistol. "Can't do that." He aimed it directly at her once again. "Nothing personal."

The gunshot filled the air with a thunderous bang and blood spattered in a bold Rorschach pattern over a wall that was the shade of bleached bone.

CHAPTER 60

"Some people have money but no sense of what art is," Damon was saying absently as he gazed at the massive abstract, which was probably a naked woman.

Or naked man.

Or a seahorse.

"I mean, I personally have no time for renegade populism. Keith Haring and his dogs. Godard's olives, Banksy's everything. But there's an inherent integrity to what they do. Or did. This? Crap. Are your ears still ringing?"

He turned back to Selina Sanchez, bound to the chair in Christopher Fisher's opulent living room. She didn't respond, but Damon guessed it wasn't from temporary deafness resulting from his gunshot to the back of Sweeney's head a few moments ago.

It would be the shock at the gore.

Maybe a bit of surprise too at Damon's sudden appearance, which put an end to the execution Sweeney had planned.

Damon walked into the kitchen and—wearing latex gloves, of course—poured and drank a glass of 2 percent milk. He was surprised to find the carton, replete with a smiling cow, in the massive Sub-Zero fridge. He figured that Fisher—a Silicon Valley venture capitalist through and through—would be an oat milk kind of guy. Or, maybe, almond. Or some esoteric grain or nut found only on a particular mountaintop in Bolivia.

Damon washed away his DNA and dried and put the glass in the cabinet.

Selina was returning to her center. Her eyes were focused, and she was calculating, he could tell.

Looking him over for vulnerabilities.

She was clearly her sister's sister.

She scanned the floor, near Sweeney's body, looking perhaps for the man's pistol. She'd apparently missed Damon tucking it away in his own pocket.

On the subjects of art and of carefully scrubbed crime scenes, no one was more buttoned-up than Damon Garr.

Then she scanned Damon, pretty damn coldly for a man who had just saved her life.

"I know you're thinking your sister will be coming to your rescue. And she will be. But, thanks to you, she didn't even know about your little investigation."

"How do you know that?" she asked bluntly.

Sharp, yes. He didn't answer. "She'll put it all together eventually. She can use the same tricks that my associate did and figure out you ended up here, in Mr. Fisher's clutches." A glance at her shattered phone. "And Verizon, or whoever, will have a record of where your pings stopped. But we'll be long gone."

"And how did *you* find me?"

"My associate? For him, the word 'firewall' is merely a 'welcome' sign. He's monitored traffic and private cams and the DMV Vehicle Tracking Service . . . Don't know about that? A lot of people don't. The state tries to keep it secret. I'm sure your sister's partner, Jake Heron? That would drive him absolutely nuts. Intrusionist . . . there's a concept for you. Are they a couple by the way, Jake and Carmen? I've observed them. It's hard to tell."

"Where's Fisher?"

He cocked his head. "Interesting you'd ask *that*. Not 'Please let me go.' Or 'No, no, don't hurt me.'"

The predator still wanted her prey. And understandably in her case. But Damon Garr could simply not comprehend how a child would want to avenge their parent's death.

"We should go."

"Where?"

"For me to know and you to find out."

He walked to the chair and, pressing the muzzle of the gun against her head with his right hand, used one of the flea market knives to cut the tape binding her hands.

She didn't resist when he pulled her from the chair and, slipping his gun away, retaped her wrists behind her back.

"You never answered my question. Where's Fisher?"

"I don't know. He doesn't figure into my calculus."

"Wait. Are you the one my sister's looking for?"

"'Looking for.' Think she has more in mind than that. But the simple answer is yes."

"You really kill people on their wedding night?"

"Around then."

"And what are you doing here? What do you have to do with this?"

He spun and looked down. "Because if I gut you like a little fish, your sister will be all, oh, fuck, what's he done to Selina?"

She gasped.

"That answer your question? Now. Move."

He took her arm.

"Don't touch me."

"Fine." He hadn't particularly wanted to.

Outside, as they walked to his Mercedes, she said, "I have to pee."

"And you couldn't have said anything in the house?"

"I had a gun pointed at me. I wasn't thinking too clearly."

He sighed. "There." He pointed to the edge of the driveway and unzipped her jeans, leaving it for her to tug them down.

"Go away."

"No."

She muttered something under her breath.

He stayed close. The same way Miss Spalding had stayed close when she'd had him pee in the bushes at the playground, rather than go into the public city restrooms ("You never know who'll be in there").

Damon did, however, look away from the girl as she squatted. Maddie Willis's body was the only one he desired.

And he was counting the minutes until he would experience it once more.

Selina got to her feet. "I have to wipe. I need a Kleenex or something."

"No."

"You're disgusting." She struggled to tug her pants up, the maneuver taking an inordinate amount of time with her bound hands.

He sighed and pulled them the rest of the way up, then zipped them. Not because he cared about her modesty, but because he wanted to get on the road. He led her to his car, helped her into the passenger seat and taped her hands to the armrest.

"You don't need to do that."

He'd seen her flinty eyes—and he remembered the articles about her gymnastics, photos of her body in the close-fitting leotards. The muscles. "Yes, I do." He got behind the wheel and started the engine, then drove down the long switchback to the highway.

She sat back sullenly and stared out the window at the desert-tinged landscape as they sped south.

Damon was suddenly aware of something. Selina wasn't curious why he hadn't blindfolded her.

The implication, of course, was that by keeping her eyes uncovered he didn't care that she saw their final destination.

And if that were the case, another conclusion was obvious: that she wouldn't live long enough to tell anyone where she'd been held captive.

CHAPTER 61

Carmen's cell phone buzzed. She pulled it out and checked the screen. Not the person she was expecting.

"Go ahead, Ryan," she said to Detective Hall.

"Agent Sanchez—uh, I mean, Carmen—Selina's not answering her cell. I'm worried. Have you heard from her?"

An icy wave stabbed her. "What are you talking about?"

"I think she followed up on Sweeney by herself."

"Why don't you back the hell up and tell me who this Sweeney is?"

"Oh, shit, I thought you knew. She didn't tell you? Wait, obviously not. I was helping Selina look into your father's murder. She told me you were busy on a serial killer case and—"

"Do you seriously think I would let my sister go after a murderer?" She saw the stricken expressions on her colleagues' faces and tapped the screen. "You're on speaker with Jake Heron, Frank Tandy and my assistant. Tell me exactly what happened."

"Sweeney's the hit man that somebody hired to kill your father."

The news struck her like a fist.

For two reasons: the fact that their theory was confirmed and that they had scored a name.

And two, that her little sister had gone after the asshole herself.

And was now, apparently, missing.

They all listened, rapt, as Ryan explained how Selina had called him after getting a client list from Carl Overton. He took them through his video call with a jailed hit man that led him to Paquito's Bar, where the bartender had given them the name of an indie gas station where Sweeney sometimes went.

"So you dropped her off at your place and expected her to stay there and wait for you?"

An awkward silence, then: "I did."

"Guess you won't make that mistake again," Carmen said.

Tandy said, "That area's in the Lost Hills Station, LA County Sheriff. I have a buddy there. I'll call him now."

"Find her, Ryan! Coordinate with Frank."

As state officers, they would have known the resources better than she would. Carmen gave Hall Tandy's number from memory. She ordered the young detective, "Move on it! And I want details on this Sweeney. Everything you've got." She disconnected. And stood with her head bowed, staring at the floor.

"Sanchez," Heron began. It was his sympathy voice, not his good-idea voice. She gave no response.

No more than five minutes passed before she received a call from Detective Paul DeSoto from the Lost Hills Station of the LA County Sheriff's Office, which covered Malibu and the surrounding area.

DeSoto said, "Agent Sanchez, I heard from Detective Hall, Riverside Homicide. He was telling me your sister was interested in a gas station called Fillups. I called the owner, who told me she'd been there, and was going to drive to the top of a mountain nearby. She asked about a red Chevy Silverado pickup that had gone that way."

"It's about a cold case homicide. Did Ryan tell you?"

"Not the details, no."

"She was playing private eye." Carmen swore. "Detective, can you get a car there?"

"Already on the way. Hostiles? Armed?"

"Probably. Proceed with caution."

"Yes, ma'am. I'll let you know what they find. This number?"

"That's right. Thank you."

Heron asked, "Detective, I'm working with Agent Sanchez. I want to see the security vids. Can you give me the gas station owner's contact info?"

The man relayed it, and Heron called and worked his magic. No warrants required when the owner of the video cooperates. And a raspy-voiced woman named Wanda was more than happy to help.

Soon he was prowling through the file on his tablet.

"Look, Sanchez."

He was scrubbing. "Red pickup goes up the hillside . . ."

Sweeney's wheels.

"Selina's car follows a half hour later."

"Shit," Carmen muttered. "Scroll, Heron."

He did.

Neither her car nor the pickup was coming down . . .

"Wait, look," Heron said.

They watched a silver Mercedes pause at the intersection, as if the driver were checking directions, then turn left and speed up the same hill. Ten minutes later, it drove back down.

"I don't care about the Mercedes. Selina's up there with the hit man. What's the ETA of the LAPD cruiser DeSoto sent out?"

"She's not up there anymore," Jake said, his voice flat, as he stared at his tablet.

"What do you mean?"

"The tag number on the Benz?"

"Yes?"

"It's registered to Damon Garr."

CHAPTER 62

Two operations were occurring simultaneously.

Carmen, Heron and Mouse were monitoring them on the computers at his workstation.

The left screen showed body cams of LA County officers approaching and entering the house of Christopher Fisher, a wealthy venture capitalist, where the body of a big redheaded man nicknamed Sweeney was on the floor, shot to death.

What happened at the house was impossible to tell for certain. Selina had possibly made the connection that Fisher was the money-laundering client and had gone to investigate. Hit man Sweeney, who worked for Fisher, had nabbed her. Then Damon had arrived, killed Sweeney and left, taking Selina with him.

As for Fisher himself, Frank Tandy had ordered officers to surveil the venture capitalist in his office downtown, but to keep their distance and not let him know he was a suspect.

The Sweeney/Fisher case was represented on the left monitor.

The right one showed four separate screens—videos from Liam Grange's tac teams' surveillance of Damon Garr's house in Malibu.

It was the logical place for Garr to go—ideally with Selina. They didn't know Garr's full story. He was the Honeymoon Killer, yes, but maybe he also had other murderous tendencies and wanted to get Selina into his house and . . .

No, she didn't let those thoughts continue.

It was all right, she told herself. There were teams in place and Garr had no idea they were onto him. The tac teams were checking presently for—

"We have the thermal readings," came Grange's deep voice.

"K." Carmen spoke the law enforcement word of acknowledgment into her earpiece.

"No living entity profiles."

Shit.

Her palms were damp, and her heart would not stop pounding. This was the only hope of finding her, and that hope dangled from a gossamer thread.

"Orders, Carmen?"

"Maintain position."

"Copy that."

"Thermals?" Heron asked.

Absently, her mind mostly on her sister, she explained, "Nothing comes in registering a human body temp."

"So, it's empty."

Carmen was vaguely aware of Mouse answering, "Not necessarily. Liam had a zero-temperature reading once and went in with the team. One of the operators got bit by a rattlesnake. Only the boot, but scared the crapola out of her. Snakes—cold-blooded, you know."

They looked over the screens displaying images of Garr's house from several angles. Of necessity, it was tac team lite. Garr lived in a lush area of Malibu, with plenty of trees, but not so many streets. It was impossible to hide a full contingent of SWAT personnel. And they were afraid if Garr was paranoid he might flee or shoot Selina at the first sign he had been made.

There was also the electronic security issue. Heron had run a signal scan, and the house was bristling with protection devices. They would instantly let Garr know his home had been breached. He probably had a go bag in his car, and at any indication of a threat he'd simply not return home and scoot to Mexico.

The thirty-year-old Garr didn't make a lot of money professionally. He was a lecturer in art history at a local university, but his father had been a successful ship charter broker and had been worth tens of millions. Garr, they speculated, would have inherited a fortune. He was also an art collector, though he did not apparently make much money that way. If you never sell the pieces you've acquired, your bottom line for that business is constantly in the red.

This echoed Heron's deductions about his resources—and about his independence in employment. A professor maybe has certain academic standards to follow but doesn't really have bosses in the corporate sense.

In the brief time since they'd known his name, they could not pull together a complete profile, but they had learned that he had been a troubled youth and had been flagged by several counselors as potentially a risk for dangerous adult behavior. His bride had died on their wedding day—ruled an accidental death.

Perhaps such a horrific loss had been the trigger that made him snap—and re-create the death now, acting it out with other victims, so that their friends and family members would experience the same sorrow he had.

A profile that had, in fact, led them to identify him at the Uffizi.

There was no criminal file on the man, not even in the Traffic Bureau. Officers and campus police had raided his office at the school, but found no leads. Then they receded from view, in case he returned to the school.

Typical of a dedicated serial killer, he had a minimal social media presence and was not active in any of the college's extracurricular activities. There was no evidence he had acted inappropriately with any of his students, though the majority were young women.

A shake of the head. "And how the hell is Garr involved with Sweeney and Fisher?"

Mouse offered, "There's no way he could have been connected to your father's death. Too much of a coincidence."

Heron said, "But we know he's targeted us—and that means he'd go after Selina. He must've followed her to Fisher's."

"Maybe, but I've taught her situational awareness. She's always checking for tails."

Tandy, from his monitor perch, nodded. "Right. Unlikely she was followed. Damon's car showed up twenty, thirty minutes after she drove to Fisher's. No, he found her some other way . . ."

Mouse said, "Maybe Garr's hacker accomplice had access to the cameras too? And tracked her that way? How many cameras are there in Los Angeles County, Frank?"

Tandy said, "More than forty thousand sending feeds to the police."

It was a good suggestion but Carmen said, "I don't know. That's one of the most cyber-secure systems in the state. They're worried an assassin might hack it to find a motorcade route to kill some official."

Then she noticed that Jake Heron's eyes were doing that thing they sometimes did that was both intriguing and scary. They went someplace else. Like he was peering into a different dimension. Carmen sometimes imagined that he was looking at a massive computer, one so big it incorporated the entire universe.

"What?" she whispered.

Heron was focusing on the right-side monitor, the one that showed the tac team's video of Garr's house.

He said one word. "Cinderella."

CHAPTER 63

Jake nodded as Su Ling strode into the Garage with her tablet in hand.

"I've got what you asked for, Jake. You want it on the murder board?"

"Yes." He resumed staring at the monitor.

A moment later some of her crisp evidence photos flashed onto the screen. Three electrostatic prints of shoe soles arranged top to bottom.

Su said, "The one on the top is HK's. Garr's. We know that from the shed at the cemetery where he rigged the booby trap with the hedge shears. The second and third are the same. The second was among those lifted from Garr's front walk by one of my people. And the third, the one it matches?" She circled it with the cursor. "It's from the case you two solved a month ago. It's Tristan Kane's."

"Jesus," Sanchez muttered, then looked at Jake. "Cinderella. The shoe. You suspected."

"We had two epic hacks in the past couple of days. Getting into our system and diverting the emails and calls to Italy. And cracking the LA camera network." He shrugged. "I could do it. Aruba could. And Kane."

"But I don't get how he became involved," Mouse said.

Sanchez snapped her fingers. "Reynolds's damned email. Kane must be constantly pinging us, searching for breaches and checking on our investigation against him. He got in, saw the HK case and—with a shitload of hacking and a shitload of money—scored Garr's identity and contacted him. He's the silent partner we were speculating about."

"For money?" Tandy asked. "Garr hired him?"

"No," Sanchez said. "I doubt it. He's using Garr to get to us. A weapon."

Mouse asked, "But CERN? The internet hub in Switzerland."

"Let me check." Jake sent a text to the authorities there asking if they'd noticed any attempted intrusions into the facility's web operations or other infrastructure.

None, the contact reported.

He told the others, "The leads to Switzerland were misdirection."

He said to Sanchez, "We've got info on Garr's vehicle. Let's get the SHIT detail on it, and the same camera network."

Sanchez sat in the chair beside Jake and began to keyboard. She frowned.

Jake asked, "What?"

"There are no hits."

Tandy asked, "Maybe he's out of the surveillance zone."

She turned to Heron and the detective's monitor. "No. It's not returning hits on *any* Mercedes. Anywhere."

Tandy muttered, "Impossible. There are as many Benzes in LA as out-of-work actors."

She lifted her palms. "Nothing."

Jake said, "Frank, can you patch me through to the system admin?"

"Sure."

In five minutes they had the answer. Jake pointed to his monitor. "Somebody hacked the system and loaded this script."

```
import java.io.File;

public class DeleteFile {
```

```
public static void main(String[] args) {

File file = new File("F;\Admin\Main\LATraf\
Surveillance\Make\Mercedes.txt");

file.delete();

    }

}
```

Tandy frowned. "The hell?"

"It deleted records of all Mercedes picked up on camera for the past hour. The admin's removing that script, but if Garr wasn't out of the surveillance zone before, he probably is now."

Jake noted Sanchez's eyes closing briefly. He could only imagine the agony she was feeling about her sister.

It was then that a man's booming voice startled Sanchez. "Guess my invitation got lost in the mail."

Fuck.

They all turned to see Stan Reynolds striding into the Garage. He added, "Of course in the digital age, the odds of any missive getting lost are rather rare, aren't they, Mr. Internet Maven Heron? No postal service issue."

Sanchez said, "Things have moved fast. We just got his ID minutes ago."

"Time is relative, as Einstein taught us." He gazed at the surveillance videos. "We are where?"

She explained about the unsub's identity.

"Well, bully for you. I'll forgive you for failing to find his assets and dig up dirt on his foreign agent registrations. And lying to me about it. No, no, no. No denial. You've saved your bacon by identifying Ivanov's hit man. Garr. Maybe short for Garritsky or something. So. What kind of Russian connections have you found?" Reynolds was staring at the video feed from Grange's tac team cameras.

That again.

"None, sir. We're convinced he's a true sociopath. He's obsessed with causing grief and sorrow. He kills, yes, but it's only so he can watch people mourn at the graveside."

Reynolds said cynically, "Who on earth would get excited about that? No, he's no serial killer at all. It's a perfect cover. We're all looking for Norman Bates in *Psycho*, and he sneaks up behind us and murders Anthony Brock. Brilliant when you think about it. But good thing I took over. We stopped him in his tracks." He pointed at the screen. "And he's holed up in his house?"

"No," Jake said. "He's not inside. Nobody's there."

"Location?"

"Unknown."

"Is he alone? Some wily GRU officer with him? Maybe his handler."

Jake glanced toward Sanchez and sensed that they'd arrived at the same decision.

"He may have a potential hostage," Jake said.

It would be a bad idea to admit that the individual was a relative of the lead agent on the case. He would likely kick Sanchez off the investigation immediately, and Jake might soon follow.

"My," Reynolds said, frowning. "Anybody official? High up? Somebody it might be suggested we were supposed to be guarding but slipped up on?"

Reynolds had gone straight into ass-covering mode. Jake boiled at his callous narcissism. "No."

"Good. Now, does Garr have any other residences?"

Sanchez said, "Not that we could find."

"So, all his records are in there." Reynolds stared at the house.

Jake said, "And he has no safety deposit boxes."

Reynolds jumped on that. "You *hardly* expect him to rent one in his own name, do you?"

A pause. Jake noted Sanchez sighing loudly. Reynolds, like most narcissists, missed the dig. She said, "Declan took that into account. He correlated visits to safety deposit boxes in a fifty-mile radius to Garr's credit card, FasTrak and license plate scans for the past month."

Reynolds was still for a moment, perhaps wondering if he'd just been belittled.

"Of course, he might've parked a mile away and walked to a bank or storage facility. Did your YouTube bot take that into account?"

Jake said, "Yes, it did, Stan."

Reynolds ignored the parry. He paced briefly, staring at the house. "All we need is one teeny-tiny bit of evidence linking Garr to Ivanov. Maybe the Russian gave him a present. A painting." He glanced at the digital murder board. "He's an artist, right?"

"No. A collector and art historian."

"All the more reason to gift him something. *Moscow at Night.* Or a landscape of Siberia. Maybe there's a shipping label. We find that and Ivanov's ghost is cooked."

"Goose," not "ghost," Jake thought. He suppressed an eye roll and said nothing, though Sanchez caught his expression.

"I think it's time to move in," Reynolds went on. "We can collect whatever evidence there is and lie in wait. Sneakily." He snapped his fingers.

Sanchez said patiently, "Heron scanned it. Lots of security outside and in. We're worried that there's a trip switch or something that will send a message to him that his house has been breached. And he'll blow out of town—maybe flee the country."

"To Russia. Then we'll get him at the border. Meanwhile, we'll have evidence on them both. Ivanov and Garr. RICO, conspiracy. I'm not worried about safes. We can always get into those. For now, I want all the devices in there." Pointing to the monitor that depicted the multiscreen version of Garr's house. "This is looking better by the minute. But keep in mind booby traps. They were popular during the Cold War."

Sanchez said, "We've been through as many internet purchase orders and other records as we can find, credit cards, debit cards. He's bought ammunition in the past six months, but no explosives or fertilizer or quantities of gasoline, anything else that would suggest a homemade bomb."

"Who's in charge there? I mean, tactical?"

"Liam Grange."

"Is he good?"

Another sigh from Sanchez. "Yes."

"Get him on the horn."

She hesitated.

"Agent Sanchez, who is running this organization?"

"You are, Stan."

It would be "sir" no longer.

He glared. "Then let's do it now. I want Garr's computers and phones. That's an order."

Then an idea occurred to Jake. But there was no way to explain. He straightened and looked at Sanchez, willing her to see his intensity.

"Heron?"

He responded with, "HTW."

"What's that you're talking about?" Reynolds asked. "HTW. Hostages Tactics Weapons?"

"Initials of an individual we've been working with," Sanchez said.

Jake said, "I need to talk to my source in private."

Sanchez seemed like she was about to object but thought better of it.

He paused on his way to the door. "Deputy Director Reynolds is right."

"Heron," Sanchez said, frowning, as if she couldn't believe what she'd heard.

"No. We need a tactical assault. How many people does Grange have?"

After a moment's hesitation she said, "A half dozen."

Heron said, "That's not enough. We need another ten or fifteen."

Drawing a satisfied smile from Reynolds.

Sanchez told him, "That'll take a half hour to put together."

"Do it," Heron said.

As he walked from the Garage, Reynolds, beaming, turned back. "The majority wins, Agent Sanchez. Democracy at work. As soon as you get those reinforcements to Garr's house, move in. And make sure there's a Russian translator there. *Spasibo!*"

CHAPTER 64

As he drove Selina Sanchez into the hills near Corbin Canyon Park, south of Tarzana, Damon was considering what lay ahead.

Thank you, Señor Picasso. I have come up with yet another variation on Serial Killing. I am on my way to *Guernica*!

He was captivated by the idea.

When it came to water lilies, Monet did the same painting over and over and over, 250 times. All the same, all different.

Variations on a theme was the bedrock of being an artist.

He pulled up into the driveway of an old house in need of paint, the yard overgrown. Small, though of two stories, with a gabled roof. In his youth he'd thought of it as resembling the house of the "Hansel and Gretel" witch.

Damon stepped out and looked around. There were no neighbors nearby and the few adjacent roads were empty. He opened the car door and led Selina out and up the front stairs, then punched the number into the padlock.

They stepped inside the dim place.

He smelled the familiar scent of laundry starch and clove (real clove, not chemicals from a spray bottle). Mold too, because this house had not been much occupied over the past few years. The single-family structure, on a scruffy one-acre lot, was fifty years old but, save for the style, might have been built last year. That was one thing about California, at least in the regions where snow didn't fall. Houses didn't age as fast as in, say, the Midwest or New England.

Also Miss Spalding, who'd inherited the house in her thirties, had taken exceptionally good care of the place. Most of the chairs and couches were covered in yellowing plastic.

One that was uncovered was the divan where the two of them would sit together and watch TV—an early model flat screen and huge for the time: fifty inches.

Thinking of all the movies he'd seen on it.

What was the first?

Friday the 13th, he believed.

Or maybe *Make Them Die Slowly*. An Italian horror flick that was truly terrible but that *did* offer up some delightfully gruesome death scenes.

Selina looked around. She was afraid, of course, but not as afraid as he would have liked.

That would change.

He was in the mood for a glass of milk, but he knew there was none fresh. That would have to wait until he was finished here. Two, three hours.

Picasso . . .

Growing yet again as an artist.

Today would see the first instance of Serial Killing 2.2.

2.0 was murdering to enjoy the mourning of families.

2.1 was further tormenting a grieving family by convincing a teen-ager that her parent was having an affair.

2.2 was not just murdering, but torturing someone to death and sending the delightful, filmed account of the victim's agony to their loved one.

His *Guernica* . . .

The horror that the family member felt would be exquisite and the only element still to work out would be somehow his witnessing that person watching the scenario in horror. There had to be a way. A hidden camera, perhaps.

He knew where Carmen Sanchez lived. Tristan Kane had given him the address. How hard would it be to hack into her security system to see the agent open the package with the thumb drive containing the video he was about to make. Kane could do it in an afternoon.

He glanced over at Selina.

Who looked pretty cocky at the moment.

This irritated Damon.

He decided to add thirty minutes to the hours of torture he had planned.

What about the screaming?

He'd forgotten to bring earplugs but maybe wadded-up tissue would work just as well.

Or he could gag her . . .

No, the screams had to be part of the show.

Tissue in his ears it would be.

"Who was she?" Selina asked, looking at the pictures of Miss Spalding on the mantelpiece.

Damon gave a brief laugh. "Are you trying to Stockholm me? You know what that is?"

"My sister's a cop. Besides everybody with a TV knows what Stockholm syndrome is. The emotional connection between hostage takers and their captives."

"And you're hoping it works the other way too. That if I tell *you* personal things, I'll be less inclined to . . . do what you're afraid I'm going to do."

"No, I don't think that at all. You're, like, a dead-eyed freak, and the last thing I want is to form any kind of connection with you. I'm just asking who's the lady in the picture looking at you in that kind of creepy way."

Damon stiffened. "Miss Spalding, my governess. And there was nothing creepy about her."

"No?" Sarcasm dripped from the word.

So, maybe Selina was aiming for the *opposite* of the Stockholm approach. She was trying to antagonize him, maybe so he'd make a mistake.

Or perhaps she figured he intended to torture her, so she was goading him to kill her immediately.

Not going to happen.

He knew enough about anatomy to make him an expert at creating many sources of pain in the human body.

He began to set up the two cameras, aimed at the chair where she sat: front angle and side. A thought occurred to him: Should he show the vid to Maddie Willis?

She was a killer. They were kindred souls. But was this a step too far? He'd have to see. Maybe he could bring up the topic tangentially. The last thing he wanted to do was alienate his newfound love.

Selina paid little attention to the preparation. "Where is Miss Spalding now?"

"Dead." The lighting wasn't quite right. He removed a lampshade.

Much better. Stark, which meant a perfect blending of form and substance.

"How did she—"

"I killed her."

After he figured out what Miss Spalding had done on his wedding day, he decided she had to die too.

His bride-to-be's death was no accident. He'd been suspicious from the start, never fully believing Felicia had slipped and banged her head on the edge of a swimming pool she swam in nearly daily and then conveniently fell into the water and drowned. The body is an amazing thing. The coughing reflex would have brought her around in seconds. Unless somebody was in the pool with her, holding her feet high.

Miss Spalding had murdered Felicia, slipping over to her house before her friends came for the hair and makeup, while Damon was at the venue.

Jealousy was the motive.

He should have known.

With a creased brow, his former governess had asked him, "Moving into a house of your own? The two of you? Without me, Little Pup? You really think you'll be happy?"

He had ignored her deliberate use of the pet name and didn't answer the question. He'd thought no more of it until a few days later when he was at the funeral with all the mourners. Everyone was dressed in black, except Miss Spalding, who wore her customary pale-gray outfit.

Tears had stung the backs of Damon's eyes—another unfamiliar sensation. He reached into his breast pocket to pull out a handkerchief. With his gaze momentarily diverted from the casket being lowered into the ground, he noticed Miss Spalding standing alone.

Clearly unaware anyone was watching, the corners of her mouth lifted briefly with the ghost of a smile.

Or had the fleeting expression been a satisfied smirk?

That was the first inkling, followed quickly by certainty, as he put the pieces together. Suddenly her choice of funeral attire made sense. Miss Spalding was dressed as if this were just another ordinary day—because she was not mourning a loss. To the contrary, she seemed pleased.

Damon's grief transmuted into cold rage as he planned his retribution. Going to the police was out of the question. With zero proof, he refused to sit through endless legal wrangling only to end up with an acquittal. Besides, the courts would never mete out the kind of justice he demanded.

Instead, he made a private vow to avenge his bride before the week was finished. He would have preferred the symmetry of doing to her what she'd done to Felicia—head trauma and drowning. But that would have been suspicious.

So, he opted for an electric dryer short in an old house without a ground-fault interrupt circuit. Electricians will tell you that 120 V will push you away from the source so it's rare to die by electrocution that way—from a lamp or toasters. But the 240 V of a dryer or electric oven?

It grabs you and doesn't let go until the muscles, including the heart, cease all function.

And that's how Hattie Spalding, who had murdered Felicia McNichol on Saturday, joined her in death the following Wednesday.

Four days later.

Setting in stone the pattern for his future murderous career.

Now, the cameras were ready.

As for Selina Sanchez's prolonged death, how should Serial Killing 2.2 unfold?

Thoughts of Miss Spalding gave him the idea of electricity. He could use house current, but that risked the inconvenience of tripping the circuit breaker. Better to schlep the car battery inside and connect lamp wire to the positive and negative and go at it.

Strip her, hook the negative lead to a toe and then touch the exposed copper strands attached to the positive wherever he wished.

Delightful . . .

But the battery was so heavy . . . he'd have to unbolt it. Too much work.

Any other ideas?

Ah, yes!

He recalled that Miss Spalding had a workbench downstairs in the basement.

His heart danced a bit at the memory, and he recalled a propane torch she'd bought to blister off paint.

Damon had been here recently and knew the red-and-black cylinder was still there.

He went downstairs to fetch it.

CHAPTER 65

Tristan Kane centered the crosshairs of the gunsight on where he knew the individual would appear from behind a building.

Unaware and vulnerable.

The weapon was a Hawk & Little Bullpup assault rifle with a sixty-round extended magazine. It had cost $14,000, but Kane didn't mind because he happened to own stock in the arms manufacturer.

"Come on, come on," he whispered.

And then the target appeared.

Kane watched Jake Heron scan the parking lot as he stopped walking.

Now . . .

A three-round burst from the Bullpup.

Every round struck its target. Blood spurted and Heron dropped. He twitched once.

And, why not? Kane let loose with another stream.

Now, the figure was still.

Kane, not a smiler, smiled now.

If only it had been real.

In his modest bed-and-breakfast two-roomer not far from Damon Garr's house, Kane was sitting in front of his Dell Alienware gaming computer with 64 GB RAM and a 24 GB Nvidia graphics card. The game he was playing was his own version of *Grand Theft Auto*. He'd scored the source code and hacked together some script that let him do deepfakes—swapping the faces of the characters in *GTA* for faces of those he wanted to shoot, bludgeon, stab, burn and blow up.

Jake Heron's avatar figured in several of his games.

So did Carmen Sanchez's.

To Tristan Kane, first-person shooter games were one of the finest creations in the history of . . . well, he was going to say the computer gaming world, but he had to expand that to one of the finest creations ever. He was too young to have played *Maze War*, the original *Wolfenstein 3D* (which put FPSs on the map) or the first *Doom*. But at eight or so he jumped on the bandwagon, and lost himself in *Homefront, Rainbow Six, Gears of War, Call of Duty, Far Cry* . . .

His favorite, though, was *Grand Theft Auto*, which started as a third-person shooter, but was now a first person. (And, yes, it was a shooter game but there were adventure and social simulation elements to it as well.) He did more than just kill prostitutes, police officers and passersby. He was active in the community. The Hawk & Little arms company was traded on the game's fictional stock exchange.

Kane could have made a million dollars a year on Twitch or another gaming channel, where people (and advertisers) paid talented gamers money while they sat on their asses and manned or womanned joystick and keyboard. But that would have meant killing only pixels. If Kane were to make a million dollars it would be from a *real* job—say, working for a hit man who needed help in breaking through his targets' security system.

Sipping herbal tea—chamomile—he reflected on what he loved about first-person shooters: they were in perfect harmony with who he had been at a young age. In a shooter game there was no delicacy, no propriety, no coddling.

Through your moves you could unapologetically destroy your opponent. Make them quiver, make them cry.

Make them dead.

And in *Mortal Kombat*, say, rip out their spines and their beating hearts.

Politeness and, by extension, mercy were a waste of time in the FPS world.

Worse, they were a show of weakness.

And in his real-life world too. This had always been the case for Tristan Kane. He spoke the truth and too bad if nobody liked it.

The meat, it's too salty. Your cooking sucks.

The dress, it's too tight. And yes, it makes your ass look big.

The sex was okay until you started faking your orgasms. Better for me if you just lie there and shut up.

I'm smarter than Dave Crenshaw, but he got an A. I know you're the teacher, but you're fucking him, aren't you?

The list of Kane's blunt observations was endless. And accurate.

Just like pulling the trigger in first-person shooters, Kane had spewed rapid-fire facts and destroyed with words people who were, to him, no different from faceless, expendable non-player characters in the games.

This philosophy informed him to his soul.

His skills took him into the world of computers and once there his outlook stood him in good stead. Unbound by propriety or the law or morality, he fell into hacking. At first for the fun of it.

Then for profit.

Setting up shop in the dark web, making a name for himself as a hired gun.

He liked that phrase. And chose handles to reflect it.

Hired gun . . .

A few years ago his online nick was "Ironsights," as in the notch and blade atop a rifle barrel. Then, more recently, he was "FeAR-15," a triple win, as it contained not only the name of the famed assault rifle, but also the word "Fear" and letters "Fe," the atomic symbol for iron, from which the first firearms were made.

And now, of course, "DR-one," the quiet deadly weapon of choice on today's battlefields (plus the twisted experimenting MD).

Whether he was hired to hack banks or crypto accounts, or to track down an elusive whistleblower a company wanted dead, he did the job efficiently, on time and with virtually no risk to his clients. Smooth sailing.

Until Jacoby Heron.

And so the real-life, blood-and-guts FPS game between the two continued. He had once thought of Heron as a thorn in his side, but that wasn't right. The man was far more dangerous. He was like one of those bullets he had once helped someone buy on the dark web—they contained a small charge of explosive.

How does it feel to kill . . .

A beeping came from Kane's smallest laptop. It was a soft sound but, to him, it blared like a Klaxon. He slid the rolling chair toward it and squinted. He was looking at seven windows on the screen, each depicting a security camera covering the front and interior of Damon Garr's house.

Well, shit.

Homeland Security Investigations and LAPD SWAT were moving up the front walkway and through the back garden.

No! Kane raged. How the hell had they found the man's identity?

And how would this affect his own reason for his involvement here in Southern California: to gain access to—yes, to intrude upon—Jake Heron and kill him?

Then he calmed and thought: Strategy?

The officers, armed with guns very much like the fictional Bullpups, were moving slowly, suspecting either armed resistance or a booby trap, neither of which was a threat.

He picked up one of his burners and sent a text to Garr, explaining his house in Malibu was compromised.

The man immediately texted back, the sloppy keyboarding suggesting utter panic, but Kane paid no attention. He could waste no time. He normally would have chained together proxies, but the officers were minutes away from breaching the door and searching the house. He began sending signals that wiped the information in Garr's hard drives and in the cloud. People think you hit the delete button and data on your computer disappears. But that's not the case. The data itself remains. A *wiping* program, on the other hand, does what a demolition company does in taking apart a house: dismantles the structure, board by board, before turning it into unidentifiable splinters.

Unfortunately, since that takes time, Kane would not be able to shred all Damon's data, but he would have the chance to destroy anything related to *himself.*

Which was all he really cared about anyway.

The bots had been released like hounds after foxes.

As he watched the progress, his anger began to grow once again.

Heron. He had to be behind it. He was the one who had identified Damon—and in doing so took him off the table as a weapon that could have been turned against the intrusionist and his likely girlfriend, Carmen Sanchez.

Thirty minutes later he was watching the police prowl cautiously through the house. He was calm. All the data mentioning him had been wiped.

Now, he could turn his attention to the question of how best to use their captive, Selina. One way would be to—

A voice behind him made his heart slam hard. "You really should have kept pinging the laboratory in Switzerland. But you didn't, so it had to be misdirection."

Kane shot to his feet and spun around.

Jake Heron stood in the doorway, lifted his arm and pointed a black device about the size of a stapler at him.

Heron did not threaten. He did not warn. Instead, he pressed a button with his thumb and fired two barbs into Kane's chest, sending him falling to the ground, wrapped in a fiery shroud of pain.

CHAPTER 66

Curious seeing your nemesis before you.

Surprising how much smaller they seem in real life.

But then baby copperheads can be more dangerous than their parents.

Jake was observing the groggy Tristan Kane gasping and moving slowly. Had he been completely still, Kane might be taken for dead, given his ashen pallor.

Wincing, breathing hard, gazing around the room, then looking back to Jake, who leaned against the battered desk in the battered room, whose key card lock had taken him half a second to defeat. The man could only stare at his captor, awash with confusion.

How Heron found this nest was an easy win. If Kane *were* the partner, as they speculated, he would be handling Garr's security. And that meant the instant he saw a takedown in Garr's house he would send signals to Garr's electronics to wipe the data.

Signals that Jake had quickly traced to the source.

Which was why he had told a confused Carmen that he supported Reynolds's plan to raid Garr's house.

As soon as that happened and Kane sent the wiping command, Heron sourced the signal's origin: this modest bed-and-breakfast near Garr's. And armed with a stun gun equipped to fire darts, he'd come to visit.

Jake had never told Sanchez about the device he'd cobbled together using batteries, a step-up transformer, an oscillator, wires, a couple of barbs and other odds and ends. He wasn't violating any laws by building a homemade stun gun. Using it, however, probably crossed a legal line.

Which was why he didn't plan to mention it. Or the stop he'd made in the HSI facility cafeteria for another piece of vital equipment.

Jake guessed that Kane had already figured out the why—and how Jake had traced him.

But there was surprise in his face still, and the reason for the reaction, Heron felt sure, was that the two men were alone. Kane was not in handcuffs, nor was he being read his rights.

What was that about? Where were the real Feds? DHS, HSI, FBI? The answer was simple. They weren't invited to the party.

This was between Jake and Kane alone.

Kane blinked again and looked around the cramped room. Then at his restraints. He sat in the desk chair. No official cuffs, but his wrists were firmly zip-tied to the upholstered arms in front of him.

Jake got straight to the most critical matter. "Now, Tristan, you and I could have quite the conversation, and we will, but now? We need to know where Garr and Selina are. And, yes, I know he has her. And that you know where. So. Tell me."

Kane looked him over with a half smile on his thin, pale lips. "Say, Jake, you working on that guilt about murdering those people in Chicago? You dream about body parts? It was quite the bomb, you know."

Jake was tempted to wipe the smirk off Kane's face by bantering in return, but he avoided that game. What's the point of one-upping the banteree? And if the lines were clunkers, the banterer himself ended up embarrassed.

"Where are they?"

"I don't know."

"Of course you do. This whole project works only if you and Garr are in regular contact. I looked at your phones and saw they're on self-wipe. It'll take me a day to get into them."

"I doubt that."

"You're right," Jake said, pretending to misconstrue him. "I could crack them in four or five hours." Which probably *was* a form of banter, but he couldn't help himself, and the dent in Tristan Kane's smugness made him glad to have done it. "But even that's too long. I'm feeling impatient today."

"I'm not saying a word."

"Where?"

Kane merely shook his head.

Jake gave it a moment, pushed away from the counter and paced slowly. He said in a cheerful voice, "UID."

Kane frowned. "User interface device. Mouses, trackballs, keyboards. What about them?"

"You hear the latest? Implanting wires in your brain, so you can *think* the cursor around the screen."

"I . . . I have. Yes. They don't work that well."

"Not yet, no. And then there's the system where your eyes control the cursor and the keys."

A slow nod. Kane looked around again, apparently growing more and more troubled about what Jake was up to, given there wasn't a single police officer present, and his nemesis was discussing computer science rather than reading him his rights.

"But the best way to talk to machines is the keyboard, don't you think? Good old QWERTY."

Referring to the first six letter keys in the alphabet lines of a keyboard.

Still keeping him off-balance, Jake asked, "How fast do you type?"

"Where's this going, Heron?"

"I myself am a solid hundred twenty words a minute, error rate of two words per hundred. And that's usually just a transposed letter or two. I'm not being modest, but when you keyboard twelve hours a day, your skill level *does* creep up, right? Come on, Kane. You've been doing this as long as I have. How fast?"

"Same, I guess, why?"

"Because I can't imagine how difficult it would be for someone to relearn how to keyboard after losing fingers."

And he lifted from his inside jacket the carving knife he'd borrowed from HSI's cafeteria.

"You fucking wouldn't."

"That was a waste of breath, Kane," Jake said. "Nobody knows I traced your signals here. Even Carmen Sanchez. I've zip-tied your arms so you can't move your hands more than a millimeter in either direction. I'm holding a knife that will cut through your fingertips with relatively little effort on my part. Something I will thoroughly enjoy doing. So in answer to your comment, yeah, I fucking would."

Kane scoffed. "They'll arrest you. You'll spend years in jail. Assault with a deadly weapon."

"Oh, forgot something." He looked around the room, noting a wrought iron desk lamp. He picked it up and, as Kane blinked in shock, flung it through the sliding-glass door opening onto a deck. Shards flew.

"What a terrible accident," Jake said, shaking his head. "I had a lead to you. I found you. But you fled and, tragically, tripped and fell into the door, shattering it. You lost two fingers. Or depending on your lack of cooperation with me, maybe three or four."

"Nobody's gonna believe that."

"There'll be so much blood, it'll seem credible enough. And besides, with your record, when it comes to whining about fairness in legal proceedings, not a soul in the world is going to care one bit about what you have to say, Kane."

He stepped closer, thumbing the razor-sharp blade.

"No . . ." Kane's eyes grew wide.

"Thumb, index, middle finger," Heron whispered. "Oh, and I have some trivia for you. Guess what part of the human body has the most pain-sensing receptor cells." He paused to allow time for Kane to process the implications. "You guessed it. Fingers."

Saying these words, Jake supposed, placed him firmly in banter territory. But as he gripped Tristan Kane's right wrist with his left hand and stroked his right index finger with the blade, Jake decided he didn't give a righteous shit.

CHAPTER 67

The three of them sped along the highway, Carmen at the wheel of her bulky but powerful Suburban.

Two passengers: one in person, one present virtually.

"You didn't really . . ." The voice coming through the FaceTime app was Frank Tandy's.

Heron, in the shotgun seat, said, "No. I just threatened. Tickled him a little with the tip of the knife. He didn't laugh."

She glanced his way and noticed his jaw tightened slightly, and she guessed he was feeling some regret that Tristan Kane had spilled Garr's location before the first phalange was snipped off. He'd misjudged her. Maybe he could have told her what he was up to.

She, of course, would never have sanctioned actual bloodletting.

But scaring the asshole?

Fair game.

Then Carmen lost interest, and she concentrated on driving. A natural behind the wheel, she liked rough roads. Trails and mountain paths.

And, as always, speed.

She hit 110 miles per hour and swerved into the left lane, slipped past a slow-moving camper and segued fast into the right once more, as the driver of the oncoming tractor-trailer yanked the air horn.

"Jesus," Tandy muttered from the device in Heron's hand. Then asked, "Where is she? Selina?"

Heron said, "Damon Garr had a governess. He didn't tell Kane much about her and I didn't have time to get the whole sordid story of their relationship. Garr uses her place as a safe house, Kane said. That's where he's got her."

It was now Carmen's turn to blare her vehicle's horn. This time the oncoming pickups pulled to the shoulder. Only two gave her the finger as she streaked past.

"Sanchez," Heron said through gritted teeth.

She grimaced and eased off the gas, remembering the motto her driver-training instructors had drilled into her when she was a new agent. "Arrive alive."

"Odds that he warned Damon?" Tandy asked.

Heron replied, "Claimed he didn't and there was no SIGINT on his phone or computer telling me he had. Might have been lying, but . . ." He shrugged.

In any event, they had done all they could—notifying local police about the Spalding house the instant Heron scored the address.

This was so very hard. Her sister's life was in jeopardy. It took every ounce of self-control she possessed to keep the speedometer below a hundred.

If anything happened to her little sister, Carmen would never forgive herself. She'd berated Ryan Hall for assuming Selina would stay home and wait for him, but hadn't she made the same mistake? If anything, her fault was far greater because they'd grown up together. Selina was smart, tough, fierce and determined. Never the type to wring her hands and let others handle problems.

In truth, it was one of many things she admired about her only sibling—and only remaining immediate family member. The thought brought another wave of dread.

She veered down a private road and announced, "We're here."

Heron said goodbye to Tandy and pocketed his phone.

Carmen skidded to a stop behind two local squad cars in front of the house that had been owned by Ms. Hattie Spalding, a former teacher and governess who had died a few years ago in a freak accident involving a defective electrical circuit. Damon Garr's Mercedes was here too, parked beside the house on the driveway.

The cruisers belonged to two local LA County Sheriff's deputies. They had exited their vehicles and were crouching behind them for cover.

WTF?

"Who's shooting?" Carmen called out. There'd been no reports of gunfire.

"No one, ma'am," one of them said. "But we heard the subject is a bad actor and figured he was barricaded inside because his car's still here. We were waiting for backup so we can secure the perimeter before going in."

The officers were following procedure. But neither of them had a sister trapped inside with a killer.

Without another word, Carmen drew her Glock and charged toward the house, calling over her shoulder, "Heron, you stay here!"

The first officer stood from his crouched position and shouted for her to wait. Then, a moment later, she heard their boots thudding up the steps of the old, shabby wood-frame structure.

Inside, she scanned the musty place, shelves filled with porcelain figurines, souvenir plates on stands, doilies and, inexplicably, old slasher movies on DVD. A lot of them. The deputies had decided to forgo protocol to back her up and were clearing the rooms as they made their way through the house, as Carmen did the same.

She broke from the kitchen into a study, called, "Clear. Main floor study." She turned and was not surprised to see that Heron had, yet again, disobeyed her orders. "We're not secure. Wait outside like I told you. Call Mouse. I want more backup."

He had just turned when a man's voice called out from a doorway in the kitchen. One of the deputies. "Found her! She's in the basement." A pause. "And you better hurry. There's a problem."

Carmen barreled down the stairs so fast she lost her footing and nearly fell on the bare cement floor. She fought to regain balance as her mind conjured horrific images of her sister on the brink of death.

Finally steadying herself, she saw Selina bound to a rickety office chair that tilted at a bizarre angle—one wheel was missing.

Selina lifted her head and blinked. She was alive. And without any apparent cuts or contusions.

Carmen lurched forward, desperate to free her sister from the duct tape securing her wrists to the arms of the chair. Carmen grabbed the SOG tactical knife clipped inside her waistband and flicked out the blade one handed.

"Hold still, mija," she said, and began slicing through the thick silver tape with the serrated steel edge.

As she worked to free her sister, an offensive—and unmistakable—odor drew her attention. Suddenly she grasped the nature of the "problem" the officer had mentioned.

Garr must have opened the valve to the natural gas line that fed the dryer or water heater. The unique stench of sulfur-tinged odorant filled the room.

Was she about to rescue her sister only to have the whole house blow them all to smithereens?

"Everyone, out," she shouted to the others. No one else needed to die.

"Think I'll stay."

She glanced up to see Heron, who had disregarded her orders to wait outside. Again. He began using his knife—with which he'd nearly amputated Tristan Kane's digits—to saw through the tape binding Selina's legs.

Both officers stayed put as well, and were working to smash open the door to the backyard, using only wooden planks. The door was metal, and using iron or steel tools risked a spark that would set off the gas.

Carmen decided to submit the cops for a commendation and reserve the ass-chewing for Heron.

"You'll be out in a second," she muttered to her sister as she cut the last strip of tape on her arms as Heron did the same for her ankles. Together they helped Selina up and pushed out the back door moments after the deputies had managed to bash it open.

Selina was unsteady on her feet at first, gaining momentum as they ran across the yard to be sure they were out of the potential blast radius.

When they finally stopped, one of the cops bent over, hands on his knees, sucking wind. "That asshole was going to gas her to death."

"Or blow the place," his partner said. "There's probably a pilot light on the water heater. When the gas got to that . . . kaboom!"

His final word reverberated through Carmen's mind like a death knell.

Kaboom.

The end of her little sister's life. The end of their family. The end of her world.

She locked eyes with Selina and saw the raw emotion that mirrored her own. It was a combination of anticipated grief. Mourning the loss of a lifetime of sisterly love that would never come to be.

Wordlessly, she and Selina flung their arms around each other and embraced for a moment before Carmen backed away and held her sister at arm's length, examining her for injuries.

Selina must have realized she needed to reassure her big sister. "I'm fine. But you need to get people to Christopher Fisher's place right away."

"They're there," Carmen said.

"He's the one who killed Dad." Selina paused. "Well, the one who paid that guy Sweeney to kill him. Fisher was the money-laundering client. And there's proof."

"Proof?" Carmen couldn't hide her shock.

"You know that fighting technique you taught me?"

Unsure where this was going, she said, "Systema."

Selina's expression was both fierce and triumphant. "I made a move on Sweeney. Knew he'd win eventually. He had a gun, after all."

Carmen struggled to keep the ice from her voice. "You fought a man with a gun?"

"Yeah, well, I figured if he wanted to shoot me, he would've done it right up front. So, I grabbed this ugly-ass statue and pretended to throw it at him. Only I made sure to hit the window. It cracked the glass."

Carmen grasped the significance of Selina's actions. "You activated the security system. It recorded everything."

"And I got Sweeney to tell me what happened with Dad and why Fisher wanted him dead."

Carmen stifled comments about how her little sister had put herself at risk. Like their father, Selina must have assumed she wouldn't survive and found a way to send a message to Carmen.

Unable to say any of this, she gave her a quick hug. Then she broke away to call Grange and request that he have his team secure the security hard drive at Fisher's.

She turned back to Selina, refocusing her attention on the fleeing suspect. "Now, Damon Garr, your kidnapper. Any idea where he went?"

"He made a call," Selina said with an even voice. "He was speaking softly, but I heard him talking to somebody about an airplane. He said, 'Executive airport, north of here.' Then something about Canada, and a wire transfer. Then he turned on the gas and ran out the door."

"Any idea which airport?"

"No."

Heron, who had been listening to the exchange, shot a glance at the pair of patrol officers standing nearby. Carmen could see his eyes narrow in thought. "Either of you shut the gas line off?"

"Me," reported the taller of the two.

Heron pursued, "How many twists of the valve did it take?"

"Not much." The cop frowned. "Maybe half a turn, I guess."

Carmen realized what her partner was getting at. This changed everything.

She turned to Selina. "Garr had no intention of killing you. He probably planned to until he heard we were onto him. Then it was all about escape."

Selina nodded knowingly. "Sure! He *wanted* me to hear the conversation so I'd send you guys in the wrong direction. The gas was just window dressing."

Carmen appreciated her sister's quick grasp of the facts. "Exactly, he's *not* going to an airport at all. He's driving. Well, to be accurate, someone else is driving him since his car's here."

"Mexico?" one of the deputies asked.

"Most likely." She gave Heron a meaningful look. He took the cue and pulled his tablet from his backpack, doubtless scanning for highway cams.

She said, "He won't be on the interstate."

"No," Heron agreed and found a camera on a two-lane highway that connected to others leading to the nation's southern border.

"Who the hell picked him up?"

Selina frowned. "There was something else. He got a call. I heard him answer it. Then he stepped away, outside, so I couldn't eavesdrop. So *that* one wasn't fake."

Carmen said, "If you didn't hear it, it won't do us any good."

"I didn't say that." Selina offered a smile.

"How do you mean?"

"The tone when he looked at caller ID and answered? And he said, 'Hey.'"

Carmen glanced at Heron before turning back to her sister. "It was romantic."

Selina nodded. "Exactly."

CHAPTER 68

Damon appreciated a beautiful woman who knew how to handle a fast car.

Maddie Willis wore shades and a baseball cap to keep her hair out of her face and gripped the wheel like an F1 driver on the track. He'd called her as he fled from Miss Spalding's house, after getting Tristan Kane's alert that his house in Malibu was being raided.

He thought again about the place.

Part of him was heartbroken, given the Demeter and all the other artwork he'd have to leave behind.

But there was no choice. Flight was his only salvation. Besides, he had plenty of hidden money. He'd settle somewhere out of the country—South America, probably—and begin his collection anew.

His avocation too.

Bludgeon, drowning, grave sites.

Bludgeon, drowning, grave sites . . .

They were barreling along one of the California highways—not a camera-rich freeway, of course—headed south. He glanced over at Maddie's profile as she whipped the vehicle through a curve. "You like speed."

"I dated a race car driver once," she said. "He taught me how to take a curve without losing velocity. You start on the outside edge of the roadway, then ease to the inside lane at the apex, then accelerate to the outside again." She gave him a wink. "He'd tell me, 'Go in slow and out fast—like sex.'"

Damn. Could she get any hotter? "I'm just glad you're putting distance between me and—"

He stopped short, unsure how to finish the sentence. He didn't want her to worry that an array of troopers would materialize in her rearview.

"I'll take care of you," she said. "Don't worry."

He began to relax. And was thinking maybe a miracle had happened—and he'd finally found the right woman. Not twisted like Miss Spalding, and not innocent like Felicia. No, Maddie was that perfect mix of sexy and cunning and homicidal that would complement his cold-blooded nature.

Overcome with uncharacteristic emotion, he turned to her. "Hey, a thought?"

"Hm?"

He was oddly reluctant to continue. It was as if a lot—a huge amount—was riding on the question. Then he blurted, "Let's run away together. Keep heading south to Mexico. Then figure out a way to get to a country without extradition."

Maddie didn't answer, and he began to worry that he'd stepped over some boundary. Then she said, "You know, I've always liked Latin America. Great food. Nice people. Beautiful villas."

After a moment she added, "As long as there's somebody to share it with."

"It'll take some time to access my accounts," he said, thinking in practical terms about life on the run.

But Maddie said, "I keep a go bag in my trunk. Fifty thousand. That'll tide us over till you can get your money." She looked at GPS on her phone and took the next left, onto a much smaller road, sand-swept asphalt.

"This is safer, back roads. I know a way to La Rumorosa."

He barked a laugh. Maddie was a constant source of surprise. He asked, "From here?" It was a long way to that dusty town in Sonora.

"I've had plans in place for a long time. I always thought someday the murders might catch up to me and I'd have to book on out of the country. Why not now?"

For a time, they chatted amiably, enjoying each other's company as the scenery blurred by. It was like their felonious pasts were forgotten, and they were just another couple.

Damon had an unfamiliar sensation he couldn't pinpoint. It took him a few minutes to realize that this must be what others referred to as . . . joy. He felt like they were a newlywed couple starting their lives together—their future as wide open as the road stretching before them.

Newlywed.

Some irony there. He smiled.

He wouldn't be alone anymore.

Maddie turned southeast, in the general direction of Sonora in Mexico, steering onto yet an even smaller and rougher road. "CHP troopers don't come this way often, and the local cops? Never."

She had made quite the study of her escape route.

He glanced around at the landscape that had become increasingly rugged and desertlike, filled with scrub oak and green-and-brown ground cover. No other cars, no homes.

As they bounded along the increasingly rough road, he joked, "Are we going to trade the car for a burro when we get to the border?"

She chuckled. "Not a burro, a *Bronco*—as in Ford. We need something that can go off road. I've got a contact here in Topanga."

She turned down a long drive and ahead he spotted a shed with a rusty tin roof. He held his questions as she drove through the open gate of a split rail fence and parked in the dusty front yard.

He saw no one and no structure that seemed to be fit for a residence.

"It's parked around back." She got out and beckoned him. "C'mon, I'll introduce you. If you're nice, he'll give you a beer. If he hasn't finished them all, anyway."

Who the hell was this contact of hers? A small part of him felt a splinter of jealousy.

Then told himself to chill. She was escaping with *him*, wasn't she?

He climbed out and joined her. They walked to the front door of the shed.

Several sharp raps with her knuckles were met with silence. She tried the handle, which twisted freely. "Looks like he might've gotten a head start on the beer," she said, glancing up at him. "Let's go roust him."

"Who exactly is this guy?"

"You'll see."

She pushed the door open and stepped over the threshold.

He followed her in, eyes straining to see in the gloom. He turned, looking all around. "I don't see anybody—"

Something crashed into the back of his skull. Hard.

Darkness engulfed him.

CHAPTER 69

She wasn't a bodybuilder, but rage had given her the strength to drag Damon's limp form out of the shed's rear door and into a shallow arroyo, where she dumped him, face up, and duct-taped his feet. Then his wrists.

Immobile. He couldn't climb out.

There was no Bronco, and no burro either. There was nothing in the shed but trash, a three-legged table and a washing machine that had spun its last load a decade ago. This property was as abandoned as property could be.

She squatted and looked down, studying him.

Damon groaned and tried to sit. Impossible.

He gazed at her, disbelief in his eyes. "No," he whispered. "I don't understand."

"You will."

"What the hell, Maddie?"

"Madison," she corrected, then enunciated the word slowly, changing the pronunciation, emphasizing each component. "Mad-eyes-on, get it?"

He blinked. "No."

"There have been eyes on you, Damon. My mad eyes. Watching you." She smiled. "And the last name, Willis. That comes out to Will-is. My *will is* for you to die."

"What the fuck?"

She saw fear creeping into his expression and laughed. Tormenting him was delicious.

"So that's not my real name. But the pun just came to me, and I went with it. 'Mad.' Although maybe *I'm* perfectly sane and the *world's* gone mad. Since a person, a *thing* like you, is part of that world."

He looked her over with an expression that was both contemptuous and wounded. "Okay, you racked your brain and came up with something clever. Good. There's a reason. Please . . ." His voice cracked. "Please, help me out. We can talk this through."

"Partly right. I'll talk. You listen."

His expression changed to one of bewilderment as he tried to piece it together. This was the moment she'd been waiting for. The moment when she could finally speak her truth.

When she could confront the monster.

His brows drew together. "But why are you doing this?"

"Notice I hit you over the head with a rock?"

He simply stared.

"Because that's what you did to my brother when you murdered him last Saturday." She leaned in close. "My real name is Lauren Brock."

CHAPTER 70

Jake wasn't great at delivering bad news, but sometimes it couldn't be avoided.

Like now.

Sanchez, who had lifted her cell phone to her ear, lowered it. "I know that look," she said. "What's wrong?"

Selina was standing beside her older sister. Both women gave him their full attention.

He checked his tablet one more time. Nothing had changed in the last two seconds. "I just linked up with the SHIT detail. Lauren Brock was moving south-southeast from Tarzana."

"What?" Her eyes went wide. "Near the Spalding house. When?"

"About twenty minutes ago, she pulled into a parking lot and picked up a passenger."

Sanchez narrowed her gaze. "Did this passenger happen to match Damon's description?"

"Yes. Well, Sanchez, you read it right. Lauren does have something going on."

"Never guessed this, though. Man."

She started to raise the phone again. "Now that we have probable cause that Lauren is aiding and abetting after the fact, we can pull out all the stops."

He held up a hand to get her attention before she called the surveillance team. "They lost her."

This was the bad news.

"No." She lowered her head briefly.

"They were on a highway, headed south. The team figured they were making a run for the border, and would eventually hit the 5 or the 405, so they called ahead to all the checkpoints and backed off a bit."

Sanchez groaned. "But Lauren took an exit ramp somewhere."

He nodded. "They've narrowed it down to two possible roads, and they've split up to check both out."

Sanchez jabbed her cell phone's screen.

"Mouse, you're on speaker. You heard?"

"Yeah, Lauren's disappeared, and she may have Damon with her."

"We've got probable cause on an A and B. Probably headed for Mexico, but they disappeared. Put out a BOLO and tell CHP and Border Patrol. Use the latest data from SHIT. It can't be more than ten minutes old."

"I'm on it."

A moment later, Mouse added, "Done, Carmen. But I don't get it. Why is Lauren Brock helping someone who killed her brother?"

"Oh, she's not helping him. She's going to murder him. I sympathize, but what she's done? It's premeditated. That'll get her a life sentence."

CHAPTER 71

Damon's head was still throbbing from the blow. His thoughts were clouded, and he struggled to make sense of the whole thing.

"I don't understand—Lauren . . . Brock?"

She peered down at him. "You didn't go to the wedding, did you? No, you just went to the hotel and waited for a chance to find a victim—my brother, it turned out—alone after the reception ended. So you never saw the wedding party."

True. He'd caught glimpses.

Bad music and worse toasts . . .

Hadn't paid much attention. He just wanted the bride and groom alone. He'd thought of killing the bride but decided Allison's bereavement would be more exquisite than Anthony's.

"I was a bit persona non grata," she continued, "and so I wandered off—to the upper garden. I didn't see you attack him. I didn't even know it had happened until later. But I did see you wearing latex gloves and acting suspicious as hell. Then I heard the screams and sirens. I went down to the koi pond and saw him." The last word was a whisper.

"And I saw you there too. In the crowd, watching. Everybody was shocked. But not you. You were almost smiling. Who the hell were you? Why had you killed him? I was about to tell the police right then, but I changed my mind. Decided I wanted you for myself. After you left, I got your license plate and paid a private eye to give me your name and address. Then you became my project. I started following you, trying to figure out what you were about."

"The blue car," Damon gasped, some from the shock, some from a parched throat.

"Oh, you saw me?" She lifted an eyebrow. "It's a junker of mine. I mostly drive a white Camry, but that day, I wanted something not connected to me." She was sweating too and wiped her brow with the back of her hand. "Damon Garr . . . You were a question mark. A professor of art, solitary and pretty damn strange. I was trying to figure out your fate when I saw you again. At the funeral! I went to say goodbye to my brother—keeping some distance from Allison and the others. Non grata, remember? And there you were. Just like watching the people at the koi pond where Anthony died, you were watching the mourners. That fucking half smile on your face! Why on earth? To gloat? I had no idea." A faint scoff. "You have me to thank for your escape, by the way."

"What?"

"The hearse. You think it moved by divine intervention? No, it was *my* intervention. I needed you free from custody."

He struggled to keep up with her logic. "For revenge. It was that important to you?"

She stretched and looked around the deserted farm, the shed, the broken posts and rails of the fences, the chassis of an old tractor sun-bleached from red to pink. "Revenge. You killed the man who saved my life." Her eyes snapped back to his, the anger inflating the sorrow and dismay and fear that seized him. "I lied about killing my rapist, but the assault was real, and I never quite recovered. Therapy was bullshit, but I liked the meds, and then when the doctors wouldn't prescribe them anymore, I went out on the street. Lost my job—and to keep myself supplied, I sold the one thing I could."

Maddie—Lauren—started to pace. He was twisting his hands in the tape bindings to see whether he could loosen them. No luck.

"My first john was my dealer," she said matter-of-factly. "He trained me, then sent me out to work off the drug debt. He kept me supplied, and I kept him solvent.

"I found out that if you're rich, people say you have a *substance-abuse issue*." She air-quoted the phrase. "But if you're poor, they call you a junkie." Her lips lifted in a smile that held no humor. "That was me. Now you see why Allison wanted to hide me in a broom closet at the wedding?

"Then I hit bottom this spring. One of the working women in our circle died, a friend of mine. A john punched her. Some argument about money. She hit her head and died. Guess what? He never got arrested. She's dead and he waltzes away. That's when I realized how my life would end if I didn't do something. So I went to see Anthony."

She slowed and leaned against a fence rail. "He had a plan that would save me, and it was going to happen when he got back from his honeymoon. The one he never took. So I lost twice. The brother I loved . . . and a chance for a new life . . . I have nothing, Damon. A boring job, a cheap rental. That fifty thousand dollars? Yeah, I wish.

"You were going down. But I had to figure you out first, so I let you talk me into going to your house. And I sure got an eyeful in that weird den of yours. All that art full of sadness and misery. Then you tell me you're an artist who finally found his true medium, but you wouldn't say what it was.

"Well, I figured it out when I remembered you at the funeral with that creepy smile. You're a sick fuck who gets his jollies watching people grieving. My brother's death was nothing to you. You could have killed Allison. You could have killed anybody. It was just a way for you to create a bunch of mourners to prey on."

He felt her words as body blows, as welts from a whipping. Yet, it was true. She had just defined Serial Killing 2.0.

And it was all shattered, the perfect union they had. All that remained was an abiding sorrow. Far worse than what he'd felt when his fiancée died.

He whispered, "Everything about you was so perfect. We were made for each other. But it was a fucking trick. You created the perfect woman for me. And then you killed her."

She'd turned him into a mourner, just like he'd done with Serial Killing 2.0.

"How does it feel, Damon? Shoe. Other foot."

Still, something didn't add up. "But I saw you half murder that man."

"Ah, you're so gullible, Damon."

He inhaled at the stinging words.

"You saw somebody I paid a thousand dollars to. Somebody I knew from the old days. We followed you to that address in Fullerton, whatever the hell you were doing there—spying on that girl, I guess. And faked the attack. He got hit a few times, mostly I missed. We had a baggie of fake blood. He's an addict. He needed money. I needed a victim."

Studying him once again. The way he might study the *Lamentation of Christ*.

"You know, Damon, we're like opposite sides of the same coin. Your medium is grief, but mine is revenge." She paused while her words sank in. "You could call us grave artists. You enjoy people standing around a grave. I'm going to enjoy burying you in one. Only I do it for justice. You're just like any other second-rate sociopath."

Tears stung in the corners of his eyes.

She noted this with apparent satisfaction.

"I'm sure that's a tough thought to live with. But you're not going to have to endure it for very long." She picked up a rusty shovel that rested on the ground nearby and with the joy of a devoted gardener began to scoop dry, sandy earth onto his body.

CHAPTER 72

Carmen had barely finished dealing with one crisis and she was already barreling headlong into the next.

Selina was safe, but now a killer was getting away.

Two killers, she reflected. Damon Garr and Lauren Brock—if she'd finished her mission to murder him.

Carmen had left her sister with Ryan Hall, taking Heron with her as she raced to the SUV to help in the search. While she drove toward Lauren Brock's last known geolocation, Heron had gotten Mouse back on the phone to coordinate communication between the satellite, CHP, Customs and the SHIT detail.

And, of course, the tireless Declan.

She had the pedal to the floor, and for once Heron wasn't telling her to slow down. She wasn't sure if it was a sign of the level of crisis they were dealing with or if he'd finally gotten used to her driving.

It was then, rounding a curve, that the white Camry came speeding right for them, over the centerline and forcing Carmen to steer onto the shoulder, which ended in a hundred-foot drop into a rocky arroyo.

Carmen gasped but controlled the skid expertly, missing the edge by inches.

Heron swore under his breath.

Back onto the faded asphalt and braking fast.

"Where'd you learn to drive like that?" he asked, as she made a quick three-point turn.

A pause. "Frank."

"Tandy?"

"It's how we met. He teaches the tactical driving course for LAPD, and the Bureau and DHS sometimes do in-service training in Los Angeles when it's not practical to go across the country to FLETC."

Peering over the side and the rocky gulf that might have been their grave, he said, "I'll have to thank him."

"Call it in," she instructed and hit the accelerator once more, sending up a plume of dust and gravel and tire smoke behind them.

Heron tapped in the last dialed number—Grange. The tactical team leader picked up at once, and Heron told him where they were and that they were in pursuit of Lauren Brock.

Grange agreed to send a tac team to cut her off and alert the highway patrol.

Lauren had the more agile vehicle, but Sanchez was the better driver, and she narrowed the distance.

"Heron," she said, frowning. "You see Garr?" She didn't think there was anyone in the passenger seat.

"No. She's alone. He's already dead."

After a longstanding moratorium on capital punishment in California, the death penalty had been reinstated, but only in special circumstances. This situation wouldn't qualify, but there were those who strongly advocated expanding the list of crimes justifying the ultimate punishment.

Carmen maneuvered the SUV through a series of tight turns and was soon on the Camry's tail. The Suburban's blue-and-white grille lights were flashing, and she could see Lauren glance into her rearview.

Lauren accelerated, and her car surged ahead on a straightaway.

Carmen caught up again when the road began to twist once more, and Lauren had to fight to control the vehicle. Carmen bleeped the siren.

Lauren didn't slow in the slightest.

Until they rounded a curve where the road was blocked by Grange's big tactical SUV and two CHP cruisers.

In addition to Grange, two of his agents and two men in highway patrol uniforms stood beside the vehicles, weapons out.

Lauren skidded to a stop.

Carmen braked and slid sideways, coming to rest across the road, blocking the Camry in. Canyon walls were on either side. Lauren wasn't going anywhere.

She climbed out, unholstered her weapon and approached. She gestured Heron to stay back, and he stopped about twenty feet from the Camry.

Carmen checked the back seat. Empty.

"Engine off, Lauren. Pop the trunk."

She did as instructed.

With a click, the lid lifted.

Garr wasn't inside.

"Get out," Carmen said. "Keep your hands where I can see them."

A pause, and Lauren slowly climbed out. Grange approached, along with his men and the CHP officers. They covered her while Carmen stepped close and frisked her. No weapons.

"Where is he, Lauren?"

She pointed her chin toward the desert.

The gesture covered about a hundred square miles.

"Is he dead?"

"Maybe."

Which could mean any number of things.

"Tell me, Lauren."

"No."

"You'll go to jail for the rest of your life. With these aggravated circumstances, there'll be no possibility of parole. You'll never see the light of day again."

Lauren's eyes became wild. "Why should I care? He took my brother away from me. The only person who lifted a hand to help me. I'm an addict and no one else gives a shit."

Carmen sensed waves of pent-up emotion rolling off her. This was clearly the tip of a very large and jagged iceberg hidden beneath the surface.

"So what you told me before, in the interview room. It was pretty much the story."

A nod.

"I'm sorry," she said. "Terrible." And in truth her heart went out to the young woman. "But it's premeditated murder."

If Garr was in fact dead.

Maybe . . .

"Sometimes you have to make sacrifices, Agent Sanchez. Whatever the consequences. Haven't you ever felt that way? I'll bet you have."

Carmen's mind instantly made the leap to her father's murder and the fact that her sister had very nearly been killed today. How would she have reacted if that had happened and she were confronting the killer?

She wanted to tell Lauren that she would have been completely professional under similar circumstances, but the words stuck in her throat.

Lauren studied her closely. Then her eyes flashed with understanding. "Exactly."

CHAPTER 73

Damon tried to control the panic.

The claustrophobia was like a poison in his soul.

And how cruel Maddie . . . no, Lauren had been . . .

She might have buried him alive completely. It would have been a horrific death, but a short one. How long can the body survive without oxygen? A few minutes tops.

But the monster hadn't been so kind. She'd buried him up to his head, then stuffed a stinking oily tube in his mouth, something from an old car. And then continued the burial process, covering the rest of his face.

He gagged and nearly puked. That would be the end. He controlled it.

He tried to lift his knees. No. He was under several feet of earth.

It might as well have been concrete.

Breathe out, breathe in.

He tried to scream, but this stole precious oxygen, and what was the point anyway? The abandoned buildings looked like no one had been there for years.

Breathe out, breathe in.

A wisp of air, but not enough.

The panic subsided for a moment. Then returned.

How could this be happening? It was like torturing Michelangelo to death. Rembrandt.

He was a genius. He was special.

Damon Garr had known it was true, from the moment Miss Spalding had come to the house and laid eyes on him.

"You're not like everyone else, are you? No, no . . . You're special. I think I'll call you 'Little Pup.' I don't mean a puppy dog. I mean a fox. Their babies are called kits or pups. And that's you, Damon. You're smart, you're clever. And you're born to hunt, aren't you? I can see it in your eyes. Can I call you that, 'Little Pup'?"

"I guess."

"Give Miss Spalding a hug."

She squeezed him so hard he could barely breathe.

Like now.

The panic unfurled like a snake within him. He screamed again. Dirt trickled into his mouth. He choked.

He shivered.

He began to cry.

More dirt trickled down.

And between the waves of panic he realized an irony. Maddie had turned the tables in more ways than one. She was killing him the way he had killed—a blow to the head and drowning. Though he would drown not by water but by earth and sand.

No . . .

But nobody understood . . .

He was special.

He was the Little Pup who had created Serial . . . Killing . . .

There was no light, of course, but behind his closed eyes one darkness became a different kind of darkness.

Two.

Point.

Oh.

And just as consciousness slipped away, he heard, or believed he heard, a sound. A chunk, chunk. Maybe his heart was giving out.

Then pressure on his leg, and pressure on his belly, on his groin.

And through his closed lids, he was aware of a haze of light.

More dirt trickled into his throat, and he began to gag in earnest.

Then the breathing tube was snatched away, and he felt hands on his body. Two, then four.

Gripping at his clothes and his hair and tugging hard. Pulling him to the surface.

He emerged from his grave, pulled up by Carmen Sanchez and Jake Heron and the huge officer he remembered from the Brock funeral. They rolled him onto his side, where he spat the sand and pebbles and dirt from his mouth and coughed dust from his lungs.

He glanced around him.

There stood Lauren Brock—no longer Maddie Willis—her hands cuffed behind her. She stared down at him as if instead of his body, the officers had just unearthed some thousand-year-old bones from an ancient site of human sacrifice.

A minor curiosity.

And nothing more.

CHAPTER 74

Carmen decided that Damon Garr did not look like a man who had just been rescued from a shallow grave.

Oh, the clothes were torn and dusty, the face was streaked with mud from where sweat met dirt. But the eyes. There was something eerily—and troublingly—despondent about them. As if he hadn't been rescued at all, but had died in the ground. And what they'd pulled out was simply a sorrowful ghost.

Human remains . . .

He was sitting in the back of Grange's HSI truck. A medical team had checked him out, given him some oxygen and doused cuts on his arms and neck with antibiotics. In a half hour he'd be processed in Central Booking and begin his journey along the road of incarceration.

She heard his voice through the partly lowered window.

"Agent Sanchez?"

She stopped and walked over to him.

"Where is she?" He was looking around.

"Lauren?"

"Yes."

The woman in question happened to be sitting in the back of a nearby cruiser, but Garr couldn't see her. A fact that he clearly found extremely distressing.

Sensing an opportunity, Carmen said, "Does this mean you're willing to waive your rights and talk to me, Damon?"

He seemed to debate whether he should give what would be an incriminating statement in exchange for one simple fact—how far away from him was the woman he'd grown obsessed with?

After a long moment, self-preservation won out. "No," he whispered.

"Do you want more water?"

He shook his head and sorrow veiled his face once more.

Carmen left him and walked to the CHP vehicle where Lauren Brock sat. She was still cuffed, but the back door was open.

Heron stood beside her.

Carmen crouched down. "Hey."

Lauren's eyes were on the horizon.

"I'll get you her number," Carmen said quietly. "The therapist. I'll make sure you can get access to her, okay?"

Lauren nodded. "She helped your sister?"

"After our father died, she took it hard. Real hard. I got her into grief counseling."

For some reason, that phrase elicited a blink of surprise.

Carmen added, "The doctor's the best. And she can set you up with addiction counseling too."

Lauren's head lowered. "Anthony was paying for rehab. I can't afford to—"

"A certain percentage of her clients are pro bono," Carmen cut in. "I checked, and she has an opening."

"I guess I should ask . . ." Lauren cast a glance toward the arroyo grave.

"About what?" Heron asked.

"I mean, what I did there. With him."

Carmen looked over the forbidding landscape. "You know, Lauren, in this line of work, it's all about facts. My world revolves around them. The gears only grind with the grease of facts."

Lauren seemed confused.

Carmen explained. "I'm known for my labored metaphors."

"She is," Heron agreed.

"But sometimes you see the results and you don't know what facts led there," Carmen went on. "Maybe there are five or six different sets of facts that could all fit. And our job is to find out which is the right one." She gave Lauren a thoughtful look. "Dr. Heron and I work with someone named Declan and one of his favorite expressions—"

"Still rather say 'its' favorite expressions," Heron cut in. Always reluctant to personify hard drives and software.

Carmen couldn't resist a chuckle. "A favorite expression is, 'It's logical.' That's essential to Declan. Logic. And I think the most logical thing is for you to be honest about everything that happened." She drove the point home. "That means *everything*. Leave nothing out."

"I don't understand."

"You'll be charged with abduction, battery, assault and attempted murder. But there are extenuating circumstances. You've never committed any violent crimes before this, although you've certainly been the victim of one. In this case, the person you assaulted murdered your brother, but in the end you decided against killing him. Those aren't legal defenses, but the prosecutor can take that into account. I'll talk to them. I'm going to recommend a suspended sentence or probation and counseling for you." She narrowed her eyes. "If they go for it, you'll have to stay clean."

"I have been. For months. And that'll continue. I promise."

If nothing else, the threat of decades behind bars should provide Lauren with all the incentive she needed to stay on the path to recovery.

Heron added, "Every day you're free and Garr's in prison is a victory. Take strength in that and your brother's faith in you."

Lauren's eyes welled. "You think I have a shot? In court?"

"Oh, yeah." Heron gestured toward Carmen. "If she vouches for you, it'll go a long way." He hesitated a beat before adding, "I know from personal experience."

Carmen cut him a quick glance. Of course, he'd been speaking of the time she'd put her reputation on the line for him, though that was not for Lauren to know.

"Thank you," Lauren whispered.

Carmen nodded, stood and started back to her Suburban, accompanied by Heron.

The cases against Damon Garr and Lauren Brock had been closed.

And yet one more remained.

CHAPTER 75

Christopher Fisher sat in the stifling West LA Community Police Station detention center interview room, listening to his shackles jingle as he fidgeted in the hard metal chair.

Fisher was reflecting that he had seen death—and he knew there was no dignity in it.

Especially when the person who had ordered that death was one Marco Mezzo.

The man called the West Coast Don was known for coming up with creative wet work that served two purposes: eliminating a soul he wanted eliminated. And instilling fear in others.

He was also known for announcing the forthcoming demise by arranging for someone to approach the victim and kiss them on each cheek. Mezzo called the gesture the "kiss of death"—a bit obvious, but the mobster was a literal man in a literal business. Once the gesture was delivered there was no stopping the sentence from being carried out.

And it just so happened that Mezzo was Fisher's boss.

So the trim, handsome, brown-haired Fisher knew he would not be cutting any deals, turning state's evidence or ratting out Mezzo's organization in any way. Better to serve a couple of decades at Club Fed than be disemboweled in his bed one night.

Mezzo was patient. He'd been known to spend years hunting down someone who had informed on the company. Fisher recalled one such former associate who'd been foolish enough to draw attention to himself while in witness protection. And Mezzo got wind of it.

The next day, the man was leaving the supermarket when a young woman dropped her grocery bag in the parking lot. He stopped to help her, and she gave him a peck on each cheek, no doubt surprising him with her gratitude for a simple courtesy.

That same night the man had been fed to a swarming horde of rats. While he was alive.

Fisher was one of several employees forced to watch the video before it was destroyed. The footage included what the man must have believed was a chance encounter in the parking lot, but was in fact a display of power and ruthlessness.

With those images burned into his gray cells, Fisher never thought for a moment of betraying Mezzo or anyone else in the company.

Which was why Roberto Sanchez had to die. The financial adviser had been too good at his job. He'd spotted irregularities in Fisher's bookkeeping and was asking a lot of questions.

Fisher couldn't go to Mezzo for help. If the boss found out he'd been sloppy, well, that would be nearly as bad as intentionally betraying him. His death might not be so grisly as being a rat entrée, but it would come just the same.

The kiss, the shuffle of footsteps behind you, the cocking gun, the slicing blade.

Rats . . .

So Fisher had trolled the dark web to find someone local to fix the problem. Unfortunately, Sweeney knew who Mezzo was, and began blackmailing Fisher. If Sweeney didn't get regular payments, he threatened to let the boss know that Fisher had botched the money-laundering operation and, worse yet, he'd covered up his incompetence and lied to Mezzo about it.

This had been going on for three years, and Fisher had already suffered a mild heart attack due to the stress. Hiring another hit man to kill Sweeney wasn't an option, so Fisher had simply sucked it up every time the man had driven to his house in that damned red pickup truck—which Fisher had paid for—to take another payment.

Now he was finally free of one burden only to find himself crushed under the weight of another. Mezzo would not be pleased at the latest turn of events.

Club Fed was starting to look like a haven.

A bead of sweat began to trickle down from his scalp. Reflexively, he moved to mop it away, only to have the heavy chains stop his arm.

He glanced up at the two-way mirrored glass in the interview room. "This is bullshit," he called out. "Where's my lawyer?"

A couple of hours ago, he'd arrived home to find cops of every stripe and flavor crawling all over the place.

Well aware they wouldn't find anything incriminating at his residence, he stepped out of his vehicle and started asking questions.

Instead of answers, he got a set of steel bracelets and a ride to the police station in the back of an LAPD patrol car.

A detective had read him his rights before explaining that someone had shot and killed Sweeney in Fisher's house, making it a crime scene. During the investigation, they recovered a home security recording in which Sweeney told Roberto Sanchez's younger daughter that Fisher had hired him to kill her father because the man had discovered a money-laundering scheme.

Well, fuck . . .

As soon as Fisher knew he was being charged with solicitation to commit murder, and maybe RICO violations, he asked for counsel. The detective had provided a phone, and Fisher had left an urgent voicemail with a defense attorney known for handling high-profile cases. Jonathan Hamilton had even successfully represented Marco Mezzo in the past.

If you were in serious trouble and you had money, Hamilton was the go-to. Fisher knew he'd be in good hands, but the wait was unnerving. They'd taken his phone and his watch, so he was guessing at how long he'd been cooling his heels. If the LAPD was messing with his head, it was working.

He glanced up at the viewing window again, wondering what the cops and the Feds were doing in there. After he'd placed the call to Hamilton, they'd immediately stopped questioning him. Fisher wasn't sure how, but he felt certain the famous lawyer would end his incarceration quickly.

The man's nickname was the "Miracle Worker."

CHAPTER 76

Standing in the cramped observation room, Carmen looked from Heron to the prosecutor, Jessica Cohen, a solidly built, no-nonsense woman with short, curly black hair. Carmen had seen her smile only when the jury came back with guilty verdicts, which almost always happened when she was presenting a case.

Carmen said, "I know Hamilton. He's going to demand witness protection. Fisher offers us a few low-level assholes, and he gets a new identity. How can I tell my sister that our father's killer will be settled in a picket fence neighborhood somewhere to enjoy his life because he's scummy enough to have helped even scummier people commit crimes?"

Cohen scoffed. "Don't worry. We're not going to roll over for him."

Carmen, who had arrested her share of dangerous people over the years, had heard such promises before. "Don't handle me, Jessica. He's got to go down. All the way, for everything. No deflated counts, no queen for a day."

The prosecutor seemed to bristle. "Not going to happen, Carmen."

"Find somebody else to dime out Mezzo. He's an asshole, but he's not part of this case. It's State versus Fisher for Roberto Sanchez's murder, and money laundering. End of story."

Cohen said, "Let's just wait for Hamilton to get here."

"Did you really say that? Did I hear you right?" Carmen said bitterly. "See? There? He's already got his foot in the door and he's not even here. I can smell WITSEC already."

The prosecutor didn't hesitate. "You're jumping the gun."

Carmen knew a few things about Jessica Cohen, who had an outstanding reputation but had not been able to secure the top spot in the district attorney's office.

A big win against somebody like Mezzo would go a long way in making that happen.

Cohen flushed and started to say something when the intercom buzzed. She pressed the button.

"Mr. Hamilton's here to see his client."

Her response was crisp. "Show him to the interview room."

Carmen turned to watch Jonathan Hamilton enter, set his briefcase on the cement floor and introduce himself. As slick as they come, Hamilton faced the one-way mirror, not to acknowledge that he knew they were being watched but to make sure his hair was perfectly coiffed. He frowned, smoothed a stray lock and then turned to his client.

"I'd shake your hand, Counselor," Fisher said, "but as you can see . . ." He trailed off, lifting his hands as far as he could in the restraints. He let out a nervous chuckle.

"That's okay," Hamilton said in a soothing tone. "I'll handle the social pleasantries." He leaned forward to kiss Fisher on each cheek.

It was a strange old-world gesture.

And the greeting did more than surprise Fisher. He blinked in what appeared to be horrified shock.

A moment later the money launderer's eyes widened. Then his face reddened. He began to gurgle as his hands formed claws, clutching at the air—unable to reach his chest. The clink of the chains was audible even in the observation room.

Hamilton stepped back, evidently stunned.

"Shit. He's having a heart attack." Cohen raced to the internal phone, hitting a button and summoning EMTs.

Carmen and Heron ran into the room and began CPR, soon to be relieved by a guard and then two paramedics.

After Fisher was wheeled out to a waiting ambulance, Carmen and Heron cornered Jonathan Hamilton, who voluntarily submitted to questioning, as well as forensic swabs.

Carmen was concerned the attorney had administered some sort of toxin during their brief contact, but there was no trace of anything on him or his client.

A short time later, Carmen called her sister to deliver the news that Christopher Fisher had been pronounced dead on arrival at the hospital.

"From what the emergency department doc said, he had an acute myocardial infarction," she told Selina. "Apparently, he had a history of heart trouble and was taking medication. The doc thinks he became highly stressed."

After a long pause, Selina said, "After what he did to us, is it poetic justice that he died of a broken heart?"

Carmen wasn't sure, but she'd take poetic justice over no justice at all.

CHAPTER 77

"Professor Heron?"

Jake, the first of the team back from the Fisher incident, was climbing from his SUV in the parking lot outside the HSI building.

He was looking at the somber man in a suit that matched his demeanor: dark gray. He was large, a bit pear-shaped, and the tension in the cloth gave him wrinkles radiating from the crotch.

"Yes."

"I'm Tony Horowitz, California Highway Patrol Special Investigations." A badge appeared.

Jake lifted an eyebrow.

"Professor Heron, have you heard from your mother lately?"

Not even trying to guess what this was about, he said, "Not directly. But yesterday she came by my apartment in San Francisco. My niece, Julia, is staying there while I'm down here on assignment."

"This I-squared thing. Yeah. We've heard about it." He looked at the Garage, which was from the outside the very definition of a dumpy, discarded, well, *garage*.

"Did she have a conversation with your niece?"

"Julia was out. My mother left a message on the security system."

"What did she say?"

"Just that she wanted to see me and that she'd be in touch later," Jake said. "She didn't leave a number or say where she was staying. What's this about?"

Horowitz said, "I'll explain. We know your mother and father, Gary Heron, have been involved in an organization known as the Family."

"The cult, right. They have been for years."

"Do you know much about the group?"

I contributed to it for my birthday.

A special day . . .

But Jake said only, "They didn't share anything. I think they wanted my brother and me to be involved, but neither of us, even when we were kids, were joiners. They gave up."

"You know the name Bertram Stahl?"

"He was the founder. Maybe he's still the head."

"He is, yes. He and members of the Family have shown up on our radar from time to time. But Stahl was smart, and nobody in the Family was ever convicted of any crime."

"No," Jake said, "it was more a personality cult than organized extortion or kidnapping. Stahl was like a secular messiah. I think he just wanted followers to worship him. The cult begged for money and sold crap online. And the proceeds went into his pocket."

"Well, for some reason, he decided to change direction. He became fascinated with the end of the world. A doomsday thing."

"Not uncommon with cults, but the leaders usually have some explaining to do when the deadline comes and goes and the world's still here."

Horowitz gave a smile. "We heard they were stockpiling guns, stealing food and supplies, vandalizing government facilities and utilities, so we opened a case. We scored an informant inside, and they told us what Stahl was doing. We got enough for RICO and conspiracy charges. We raided the cult's main operation in Mendocino. Stahl got away. He took a half dozen of the most ardent followers with him. They're armed and on the run."

"And my mother?" Jake's face screwed up with disgust. "She had to be part of it. She and Stahl escaped together, I assume. That's why she came by my place. She was hoping to hide out in my apartment. Both of them."

"No, no, no . . ." Horowitz shook his head. "Your *mother* was the informant I mentioned."

"What?"

"She's the one who turned in Stahl and the others. She didn't want anything to do with the direction Stahl was taking the cult. Stahl found out she betrayed him and went after her, but she got away in time." He hesitated. "I'm not happy saying this, Dr. Heron, but I have to. Your father tried to stop her. He was going to hold her in their barracks until Stahl could get her."

Jake had only a vague notion of Gary Heron, an impression that had been sanded down over the years so that his father had moved from nondescript to near obscurity. He was a character in a science fiction movie slowly becoming invisible.

Lydia was always the instigator. The force.

But for him to turn on her?

Peer pressure—like that exerted in a cult—was one of the most insidious forms of intrusion. And among the hardest to resist. He guessed his father had been brainwashed, in a way.

"Your mother's a hero, Professor. She saved a bunch of lives. So, we're trying to find her. There're no charges. We want to get her into protective custody. Probably set her up in witness protection until we can find Stahl and his people. So do you have anything that could help us?"

He was stunned by the news. It took him a moment to focus. "I don't, no."

Horowitz produced a wallet and gave Jake his card. "If you hear from her again."

The CHP investigator stepped away. He paused and turned back. "I'm sure your parents gave you a real crappy childhood, Professor. But all my years in this job, one thing I can say. People can change. I've seen it a thousand times. And you know where it happens most often?"

"Within families."

"You got it, Professor. You got it."

As the officer left, Jake noted several vehicles pulling into the lot. Sanchez and Selina.

He had a fast thought, a rare sentimental one. They had solved the case about Roberto Sanchez, clearing his name and getting justice in the process.

Now Jake wanted to share the story Horowitz had just told him.

Your mother's a hero, Professor . . .

He walked forward to join them, wondering where this new information would lead—and how soon they'd be able to embark on another unauthorized freelance investigation.

CHAPTER 78

"So it's done, completed, *finis* . . . kudos to you both!"

Carmen glanced up impatiently at Stan Reynolds, who hovered in the doorway of the Garage.

The deputy director gave an exaggerated wince. "But I'm afraid I do have a tad bit of bad news for you."

She had been writing up the after-action report with Heron, Selina and Grange.

Then Reynolds frowned, looking at Selina. "And you are . . . do you work here?"

"She's my sister," Carmen said, and did not tell him that she was the kidnap victim they'd alluded to earlier.

Reflecting that the man had not even asked about the condition of the abductee.

Stan Reynolds, true to form.

"I know you and your erstwhile leader, SSA Williamson, were a touch skeptical of my theory that Sergei Ivanov was behind the Brock murder."

Heron whispered, "'Tad.' 'Touch.'"

Carmen tried not to smile.

"But we dug deep enough and found, guess what, the dear departed bridegroom, *did* send an encrypted message to a known asset in the

Russian embassy in Washington. It came from, ta-da, Brock's house."
His eyes were triumphant. "I ordered agents to bring Ivanov in for
questioning."

She frowned. "What charge?"

"He wasn't arrested. Only brought in for questioning. As I just said.
But we'll break him. I know you tried, did your best. Points for that.
But I'm afraid there will be consequences for dropping the ball."

All of Reynolds's skills were on full display—not as a law enforcer
but as a master *political* operator. On these facts, he would have an
easy time bringing I-squared within his own orbit. Organizations—
and personnel—often never recovered from national security oversights
like this.

The hollow feeling within her spread.

She glanced at Heron, who appeared as troubled as she was.

How had they missed it?

Well, if I-squared were taken away from Williamson, which now
seemed likely, and brought under Reynolds's direct control, she'd quit.

Simple as that.

And what about Professor and Intrusionist Jake Heron? Williamson
was the only official in the federal government with the cojones to enlist
the help of a civilian consultant with his background, however brilliant.

This would be the end of their working relationship.

And perhaps the end of any relationship at all.

Reynolds said, "We'll congregate in the morning about what comes
next. Ciao."

He strode triumphantly out of the Garage.

Selina muttered, "Dude is a total prick."

No one argued with her assessment.

Carmen finished the last paragraph of her report and hit Enter,
sending the file to the powers that be. It described in detail Damon
Garr's unique profile as a killer. Also contained was the disposition of
Tristan Kane—in a maximum-security holding facility, where he would
have zero access to electronics. Lauren Brock's statement, along with

Carmen's notes about her history and the extenuating circumstances of her relationship with Garr, were included too.

Footnotes described the crimes in Verona and Florence.

Not a single word of Russian conspiracy was included.

Heron said firmly, "I've had it, Sanchez. I need a drink."

"Me too," Selina chimed in.

"No," Carmen said instantly.

"I'm almost twenty-one."

"Which is like being almost pregnant. Either you are or you're not."

Selina pouted but Carmen could tell she wasn't truly upset. She knew that her gymnastics always came first, and rhythmic routines and alcohol do not mix.

Carmen suggested, "Virgin strawberry margarita?"

"That'll work. If there are chips and salsa involved."

"Deal."

The three of them said goodbye to Grange and Mouse and walked from the facility into the cool night air.

In the parking lot, they made their way toward the Suburban and Jake's Nissan, parked side by side. She had yet to repair the bullet hole in the back window that she'd placed there the other day as a prelude to the set in Santa Monica that had yielded Tristan Kane's account information.

"I'd leave it," Heron said, noticing she was eyeing the damage. "Nobody'll park near you at the mall."

She chuckled.

It was then that Carmen was vaguely aware of a dark SUV pulling into the lot and moving slowly their way. It stopped not far away, though at an odd angle, outside the white lines of a parking space. The door opened.

The driver was Allison Brock, Anthony's widow. Her stern visage slipped away, and she smiled, waving a greeting. Carmen supposed she had come with information about Lauren, her sister-in-law, perhaps not knowing they had already cracked the mystery of Ms. Person of Interest. Or was maybe curious about what else the investigation had revealed.

Carmen waved back.

There was a beat of a moment.

And then Allison raised an Uzi machine pistol. She aimed toward the trio, pulling the trigger and sending a fusillade of bullets their way.

"Down!" Carmen cried as the others dropped to the asphalt. She went for her gun but saw that she could not get a bead on Allison, who was using the open door for cover.

Then Allison spotted another target, one she could hit without exposing herself to return fire from Carmen.

Mouse had just walked from the building and stood fifty feet away, frozen in place.

Allison aimed at her, as Carmen tried to acquire a clear-sight picture—but she had no workable shot.

Uzis have short barrels and fire a small-caliber bullet, but they're accurate—and lethal enough at this range.

"Mouse!" she called out to her. "Down."

The woman crouched but was still an easy target.

Just as Allison centered her weapon, another vehicle skidded to a stop inside the gate to the parking lot. It was a small SUV, a black Ford Edge. The door swung out and a towering mountain of a man wearing a black leather jacket stepped out fast, smoothly drawing a pistol as he sank into a tactical stance. Unlike Carmen, he had an unobstructed view of Allison Brock, and he fired three times. She grabbed her chest, dropped her gun and slumped to the ground.

Carmen shifted her Glock toward the unknown shooter, who lowered his gun and shouted, "I'm a friendly."

"Weapon on the ground, step away."

"Yes, Agent Sanchez."

He knows me?

The man followed orders, placing the pistol at his feet and taking two steps back with his hands in the air, one of which held an open wallet.

As Heron called 9-1-1 and Mouse returned to the Garage to summon help, she approached and secured Allison's gun and then examined the ID that the newcomer displayed. His name was DeLeon Blake, and he was a security consultant. His license to carry a firearm was in order.

Accompanied by Mouse, Liam Grange ran from the building, weapon in hand. Then slowed after assessing that the danger had been neutralized.

"Explain," Carmen said to Blake.

"I work for your late father's boss, Carl Overton. After Selina came to him asking about your father's clients, he hired me to keep tabs on her. She told him a stalker was following her, and he was worried about her safety." He grimaced. "Did the best I could but she gave me the slip."

"What's this about a stalker, Sel—?"

Carmen turned to her sister.

And gasped.

"Carmen . . ." Selina's voice was weak. She removed her hand from her chest, revealing the hole from one of Allison's bullets. It was just above her heart.

"I think . . . maybe I should . . ."

Selina slumped to her knees.

CHAPTER 79

Jake and Sanchez sat side by side in identical orange chairs of the UCLA Medical Center emergency room.

They'd been here for a half hour but, to Jake, it seemed like forever.

He was aware of another visitor entering the area and walking their way, but he was visible only in silhouette.

Jake supposed that the person would take one of the many chairs—most were empty—and sit solemnly, riddled with anxiety, waiting for news of a loved one.

But instead he walked directly up to them.

"How is she?"

He looked up to see Eric Williamson.

Jake rose. Sanchez too.

No hands were shaken, and there were no embraces.

Sanchez answered, "Still in surgery. Trying to save her heart."

Williamson sat. He looked at them and gave a faint smile. "Wondering what I'm doing here?"

Jake said, "We thought you'd been put out to pasture. Thanks to us. We missed the Russian connection."

"I always wondered about that expression. It's supposed to mean 'retired,' I guess, but aren't all cows put out to pasture every day? It's not like they have desk jobs they retire from."

Sanchez didn't laugh. Nor did Jake.

At that moment, the double doors to the emergency suite opened and a doctor approached. He was tall and slender and seemed extremely focused and no-nonsense. His name, according to the ID on a lanyard, was J. Singh.

"Doctor," Sanchez began.

The man had surely delivered unfortunate news dozens, if not hundreds, of times, and Jake recognized that his face had slipped into an expression he undoubtedly used at moments like this.

He knew what was coming.

"I'm sorry. We did everything we could."

Jake had heard that before. It was word salad. Would any doctor admit they'd done *less* than they could?

Sanchez sighed. Then she said, "I'll need her effects."

"Of course."

"Thank you, Doctor."

He nodded, turned and left.

"Shit, Heron—"

Williamson was shaking his head, and he remained silent.

A moment later a voice from behind them, in a woman's bright lilt, asked, "Hey, why so glum?"

Jake turned to see Selina Sanchez walking toward them.

He asked her, "How are you?"

"Broke a damn rib," she muttered, gesturing toward her chest, where the bullet hole in her sweater was still evident. Allison Brock's bullet had been stopped by the ballistic vest Ryan Hall had given her when she started to play amateur detective. But rounds from an Uzi 9mm submachine gun still travel at 1,300 feet per second. In a battle between bone and lead, the former often loses, even with Kevlar blunting the force of impact.

Selina had been in another part of the ER—that side devoted to non-life-threatening injuries.

Sanchez hugged her sister gently before responding to her question about everyone's dour expression. "Allison Brock, the woman who shot you, just died."

"Died?" Selina whispered softly, "I'm so sorry to hear that."

Jake frowned. "Well, Selina, you don't need to be *too* sad about it. She *did* shoot you, after all."

She waved the comment away. "Oh, I'm not upset about *her*. I'm pissed for you, Carm. I'm sure you wanted a chance to interrogate the crap out of her."

Jake had to smile.

Then Williamson turned to his employees. "You might be interested to know that Reynolds was recalled to Washington. He'll be in the penalty box for a while. He got it partly right. Yes, there was an encrypted message from Brock's house to the Russian embassy. A burner phone."

Jake immediately arrived at the only logical conclusion. "But it was *Allison* who called them."

Sanchez put a hand on her hip. "Shit. *She* was the Russian agent."

"Part of a sleeper cell," Williamson confirmed. "Anthony Brock knew nothing about it. In fact, she'd latched on to him for intel. He was low-level GAO when they met but was in the process of getting a top-secret clearance, which takes about six to nine months."

"So Allison was positioning herself for future access," Sanchez said, "and she worked with Sergei Ivanov?"

Williamson chuckled. "Now *that's* the funny part. Not ha-ha funny. But weird. Ivanov was a CIA asset. It took years for the Agency to cultivate him."

"Hell," muttered Sanchez. "Reynolds blew his cover."

"It's the only reason I can tell you about it. Picking him up drew attention to him in Moscow. He's burned." A sigh. "Five years of actionable intel, but the pipeline's cut off now. Not likely we'll ever find someone else in his position willing to cooperate."

Sanchez gave a humorless laugh and turned to Jake. "Remember when Allison said after her husband died, she'd have to start all over again? She wasn't talking about a new relationship or husband. She meant getting her hooks into another patsy in the government to use for her spy game."

Jake asked, "Eric? What about Congress? I-squared?"

"The subcommittee apparently liked my answers. They didn't even seem to mind when I asked a few questions of my own. Like: 'Could you explain why, in detail, you aren't willing to fund us at the level I've requested, Ms. Committee Chair?' I think some of them were intimidated."

Eric Williamson was, Jake knew, a master of intimidation.

Their supervisor lifted his palms. "So I-squared's permanent. Or as permanent as anything ever is in Washington."

"And staffing?"

"No action on that. Afraid it's still just the two of you for the time being. Well, Mouse and Declan, of course." He got a text and read it, nodding slowly. "Hm. Okay. I've got work to do," the big man grumbled. Without a goodbye, he walked from the ER, texting as he went.

A nurse entered from the operating suites and handed a manila envelope to Sanchez. Allison Brock's personal effects, which might, or might not, contain earth-shattering secrets about the life of a sleeper agent.

Sanchez dug in her jacket pocket. Jake smiled, reflecting that very few people have official law enforcement evidence bags sitting beside a tube of lip balm.

After she'd bagged everything, they started for the door, Selina beside them.

Sanchez offered, "So, cocktail hour?"

Selina frowned. "I think I'll pass."

"Why?" Sanchez asked. "You feeling all right?"

"Oh, I'm fine." She turned to face Jake. "But if you're not going to ask my sister out, apparently somebody's got to take charge. You two run along." A wink. "And Jake? Have her home by midnight."

"Lina!"

Jake felt the warmth of what might have been his first full-on blush.

Selina slung her bag over her shoulder—wincing slightly—and strode out the door, leaving the two I-squared operatives alone.

Sanchez looked up into his eyes. She whispered, "Heron?"

"Hm?"

"Have a question."

"Okay."

"Back at the Chinampas Grand Resort? When we were on the deck outside the honeymoon suite?"

His cheeks grew hotter. "Vague memory."

"Yeah, right." She lowered her voice. "Getting close, playing newlyweds. I want to know something."

"Go on." He was whispering too. Noting his heart had started tapping a bit faster. He swayed closer.

She frowned. "Didn't you think the bathrobes were pretty cheesy, considering what the place must've cost?"

"It was the only thing on my mind."

Then she took his hand and pulled him close.

That lavender smell again.

He lowered his head toward hers.

Which was when their phones buzzed with simultaneous texts, the tones slightly different but each urgent in its own way. They eased apart and retrieved their devices.

"Mouse?" Jake asked.

"Mouse," Sanchez confirmed.

He read:

I don't know if you two are doing anything important at the moment but Williamson's back—did you hear? There's been an incident. A big one. He needs to see you both, immediately, if not sooner.

The two shared a smile and, after sending brief replies, walked toward the parking lot, where Sanchez's Suburban was ready to transport them back to HQ, and whatever awaited in their future.

ACKNOWLEDGMENTS

Writers keep odd hours, have odd thoughts and even odder conversations. Their families, who are on the front lines of all the mayhem, deserve special recognition. Jeff finds constant support from sister Julie, Madelyn and Robby, Katie and Kyla, not to mention Blush (as long as he feeds her on time). Isabella has the unswerving support of her husband, Mike; her son, Max; and her writing muse/dog, aptly named Buddy. Our gratitude includes, of course, a hugely understanding group of extended family and friends.

We are fortunate, too, to have an outstanding publishing team at Thomas & Mercer. Editorial Director Megha Parekh, who shared our vision; Charlotte Herscher, who helped shape it; and the editing team who polished it to a shine, including Miranda Gardner and ace copyeditors Jill Schoenhaut, Heather Rodino, James Gallagher, Sarah Vostok and Robin O'Dell.

Finally, our heartfelt thanks to our agents, Deborah Schneider, Liza Fleissig and Ginger Harris-Dontzin, a.k.a. The Dream Team. When we approached them with the idea of a partnership, they swung into action and brought our goals to fruition.

ABOUT THE AUTHORS

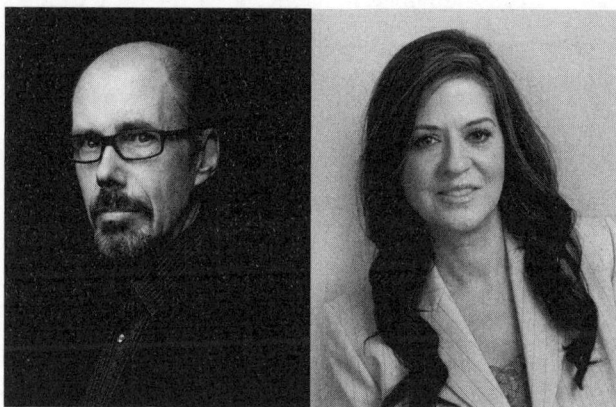

Jeffery Deaver is the award-winning international and #1 *New York Times* bestselling author of numerous series, including Lincoln Rhyme, Colter Shaw, and Kathryn Dance, as well as the Sanchez & Heron series with Isabella Maldonado. Deaver's work includes fifty novels, more than one hundred short stories, and a nonfiction law book. His books are sold in 150 countries and translated into twenty-five languages. A former journalist, folk singer, and attorney, he was born outside Chicago and has a bachelor of journalism degree from the University of Missouri and a law degree from Fordham University. He was recently named a Grand Master of Mystery Writers of America, whose ranks include Agatha Christie, Elmore Leonard, and Mickey Spillane. For more information, visit www.jefferydeaver.com.

Isabella Maldonado is the award-winning international and *Wall Street Journal* bestselling author of the Nina Guerrera, Daniela Vega, and

Veranda Cruz series, as well as the Sanchez & Heron series with Jeffery Deaver. Her books are published in twenty-four languages. Maldonado wore a gun and badge in real life before turning to crime writing. A graduate of the FBI National Academy in Quantico and the first Latina to attain the rank of captain in her police department, she retired as the Commander of Special Investigations and Forensics. During her more than two decades on the force, her assignments included hostage negotiator, department spokesperson, and precinct commander. She uses her law enforcement background to bring a realistic edge to her writing. For more information, visit www.isabellamaldonado.com.